ALSO BY KATHERINE WOOD

Ladykiller

SUNBURNED

SUNBURNED

A Novel

KATHERINE WOOD

BANTAM
NEW YORK

Bantam Books
An imprint of Random House
A division of Penguin Random House LLC
1745 Broadway, New York, NY 10019
randomhousebooks.com
penguinrandomhouse.com

Hardback ISBN 978-0-593-72647-1
Ebook ISBN 978-0-593-72648-8

Printed in the United States of America on acid-free paper

1st Printing

First Edition

BOOK TEAM: Production editor: Ted Allen • Managing editor: Saige Francis •
Production manager: Samuel Wetzler • Copy editor: Emily DeHuff •
Proofreaders: Claire Maby, Amy Harned, Al Madocs

Book design by Caroline Cunningham
Palm tree photo by Caroline Cunningham

The authorized representative in the EU for product safety and compliance is
Penguin Random House Ireland, Morrison Chambers, 32 Nassau Street,
Dublin D02 YH68, Ireland. https://eu-contact.penguin.ie

For:

Jessica, Windsor, Rachael, Katie, Kristin, Kristen, Jennifer,

Taylea, Stephanie, Laura, Lindsay

Man is condemned to be free. Condemned, because he did not create himself, yet is nevertheless at liberty, and from the moment that he is thrown into this world he is responsible for everything he does.

—JEAN-PAUL SARTRE, "EXISTENTIALISM IS A HUMANISM" (1946)

SUNBURNED

PROLOGUE

T he shivers that racked my body were not from cold, but shock.
I wasn't cold. Far from it. This was St. Barth's in March—
sunny and dry, a gentle swell from the east. Great visibility beneath the
clear water, the current not too strong. Perfect conditions for diving.

My hands trembled as I wrapped my towel tighter around my waist
and gripped the railing of the yacht, my eyes fixed on the Search and
Rescue boat tied to the mooring ball closest to the giant rock that
marked the edge of the reef. The others huddled in pairs, watching the
surface of the water for signs, their heads bent together, murmuring,
crying. I did not know them well enough to share in their grief, if
that's what it was.

We didn't know. We didn't know yet. But we would soon. There was
only so much time a person could stay down there before the tank ran
out. The window was closing, if it hadn't already.

My hair dripped seawater, cool against my sun-warmed skin. A
bird glided on the breeze, then plunged to the water, coming up with
a silver fish wriggling in its beak.

This wasn't my first encounter with earth-shattering tragedy, but
that didn't make it any less shocking. Though the out-of-body sensa-

tion may have been familiar, it was not comforting watching myself from above, both here and not here, feeling and unfeeling, the scene vivid and distant. Surreal.

A disturbance on the surface drew my eye to the water near the back of the rescue boat. A head bobbing in the waves, black against the reflection of the sun on the sea, and then another. Three more at once. The five who'd gone down. They were struggling with something odd-shaped and heavy, a silver tank still strapped to its back.

I leaned over the railing and hurled into the glinting water.

PART I

CHAPTER 1

I'd said no. Of course I'd said no.

I'd never wanted to see Tyson Dale again, much less spend his birthday with him at his compound in St. Barth's. And yet here I was on the tarmac at Miami Executive Airport, his sleek jet looming above me in the noonday sun like a dog sent to fetch a toy for its master.

It did not escape me that I was the toy.

The driver had only just popped the trunk of the chauffeured Suburban that Tyson had dispatched to collect me from my house this morning when a uniformed attendant appeared and took possession of my roller bag. "Is this everything, Ms. Collet?"

I'd been sure I'd grossly overpacked for what was to be only a five-day trip, but his question made me wonder whether I should have brought more. Regardless, it was too late now. "That's it. Thank you," I said.

Though I'd already hugged them goodbye, my ten-year-old boys bounded out of the SUV like a pair of puppies, salivating over the sight of the aircraft, and I suddenly understood why they had insisted on accompanying me to the airfield.

"Can we go on it, Mom?"

"Please?"

"Pleeease, Mom?" they pleaded in unison.

Their identical faces were like mine, sharp-featured with a straight nose, though their lips were wide while mine were bow-shaped, their eyes brown to my blue. They countered their indistinguishable appearance with opposite style, Benji the more clean-cut of the two, his nearly black hair spiky and short, while Alex's long, straight mop fell in his dark eyes, but their mannerisms mirrored each other's, and they often spoke as one, as they did now.

"Pleeease?" their voices chorused again.

They'd shot up so much this year that I didn't have to bend to look them in the eye as I placed a hand on each of their shoulders, shaking my head. "We talked about this."

But the pretty stewardess at the bottom of the airstair had different ideas. "We have plenty of time until wheels up if they'd like to explore the plane," she said, smiling sweetly at the boys.

They whooped and high-fived, sprinting up the stairs before I could so much as protest, the stewardess on their heels. "Is it okay if I give them juice? It's fresh-squeezed mango, pineapple, and orange. Tyson's children's favorite."

Tyson's children. I was startled to hear the words come out of her mouth, but of course he was the father of two sons by his ex-wife and a daughter by another woman. A lot had happened in the decade since we'd last seen each other. Well, a lot had happened to him.

Less had happened to me.

"Sure," I acquiesced, forcing a smile.

"You were right," Rosa said, getting out of the car to stand beside me in the shadow of the jet. "We should've asked for more money."

"Told you."

Rosa tucked a brunette curl behind her ear and grinned, displaying her dimple. She'd recently cut her hair to just above her shoulders, and it suited her face, accentuating her large dark eyes and rosy cheeks.

Rosa was named Friendliest in high school, her warm smile always at the ready, while my RBF had earned me the moniker Ice Queen, my introversion mistaken for aloofness. We might never have become friends if her family hadn't moved in next door to my mom and me when we were in ninth grade. Now more of a sister, she was my children's honorary auntie, and, since she left the police force a year ago, my business partner at Sunshine Discovery Agency.

No, we're not spies, though spying on people does come with the territory.

Discovery agents are most often employed by attorneys to collect pre-litigation information before cases go to trial, though we are sometimes hired by corporations or individuals to gather intelligence privately. As a computer systems expert, I specialize in the digital side of things, while Rosa handles the human half, a division that plays to our natural strengths. In normal circumstances, Rosa would be the one jetting off to St. Barth's to meet with the client while I gladly stayed behind to provide digital support from the comfort of my office.

But Tyson Dale was no normal circumstance.

The money wasn't why I was going. I had my own reasons—reasons that Tyson was quick to remind me of when I'd initially turned him down. But he understood that Rosa hated him and would never have let me go had he not offered a generous sum for our services that would allow her to buy the new car she so desperately needed. He was smart like that, always acutely aware of pressure points and unafraid to take advantage of them.

So for once, I was the one boarding the plane while she stayed behind to watch my boys.

"Not gonna lie, I kinda want to see the inside of the jet too," Rosa said.

I sighed and waved for her to follow as I started up the airstair.

We found the boys in the cockpit peppering the good-natured pilots with questions, their faces aglow. They were enjoying the attention, and there wasn't room for all of us in the small enclosure, so I gratefully accepted the cold towel the stewardess offered and followed her into the elegant cabin of the plane.

The closest I'd ever been to a private jet was seeing one on television, but I knew better than to gape as I took in the buttery cream leather seats and glossy wood accents, realizing as I cleaned my hands with the rosemary-scented towel that it was likely more for the plane's benefit than for mine.

Rosa sank into a captain's chair, rubbing her palms over the smooth armrests. "I could get used to this," she said. "Why'd you guys break up, again?"

I glared at her and she laughed, accepting a glass of champagne from the stewardess as I politely declined, not exactly in a celebratory mood.

"Joking, of course," she said, sipping her bubbles. "His ego is definitely not worth a billion dollars. Though, I mean, he does travel all over the world for work, right? How much would you really have to see him?"

Her cell rang, and she raised it to her ear. "Sunshine Discovery Agency . . . No, this is Rosa Rodriguez, I'm her business partner. What is this concerning?"

Her eyes met mine as she listened, her brow furrowing. "No comment. Please do not call here again."

"What was that about?" I asked as she hung up, jamming the phone into the pocket of her jeans.

"That was a reporter, hoping to talk to you about your relationship with Ian Kelley."

I grimaced. "Shit, that was fast."

"Brace yourself. It may be a shitstorm by the time you get back."

The thought made me physically ill.

The stewardess appeared with my boys on her heels, now sucking on lollipops. "It's time to prepare for takeoff."

Rosa chugged half her glass of champagne and rose, wrapping me in a hug. "See you in five days. I'll keep the wolves at bay while you're gone. And seriously, anything you need, just say the word. I can't wait to hear what it is Tyson's willing to pay us a hundred grand for."

"Yeah, same," I said, kissing my boys on their foreheads.

But I had an idea.

* * *

Thirty minutes later, I was airborne, the lone passenger on the jet as we soared southeast through the endless blue, the line between the sea and sky indistinguishable out the large oval windows.

I dropped my gaze to my laptop, once more going over the trove of information on Tyson and his company that I'd scraped from the internet in the twenty-four hours since he'd hired us. Until now, I'd done my best to steer clear of any mention of him or his success in the decade since we broke up, though I couldn't help but see the headlines over the years:

TYSON DALE WANTS TO SAVE THE WORLD WITH NEW
    DESALINATION TECHNOLOGY
COULD DE-SAL BE THE NEXT BIG THING?
WASTE WAS THE BIGGEST PROBLEM WITH DESALINATION. THEN
    DE-SAL CHANGED THE GAME.
MIAMI FIRST CITY TO UTILIZE DESALINATION TO PROVIDE OVER
    HALF ITS CLEAN WATER.
BRAZIL, AN EARLY ADOPTER OF DE-SAL, GOES ALL IN.
TOP 40 UNDER 40: #1, TYSON DALE.

De-Sal had skyrocketed to success, and Tyson had been widely perceived as one of the hottest bachelors in America, until he married his yoga instructor six years ago. They divorced while she was pregnant with their second child, after he knocked up another woman. The press had been vicious, and it was around that time that Tyson had retreated from the public eye, allowing his business partner, the former Olympic swimmer Allison Zhu, to become the face of the company. His brother, Cody, worked with him as well, but Cody had never been one for the spotlight, and though he held the position of COO, he was rarely mentioned online.

Tyson had remarried—a Belgian model named Samira Maies—just over a year ago, and while it was easy enough to locate images from the campaigns she'd done for brands like Prada, Dior, and Omega, it seemed she was also very private about her personal life. Or more likely Tyson had quietly had her history wiped from the internet.

I'd heard rumors of his new strangeness, his paranoia, but it was hard to weed fact from fiction online, and I hadn't been surprised when he refused to talk about his reason for calling me over the phone. I wasn't in a position to press.

"We've reached cruising altitude, if you'd like to move about the cabin, Ms. Collet," the stewardess said as she approached, bearing a small silver tray of mozzarella balls with fresh basil atop sliced tomatoes, which she set on the table before me. "I'll refresh your water as well," she added, noticing I'd already finished my bottle. "Is there anything else I can get you?"

"Please, call me Audrey," I said. "And no, I'm fine."

Though I hadn't felt fine for over a week now.

The news had arrived last Friday, during Rosa's and my weekly visit to the outdoor shooting range on the edge of the Everglades.

It was early March in south Florida, and the day was downright delightful, sunny and seventy, with low humidity and a light breeze. The kind of day that makes you feel you can fly. Spindly pines arched overhead, and I could hear water trickling on the other side of the embankment behind the targets.

I focused on the black-and-white concentric circles, stilling my breath as I squeezed the trigger. Power reverberated through my body as I absorbed the kick of the gun with my elbows and shoulders, watching the bullet rip through the paper target two inches above the center.

"Nice!" Rosa enthused as I fired off another four shots in rapid succession.

All of my shots hit their mark. I lowered my weapon and winked at her, and she laughed heartily.

"And to think, five years ago you'd never touched a gun," Rosa said as she reloaded her clip.

It was true, I'd never been much of a fan of guns—still wasn't—and hadn't carried one in my first few years on the job, until I'd gotten

myself in a sticky situation gathering evidence against a human traf-
ficking organization. Rosa, then a rookie cop, had gifted me a Sig
Sauer P226, the same weapon she carried, with a gift certificate for a
gun safety course. I'd balked at first but had eventually caved, and I'd
made it my business to become a sure shot.

While I only rarely had to use my weapon on the job, target practice
was an important part of gun safety, not to mention a fantastic way to
blow off steam at the end of a long week.

Though actually it had been a good week, and I'd had little steam
to blow off—until Rosa's phone rang. "It's Deanna," she said, raising
the phone.

Deanna, our friend and primary contact on the police force, whose
calls we always took. I held my gunfire as Rosa answered, her face
shifting to an expression of concern while she listened. I could tell
from her questions that this was no routine call.

"What is it?" I asked as she hung up.

She shook her head with disgust. "Another foot."

I grimaced. The discovery was grisly, but not unusual. Something
about the sturdy construction of athletic shoes combined with the
current in the canals preserved and regurgitated the feet when the rest
of the body had long since been devoured by the bounty of life in the
Everglades.

"Nike Air Jordan high-top," she specified. "Caught in the wreckage
of a car that had been sunk separately, they're pretty sure."

Also not uncommon.

"But here's the catch," she continued, loading her clip. "It had a set
of keys tucked into the lining of the shoe."

I frowned. "And?"

"The key chain had a metal tag on it with the initials engraved."

A tingle at the back of my scalp. "Go on."

"Remember Ian Kelley?"

I felt the blood drain from my face as I nodded.

"The initials were I.J.K., as in Ian Jason Kelley, and the shoe was
exactly his size."

"Shit."

"They have to do testing on the remains to confirm, but if it's actually him . . ."

She didn't have to finish that sentence. There'd been no murder investigation after Ian disappeared, because there'd been no body.

But that was about to change.

could hear the music a block from the club.

"We can get out here," I volunteered as my mom slowed for a stop sign.

She pulled her Honda over to the curb, her eyes twinkling beneath the turquoise scarf wrapped around her head. "What, you don't want people to see your mom dropping you off at the club for your twenty-first birthday?"

I chortled. "Yeah no."

"Ugh, these stilettos were not made for walking," Rosa complained as she pushed open the back door.

"Just for dancing?" I teased.

I climbed out of the car into the balmy evening and adjusted my short, sparkly dress, my birthday present from Rosa, who had also done my makeup, and tamed my perpetually tangled long brown hair into glossy curls.

"Wait!" my mom called before I could shut the door. She raised her phone. "Strike a pose."

I rolled my eyes but Rosa and I did as instructed, posing like Charlie's Angels on the sidewalk until the driver of a pickup truck rolled down his window to whistle.

"Bye!" I said, slamming the door to my mom's car and blowing her a kiss.

"Thanks for the ride, Alex," Rosa called as we started down the street.

I could see my mom laughing as she drove away.

The sidewalk outside Starfish was teeming with people waiting to get in. But the bouncer, who'd been on the football team at our high school back when Rosa was a cheerleader, lifted the velvet rope as we approached. "Birthday girl in the house," he said into his walkie.

After a moment, the black-suited manager appeared in the doorway and ushered us inside. Dance music pounded through the speakers, flashing blue and silver lights reflecting off the disco balls that hung from the rafters as he led us past the bar and around the dance floor to a booth in the corner.

"Drinks are on the house tonight, ladies," he said, gesturing to the vodka and juices in the center of the table. "Happy birthday."

As he disappeared into the crowd, Rosa pulled me toward the booth. "Corner table so you can lurk in the shadows. No balloons, as promised. And I didn't even invite anyone. Though I may have told a few people we'd be here. But only people you like."

"Jesus, am I that bad?"

"I'm just messing with you. You know I love you."

Her eyes narrowed as they caught on someone across the room. "Is that . . ." She snapped her fingers, searching for a name. "The squirrelly guy that was your lab partner senior year—"

"Ian Kelley?" I looked over to see two guys leaning against the wall near the hallway that led to the bathrooms. It took me a minute to register that one of them was, in fact, Ian. He was taller than he'd been in school, and even thinner, looking more like a ferret than a squirrel now with his new tattoos and all-black clothes, his dyed black hair shaped into a mullet. "Yeah, that's him," I said.

At first it looked like he and the other guy were just talking, until I noticed an exchange pass between their hands.

"Is he dealing?" I asked, thrown.

"Looks like it."

Ian and I hadn't exactly been friends in school, but we'd been friendly. He was smart and we were in a few AP classes together, occasionally paired to work on projects. Most people thought he was a weirdo—but then so was I, though I kept my weird more on the inside. I'd never liked to be the center of attention.

"Damn," I said, shaking my head. "That's sad."

"Not super off-brand, though," Rosa said.

It was true he'd been a pothead, and I remembered rumors that his home life wasn't great. Dad in jail, that kind of thing, though we'd never discussed it.

"But he had a scholarship to . . ." I racked my brain, but couldn't remember where.

Rosa shook her head. "I heard he lost it." She leaned in, cut her eyes toward the bar, and whispered, "Look what the cat dragged in."

My heart caught in my throat as my gaze landed on Tyson Dale, leaning against the bar. He was wearing a fitted black T-shirt that showed off his toned biceps, his dark hair long enough to tuck behind his ears.

Damn. He looked good.

My face must have given me away because Rosa immediately shook her head. "No, Audrey. Absolutely not. He is bad for you. Look away."

I obeyed, turning my back on him as I poured myself a vodka cranberry. I knew Tyson was bad for me, had always known Tyson was bad for me. But that had never stopped me from going there. He was my first boyfriend, my first love, the one I'd lost my virginity to, the one who'd broken my heart—more than once. Our history was long. Too long for a pair of twenty-one-year-olds.

"Ryan's with him," she reported. "They must've just gotten home for the summer."

"Yeah, Tyson got in yesterday," I said before I could stop myself.

"You've talked to him?" she asked incredulously.

"He texted me."

"And you responded."

I shrugged. "He's one of my oldest friends."

"*Friends*." She snorted. "Did you tell him you were going to be here tonight?"

I winced. "Maybe."

"Audrey!"

"I know, I know—"

"Do I need to remind you he stood you up on prom night?" she demanded.

"That wasn't his fault. The boat—"

She held up a hand to stop me, letting out an exasperated sigh. "Just don't say I didn't warn you."

Rosa's gaze shifted over my shoulder, and I spun to see Tyson and Ryan prowling toward us. Tyson's dark eyes were fixed on me, his square jaw flexing as he landed at our table. "Happy birthday, gorgeous," he said, pulling me in for a hug. I caught a whiff of the intoxicating cologne he'd worn since high school, which I knew I was supposed to hate. But that was not my Pavlovian response. "You look incredible," he whispered into my hair, his hand lingering on my hip.

"Thanks," I said. I ripped my eyes from him to give Ryan a hug. "Good to see you guys."

Tyson slid into our black leather booth, pulling me with him.

"Please, join us," Rosa said, her tone spiked with sarcasm.

My eyes caught on Tyson's Coors Light. "I see your taste hasn't changed."

He eyed me. "No. It hasn't."

"How's Boston?" I asked, ignoring his innuendo.

He shrugged. "Fine."

"Fine?" I asked. "That's all?"

"I just wonder how much you can learn in a school environment, you know?"

"I'm sure your parents would be thrilled to hear that with the amount they're spending on tuition," Ryan ribbed.

"Spending the money makes them feel better about how little they're involved in my life," Tyson said bitterly.

"How long are you here for?" Rosa asked.

"Two, three months? I'm watching the house for the summer while they do whatever it is they do."

"That's very nice of you," I said. "What's the real story?"

"I had an internship lined up in New York, but the company went under and it was too late to get anything else," he admitted. "So here I am. All by myself in that big house." He focused on me. "I'm gonna get lonely."

"You could get a job like the rest of us," Rosa suggested.

"Do you have a job?" Tyson asked, his eyes still on me.

I nodded. Taking care of my mom was really my full-time job, but as her disability insurance paid barely enough for us to scrape by on, I'd had to find some way of making money that would allow me to make my own hours. Fortunately, my skill set was suited to that kind of arrangement. "I'm working for a DevOps company."

"What does that mean?" Ryan asked. Tyson laughed and Ryan held up his hands. "Pre-law over here. I have no idea what you smart people do with computers."

"I analyze systems software and engineer automation maintenance and virtual services," I explained.

Ryan and Rosa exchanged a glance. "Yeah," Rosa said. "I don't get it, either."

The song changed, and Ryan stood up, offering Rosa his hand. "Wanna dance?"

"But you're going back to school in the fall," Tyson said once they'd gone.

I swirled the ice in my drink with my straw. "We'll see."

"What do you mean, you'll see?" Tyson asked. He'd never known when to leave well enough alone. "You need to be registered already if you intend to go back."

"I can't go back in the fall, okay?" I snapped. "I have to take care of my mom."

"Can't you—" he started, but I cut him off.

"There's no one else."

"But you'll lose your scholarship if you—"

"I already did." I took a long draw of my drink. "I couldn't keep my grades up with driving back and forth all the time."

He stared at me. "But can't they make some kind of exception for your situation?"

I shook my head. "Believe me, I tried."

He nodded, and I could see the wheels turning in his brain as his eyes swept the room. He focused on Ian, who was now sitting at the edge of a crowded booth, his head bent in what looked like serious conversation with a guy in his thirties. "Great," he said dryly.

"What?"

"Just—Ian. He's renting that trailer on the land behind our house. He came around to see if I wanted to go out tonight, and I said I was too tired."

"Is he not in school anymore?"

Tyson shook his head. "He's been renting the trailer since Christmas. I don't know the full story."

He angled his face away from Ian, returning his attention to me. "So. What are you gonna do?"

"I don't know," I answered honestly. "I'll figure that out once my mom gets through this. I'm not even totally sure I want to work in the tech sector anymore."

Even in the semidarkness, I could see the confusion on his face. "Why? You're so good at it."

"I like identifying a problem, finding a way in, figuring out a puzzle. But doing it for a company is . . . I'm bored out of my mind. And as much as I love computers, being in front of one all day is draining."

"I get that," he agreed. "I hate school. But it's just a stepping-stone. Some of the people I'm meeting will be useful, and investors like to see a pedigreed background."

"Investors in what?"

"Whatever company I start."

"Are you developing some amazing tech I don't know about?" I asked.

"I'll figure that out," he said.

He sounded so confident, so self-assured. Was that what being raised with a security net gave you? Or was it just his personality? Maybe that was what attracted me to him, I thought as he placed his hand on my leg beneath the table.

My gaze collided with his. "So what's the goal?" I asked. "World domination?"

A sly smile crept across his face as he leaned in and whispered, "One day they will all bow down to their king."

I laughed. "Me too?"

"Oh no. You'll be queen." He placed his empty beer bottle on the table, his gaze dropping to my mouth. I could feel the familiar magnetism of him, pulling me closer against my better judgment. I shouldn't get involved with Tyson. I knew that. But I was only twenty-one. "I've missed you," he whispered.

I went home with him that night, and we didn't sleep a wink.

CHAPTER 2

" H ere we go."

The deeply tanned pilot of the twelve-passenger prop plane grinned as we rose into the air, adjusting the captain's hat perched atop his shock of white hair. There was no co-pilot for the short hop from St. Martin to St. Barth's, and I'd readily accepted the opportunity to sit up front when he offered.

"How many times a day do you do this?" I yelled over the hum of the engines.

"Depends on the season. Twelve today."

I looked out over miles and miles of deep blue sea, dotted with white-ringed islands edged by turquoise shallows. Tyson's jet had gotten me as far as St. Martin, but jets couldn't land on St. Barth's, so here I was on the commuter plane to the famed island playground of the wealthy, where I was to meet Tyson.

I hadn't seen him since long before De-Sal took off, and I had no idea what to expect. I'd reached out to our old friend Ryan, who was now an attorney in Charlotte, hoping he might have some insight to share, but he hadn't seen Tyson in years either. He did report that last time they'd hung out, he found that Tyson had become obsessed with the occult, with vibrations and energy. That tracked with something his ex-wife's nanny had said in one of the many tell-all articles on him that I'd consumed since I'd agreed to this trip, about his fasting and chewing khat leaves until he heard voices that gave him direction from a different dimension.

In most individuals, this might be seen as a mental break, but people were used to tech titans behaving strangely and the consensus was that the ideas the voices gave him on desalination and natural energy could quite literally save the world, so it was hard to argue that he should stop.

As we drew closer to St. Barth's, I could make out rocky cliffs giving way to sandy shores around the ragged edges of the mountainous island, a mix of green- and red-roofed houses scattered over ridges and valleys and clustered around the port where yachts were stacked like bricks in the azure water.

"You ready for this?" the pilot asked.

Suddenly the harbor was beneath us, the earth rising alarmingly fast in front of us. My heart leaped to my throat as we crested the steep spine of the island then plunged with the slope of the hill to the runway, touching down front wheel first and skidding to a halt at the edge of the turquoise sea.

The sound of propellers filled the air as I climbed down from the plane into the strong sun, holding my panama hat on my head so it wouldn't blow away in the steady wind. Benji and Alex didn't have phones yet, but I texted Rosa to let them all know I'd landed safely, then collected my compact roller bag from the plane's belly and dragged it into the small, uncrowded airport, past the lone passport control stand, where the remarkably handsome immigration officer obligingly directed me to the exit.

As I exited through the glass doors and wandered toward the taxi stand, I couldn't help but notice that, like the sexy immigration officer, the tourists and locals loitering in the shade outside the airport trended toward good-looking and well-dressed. More than trended. If someone snapped a photo and printed the name of a luxury fashion brand at the bottom, the scene would be believable as a fashion ad. But of course, this island was a territory of France. I heard snippets of French and caught a whiff of cigarette smoke. At home, I would have made a face and waved the smoke away—even in college I'd never been more than a social smoker, and it had been years since I'd so much as taken a puff—but here, I was surprised to find I kind of wanted one, preferably paired with a cold glass of rosé.

Hot in the layers I'd worn on the plane, I stuffed my sweatshirt into my purse and tied my long hair back with the rubber band I always kept around my wrist. I felt underdressed in my ripped jeans and T-shirt, and was immediately glad I'd allowed Rosa to talk me into packing my most fashionable clothes. The clothes I so seldom had occasion to wear in my regular mom life.

"Bonjour, madame."

I turned to see a ridiculously sexy Frenchman, dressed in a crisp white button-down shirt and black trousers, smiling at me. His skin was bronzed, his high cheekbones accentuated by his close-cropped beard, his tousled hair the kind of rich, multidimensional brunette that women paid a fortune for in the salon.

He took off his sunglasses, revealing eyes of mesmerizing blue. I mean, shit. My eyes were blue, but they were more of a standard midnight blue. His were stop-you-in-your-tracks blue, as electric as the sea I'd just flown over. "You are Audrey Collet, yes?" he asked in a lilting accent.

I nodded as he leaned past me to easily lift my suitcase. He smelled faintly of cologne and cigarettes.

"I am Laurent." He deposited a business card printed on thick stock into my hand, and my eyes slid over the type, something about executive services. "Here we are."

He loaded my suitcase into the back of a Mercedes Sprinter van, then reappeared at my side, deftly taking my hand to help me up into the back seat. My heavy bag threw me off balance and he caught me, his muscles flexing beneath his shirt, his arms surprisingly strong for his slight frame.

"*Merci,*" I said breathlessly, allowing him to deposit me into the cool leather interior before he climbed into the driver's seat and started the engine.

I smiled to myself as we turned onto the two-lane road that ran up the hill next to the airport. Clearly I needed to get out more, if an interaction as innocuous as that could make me flush the way it just had.

I didn't date much. Rosa accused me of being jaded, and perhaps I was, a little bit anyway, but it was more that I liked my life just fine and didn't see any reason to rock the boat. After all, I didn't just have myself to think about. Any man I spent time with needed to be right not only for me, but for my boys. And I didn't exactly have the greatest track record with men. Tyson had shattered me, and I'd in turn shattered a string of boyfriends afterward. I'd learned the hard way that it was better to keep my occasional entanglements casual and brief, with no risk of anyone's getting shattered.

Now that I was here, I suddenly realized how nervous I was about seeing Tyson again. Not because I was still in love with him. No, that had ended a long time ago. But because he'd always known which of my buttons to push, and now I had an added vulnerability in the form of two ten-year-old boys I loved more than life itself.

I was older now, I reminded myself. I wouldn't allow him to manipulate me the way he used to.

Laurent glanced in the rearview mirror, his bright eyes mercifully hidden by sunglasses. "Is this your first time to visit St. Barthélemy?"

"Yes," I replied, glad for the distraction.

"It is a special place."

We skirted the roundabout at the top of the hill, where a bronze statue of a man in a loincloth stood, spear in hand, blowing into a conch shell. "This statue honors the Arawak, the first tribe to inhabit the island," Laurent explained.

As we bumped over the narrow road that ran along the ridge of the island, I noticed that the landscape was more arid than tropical, with cacti and succulents rooted in the dry, rocky soil. The views on both sides were spectacular, jagged green hills embracing red-roofed seaport villages and white sand beaches, the electric blue sea beyond marked with sailboats and yachts. In the distance, the islands of St. Martin and Anguilla shimmered on the horizon.

"It's beautiful," I said. "Have you always lived on the island?"

"No. I came from France five years ago."

"What brought you here?"

"There was a girl," he said with a sly smile. "But I stayed afterward because I like the lifestyle. Also, the surfing is not so bad for the Caribbean."

I smiled. "Really?"

In the rearview mirror, I saw I'd caught his attention. "In the winter is best, but we can get swells any time of year."

"I've got kids, so I don't get to go as much as I used to, but I grew up surfing in south Florida. Same thing. Not as reliable as someplace like Hawaii, but you can still have a good time."

"How old are your children?"

"Fourth grade. Twin boys."

He raised his brows. "I hope you don't mind my saying, you seem very young to have children this age."

"I had them young," I said.

"I coach some boys this age in surfing," he said. "It is a good age."

The van came to an abrupt stop, and I leaned forward to see a pair of rust-colored chickens crossing the road.

"Have you worked for Tyson long?" I asked.

"I work for a company that manages many houses. His is one of them." He made a hairpin turn off the main road, down a steep one-way street that hugged the side of the mountain. "I handle his house when he is in town because I understand his needs."

"Which are?"

He flashed a smile. "Many."

"Sorry," I returned. "I just don't know what to expect. It's been a while since I last saw him."

"Yes," he said. "He told me."

"What else did he tell you?"

He pulled through a modern wooden gate emblazoned with LE RÊVE in sleek silver capitals and parked the van, turning back to talk to me over the seat. "That I'm to help you with whatever you need."

I considered him, gauging what I could say. "Did he . . . say anything else?"

"He's in a meeting now, but asked to see you in his quarters at seven."

I nodded. So either Laurent didn't know why I'd been called here, or he'd been instructed not to share whatever he knew with me. "Who else is here?"

"His wife, Samira, her friend Gisèle, his business partner, Allison, his brother, Cody, and Cody's girlfriend, Jennifer."

So, seven people, including Tyson and me, only four of whom I hadn't met. That wasn't so bad. And I was glad Cody would be here. No matter what had happened between us, Cody had always been kind to me.

"Are you ready?" he asked.

I placed my hat on my head. "Ready as I'll ever be."

ELEVEN YEARS AGO, JUNE

"I'm sorry I don't have better news," my mother's doctor said.
The slanted afternoon light through the window caught in Dr. Weisman's blond bob, illuminating it like a halo.

"Six months," my mom echoed softly.

Death hovered in the corners of the room as I squeezed her cool hand, forcing back tears. "Is there anything we can do?" I asked.

The doctor's eyes were full of compassion as she leaned her elbows on her desk. "There is an experimental new treatment—"

"Yes," I said immediately, glancing at my mom's gaunt profile.

"Experimental, meaning it hasn't been proven," she said carefully, her face solemn. "And it also isn't covered by insurance."

"But it could save her?" I asked.

Dr. Weisman shook her head, focusing on my mom. "It might give you more time."

"A year?" I asked. "Ten years?"

"I don't know," she said. "It's at a hospital in Naples, but I could refer you. They'll have to determine whether you're a good candidate."

"Okay," I said. I knew my mom was a good candidate; she was only forty-nine, and she'd beat this hellish diagnosis once before. If an experimental treatment could work for anyone, it could work for her. "Thank you."

"Wait," my mom said, patting my hand. "How much does it cost?"

The doctor slid a folder across the desk and I grabbed it, rifling through the pages until I located the printout of the costs on the very last page. My heart sank. "Each treatment is $146,000?" I asked, incredulous.

"I know it's a lot," Dr. Weisman said.

"How many would my mom need?" I asked.

"The treatments are in monthly cycles," Dr. Weisman said. "Often, to start, treatment is recommended on an ongoing basis."

"It's okay," my mom said with a bitter smile. "We don't have that kind of money."

A sob escaped my throat. "It's not okay, Mom."

She looked at me, her eyes unnaturally wide without their lashes. "Maybe it's just my time, honey."

"No," I said, shooting to my feet. "Send us the referral. I'll find the money."

"What did your dad say?" Tyson asked that evening, taking a pull on the joint that burned between his fingers.

We were on the covered porch of his parents' giant hacienda-style house at the far edge of the suburbs, overlooking their pool and the orange groves beyond as the sinking sun turned the sky tangerine.

"Dad said he couldn't afford to help." I took the joint from Tyson and inhaled deeply, hoping the marijuana might numb the mixture of despair and panic that had been coursing through me since the meeting with my mom's doctor. "He has three children with his new wife."

I could count on one hand the number of times I'd met my half-siblings. It was a sore point.

"I thought his family was rich or something," Tyson said.

I shook my head. "His parents have some money, but most of it is tied up in real estate."

My dad was Swiss and lived in Geneva, where we'd lived until my parents divorced when I was ten and my mom and I moved back to Florida, where she was from. Because he wasn't American, he wasn't subject to American child support laws, but his parents did buy a house for us to live in—the house my mom still lived in—which was why we couldn't refinance or sell it to pay for her treatment. It belonged to them, not to us.

"You could do one of those GoFundMe's," Tyson suggested.

I snorted. "Are you kidding me? My mom would rather die. Literally."

I got up and went to the railing, silently watching the sun melt into the horizon. Only Ian's trailer marred the pastoral view. Originally intended to be a caretaker's home, it sat on the far side of a small pond behind the house, out of sight from the street but fully visible from our vantage point.

"There are other ways to get the money," Tyson said, casting a glance at me through the smoke that hung in the humid air. "You have a very specific set of skills."

"I'm not Liam Neeson, and this isn't a movie," I said.

"I'm not saying that it's what you want to do, or what you should do." He sucked on the joint, studying the beat-up Toyota Corolla bumping along the gravel road to Ian's trailer. "But you're so talented. It's what I would do, if I were you."

It was true I was good at hacking. Very good, my skill born out of an early obsession with gaming that had led me down the rabbit hole during the endless days spent in my mother's hospital room after her first diagnosis, shortly after we moved back to the States. Some kids might have lost themselves in books or movies, but I had more of an engineering brain and loved the puzzle of computers, the black-and-white cause and effect. Humans were mercurial, computers were predictable; life was messy, but the digital landscape was infinitely organized—which was comforting when you were a child in a strange land with your mother wasting away in a hospital bed.

But even though I could use my skills to steal the money for my mother's treatments—and I could, I knew I could—it wasn't an option I was willing to consider. "Even if I was okay with that, Mom wouldn't be," I said. "And not just because of the morality. She cares more about my future than her own. She'd never let me risk going to jail for her."

"How is it any different than hacking into a government database to wipe my DUI?" he asked.

I winced, thinking how dumb I'd been to agree to do that our senior year in high school. "I was stupider then," I said. "And she didn't know about that. Plus, the government is notoriously disorganized."

"Well," he said, pulling me into his lap, "I think we've found our target."

"I am not stealing from the government!" I protested, swatting his chest.

"Doesn't have to be the government," he said, watching as the Corolla parked between the pond and Ian's trailer. "Any big company will do. You know Cody is working for American Drugs now." He nuzzled my neck. "He's always had a thing for you. He thinks I don't know, but I know."

I didn't try to deny it.

Where Tyson was fire, his older brother Cody was earth. Solid, reliable, prone to getting stepped on. He wasn't as magnetic as Tyson, but he was a good guy, and I liked him. Everyone liked him. He was likable. Unfortunately, next to his brother, he fell into shadow.

In front of Ian's trailer, a girl emerged from the Corolla. We were too far away to make out her features, but she was slim with short dark hair, and looked to be about our age.

"Looks like Ian's getting laid," Tyson commented.

I recoiled. "How do you know she's going over there to sleep with him?"

"True, she could be buying drugs. But this is the third time this week I've seen her over there, and the other two times, her car was there all night. So either she has a drug problem, or he's getting laid."

Or both. "Why do your parents let him live there?"

"They like having somebody there to watch the place when they're out of town. They don't know about the drugs. And this weed is pretty good, so I'm not gonna tell them. I'm sure he'd rather be hacking into a drug company if he had the opportunity."

"Ha-ha," I said, shaking my head. "It's not for lack of skill, that's for sure. He was smarter than any of us."

"Remember that program he designed to bypass the pay option on the vending machine outside of Mr. Gutierrez's room so that it was free?"

I nodded. "He had so much potential. What happened to him?"

"I think it's pretty obvious," he said, drawing on the joint. "Drugs can really fuck shit up." He grinned, holding the roach out to me. "Want the last hit?"

Yeah, Tyson was definitely missing a sensitivity chip. I waved the joint away, the pleasant light-headedness threatening to turn on me with all this talk of Ian.

"Cody's coming into town this weekend," he went on. "I'll talk to him about it."

"No," I said, rising to go to the railing. "Even if I wanted to be a criminal, it's not like you snap your fingers and money is in your account. You'd have to come up with a plan, a program . . ."

"Now you're thinking," he said.

"I'm not," I said, staring down at the reflection of the sky in the pool.

But I was.

CHAPTER 3

Le Rêve was stark, white, and modern, with no windows facing the driveway.

"Shoes," Laurent said, indicating a row of cubbyholes nestled beneath a bench just outside the door. "Never wear them in the house."

"Got it," I said solemnly as I slipped off my trainers and stowed them in a cubby.

He pressed the silver latch of the door and it swung noiselessly inward, revealing a view of the sunlit sea beyond. The house was high enough on the hill that the vista was uninterrupted, the entire front wall open to the rectangular infinity pool and panorama of calm blue sea, where three jagged rocks jutted out of the water like the spines of a giant dragon about to emerge from the bay.

To my right was a spacious living room featuring chic low-slung couches, to my left a long wooden dining table, and beyond that, a bright, streamlined kitchen. The interior was understated and elegant and flowed naturally into the shaded exterior living area. The space had clearly been designed to be unobtrusive, stepping out of the way for the true star of the show, the view.

Motion drew my eye to the row of loungers along the pool, where a topless blond sunbather sat up, gazed in my direction from behind gigantic sunglasses, then unceremoniously turned onto her stomach. Next to her, another long-limbed, similarly clad girl, this one caramel-skinned with lush dark curls, lifted her head to look at me before muttering something unintelligible to the first girl. They turned away, bored by my very presence, as I stood there awkwardly, wondering whether to introduce myself.

Though I'd worked hard to overcome the social anxiety that had crippled me when I was younger, meeting new people still did not come naturally to me. I preferred the solitary side of my career, sitting behind a computer for long hours, while Rosa thrived in social situations—one of the reasons we made such good partners. I wished she were here.

Laurent beckoned me to follow as he rolled my suitcase past the dining table, into the far corner of the kitchen, where he pushed open a door on the view side of the house. Inside was a short hallway that led into a well-appointed bedroom featuring a platform bed and a wall of windows overlooking the view. "Tyson's wife, Samira, is the blonde, Gisèle is her friend," he said. "They are Belgian."

He said it as if that should mean something, and I nodded, but whatever the implication was went right over my head. "Models?" I asked, though I knew from my cursory research that at least Samira was.

"Yes." He approached the sliding glass door, indicating the sun deck beyond, where four chairs were arranged around a fire pit. "This deck is at the spa end of the pool, but you have a more secluded outdoor space through here." He went around the bed to open a door that led to another deck, this one shaded by a flowering tree with orange blossoms. "Be aware you're directly over Tyson's private garden, where he likes to meditate. The entire ground floor is his personal space. Don't go down there unless you are invited."

I nodded as he opened the cabinet next to the television that faced the bed. "Here you have a printer, and extra sheets and towels."

"Where are the rest of the bedrooms?"

"Allison's suite is on the other side of the living room, and the rest are upstairs."

I nodded, forming a mental map. "You don't stay here?"

"No." He met my eye with a small smile that said *Absolutely not, thank God.* "I'll let you unpack." He checked his watch. "It's nearly six. Dinner is at eight, but you have had a long travel day. Would you like anything to eat now?"

I nodded gratefully. "Please."

I glanced toward the pool as I followed him into the kitchen, but Samira and Gisèle had disappeared, replaced by a pretty young maid cleaning up after them. Laurent opened the gargantuan stainless steel refrigerator, revealing neatly stacked glass containers of food interspersed with orderly rows of Perrier, fresh-squeezed juices, and French wines. The bottom shelf of Coors Light stood out like a Big Mac in a Michelin-starred restaurant. I had to smile. However many other ways Tyson might have changed since I last saw him, he was apparently still drinking Coors Light.

Laurent took a handful of containers from the refrigerator and set them on the island as I grabbed a large Perrier. By the time I'd quenched my thirst, he was sliding a plate of freshly cut fruit and a smoked salmon sandwich toward me. "You're an angel," I said.

I'd just stuffed the first delicious bite of sandwich into my mouth when I heard voices and turned to see two men in polos coming up the stairs. One was in his twenties with a backpack on his shoulders, the other in his fifties carrying a briefcase. They nodded to Laurent and me as they cut across the room toward the front door.

"Tony," a female voice called out, and the older man turned to face the woman who emerged from the stairwell, holding a folder. "You left this," she said, handing him the folder.

Allison Zhu was just as broad-shouldered and svelte in a figure-hugging black dress as she had been in a Speedo when she shot to fame as a gold medal swimmer in the 2012 and 2016 Olympics, her perpetual poise and endorsement deals with Under Armour, Verizon, and Dove making her a household name. Her features were sharper than they had been when she was younger, her formerly long straight black hair now blunt-cut in a chic bob, but she radiated the same cool control that had been her trademark all those years ago.

She and Tyson had met in college, but this was the first time I'd encountered her, and she was nothing if not intimidating as she turned her attention to me when the men left. "Hi," she said, approaching with her hand extended. Her grip was strong, her dark eyes penetrating. "I'm Allison. You're Tyson and Cody's friend?"

So they'd called me a friend. That was a good sign. "Audrey," I replied. "Nice to meet you."

I'd learned in my brief research that after she'd retired from competitive swimming, Allison had gone on to business school, and, looking for something to do with the millions she'd made on her endorsement deals, had partnered with Tyson to create De-Sal. Tyson may have been the creative genius who patented the technology, but it was clear from everything I read about her that Allison was a shrewd businesswoman who had turned the company into the behemoth it was today, with more than a hundred desalination centers all over the world.

"We're still wrapping up for the day downstairs, but I'll see you at dinner?" she asked as she withdrew her hand.

"Yes," I said.

Laurent turned to me as Allison jogged down the stairs. "I have to pick up Jennifer at the spa," he said. "You will be okay?"

I nodded. "I'm pretty tired. I'll probably try to take a nap."

"I'll wake you at six-thirty."

"You don't have to."

He smiled, a hint of mirth in his bright blue eyes. "Unfortunately, I do."

"Ah," I said, understanding. *Tyson. Of course.* "Well, then, I'll see you at six-thirty."

Back in my room, I closed the drapes against the bright day and lay on the soft bed, wondering what the hell I'd gotten myself into.

But it was only five days. I could handle anything for five days, and I'd been clear when I accepted this invitation that it was the one and only time I'd respond when Tyson called in a favor. He'd agreed, of course, but I knew better than to take Tyson at his word. No, if I wanted Tyson Dale out of my life for good, I'd have to find a way to make that happen.

Fortunately, I was resourceful.

ELEVEN YEARS AGO, JUNE

The sun had not yet dropped beneath the horizon when I tucked my mom into bed and biked the two miles over to Tyson's. It was so humid I should've borrowed her car, but I got so little time to myself that the twenty minutes alone with my thoughts was worth showing up damp with perspiration.

I found Tyson and Cody poolside in the soft evening light tending the smoking grill, longnecks dangling from their hands. Cody was slightly taller and broader than Tyson, but somehow took up less space, his personality as reserved as Tyson's was brash, his sense of style trending toward traditional—like the golf shirt he now wore—while Tyson was more of a rock 'n' roll kind of guy.

"Hi, gorgeous." Tyson lifted my backpack from my shoulders and set it in a chair. "Does this mean you're staying the night?"

I smiled. "Maybe."

I didn't usually spend the night with Tyson, because I wanted to be there to help Mom if she awoke in the night in pain, but I knew that after the amount of energy she'd expended while we were at the beach today, she'd be out cold until morning.

He pulled me closer, slipped an arm around me, and kissed me.

"Mmm . . . salty." I pushed him away, stripping down to my bikini to dive into the pool.

I emerged refreshed and Tyson handed me a towel with a naughty grin as I approached the grill, wringing out my long hair.

"What do we have here?" I asked Cody.

He gave me an affectionate pat on the shoulder. "Shrimp, bell pepper, and pineapple skewers."

"Yum. What's that?" I asked, pointing at the palm-size packets of tinfoil.

"Marinated lionfish we caught diving today," Tyson said.

I raised my brows. "Are we going to die tonight?"

"I watched a video online on how to fillet it," Cody said. "It's supposed to be good. And it won't kill you, even if I did it wrong."

"A ringing endorsement," I said dryly.

But when we sat down to eat at the table on the covered porch, we all had to agree that the lionfish was actually quite good, white and flaky and slightly buttery, similar to mahi-mahi.

After dinner, Cody topped up our glasses of white wine as Tyson popped the cap on another Coors Light. "Sure you don't want to drink something that doesn't taste like piss?" Cody teased.

"One man's piss is another man's wine," Tyson quipped.

"Ew," I said, rising to walk out to the glowing pool. The pavement was still warm with the heat of the day as I sat on the edge and dangled my feet in the soft water.

Behind me, a phone dinged. "I'm gonna run over to Ian's and pick up some weed," Tyson said.

As he went out the back gate, Cody sat down next to me, lying back on the pavement with his feet in the pool.

All week I'd been going back and forth over the idea Tyson had planted about hacking to get the money for my mom's treatments, fearful of losing her but equally fearful of crossing a line I couldn't uncross. But something had clicked inside me today when we were at the beach, and I now knew I'd do whatever it took to save her.

"Did Tyson tell you about my mom?" I asked, afraid to look at Cody.

He nodded. "I'm so sorry, Audrey."

I bit my lip, holding back tears. "It's not fair," I said to the sky.

"No, it's not," he agreed. "Tyson told me about the treatment she needs, and how much it costs." He let out a sigh. "I don't know if I can help."

I closed my eyes as my heart imploded.

"But I want to try," he finished.

My head snapped toward him. "What do you mean?"

"I can get you into the system. The rest is up to you."

"Seriously?" I asked, my heart beating erratically.

He nodded. "It's big and disorganized with very little oversight, and honestly the company is doing enough shady shit that while I don't like to break the law, I also don't feel like it's morally wrong. Alex needs the money more than their billionaire CEO does."

I blinked at him, flooded with gratitude. "Thank you."

"Poke around, come up with a workable plan, then we can go over it together."

"Okay. I'll be careful, I swear. If I think there's any chance of getting caught, I won't do it."

"I trust your judgment."

I grabbed his hand and squeezed. "Thank you, Cody."

The gate on the far side of the patio swung open and Tyson entered, a look of annoyance on his face. I realized why a split second later, when Ian followed him through, letting the gate slam behind him.

"Oh shit," Ian said as the metal clanged, turning back so quickly that he almost lost his balance. He was barefoot in basketball shorts and a dirty sleeveless T-shirt, and as he drew closer, I could see that his pupils were as big as saucers. "Whassup?" he said, reaching down to give Cody and me sloppy high-fives.

"Careful," I said as he tottered near the edge of the pool.

"Audrey," he crowed, collapsing to the concrete next to me and plunging his feet into the pool. "It's good to have you home." His words were slurring, and when he threw an arm around my shoulders, his body odor was so pungent that it was all I could do not to recoil.

"Everybody else was dicks to me in high school, but you—you! You were always nice."

"Thank you." I patted his hand and removed his arm from my shoulders as I stood, going to the table to retrieve my wine as an excuse to escape the acrid scent of him.

Cody eyed Ian. "Ian, what's going on?"

"Oh you know," he said. "Ran outta beer. Tyson thought I shouldn't drive to the store, so he was kind enough to offer me some of yours."

Tyson approached him with a half-full case. "Here you go."

"Thanks, man, I'll pay you," Ian said, fumbling in his pocket, producing some change, a receipt, and a baggie of white powder. "Oh shit, here, take this," he said, tossing the bag of powder at Tyson. "It's good coke."

Tyson shrugged and pocketed it while Ian pulled out his other pocket, producing a wadded-up bunch of ones and a set of tiny keys. "Oh damn," Ian said, dangling the keys from his finger. "Don't want to lose these."

None of us said anything, not wanting to give him reason to stay, but he wasn't discouraged. "Got a lockbox," he went on. "A security . . . Secure . . ."

"A safety deposit box?" I asked.

He pointed at me. "Where I can lock up my secrets safe."

A receipt fluttered to the pavement, and I picked it up and handed it to him, noticing that it was a teller's receipt from Bank of the South, but curious as I was, I stopped myself from checking the balance.

"I can walk you back," Tyson said, helping Ian to his feet.

Ian reached for the case. "I'll stay and have a beer."

Tyson jerked it away and Ian again teetered dangerously at the edge of the pool. "We're going to bed."

"What, we're not friends anymore?" Ian whined.

Tyson clenched his jaw, taking Ian by the elbow. "Let's go."

"You don't wanna cross me," Ian snapped, wrenching his arm from Tyson's grasp to grab the box of beer. But he didn't protest further as Tyson ushered him roughly to the gate.

"Thank God," Cody muttered as it clanged shut behind them.

But I felt no sense of relief as they disappeared into the night. Maybe I should have been worried about the felony I planned to commit to get the money for my mom's treatment, but the bad feeling tugging at my gut had nothing to do with that.

Trouble breeds trouble, and as bad as I may have felt for him, Ian Kelley was trouble.

CHAPTER 4

By early evening, I was revitalized by a power nap followed by a shower and an espresso—thanks to Laurent, who'd had the wherewithal to inquire whether I'd like one when I came out of my room wrapped in the white waffle robe I'd found hanging in my bathroom, unable to shut off the shower. He gamely followed me into the bathroom and cut the water with a pressing rather than a pulling motion, impervious to the spray that soaked through his white buttondown, leaving it stuck to his toned chest.

He ran his hand through his wet curls as he stepped out of the shower and for a moment when our eyes met, I felt almost as though he'd reached out and touched me. I turned away quickly, wondering as I led him to the door just how many women had asked him to fix their showers when they weren't broken, and of those women, how many might not have kept their robes on.

I'd just finished dressing in a strapless black jumpsuit when there was a light tap on my door and I opened it to find Mr. Sexy Butler there with a freshly brewed espresso in hand. He'd changed into a fitted black T-shirt that somehow looked even better on him than the button-down, the tail of a tattoo peeking out beneath his sleeve. "Tyson wants you," he said.

It was fifteen minutes before the time Tyson had specified, but I was ready. I downed the espresso, then grabbed my backpack and slung it over my shoulder as Laurent reached for it. "I can take that," he said.

"I've got it," I assured him.

I followed him into the onion-and-butter-scented kitchen where two white-uniformed chefs were preparing our meal, while on the deck, one of the staff lit candles in hurricane lamps as the light bled from the evening sky.

My heart rate increased steadily as Laurent led me down the stairwell to Tyson's private terrace, where he rapped gently on the wide wooden door. After a moment that felt like a lifetime, the door swung open, revealing the man I'd once been in love with.

He was barefoot, dressed in loose natural linen pants and a matching collarless button-front shirt, a mixture of leather and silver jewelry around his neck and wrists, his dark hair Jesus-long. He was gaunt, his formerly tawny skin sallow, the hollows beneath his eyes giving him a haunted appearance. He looked like he hadn't slept in a week.

I covered my shock with a smile as he ran a hand through his hair, looking me up and down without comment. "Tyson," I said. "Good to see you."

When he didn't reply, Laurent filled the silence. "Dinner will be ready at eight."

Tyson opened the door wider and retreated into the depths of his suite without a word, leaving me to throw a distressed glance at Laurent. "Don't take it personally," he said quietly.

I could smell sage burning somewhere as I crossed the threshold and closed the door behind me, allowing my eyes to adjust to the gloom. Only one side of the vestibule was open, so I went that way, coming around the corner into another full kitchen open to a dining room.

It wasn't just the heavy blackout drapes covering the windows that made it darker down here. The surfaces of the kitchen were gunmetal gray, the cabinets above sleek and black. A modern brass chandelier burned low above a black walnut dining table, where Tyson was seated at the head of the table, a glass of something that looked like sludge before him.

The temperature was somewhere in the vicinity of iceberg, and goosebumps prickled my arms as I pulled out a chair and sat, placing my backpack in the empty seat between us. He looked at it as though it might contain venomous snakes. "Leave that outside," he said quietly.

"It has my computer and my notebooks—"

"You don't need it. Leave it outside."

I frowned, assessing him. It wasn't just his physical appearance; his whole aura was different. Darker. Still just as magnetic, but with a heaviness that hadn't been there before.

I rose and hefted the backpack. Once I'd dropped it outside the door, I returned to the table, but he stopped me before I could sit. "Put your arms out," he said, rising.

"What?"

He sighed as though exhausted. "I need to make sure you're not wired."

"Wired?" I laughed. "Would you have called me here if there was any chance I'd be wearing a wire?"

He held his ground, and I extended my arms, trying not to cringe while he felt around my torso. He paused with his hands on my back, inhaling me the way a wolf does a rabbit, and I shuddered to think I used to crave those cold hands on my body. "You'll need to wash those harmful chemicals off your skin," he said gruffly, letting me go.

"What?"

"It's bad for your health and the odor gives me a headache. Laurent should have told you."

Gathering that he was referring to my perfume, I nodded, dropping into my seat. No wonder he smelled different now, his formerly ubiquitous cologne replaced with whatever herbs and supplements were leaking through his skin.

"Are you unwell?" I asked gently. That would explain a lot.

He snorted, those dark eyes flashing. "I'm healthier than I've ever been."

I nodded, crossing my arms. So that's how this was going to go. "Why am I here?"

He slid a long white envelope across the table to me. I picked it up, noting it was addressed in neat block lettering to him here at Le Rêve. There was no return address, but it was postmarked with my home zip code, which had been his parents' as well until they sold their property after Hurricane Irma ripped the roof off their house and destroyed the orange grove. "Open it," he instructed.

I lifted the flap and extracted a clipping of a newspaper article with the headline LATEST FOOT IDENTIFIED AS MISSING MIAMI-DADE COUNTY RESIDENT IAN KELLEY.

"I've read this," I said.

His eyes bored holes in me. "Why did you send it to me?"

"What?" I asked, thrown. "I didn't send this to you."

"Then who did?"

"I have no idea." I placed the envelope on the table between us, shaking my head. "Wait. Back up. Is this why you called me down here?"

"What do you want from me?"

I blinked at him, trying to gauge where he was coming from. "What are you talking about?"

"Money? A job?"

"What? No. You invited me—"

"You may think you have the upper hand here, but we go down together," he growled. "What would your sons do then, huh?"

I pushed back from the table, my chair scraping over the tile as I shot to my feet. "What the fuck, Tyson?" I was shaking. "I don't want anything from you. And I didn't send you that article. Though I do think we should talk about its contents—"

"Why, so you can record our conversation? Are you working with the feds?"

"The *feds*?" I shook my head. Talk about paranoia. "I don't know what is going on with you, but I had nothing to do with any of it. Keep your money. I'm going home. I'll find somewhere else to stay for the night."

Anger roiled in my veins as I stormed toward the door. To think I'd come all the way down here for him to accuse me of—what? I wasn't even sure.

"You're forgetting I have evidence," he said without rising.

I spun to face him. "Of what?"

His face was placid. "The statute of limitations may be up, but you think the attorneys and law enforcement agencies your little firm works with will continue to trust you with their confidential information once they know you're a thief and a liar?"

It was all I could do not to smack him. "I know your secrets too," I said through gritted teeth.

"Yes." He smiled. The asshole. He was actually enjoying this. "But it would be very difficult for you to spill them without implicating yourself. And once I destroy your reputation, who do you think people will believe?"

"Fuck you, Tyson," I spat. "What do *you* want from *me*?"

"Now we're getting somewhere." He pointed at the chair opposite him. "Sit down."

My knees wobbled as I sat heavily into the chair, staring daggers at him.

"If you want me to believe you didn't send this," he said, tapping the envelope, "then tell me who did."

"I told you, I don't know!"

"Discovery agent," he scoffed, making air quotes with his fingers. "What does that even mean?"

I glared at him, cursing myself for being stupid enough to think coming here was a good idea.

He thrust the envelope at me. "Discover who sent this, and your secret is safe."

"Why do you care?" I appealed. "It's just an article. Public knowledge."

"I think we both know there's more to it than that."

I shook my head. "Anyone who was around at the time Ian disappeared knows he'd been living on your property, and they know how successful you are now. Someone is just fucking with you." I rubbed my hands up and down my arms to warm myself. "What we should be talking about is what we're going to say to the police when they call us for statements."

"We already gave them statements."

"Ten years ago, when it was a disappearance. There's a body now. If they open a murder investigation, we're going to have to answer questions all over again."

"So, I'll tell them what I told them then." He leveled his gaze at me. "Unless you give me reason to change my story. You have five days to figure out who sent me this, or I'll have to assume it was you."

I'd promised myself I wouldn't let him manipulate me, and within ten minutes, he'd turned me into his bitch.

CHAPTER 5

I steeled my nerves, hardening my face as I stared across the table at Tyson. How was it possible that just ten short years ago I'd been smitten with this black hole of a human being? The thought was revolting.

But he'd been different then. Not perfect, by any means, but not . . . this. The venom I'd seen only glimpses of when we were together had clearly spread like a fungus within him, turning Jekyll into Hyde.

"If we're going to play this game," I said, crossing my arms over my chest, "who—besides me—do you think might have sent you this article?"

"Someone in my inner circle," he said darkly.

"What makes you think that?"

"This address is private. Only people close to me would know it."

I raised my brows, turning on the sarcasm. "Like me?"

"You're a 'discovery agent,' right? I think we both know you could easily have discovered it."

"As could any number of other people. Not to mention anyone that works here or has seen you come and go," I added.

"So, you'll need to narrow down the list."

I swallowed the acid in my throat. It was true that he could ruin my life with a lot less self-sabotage than would be necessary for me to ruin his. If I was really going to stay here—which I would decide once I had a moment to parse out whether his threat held water—I needed to blunt the sharp edges between us before this turned into a bloodbath.

"Let's start over," I said, composing myself. "You mentioned your inner circle. Is there anyone you're close to that you suspect could mean you harm?"

"All of them."

I refrained from pointing out that if he treated them anything like the way he was treating me right now, he deserved it. "I'm gonna need more than that."

He took a slurp of his green drink. "The board wants to take the company public, and I won't let them."

"Anyone specific, or the board in general?"

"Most of them are too scared to cross me. They saw what happened last time someone did that."

"Which was?"

"Suffice it to say his career is over."

I narrowed my eyes, wishing he'd allowed me a pen and paper. "Could he be the one behind this?"

Tyson shook his head. "He's dead."

I gaped at him.

"Not my fault he decided to off himself," he muttered.

"Jesus, Tyson." His cruelty was one thing, but this level of antipathy was something else entirely. "So, who is most adamant you take the company public?"

"That conversation is tabled," he said. "Now it's about bringing in additional investors. I don't have any interest in diluting my shares further, but Allison needs the money."

"Why?"

"She made a bad investment and now she owes the bank eighty million. She's getting desperate. She already sold her house in Aspen. Lately she's been trying to talk me into buying her out or allowing her to sell some of her shares to an investor. Like I'm responsible for her bad decisions."

I swallowed my impulse to comment on Tyson's blatant insensitivity. "So, you think she could be planning to blackmail you to get money out of you?"

He shrugged.

"Okay," I said evenly. "Who else?"

"My brother hates me."

I tilted my head. "Why?"

"He thinks I don't respect him."

"Do you?"

"No."

"But would he send you this article, specifically?" I asked, tapping the letter. "It doesn't seem likely. Have you talked to him about it?"

"No."

"We should—"

"No," he said firmly. "If it's him, I don't want to give him the satisfaction."

"Okay," I said, furrowing my brow. "Anyone else you think it could be?"

"It could be his girlfriend, or my wife, or her best friend."

I was beginning to see a pattern. "They hate you as well?" I asked.

"Samira gets nothing from me unless we're married three years. I made my expectations clear before we married and she was fine with it in the beginning, but lately she's started . . . acting out."

I didn't blame her. "How long have you been married?"

"Fourteen months."

I evaluated him. "If they all hate you so much—and I'm gonna go out on a limb here and say you hate them too—why are you all on vacation together?"

"We're not on vacation, we're here to open a De-Sal center. St. Barth's is a territory of France, and we've had a hard time breaking into the E.U. with all their environmental regulations. If this works, we'll be in France by next year, and the rest of the E.U. will follow suit. If it doesn't work, we'll have to revisit taking the company public or bringing on investors, which, like I said, I don't want to do."

"But Allison does."

He nodded.

"Again, why are all these people you hate staying in your house?" I pressed.

"Security reasons."

Frustration prickled beneath my skin. "Is there a security threat?"

He pointed his eyes at the letter.

"So, you gathered everyone you suspect might be out to get you here, in your home?" I pressed.

"The house is gated and free of outside listening or viewing devices, my staff is vetted, my Wi-Fi is secure, and I can keep an eye on everyone with the cameras hidden in all public areas of the house. So yes. It is best that they, and you, stay here."

"I'll need access to those cameras."

"I'll arrange it. Anything else you need, ask Laurent."

"Does he know about the clipping?" I asked, tapping the envelope.

"No. And I trust you won't tell him, or anyone else."

I nodded. "What does he know?"

"That you're a former friend, here to help me solve a personal problem."

"You trust him?" I asked. As paranoid as Tyson obviously was, his apparent faith in Laurent seemed inconsistent.

He smiled faintly. "I know enough of his secrets that I feel confident he won't risk crossing me."

So Laurent had secrets too. Fascinating.

"Anything else you think I should know?" I asked.

"The developers who own the land that overlooks the site of the future De-Sal center are trying to tank it. They bought the land before the De-Sal project was announced and believe they won't recoup their expense because the center will mar the view."

I nodded. "Lemme guess, they hate you too."

"Yes." Tyson's watch buzzed and he rose, gesturing to the door. "That's all the time I have."

I stood, kicking myself for being naïve enough to think his reasons for inviting me down here were benign.

But I was no pushover, I thought as I stepped into the sunlight, gathering my bag from where I'd left it beside the door. He might have the upper hand right now, but only because his accusation and threats had caught me off guard. I just needed a moment to recalibrate.

My head spun as I trudged up the stairs. Did he truly think I'd sent that article to him? Was this even really about the article?

If this were an actual job, I would walk. There simply wasn't enough to go on, other than Tyson's paranoia about who hated him and why, which might very well have no tie to reality. It certainly didn't where I was concerned.

Regardless, it was in my best interest to stay on his good side, and if someone really was blackmailing him, it concerned me as well. As much as I hated it, our fates were intertwined.

Cody and Tyson hovered behind me at the desk in Tyson's father's office, staring intently at the two computer monitors displaying the program I'd designed.

"American Drugs has contracts with thousands of vendors whose products are sold in their stores," I said, pointing to the list on the screen. "Every time a sale is made, there's a split with the manufacturer. The program I've designed is a sales deflation program—or SADEP. It deflates sales by an infinitesimal amount on a random, rotating basis, so AD is paying out the same amount of money, but a tiny fraction of it falls through the cracks into our hands."

Tyson peeled an orange as Cody crossed his arms over his chest. "So we're not actually stealing from AD."

I shook my head. "And we're not stealing a large amount from any one company, but a tiny amount from thousands of companies. An imperceptible amount to them, but a lifesaving amount to my mom."

"That's fucking brilliant," Tyson said, popping an orange wedge into his mouth. "You're fucking brilliant."

I spun in my desk chair, looking up at Cody. "What do you think?"

"He's right," Cody said. "It's brilliant. I wish I were half as smart as you."

I laughed, relieved that he approved of the idea. "You make a girl blush."

"How long will it take to get the money you need for the first round of treatment?" Cody asked.

"Depends on sales and how bold we want to be with the numbers," I said. "I want to be safe about it."

"Of course," Cody said.

"But you need the money now." Tyson offered me a piece of orange, and I shook my head.

It was a new thing, this orange obsession. He'd begun eating them morning, noon, and night, in conjunction with meditating in the rays of the rising and setting sun. He'd explained the supposed health benefits to me, but I knew he'd likely be into something else within a week.

"If sales remain steady and I run the SADEP at a moderate level, I can have the money in a week," I said. "After which I would pause it until I need to run it again."

"Or just keep it running," Tyson suggested. "You could run it for years and no one would notice."

Cody and I both shook our heads, unamused, and Tyson held up his hands. "I'm just saying, Audrey could go back to school. I could buy a boat. Cody could pay for hair plugs."

"Fuck off," Cody said, running his hand through his hair. It was only slightly thinning, but Tyson loved nothing more than to razz him about it.

"Better check your fingers," Tyson ribbed. "You just lost another fifty strands."

"Tyson, enough," I said. "We're not in this for profit."

"Why not?" he asked. "You're committing the same crime either way. If you get arrested, the police aren't going to care why you were stealing, or what you used the money for, or even exactly how much you stole. You might as well enjoy some of the rewards."

Cody snorted. "You mean *you* might as well enjoy the rewards."

"I am the one that suggested it. Seems only fair." He grinned, tossing an orange wedge into the air and catching it in his mouth.

"The reward is my mother living," I said. "I'm not doing this for me."

Cody shot eye daggers at Tyson. "And I'm not going to allow *you* to make it about *you.*"

"You don't get to *allow* me to do anything, big brother," Tyson returned. "You don't control me."

"For this, he does," I rejoined. "He controls us both. He's the one taking the most risk, so he makes the rules."

Tyson laughed. "Jeez, you guys are so serious."

"This is serious business," Cody said. "If we get caught, we could face serious consequences. Jail time. The only reason I'm even considering this is to save Alex's life. Not so you can buy a fucking boat."

Tyson crossed his arms. "Don't you want Audrey to be able to go back to college?"

"For the last time, this isn't about me," I snapped, standing. "I'm going to get some air."

I strode out of the room, leaving the desk chair spinning in my wake.

Outside, the day was sweltering. It had rained all night and the air felt heavy as the moisture evaporated in the beating sun. I stripped down to my swimsuit, leaving my dress in a pile on the concrete as I dove into the pool, which was almost too warm to be refreshing.

I swam a few laps to clear the irritation buzzing inside me, until I sensed I wasn't alone and surfaced in the shallow end, ready to tell Tyson off for the way he'd treated his brother. Only it wasn't Tyson that was standing at the edge of the pool smoking a cigarette.

"Hey, Audrey," Ian said as I looked up at him. He was barefoot, as usual, and muddy.

"Ian," I said, trying to sound friendly. "What's up?"

"The water in my trailer isn't working."

"Okay," I said, annoyed. "I'll go get Tyson. I'm sure they have someone that can see about it."

I noticed his hand was shaking as he raised the cigarette to his mouth. "I've been working on it."

"You've been working on the plumbing?" I asked, mounting the steps in the shallow end. "I don't know if that's a good idea. Is that why you're muddy?"

"The pipes are under the house."

I grabbed a towel off a lounge chair and wrapped it around myself. "Do you know about plumbing?" I asked.

He sucked on the cigarette like it was his job. "Enough."

"Ian," Tyson called out as he emerged from the house. "You look like a pig in shit."

"He's been trying to fix the water for his trailer," I said.

Tyson crossed his arms as he approached, looking Ian up and down. "What's up with your water?"

"It's dirty."

Tyson gestured toward Ian's trailer. "Why don't you show me what we're working with, and we'll take it from there."

I snatched my dress off the pavement and headed inside as they exited through the back gate. The air conditioning on my wet skin was a welcome relief, the beige marble slick beneath my feet.

"Hey," Cody called from the open kitchen as I cut across the great room toward the stairs.

I changed direction, meeting him at the kitchen island.

"You feel good about the VPN you're using?" he asked.

I nodded. "It's secure."

"And the bank account?"

"A numbered account in Switzerland. It was opened using residential papers, so ownership is protected."

Opened thirteen years ago by my dad to funnel money to me on Christmas and my birthday without having to involve my mom. Only he and I had access to it, and I knew he only ever checked it when depositing the thousand dollars he gave me on those days. My birthday had just passed, and Christmas wasn't for another seven months, so I felt safe using the account for our deposits for now.

I could see Cody trying to work out how I'd opened an account overseas, but I laid a hand on his arm. "Probably better you don't know. You're risking enough."

Cody was a good man, and I felt guilty for the risk he was taking on my behalf, but I'd been over and over it, and this was the only possible way I could come up with the money I needed quickly enough for it to make any difference.

"Like I said upstairs, you're in control," I said. "You say the word, I shut it down."

"I trust you, Audrey," he said, his dark eyes clear. "It's my brother I don't trust."

I forced a laugh. "His moral code is certainly questionable."

He looked at me for a moment, his brows tugging together.

"What?" I asked.

"I just don't understand what a girl like you sees in him."

But as infuriating as Tyson could be, he also made me feel good about myself. He wanted my opinion, gave weight to my viewpoint. In a world where I was no longer the star student—or a student at all—he told me I was brilliant. He had faith in me even when I didn't.

A year ago, my life had seemed like a river flowing toward a secure future, but the reappearance of my mom's cancer was like a storm that had washed me out to sea and left me adrift alone in a churning ocean. Tyson was a life raft.

But I couldn't say that to Cody. Instead, I simply shrugged. "Sometimes I wonder that myself."

CHAPTER 6

Once I'd written down everything Tyson told me in my notebook, vomited my vitriol toward him on Rosa via text, and fought my way through a ten-minute guided meditation on releasing anger, I felt marginally better. I still had no desire to dine with Tyson's entourage, much less Tyson himself, but I couldn't yet see a better way out of this mess than to determine which of Tyson's inner circle had sent the offending article.

If it were in fact one of them at all.

If not? Well, I'd cross that bridge when I came to it.

Regardless, I needed to get to know the players. So, dinner it was.

I felt like I was putting on body armor as I applied a bit more smoothing cream to my tousled waves to ensure they didn't turn into a lion's mane, hooked sparkly earrings through my ears, and traced the water line of my eyelids with the navy eyeliner Rosa had promised would make my eyes pop against the chestnut color of my hair. I didn't usually wear much makeup and had been doubtful of the color, but as I evaluated myself in the mirror, I saw that she was right, and I could almost imagine she was there with me, soothing my rattled nerves.

I entered the fragrant kitchen to find a woman in a chef's white coat carefully slicing tomatoes. She looked up and smiled. "Bonne soirée, madame," she said.

"Bonne soirée," I returned, wondering briefly when I had graduated from mademoiselle to madame, despite my bare ring finger. "It smells amazing in here."

"I hope you will enjoy."

Though it was eight on the nose, I appeared to be the first guest to arrive. The lights were dimmed, and candles flickered in hurricane lamps on all the tabletops, nestled among tasteful displays of pale pink roses. A soundtrack of chill beats pulsed over the speakers, the pool lights changing color in sync with the beat.

A server dressed in black appeared at my elbow. "Good evening, madame. Would you like a glass of champagne?"

I normally didn't drink when I was working, but after my encounter with Tyson, I could use something to take the edge off. "Yes, thank you," I said.

He took a bottle of Dom from an ice bucket, allowing the bubbles to dissipate as he eased the pale gold liquid into the flute. I took a sip and wandered toward the view, enjoying the soft fizz of effervescence over my tongue.

Tyson could make fun of my line of work all he wanted, but I loved what I did, and I was damn good at it. While I'd started out selectively accepting jobs that required only my computer skills, over the years I'd gotten bolder. Yes, I still did a lot of hacking, but I'd also developed other talents—like stealth and deception—to get the information I needed. I thrived on the adrenaline rush of it, and as long as I stayed within the law, I was not held to the same standards as law enforcement, which made it that much easier for me to uncover the evidence necessary to bolster the cases of the attorneys that hired me.

This assignment—which was how I needed to think of it to avoid scratching Tyson's eyes out—was one that would require every ounce of my people skills. My weakest skill set, to be sure. I wished more than anything that I could call Rosa and get her take, but I couldn't.

Not about this. There was too much she didn't know. That she didn't need to know. I was on my own.

When I reached the edge of the pool, I saw I wasn't in fact the first to arrive. A couple stood at the railing on the deck beneath the infinity pool, looking out over the dark ocean toward the lights of St. Martin glittering on the horizon.

The man was Cody, I realized as he turned his face.

Where Tyson had shrunk, Cody had grown. He had a short beard, his dark hair thinning, and he was bulkier now—not overweight, but thick—in a polo shirt and shorts. The woman was blond, though she didn't have Samira's lanky, effortless cool girl vibe. She was of medium height, her hair carefully curled, her compact, tanned, and gym-toned body wrapped in a tight Pucci print.

She must have sensed my presence because she turned and looked up at me, flashing a smile. Feeling as though I'd been caught eavesdropping, I waved. Cody's face went slack for a moment as he saw me, then he also smiled.

"Cody," I called, genuinely glad to see him. "So good to see you."

"Audrey, welcome," he replied as they approached. I'd kept loosely in touch with Cody for a few years after Tyson and I broke up, but we'd lost touch as De-Sal took off. Now I stood on my toes to give him a hug and he studied my face as we pulled apart. "You look incredible."

"Thank you."

"Hi," the woman said, not to be left out. Up close she had the symmetrical beauty of a newscaster: perfectly arched brows, pert nose, Crest-white smile, skin contoured and scoured of any blemish. She'd definitely had work done, though it was good enough work that it was hard to determine what exactly had been altered. "I'm Jennifer. His girlfriend."

Something about her was familiar, though I couldn't quite place it. "Audrey," I said, extending my hand. "Have we met? You look so familiar."

She shook her head. "I don't think so. Unless you've lived in Wisconsin or San Francisco?"

I shook my head and turned up the wattage in my smile, waving it away as I offered up the friendliest version of myself. "Anyway, it's lovely to meet you."

Acting was as necessary a part of my tool kit as hacking or self-defense, and while I'd never had any desire to perform on stage, I found it freeing to slip into character on a job. It allowed me to disassociate, keeping my true self hidden behind a mask so that I could focus on the task at hand without giving too much of myself away.

Here I'd be more gregarious and less reserved than I was naturally. I'd keep my sarcasm to myself, smile often and chatter affably—make them like me, want to confide in me. It would be trickier to pull off with Tyson and Cody around, but it had been a while since they'd seen me, and Tyson had bullied me into doing this shit for him, so I doubted he'd challenge my faux geniality.

"Excuse me, Monsieur Dale?" called one of the chefs, her hands clasped before her as she lingered at the edge of the kitchen. "I would like to ask you a question about the dinner."

"Excuse me," Cody said, patting my shoulder as he took leave of us to follow her into the kitchen.

Jennifer leaned in, her floral perfume heavy in the humid night air as she whispered, "I hear you and Tyson dated."

I choked on my champagne, the bubbles sharp in my nose. "A long time ago."

She leaned closer. "I hear it didn't end well."

I raised my brows. "I can't argue with that."

Before I could inquire what else she'd heard, Samira and Gisèle came tripping up the stairs in minidresses, a tangle of long legs, beach waves, and supple skin, their heads bent together as they murmured in French too low for me to make out.

"Do you speak French?" Jennifer asked.

I briefly considered lying, but Tyson and Cody knew too much about me. "Yes. My father is Swiss."

"Well then, you'll fit in here better than I do."

I had to laugh. "I doubt it."

She gave me a conspiratorial wink as a server poured Samira and Gisèle glasses of Dom, which they clinked, never casting a glance in our direction as they settled into seats across from each other at the end of the table.

Jennifer's phone dinged with a text and she raised it. "My son," she said as she keyed in a response. "He texts me good night anytime I'm away."

She turned the screen of the phone to face me, displaying an image of a dark-haired boy about my sons' age, and my heart squeezed with longing for my own boys as I smiled. "I have twin boys about the same age."

Jennifer sighed. "It's like I can see him slipping away into teenager-land in front of my eyes."

"I know, right?" It truly was hard, watching my sweet boys turn into surly teenagers before my very eyes, but I was also aware that bonding with her over our similarities would make her more comfortable with me. "It kills me. They won't even let me hug them in public anymore."

"It's the worst," she agreed, then wrinkled her nose. "And he's starting to smell like a teenager too."

I laughed as Laurent approached, touching me lightly on the back and gesturing to the thick oak dining table, which was big enough for twelve but set for only seven, leaving an awkward amount of space between the settings. "Dinner will be served shortly."

And then he was gone, my skin tingling where his fingers had grazed. *Too bad he works for Tyson*, I thought, realizing with embarrassment that Laurent had likely already told him all the questions I'd asked in the car. No wonder Tyson had been so smug.

"How incredible is he?" Jennifer whispered, her gaze tracing the curve of Laurent's ass in his fitted black pants as he returned to the kitchen.

"He is very helpful," I agreed.

"Oh yes, I'd love his help with all kinds of things," she insinuated.

Normally, insta-friend oversharer types struck me as ungenuine and gave me anxiety, but in this scenario, I realized Jennifer could turn out to be quite useful. I laughed again and threw her a wink as we made our way to the table, where she took a seat next to Cody and I settled myself across from her.

Allison emerged from her suite on the other side of the living room, typing madly on her phone as she slid into the seat between me and Gisèle, an arm's length away. The server filled her glass with white wine, and she locked eyes with Cody, saluting him with her glass before she took a sip. I could feel the tension radiating off her, and as she set her phone facedown on the table without so much as a glance in my direction, I had the distinct feeling that whatever shit she was mired in, Cody was in it with her.

Tyson was yet to appear, but no one commented on his absence as Laurent went over the menu for the evening while a waiter whisked away my champagne flute, which I was surprised to find was empty, then filled my wineglass with a chilled white that was crisp and dry on my tongue.

Across the table, I noted that Jennifer covered her wineglass with her hand when the waiter approached.

"Is Tyson coming to dinner?" I asked as small plates of ahi crudo were placed before us.

"He'll be here," Cody said, spearing a chunk of fish with his fork. "But we don't wait for him."

"He's on a liquid diet," Jennifer divulged. "Stirs this nasty green mix some health guru gave him into alkaline water morning, noon, and night."

I nodded, remembering the green sludge he'd been drinking earlier. "But he still drinks Coors Light?"

Allison's sheath of glossy black hair gleamed in the candlelight as she turned to me with a wry smile. "I guess by comparison the green shit tastes good."

Cody chortled, catching my eye. "One man's piss—"

"—is another man's wine," I finished, raising my glass to him.

The shared humor at Tyson's expense elevated the mood at the table enough that Jennifer took a stab at interrogating Samira and Gisèle about the paddleboard yoga class they'd taken earlier. She didn't get much out of them beyond giggles, but I had to admire her moxie as I swallowed a delicious bite of ahi and took another sip of my wine. This was not my usual twelve-dollar bottle from Publix. No, this was the good stuff. The sunshine-in-a-glass stuff, and I would have had no trouble drinking the entire serving in one gulp. Which would be ill-advised, seeing as I was already starting to feel lighter in my seat.

Allison was again typing at her phone while Jennifer complained about how crowded the spa at Eden Roc had been today when the table quieted and eyes shifted toward the stairwell behind me. The giddiness of the wine soured in my stomach at Tyson's approach, his presence pulling at the fabric of the room like dark matter as he took the seat next to me at the head of the table.

Laurent placed a can of Coors Light in front of him, and he sipped it calmly while the table seemed to hold its breath. I didn't dare meet anyone's eyes for fear my internal smirk at the Coors Light would mar my face, drawing Tyson's ire.

After what felt like ages, Tyson spoke. "How are Alexander and Benjamin?" he asked, flashing his most charming smile at me, as though he hadn't just threatened to ruin their lives half an hour ago.

I sensed the others relax as they registered Tyson's mood as non-threatening, but like a mother bear sniffing out danger, I felt the hair rise on the back of my neck at the mention of my boys. "Good," I said, returning his smile without elaboration.

"Oh, come on, you can do better than that," he said with a laugh. "Show us some pictures! I'm sure Cody would love to see them as well."

Cody nodded as he looked from Tyson to me, but I could see the unease behind his smile.

Mechanically, I raised my phone and showed Tyson the lock screen.

"They surf," he commented, taking it from me to study the picture of the boys standing on the beach, surfboards under their arms. "Like you. I bet they're smart, too, aren't they?"

I nodded as he returned the phone. "They are. They're hard workers."

Jennifer reached for the phone. "Oh, they're so cute!" she gushed.

"What are their favorite subjects?" Tyson pressed.

"Alexander's a math whiz, Benjamin's more of a science guy," I answered.

His eyes lingered on my face as he nodded. "That tracks. Kind of like me and Cody. I'm the ideas guy, he's got the business sense."

"As does Allison, I'm sure," I said with a smile in her direction.

Allison and Cody again locked eyes across the table, and Allison nodded ever so slightly.

"Speaking of work, I got the list of council members who will be at the hearing tomorrow," Cody said, directing his voice at his brother.

"Hearing?" I echoed. Tyson hadn't mentioned a hearing earlier—I would have remembered that.

"City council meeting," Allison clarified. "It's not really a hearing. Some assholes don't want the De-Sal center marring their view. Though the footprint is barely the size of one of the yachts you see out there."

"It happens every time we're breaking ground," Cody added. "Some of them are worse than others."

As Allison signaled the waiter for another glass of wine, I couldn't help but notice the sleek curve of her bicep. I would kill to have arms like that. "The richer they are, the worse they are, and this is St. Barth's, so these should be pretty awful," she said.

The irony of this group's complaining about the awfulness of wealthy people was not lost on me. But this meeting might be a good opportunity to meet the developers Tyson claimed hated him. "Is the meeting open?" I asked.

Allison shook her head.

From outside came the sound of an engine as headlights swept the fogged glass slats in the front door. *"That's our car,"* Samira said in French, rising.

"Where are you going?" Tyson asked, switching to English. He was still smiling, but something dark lurked behind his eyes.

"Into Gustavia," Samira answered, sticking to French as she and Gisèle gathered their palm-size purses from the kitchen island.

"I don't think so," Tyson said lightly.

Samira put her hand on her hip. *"We talked about this earlier. We're meeting friends."*

"Who?" he asked.

"You don't know them."

He sipped his Coors. "Then they're not your friends."

"I'll tell the driver to wait," Gisèle said to Samira, starting for the door.

"Go ahead, Gisèle," Tyson returned calmly. "Samira won't be joining you tonight."

Samira's jaw dropped. *"Don't be ridiculous."*

Tyson stood. He didn't have to threaten her. They both knew he had all the power. "We're not having this conversation here."

Gisèle stood unmoored halfway to the door, her pretty face crumpled at the idea of being separated from her friend. "It's okay," she said. "I can stay."

"No. Go," Tyson instructed, waving her toward the door with his hand while keeping his eyes trained on his wife.

After a long moment, Gisèle threw Samira an apologetic glance as she scuttled out the door, quickly waving goodbye with a pinched forehead.

Samira snatched her purse off the island, her face dark. "You don't own me," she levied at Tyson in English for everyone's benefit. She grabbed a bottle of wine from an ice bucket and spun to march toward the stairs down to their room, Tyson on her heels.

"He kind of does, though," Allison said under her breath once they'd disappeared down the stairs.

I felt a pang of sympathy for Samira.

Tyson had always been a blend of light and dark, but he'd kept his dark side tightly tethered when I'd known him, masked by the charming face he showed the world. Now it seemed the tables had turned.

The four of us who remained at the table didn't speak again of Tyson once he had left the room, but words weren't necessary to convey the feelings written on their faces.

Tyson might be paranoid, but he was right about one thing: Everyone in this house hated him.

CHAPTER 7

After dinner, I collapsed on the cloudlike bed in my room and opened my phone to find an invitation from a security app with a text from Tyson that the username was my middle name, the password my birthday. Shocked that he remembered either of those details, I logged in and navigated to the cameras, watching from the comfort of my bed as Jennifer got up from the table and retired to her room.

The audio was just as crystal-clear as the video, and I could hear every word Allison and Cody uttered as they groused over glasses of whisky about the problems they were having with the De-Sal center in Monterey, California.

A text from Rosa pinged my screen, replying to the rant I'd sent her about Tyson earlier. The boys were in bed, and she was dying to hear the details of the mysterious job he'd paid us a hundred thousand and flown me down here for. My thumbs hovered above the keyboard for a moment before I typed:

All good here. Worried I may have gotten a little sunburned though.

"Sunburn" was the code word we used to let the other know we were being monitored and couldn't talk. It was partially true at least, I couldn't talk. I could've texted, if I wanted to. There was no way my phone was being monitored; I'd had it with me since I arrived. Rosa wouldn't question my message, though. She trusted me.

Which made me feel that much worse about lying to her. But it was for her own good, I reasoned.

I turned off my bedside light and returned my attention to the security cameras, following as Cody and Allison moved from the dining table to the fire pit on the deck just off my room, where they lit cigars. The audio wasn't any good with the noise of the waterfall from the spa muddying the sound, and it struck me that even if Tyson was watching the cameras, he wouldn't be able to hear their conversation over it.

Fortunately, the slatted window to one side of my sliding glass door was open to the night air, and their voices floated toward me on the breeze, clearly audible if I lay still enough.

"I've given him multiple options," came Allison's voice a fraction of a second before her mouth moved on the screen of my phone. "If he doesn't want to dilute his shares by bringing on an investor, he won't have to. I'll sell some of mine."

"Rick Halpern would be a good fit," Cody agreed.

"The king of green energy," Allison emphasized. "He's perfect."

I googled the name as Cody replied, "I think Tyson's worried about the due diligence."

I scanned Rick Halpern's bio, copying and pasting the pertinent bits into my notes app. A reclusive billionaire who had made his money in wind and solar farms, he was indeed the king of green energy.

"I don't think one report will be a deterrent for Halpern," Allison said, "but it should slow things down enough that Tyson would be open to his investment."

"If anything holds up the installation here, he won't have much choice," Cody said, giving Allison a meaningful glance.

Allison's phone dinged and she glanced at it. "I've gotta head out."

"Where are you meeting?"

"Le Ti."

I could see Cody nod, muttering something I couldn't make out as Allison rose, putting a hand on his shoulder. "See you in the morning."

"Keep your head down," Cody cautioned.

Allison exited, leaving Cody staring into the fire, and I sat up in bed, adrenaline suddenly pulsing through my veins. I wasn't sure what Allison was up to, but it was something clandestine, something for which she'd need to keep her head down.

I grabbed my purse and dug through my wallet, pulling out Laurent's card. Laurent who had secrets. I spun it between my fingers, considering. Tyson trusted him, had said I could trust him. Which meant I couldn't trust him at all, of course. But he would almost certainly help me with what I needed.

Before I could second-guess myself, I keyed in his number and tapped out a message to him.

I had to wait only ten seconds for the three little dots to appear.

ELEVEN YEARS AGO, JUNE

It all happened quickly: A week after Cody approved my SADEP, I had the money to pay for my mom's first treatment, and a week after that, we were in a hospital in Naples and she was receiving infusions.

She'd asked where the money had come from—of course she had—and I'd told her it had come from Dad, which was the same thing I'd told Rosa and anyone else who asked. I'd also fabricated a story about his not wanting Mom to know, so that she wouldn't try to reach out to thank him.

Any qualms I had about lying to her were erased after the first week of treatment. Her energy had improved after only a few days, and by the time we left, she was the closest I'd seen to her old self since her cancer had reappeared a year ago. Her hair had started to grow back in a soft fuzz of silvery brown, her coloring was better, her eyes less sunken. She looked alive.

In the car on the two-hour drive home, we listened to all her favorite eighties bands—Depeche Mode, Talking Heads, Madonna—and she sang along, her face upturned to the sun. Whereas chemo had left her unable to eat, the new treatment made her ravenous, and we stopped for burgers at a roadside diner, taking milkshakes to go when we were finished.

My phone dinged with a message as we were pulling out of the parking lot, and my mom saw Tyson's name pop up on the screen. "Doesn't seem casual," she said with a smirk.

"We're just hanging out," I protested.

She laughed, shaking her head. "Hormones and pheromones."

"We have things in common, too," I protested.

She held up her hands. "Enjoy your youth, honey. I of all people know it won't last forever. I just don't want you to get hurt."

"I know," I said. I gave her what I hoped was a convincing smile. "You don't need to worry."

Tyson and I hadn't talked about what would happen at the end of the summer, but he regularly made references to our future together, and he'd reached out every day I was gone to check on me.

I was excited to tell him about my mom's progress, so once I'd put her to bed that evening, I biked over to his house like we'd planned. But when I arrived, I found the house empty and the doors locked.

"I'm at Ian's," he answered when I called. "Come over."

I sighed. I was far too worn out to be around people tonight. "I'm only coming to get the keys."

Leaving my backpack on the porch, I pocketed my phone and went out the back gate. The sun was setting as I followed the path through the long grass and around the muddy pond to the mobile home, where Ian's old pickup truck was parked next to the beat-up Corolla I now recognized as belonging to the girl he was dating. What looked to be a generator was making a loud noise on one end of the trailer, and some kind of pump contraption was humming next to the warped wooden steps up to the front door.

As little as I wanted to be there, I'd never seen inside Ian's place and was curious. I could smell the weed through the door as I knocked on the fogged glass. After a moment, the door swung in, revealing my boyfriend, a joint in one hand and Coors Light in the other, his eyes at half-mast. He pulled me close, planting a kiss on my mouth. "How's your mom?" he asked.

"Better," I said. "She ate a double bacon cheeseburger for lunch and sang 'True Blue' all the way home."

"That's good to hear," he said. "I missed you."

As he released me, I took in Ian's eclectic décor: plastic-framed posters of Che Guevara and Steve Jobs hung on the walls above a stained La-Z-Boy and a floral-patterned couch that must have belonged to Tyson's parents, engineering textbooks piled on the side table. An empty microwave box served as a coffee table, on which was an ashtray filled with at least fifty cigarette butts. Either he wasn't a very successful drug dealer, or he was investing his money elsewhere, because he certainly wasn't spending it on his décor.

Ian was on the couch eating a piece of pizza out of the open box that rested on the makeshift coffee table. "There's pizza if you want it," he said, gesturing to the box.

"I just ate," I said. "I've had a long day. I can't stay. I'm just grabbing the keys to the house."

At that moment, the door at the end of the hallway burst open and the girl stumbled out, rubbing her eyes as if she'd just woken up. She was mouselike, petite and pale, her dark hair cropped to chin length, a fringe of bangs falling in front of her eyes.

"The motor's making a funny noise," she said to Ian without moving from the doorway.

There was a twang in her voice, a flatness to her vowels. Australian, maybe?

"What kind of noise?" he asked, peeking through the blinds over the window behind the couch.

"I don't know, like grinding or something," she said.

Yes, her accent was definitely Australian. I wasn't sure why I was so surprised, but I was.

Ian sprang to his feet and pushed open the front door, bounding down the steps into the gloaming. Tyson trailed behind him, the joint still burning between his fingers.

"Keys," I reminded Tyson, following.

"I'm coming with you, I just want to see what he's got back there," he said as we reached the bottom of the steps.

"What is all this shit?" I whispered, gesturing to the pump contraption.

"Water filter," Tyson said, starting along the path around the trailer.

"Do your parents know about it?"

He shook his head. "Whatever, it's stopping them from spending money on a plumber to fix the pipes."

Curious, I followed them out to the back of the mobile home, where two plastic kiddie pools filled with water were connected by a series of pipes and pumps, one of which was indeed making a grinding noise.

"Fuck," Ian said, bending over it. "It's a snake."

"Where?" I jumped back instinctively.

He shone the flashlight of his phone up inside the machine. "It's dead," he said. "It must've slithered up there and gotten stuck in the motor. Now what's left of it is clogging the filter."

"What is this thing?" I asked.

"Gonna be hydroponics if I can get the brine to power the system."

"Brine?" I asked, blinking at him. Somehow, between the drug use and the squalid living arrangements, I'd forgotten how smart Ian was.

"The leftover mix of salt and chemical rejected by the membrane." He pointed to a bucket filled with sludge beneath the contraption where the snake was caught.

"Does it work?" Tyson asked.

"Partially," Ian said.

Tyson squatted next to the filter pump, inspecting Ian's work. "I didn't know this was back here."

"Dude," Ian said, seeming to remember Tyson was his landlord. "Please don't make me move it. I'm getting rid of the chemicals so they're not hurting anything, I swear."

Tyson considered him just long enough to make him squirm, then grinned. "Shit, man, just give me a bag of that weed, my lips are sealed."

Ian relaxed. "Sure thing." He flipped a switch and the grinding noise stopped as the machine powered down. "It's too dark for me to deal with it tonight. Andie and I are gonna head to Starfish if you guys wanna come."

"Is Andie Australian?" I asked.

He nodded, lighting a cigarette as he led us to the front of the trailer.

"Where'd you meet her?" I asked.

"School."

"But you're both . . . taking a break?" I asked.

He nodded. "She's on a student visa, so she'll need to reenroll in the next few months if she doesn't want to go back to Australia."

"Or you could marry her," Tyson ribbed.

Ian exhaled a line of smoke, shaking his head. "If you'd grown up with my parents, you wouldn't ever wanna get married either."

Andie opened the door of the trailer and poked her head out. "We gotta leave in fifteen," she said.

I opened my mouth to introduce myself, but before I could get a word out, she'd let the door slam shut.

Ian went into the trailer, disappearing from our line of sight for a moment before returning with a gallon-size bag of weed. He handed it to Tyson, who opened the bag and inhaled deeply. "Sweet," Tyson said. "Lemme know when you get that hydroponic system up and running. Maybe we could go into business together."

Ian nodded as he mounted the steps to his front door. "Cool," he said as he slipped inside. "See ya."

"He always was a fucking smart kid," Tyson said as we walked the path through the long grass back to his house.

"Yeah," I agreed. "But you are not going into business with him growing pot."

He shrugged, lacing his fingers through mine, and I could see the gears turning in his brain. "It's a lucrative business—"

"No," I said, giving him the side-eye. "You have too much to lose."

He elbowed me playfully. "Not all of us can be as brilliant as you.

The rest of us have to keep our eyes open if we want to start a multi-billion-dollar company someday."

"That's a kind of brilliance too, though, isn't it?" I said, pushing open the gate. "Thinking in terms of multi-billion-dollar businesses?"

He spun me around so that my back was against the wall and pressed his body into me, running his hands up beneath my shirt. "Talk to me like that, we're not gonna make it to my bed," he growled into my ear.

"You like having your ego stroked, don't you?" I teased.

I was laughing, but I realized as I kissed him just how much truth there was to it. Tyson's liberal compliments were boomerangs, designed to retrieve praise to inflate his delicate ego. That delicate ego was why he needed to show up his brother at every turn, why he constantly craved credit for his ideas. It was basic psychology: His parents may have given him cash, but they certainly hadn't given him enough attention, so he sought it elsewhere.

Perhaps that realization should have rung a warning bell somewhere inside me, but as he lifted me and carried me across the pool deck to the covered patio where we tumbled to the couch in the dark, I had other things on my mind.

CHAPTER 8

Stilettos in hand, I stealthily slipped out the door to my private side deck and through the slatted wooden gate that led to the exterior servants' quarters. Sticking to the shadows at the edge of the driveway, I scurried down the hill barefoot and let myself out the pedestrian entrance, where I found a dark green vintage Land Rover idling. I peered into the window to make sure Laurent was in the driver's seat before opening the passenger door and climbing inside.

He was freshly shaved, his curls damp from the shower, and while I was still in the black strapless jumpsuit I'd worn at dinner, he'd changed again, now dressed in a cream linen button-down with the sleeves rolled up, paired with chinos. He looked good enough to eat—which was exactly what I would not be doing tonight, obviously. But it had been years since a man had had any effect on me, much less turned my blood to lava with a glance, and it was a nice reminder that part of me wasn't totally dead. Of course, it wasn't just me he had this effect on, I realized. Jennifer clearly had the same response, even with her boyfriend standing right beside her. It must be Laurent's superpower, melting women.

I smiled to myself as we roared up the hill that led away from Le Rêve. "Nice ride," I commented.

"I inherited it from a client I was close with." His eyes flicked toward me. "Can I ask why you need to go to Le Ti?"

I hesitated. But I didn't see how I could keep it from him, with what I was asking of him. "I'm following someone."

He raised his brows. "For Tyson?"

I nodded. I wanted to qualify it, to explain myself, but aware that whatever I told him he'd likely take straight back to Tyson, I didn't.

"You know Tyson's guests at the house pretty well?" I asked.

He shrugged. "As well as you can know anyone, when you are working for them."

The SUV vibrated beneath us as he slowed, letting a car pass before merging onto the main road. "I would guess they let things slip around you that they might not in front of other people," I said.

"Yes."

"Do you think any of them wish Tyson harm?"

He chuckled. "What do you think?"

"I don't know them, that's why I'm asking you."

He cut his eyes briefly toward me. "But you know him."

"Not really," I demurred. "Not anymore, I mean. I did. But he's different now."

"He was kind to you this evening when you spoke?"

His gaze was fixed on the winding road, and between his accent and the darkness of the car, I couldn't quite gauge where he was coming from, so I held my tongue, waiting for more information.

"So, no," he said after a moment.

"No," I admitted as he turned off the main road to weave down a narrow street that cut through a neighborhood.

"The staff call him *la bête noire*," he said. "The black beast."

"Ah," I said, relaxing a little.

"Yes." He turned onto a side street and parked the Land Rover, his face in shadow as he focused on me. "I will be able to help you better if you tell me what we're looking for," he said.

"You don't have to help me," I said automatically. "I can handle it."

"I'm sure you can," he agreed. "But I know Le Ti and everyone who works there. I could make things easier for you, and I'd like to help you, if you'll let me."

He held my eye as I assessed him. Was there any reason why I shouldn't let him help me? I wasn't doing anything I didn't want to get back to Tyson—after all, he was the one who'd said I could trust Laurent—and it would make my night easier.

"Allison is coming here to meet someone, and I want to find out who," I said.

He nodded, taking it in stride. "So, you don't want her to know you're following her."

"No."

"Well, then, it is good it is a costume bar, and I am friends with the girl who runs the closet."

Ten minutes later, Laurent returned to the Land Rover with a bag in hand.

"What have you brought us?" I asked as he closed the car door behind him.

I looked on with increasing interest as he pulled out a multicolored clown wig, followed by a Mexican poncho, a pink princess dress, a Zorro mask, a blond wig, a bridal veil, a sorcerer's hat and cape, and a cowboy outfit.

I laughed as he placed the cowboy hat atop his head, glad he was game to play along. "Perfect."

A Zorro mask paired with a fringed vest and cowboy gun belt completed his look, while I donned the navy sorcerer's cape to cover the outfit I'd been wearing at dinner and fastened a purple Mardi Gras mask over my face.

Once we got out of the car, I placed the tall sorcerer's hat on my head, lifting the long robes as we walked down the street. "This has to be the most ridiculous disguise I've ever worn," I said, scurrying to keep up with his long strides.

He flashed a sly smile, his eyes catching on mine. "I like to please."

Okay, cowboy.

I turned away, hiding my smile. I knew he meant he *aimed* to please, knew it made sense in context, but the way he said it made me think of something very different. And here I was, thousands of miles away from home, no need to worry about messy entanglements. If the circumstances were different, I had a feeling this could be a very enjoyable evening indeed.

But they weren't.

We approached the back of the building, where a guy and a girl dressed in black were leaning against the wall next to the door, smoking cigarettes. The guy chortled as we drew closer, and the girl stubbed out her cigarette, approaching to adjust Laurent's hat. *"Very nice,"* she said in French as he handed her the bag of extra costumes. *"Of course you would make a dashing cowboy."*

"Thanks for the costumes," he said, switching to English for my benefit.

"Is this the pretty American you picked up this afternoon?" the guy razzed Laurent in rapid French. *"You work fast, my man."*

So he'd spoken about me to this guy. Called me pretty. I felt heat creep into my cheeks.

"Fuck off," Laurent returned with a laugh. *"It's not like that."*

I rose to the occasion, playing the one card I had up my sleeve. *"How could I turn down such a dashing cowboy?"* I asked, matching their French as I linked my arm through Laurent's.

His head snapped toward me as the other two's eyes widened. *"Oh shit,"* the girl said, laughing.

"Have a nice night," I said, relishing their surprise as I tugged him through the door into the kitchen.

"This way," he said, leading me past the staff who appeared to be cleaning up from dinner service, through a door, into a dark, cave-like room with flashing lights and pounding bass. Tables circled a dance floor, and a small raised stage was crowded with beautiful people in costumes, moving in rhythm to the deafening house music.

He pulled me to the side of the room, placing his mouth next to my ear to be heard over the music. *"You didn't tell me you spoke French,"* he said.

Damn, I was a fool for a good cologne, and his was excellent.

"You didn't ask," I replied.

He laughed, pulling back to look at me with a slight shake of his head, the colored lights sliding over his skin. "So tell me, Audrey. Why do you speak French like a native?"

"I was born in Geneva," I said. "I lived there until I was ten."

"Ah," he said. *"You are full of surprises."*

I laughed. "But then, so is anyone you've just met, right?"

He shrugged, his eyes lingering on mine. "In my line of work, I meet a lot of people, and I am seldom surprised."

Just then, the girl we'd spoken to in the alley pushed out of the kitchen, setting her tray of shots on the table next to us. Without a word, she handed one to each of us, raising her own. "Clase Azul," she said, clinking her glass to ours.

What the hell, I figured. It wasn't every day I had the opportunity to drink tequila that good. I closed my eyes as the liquor burned down my throat. Laurent and I were both working, I reminded myself. For *la bête noire,* no less. It wouldn't do to get that confused, as much as I might like to. What I needed was to figure out who was blackmailing Tyson, so I could get off this island and out of his life.

"We should find Allison," I said, pushing off the wall to scan the room. If she was wearing a costume, she could be hard to spot.

"Want to dance?" Laurent asked.

I frowned. I very much wanted to dance with Laurent. Which meant it was a terrible idea, especially with the expensive tequila now coursing through my veins.

He nodded toward the stage. "We'll have a better vantage point up there."

He was right. But I shook my head, sticking to my guns. "She's not here to dance. Let's check the booths. Is there a patio?"

He nodded and pointed, reaching back for me as he started along the row of booths that edged the dance floor. I ignored his outstretched hand, keeping my gaze focused on the faces of the revelers around us, none of whom bore any resemblance to Allison.

I lifted the hem of my robes when we reached the steps up to the patio, but as I raised my foot, the fabric snagged on my stiletto, and I tripped forward. Laurent thankfully caught me before I could face-plant, his hands on my waist as I gripped his biceps to steady myself.

Never in my life had I been a person who could be described as clumsy, but this would make the second time today I'd found myself gripping his remarkably strong arms. Behind his mask, his eyes found mine. "You good?" he asked.

I nodded. "It's these stupid robes."

His hands lingered on my waist as a clown and a pirate shoved past us, pushing him into to me. Neither of us moved to pull apart. "We should check the bar," I murmured, so close that my lips brushed his ear.

"Good idea," he whispered.

I pulled away from him, grateful for the masks that hid our faces, and strode blindly onto the patio. *Allison,* I reminded myself. *Look for Allison.*

The patio outside was cooler and much less crowded than the dance floor. I twisted my hair over my shoulder as I slid into a seat at the stone bar and ordered a glass of water. Laurent leaned his back against the bar, scanning the tables of revelers from behind his Zorro mask, while I scrutinized the groups of laughing people standing around the entrance to the gift shop.

The crowd parted for a gaggle of gorgeous women in rhinestone outfits that left little to the imagination, and my gaze landed on a group of three seated at an out-of-the-way table partially hidden by a potted palm. The sole woman at the table was slender but muscular, her only attempt at costume a pair of heart-shaped pink sunglasses and a fedora that did little to disguise her identity.

I elbowed Laurent. "There," I said, nodding my head toward her.

The other two men at the table wore more thorough disguises, but the one dressed as a knight was thin and tall, and the other one was older, salt-and-pepper hair peeking out from beneath the pope hat he was wearing, a simple black mask covering his eyes.

"Do you know those men?" I asked.

He shook his head. "It's hard to tell with the costumes."

They were clearly having an intense discussion, leaning forward in their seats and taking no notice of anyone else in the bar.

"But they'll have to take them off before they leave," I said. "So all we have to do is wait."

Laurent signaled the bartender and ordered two glasses of Clase Azul on the rocks. I started to protest, but he shook his head, sliding a card toward the bartender. *"We may be here a while, we might as well enjoy ourselves,"* he reasoned.

I took out my phone and pretended to check my makeup on the screen while capturing pictures of Allison with the two men.

The bartender slid our drinks toward us, and I raised my glass to Laurent. "Thanks for escorting me."

He tipped his glass to mine and we both drank.

"I have to ask, but you do not have to answer—" He evaluated me, his eyes unreadable behind his mask. "Why has Tyson asked you to follow Allison?"

"Oh, it's—" I racked my brain for how to say it without giving anything away. "I owe him a favor, and it's kind of what I do for a living."

He raised his brows. "You follow people?"

"I help attorneys get information that could be useful at trial, which, yeah, sometimes involves tracking people."

He cocked his head. "How did you get into that?"

"It's a long story."

"I have all night."

"Short version, I'm good with computers," I said. "I used to work in cybersecurity and one of my clients was a law firm. I helped them track down some digital information they needed for evidence in one of their cases, and it grew from there."

"And you also track people?"

I shrugged. "Believe me, I never imagined it would be part of what

I did, but sometimes the information I need can't be obtained digitally. And honestly, it's kinda fun."

"Is it ever dangerous?" he asked.

"It can be."

"Do you carry protection?" he asked.

I nodded and he drew back, impressed.

"I'm also trained in self-defense," I added. "But fortunately, I haven't had to use either on the job yet."

"Damn," he said, the corner of his mouth quirking into a smile. "You are kind of a badass, aren't you?"

I grinned and shrugged, my pride swelling with his compliment. "Don't worry, I can protect you if we get into any trouble tonight."

He laughed as on the other side of the patio, Allison rose from the table, shaking hands with the men. We watched as she quickly walked toward the exit, discarding the fedora and glasses on a table by the door before she slipped into the night.

Laurent nudged me, and I turned to see the pope and the knight headed inside. We grabbed our drinks and followed them past the dance floor into the darkened dining room, across the cheetah print rug to the costume room at the back. "There's only one entrance to the costume closet," Laurent said, grabbing my hand to stop me before I could mount the steps.

His palm was rough against mine as he pulled me into the shadows, where we leaned against the wall outside the door, waiting for the men to emerge. We were standing so close, our hips were touching, and again, neither of us moved to pull apart.

"You have calluses," I commented inanely.

"I lift some weights." He opened his hand between us, tracing the calluses with his fingers. "Is worse on my fingers."

He gripped my wrist gently, lifting the sleeve of my robe to trail his fingers down the inside of my arm. Shivers cascaded all the way down my body.

"From the guitar," he explained. My breath grew shallow as he ran my fingers along his other hand. "Feel the difference?"

I nodded, allowing myself a glance up at him, again grateful for the masks covering our faces. "What kind of music do you play?"

"Everything. Reggae, rock, flamenco."

I was too hot, I had to get out of these robes, and now that Allison was gone, I didn't need to worry about anyone recognizing my jumpsuit. I ripped my hat off, handing it to Laurent as I pulled my sorcerer's costume over my head. I sighed, dropping it to a chair next to me.

Laurent's gaze swept over my bare shoulders before our eyes met again. Chemistry like this couldn't be one sided, could it?

Not that it mattered. Nothing could happen between us.

Movement behind me drew his attention, and I turned to see two men descending the stairs. The tall, thin one was perhaps forty, his light brown hair swept back from his forehead, his nose prominent. The older one was maybe sixty, ruddy-skinned with a paunch and long, wavy gray hair.

"Do you know them?" I asked as they cut across the room.

He nodded. "David Barbier and Charl Michel. They're both on the city council."

"The council Tyson's meeting with tomorrow?" I asked.

He nodded. "I wonder if Allison was bribing them to approve the center."

"Maybe," I said, thinking back to the conversation I'd heard between Allison and Cody earlier. But I wasn't about to share that with him.

He untied his mask, and I did the same. It felt oddly intimate, revealing our naked faces to each other.

"Let's keep this between us for now," I said. "I don't know yet what it means, and I want to find out more before I say anything to Tyson."

He nodded. "You can trust me."

Our eyes caught, and I wished more than anything that that were true.

CHAPTER 9

I'd just started to drift off between the crisp white sheets of my bed when the sound of crashing glass startled me awake. I turned to check the clock: 2:52 A.M.

The kitchen light shone yellow beneath the door to my room. I heard the clicking of heels and soft laughter. Gisèle, returned from her evening out, I figured. Probably drunk and stumbling around the kitchen. It was a good thing I hadn't returned any later; we might have run into each other in the driveway.

After a moment, Samira's voice broke the silence. *"What are you doing?"* she asked in French. *"You could have woken Tyson."*

"Doesn't he wear those stupid headphones?"

"Take your shoes off. You're trashed. Noise cancellation doesn't help if there's an elephant in the house."

I snickered quietly in the dark. Miss cool girl had some bite to her.

A giggle-hiccup from Gisèle. *"Who are you calling an elephant?"* The thunk of shoes hitting the floor. *"Have a drink with me."*

"I've been asleep for hours."

"You're mad I went out without you," Gisèle pouted.

"I'm not mad." I could practically hear her eye roll.

"I saw Laurent. He was wearing a ridiculous cowboy costume."

My pulse quickened. We'd thought we were being so careful.

"You went to Le Ti? I thought you were going into Gustavia."

"I changed my mind."

"Who was he with?"

Another hiccup. *"Some girl I didn't recognize."* I breathed a sigh of relief. My costume, at least, had been successful. *"They looked like they might fuck right there in the club."*

My eyes went wide in the dark. I hadn't even been totally sure what we were doing could be considered flirting, and yet it looked like we "might fuck right there in the club"? On the bright side, that meant the attraction definitely hadn't been one-sided—but what the hell had I been thinking?

Thankfully we'd been wearing costumes, but I couldn't be so careless again.

"Did you see Bryan?" Samira asked.

Gisèle must have nodded because Samira added, *"And?"*

"He's doing a series of black-and-white nudes on the beaches around the island. It's a sirens theme. He wants us for it."

"Go for it."

"I don't want to do it without you." Hiccup. *"Michelle did that series with him last year and she's the new Bond girl now."*

"I don't think those two things are related."

"But they're not unrelated."

A pause. The sound of liquid splashing into a glass. *"You know he's never gonna let me do that,"* Samira said.

"What man wouldn't want to be married to the next Bond girl?"

"Are you joking?"

"But when you married him, he said—"

"He said all kinds of things when I married him," Samira hissed.

"But you're such a talented actress—"

A chair scraped over the floor. *"That part of my life is over!"*

Earlier today I'd been intimidated by Samira's burnished exterior, but hearing the pain in her voice now, I felt sympathy toward her. She was only twenty-five, and she sounded so jaded. I knew nothing about what she'd been through, but something had compelled her to fortify her walls at such a young age, and I did know what that was like.

"*Do you know what a hundred million broken down over thirty-six months comes out to per month?*" Samira demanded. "*Two point eight million. That is far more, I guarantee, than a fucking Bond girl makes.*"

So Tyson was right. Samira was with him for the money, though she'd clearly gotten more than she'd bargained for in marrying him.

"*Twenty-two more months. You know the deal. I walk away now, I get nothing,*" Samira concluded.

Another hiccup from Gisèle. "*But you're miserable.*"

"*I'd be more miserable if I were poor.*" Samira's tone was caustic.

"*You'll never be poor,*" Gisèle protested, clearly too inebriated to know when to quit. "*You were a successful model before all this—*"

"*Before William,*" Samira stopped her, putting an emphasis on the name that told me he was important. "*You think any brand wants to be associated with me now? I'm radioactive. It's a miracle Tyson wanted any part of marrying me.*"

I made a mental note to find out who this William was as Gisèle softened her voice. "*I just want the best for you.*"

"*Then back off. You're here because—*"

Gisèle giggled. "*He likes what I can do with my tongue.*"

My jaw dropped. Had I heard that right? Gisèle's voice was low enough, perhaps she'd said something else.

"*Yes,*" Samira answered, dispelling any doubts I'd had about what I heard. "*And to keep me happy.*"

"*You also like what I can do with my tongue,*" Gisèle purred.

Oh, I'd definitely heard correctly.

Silence for a moment, followed by a distinctively sexual sigh. "*He doesn't like it when we—*"

"*Shh . . .*"

The sound of something sliding across the counter. A moan. "*He has cameras.*"

"*He's asleep.*"

I pulled my pillow over my head. It was clear there was going to be no more conversation I needed to hear tonight.

ELEVEN YEARS AGO, JULY

Rosa tilted the blender to her lips and swallowed, passing it to me. "I think it needs more tequila," she said.

"You always think it needs more tequila," I teased as I took a sip. My eyes popped and I gave a shudder so dramatic my towel slipped off my shoulders, leaving me in my bikini. "Definitely doesn't need more tequila."

She laughed as I scooped my towel off the sticky marble floor of Tyson's parents' kitchen and wrapped it around my waist. I held out my red Solo cup and she filled it, peering out the window above the sink. "Who are all these people?" she asked.

Tyson's Fourth of July party was in full swing, the patio full of revelers in red, white, and blue splashing into the pool in the golden afternoon light. Smoke rose from the grill where Cody was cooking hamburgers and hot dogs, while Tyson held court on the top step in the shallow end, his Coors Light splashing into the pool as he gesticulated wildly with his arms, causing two girls in matching American flag bikinis to giggle.

"I don't know half of them," I said, joining her at the window.

"You're too good for him," she said, focusing on Tyson.

"We're twenty-one and it's summer," I said, shrugging off her concern just as I had my mom's. "I can make mature decisions when I'm older."

"Yas, bitch," Rosa said, raising her Solo cup to mine.

I wished I were having as much fun as I was pretending to right now. But my mom had recently gone in for her four-week evaluation and been told she needed another round of the wildly expensive experimental treatment as soon as possible. I'd been surprised; she'd seemed to be doing so well. Her energy had been better, she was gaining weight. We'd been gardening again, and had even gone snorkeling and kayaking a couple of times.

Mom had been hesitant about doing the treatment again, preferring that I use the money to complete my education rather than to extend her life by probably only another couple of months. In the end I'd convinced her to try another round, but she felt compelled to at least call my grandparents and thank them. I persuaded her to write a note instead, which, rather than mailing, I tucked into a shoebox in my closet.

I was lying to her for her own good, I told myself again as I restarted the sales deflation program. But I never felt good about it.

My dad, however, hadn't so much as inquired about my mom since he told me he couldn't help, so there was no need to lie to him.

"I'm gonna run up to the restroom," I said. "I'll meet you out by the pool."

I padded across the reflective marble floor and mounted the stairs, shivering in the blasting air conditioning as I paused on the landing, considering the cracked door of Tyson's dad's office. I was certain I'd left it closed. I froze in place.

Tyson's parents weren't coming back until the end of the summer and their computer wasn't used for anything else, so I'd left the SADEP running on it. It was hidden behind the desktop, but wouldn't be terribly difficult for anyone with minimal computer skills to locate. Which would be very, very bad.

As I pushed open the door, my heart leaped to my throat.

Ian was seated in the desk chair, the SADEP open on the screens before him, a Bud Light sweating next to the keyboard, his phone in his hand. He swiveled to face me, a grin spreading across his face when he spied me frozen in the doorway. His eyes were bloodshot, his pale skin pink from the sun.

"What are you doing?" I demanded.

"I was just admiring your work."

I opened my mouth to protest, but nothing came out.

"It is yours, isn't it?" he asked, spinning back to look at the computer. "Tyson couldn't have designed anything this elegant, and I doubt Cody could, either. Though he must have keyed you into the system."

"Please," I said, shaking. "Leave."

"Audrey," he whined, drawing back. "I'm hurt. I thought we were friends."

"You shouldn't be in here," I said, my voice strangled.

"But I am."

"Please go. For both our sakes."

"Hold on now," he said, taking a swig of his beer. "It doesn't seem fair you're making roughly two thousand dollars an hour without lifting a finger while I risk my life to make half that in a week."

I shut the door behind me and pulled out my phone to text Tyson and Cody:

911 office now

I turned back to Ian, whispering urgently. "I have to pay for my mom's cancer treatment."

"I don't give a shit what you use the money for," he returned. "Just that you give me my cut."

"What?" I gaped at him, shaken. "No."

"I get a cut weekly, and I keep my mouth shut."

Life in prison flashed before my eyes as we stared at each other, my panic escalating with every passing second. "Ian, please—"

At that moment, the door flew open, and Tyson and Cody burst into the room. Tyson was dripping wet, a towel around his waist, and Cody still had a steel spatula in his hand.

"What the fuck is going on in here?" Tyson demanded, pulling Ian out of the chair by his shirt collar and pinning him against the mostly empty bookshelves.

Cody kicked the door shut as Ian squirmed.

"I found him snooping on the computer," I said.

Cody dropped the spatula to the desk as he sat in the chair vacated by Ian and rolled it to the computer, scanning the program open on the screen.

"I want a cut," Ian growled.

"Fuck you," Tyson spat in his face, grabbing the spatula Cody had deposited on the desk. He jabbed the sharp end into Ian's neck.

"Are you gonna kill me?" Ian choked out.

"I'm thinking about it," Tyson said, pushing the spatula so deep into his neck he drew blood.

"Tyson," I warned.

"I have video," Ian threatened, wincing.

"Give me your phone," Tyson demanded.

"Do what you want, it's already in the cloud," Ian spat as Tyson wrenched Ian's phone from his hand, tossing it to Cody.

"Password," Cody said.

"No," Ian said.

Tyson tightened his grip on the spatula, and Ian choked. "Twenty percent," Ian said.

"Fuck you," Tyson whispered in his ear, slamming his head into the shelves.

Ian kicked at Tyson as Cody pulled the protective covering off Ian's phone and whacked it against the corner of the desk, cracking the screen. When he was satisfied, I took it from him and opened the window, tossing it onto the driveway below, where it splintered. A group of people I didn't know looked up briefly from where they were seated on the tailgate of someone's pickup truck, then continued their conversation as though nothing had happened.

I slammed the window shut as Ian scrabbled to get hold of Tyson, who was bigger and stronger. "Twenty percent," Ian repeated. "Or I send Cody's company the video I shot."

Tyson slammed his fist into Ian's face and he groaned.

"Five," Cody said, pulling his brother back.

Ian spat blood on the beige carpet. "Fifteen."

"Why are you fucking negotiating with him?" Tyson demanded of his brother.

"It's my job on the line," Cody said gruffly. "Not yours." He turned to Ian. "Ten. For the length of the summer only. When Tyson goes back to school, this is over."

"Deal," Ian said.

"Let him go," Cody said to Tyson.

Tyson swiped the blade of the spatula along Ian's neck as he released him, leaving a line of blood across his pale skin. Ian covered it with his hand, glaring at him.

"Now get the fuck out," Cody said, pointing at the door.

"And if you ever step foot inside this house again, I will kill you," Tyson added.

In that moment, I believed him.

CHAPTER 10

I must have miraculously fallen asleep again at some point, because I awoke to the sound of a rooster crowing and sun streaming through the sheer curtains. I smelled pastries and heard voices. I was desperate for caffeine, but remembering Gisèle and Samira's conversation last night, I pulled my computer into my lap and googled "Samira Maies + William."

My jaw dropped as the screen populated with articles, mostly in French, from publications in Luxembourg, Belgium, and France.

WILLIAM NICOLAUS, COUNT VON TURENBERG. DEAD IN
   HUNTING ACCIDENT
SAMIRA MAIES QUESTIONED IN HUSBAND'S DEATH
MURDER OR MISHAP?

Scanning through the articles, I discovered that William was the handsome fifty-year-old Luxembourgish count Samira had wedded at the age of twenty-two, a marriage that had lasted only four months before he was tragically killed in a hunting accident on his estate.

So my hunch had been right: Tyson had indeed manipulated the search results of his wife's name not to include any mention of her first marriage. But he couldn't scrub the internet of every article written about her, which meant that if you knew what to google, all the information was still there. And it was a lot.

Not only had Samira been in the hunting party on the day her first husband met his end, she'd been the one to discover his body, slumped over a fallen log in the dense woods, the back of his head blown clean off. Although she denied any part in William's death, accidental or otherwise, and had been cleared thanks to the testimony of none other than Gisèle, who had been by her side the entire day, his grown children and ex-wife had been so sure Samira was responsible that they'd managed to cut her entirely out of any inheritance.

William's death had eventually been declared accidental, with a close friend of the family asserting that whoever had mistakenly shot him might never know they'd been the one to end his life, but media speculation about Samira's involvement was so rampant that she'd fled to New York, which was where she met Tyson.

Jesus. Samira had been a suspect in a murder—seemingly cleared only because of Gisèle, who plainly would do anything for her.

So why hadn't Tyson mentioned any of this to me?

Once again feeling backfooted, I quickly pulled myself together and changed into a sundress, taking a moment to tone down my annoyance before sliding open the glass door and stepping onto the front deck. The day was balmy and blue-skied, the sea at the bottom of the jagged hills sparkling in the morning sun.

Allison sat at the oak dining table eating fruit and scrambled egg whites, while Jennifer and Cody lounged on the low white couch facing the view, and Samira and Gisèle sipped espressos at the sleek island they'd desecrated the night before. It was hard not to stare, considering what I'd just read—not to mention what I'd overheard last night.

Samira muttered something, and Gisèle looked at her with such tenderness that I couldn't believe I hadn't seen it before. Had they been lovers when Samira's first husband was killed? And was Tyson aware that their romantic involvement wasn't purely for his benefit?

"Good morning." Laurent's voice vibrated pleasantly in my ear.

"Good morning." I turned, my fingers brushing his as he deposited a cup of coffee in my hand, made just the way I liked it. "Merci."

"There are pastries, eggs, and fruit if you're hungry." His blue eyes held a hint of mischief. "Did you sleep well?"

I nodded, desperate to tell him Gisèle had spotted us. But that would have to wait. "The bed is comfortable."

"The rooster didn't wake you? I should have told you, there are earplugs in the drawer by the bed, and the clock is also a sound machine."

"I had a pillow over my head," I said. I could see the question in his face, and I let my gaze flit quickly to Gisèle. He understood. "But tonight that will be helpful. Thank you."

He ran his tongue over his bottom lip and I heard Gisèle's purr, *You like what I can do with my tongue.* Heat crept up my neck and I quickly turned away.

"Morning," Allison said as I approached the table. Her benign expression made it clear she had no idea I'd followed her to the club last night. "Laurent," she called. "As soon as Tyson gets here, we're ready to go."

"Okay," Laurent said, checking his watch.

His eyes flicked up and I turned to see Tyson prowling across the outdoor living space, his black hair swept back from his forehead, aviators perched on his nose. My stomach clenched. Samira stood as he approached and met his lips with a kiss, while Laurent scooped a green powder from a jar and stirred it into water, hastening to deliver the concoction into Tyson's hand.

Tyson stalked over to the table, where he lingered at the head, his hand resting on the chair back. He was smiling. It was unnerving.

"Good morning," Allison said, her countenance impassive.

"It's the vernal equinox," Tyson said softly. He dropped a handful of polished black rocks on the table. "Keep these in your pockets today for grounding."

I noticed then that he had what appeared to be the same sort of rock on a leather string around his neck, as did Samira. He had always loved his charms.

"Thanks," I said, swiping a rock off the table and pocketing it as Gisèle did the same.

A trace of disdain marred Allison's placid face as her gaze lingered on the rocks. "Let's go," she said without picking one up.

"We'll dive tomorrow," Tyson murmured. Across the kitchen, Laurent's ears pricked up and he was at Tyson's elbow in lightning speed.

"How many will be diving?"

"All of us," Tyson said. "You'll figure it out."

"What time would you like to go?"

"The water will be clearest in the afternoon. We'll need the boat. We can have dinner on board afterward, and spend the night."

"Of course," Laurent said.

"Did you bring your dive gear?" Tyson asked, fixing his eyes on me.

I shook my head. I didn't get to dive as much as I liked and would've loved nothing more than to dive here in St. Barth's, even if it meant diving with Tyson. "I'm sorry. I didn't know."

"Go to Gary's."

"Gary's?" I echoed.

"It's a dive store in Gustavia," Jennifer clarified, rising from the couch. "They have everything."

I nodded, but from what I'd been told about the prices on the island, the idea of my being able to afford anything there was preposterous.

"Put whatever you need on my account," Tyson said.

"Thank you," I replied, surprised.

As he strode for the front door, I thought about calling out to him, pulling him aside to ask about Samira's dead husband. But Allison and Cody were already following him out of the house, Laurent close on their heels. I'd have to find another time.

The second the door closed, Gisèle and Samira disappeared down the stairs, leaving Jennifer and me alone.

"That was generous of him," I commented.

"He has his moments." She took a rock from the table and rubbed her thumb over its smooth surface. "He was different, when you dated?"

I nodded. "I mean, he was ambitious, and morally flexible, and into this kind of shit—" I gestured to the rocks. "But he was also charming and fun. Even sweet, sometimes."

"I guess success has really done a number on him," she said.

I murmured agreement, but I knew she was wrong. It wasn't the success that had done this to him, it was the guilt.

CHAPTER 11

By the time Laurent returned to collect me from Le Rêve, the sun was high in the sky, bouncing off the white yachts that sailed silently on the deep blue sea below. No one was around when I emerged from my room with my sandals in hand to find Laurent waiting for me in the kitchen, wiping down the spotless countertops.

His lips parted slightly as his eyes met mine, and I completely forgot for a split second why I was there. What was it about the way he looked at me? It wasn't flirtatious or seductive, nothing that obvious. It was more . . . open? Unguarded. Like he saw me. Which was ridiculous. I didn't even know his last name. But that didn't change the fact that his slight smile felt like an invitation intended only for me.

"Ready?" he asked. "It's just us."

Just us. I liked the sound of that entirely too much.

He led me to the front door, his shoulder brushing mine as he reached past me to open it. Outside, I stepped into my wedge sandals before continuing to the car. He clicked the key fob and the side door slid open. I hesitated. "I'll sit up front with you, if that's okay," I said, my heart beating like I'd just propositioned him.

"Of course," he said.

I came around the back of the van to the passenger side as he came around the front, both of us reaching to open the car door at the same time. I laughed. "I'm used to opening my own doors."

He stepped back and gestured for me to open the door. "It's heavy," he warned.

I dragged my gaze away from his to locate the door handle and pull. The door was in fact surprisingly heavy, the driveway slightly slanted, and I wobbled backward on the uneven pavement in my wedges, my back landing against his chest. "Sorry," I said automatically, mortified.

That made three times since I'd arrived here. I was beginning to think gravity was conspiring to push me into his arms.

"Will you let me help you into the car?" I could feel his voice reverberating in his chest.

"That would be lovely."

He placed one hand on my back, taking my other hand in his to lift me into the van.

"Thank you," I said, allowing myself to meet his amused gaze before he closed the door.

I took a breath, busying myself with my phone as he walked around to the driver's side and swung himself up into the van. He extracted a pair of sunglasses from the visor before expertly executing a three-point turn in the small space to point us in the right direction.

"You are a diver, Audrey?" he asked as we pulled out of the driveway.

I nodded. "I grew up diving. My mom loved to dive."

"So, it is in your blood."

"Yeah." I could picture my mom clear as day, grinning and tan, her dive mask pushed up on her forehead, her braid dripping seawater as she spouted off the Latin names of the fish we'd seen down below. In her element. The image made my heart both sing and bleed. "What about you?"

"I have been obsessed with the sea since I was a boy. My brothers and I spent summers with my grandparents on the west coast of France, near Biarritz. But I did not start diving until I moved here."

"Because you were always surfing?" I guessed.

He nodded. "Biarritz has very good surfing."

"What's the biggest waves you ever surfed?"

"Nazaré, in Portugal," he answered immediately. "The waves are so tall they tow you out on a Jet Ski."

"That's terrifying."

"Yes." A glimmer of a smile flashed across his face. "But it is nice to be terrified sometimes, no? Makes you feel alive."

"Yeah," I agreed. "Totally."

He glanced over at me, and I was glad for the sunglasses covering his bright eyes. "Last night was fun."

I nodded, flushing. "Oh, I meant to tell you Gisèle saw us."

"At Le Ti?"

"She recognized you but not me. She didn't suspect anything." I held my tongue about the part about our looking like we were going to fuck right there in the club. "I overheard her telling Samira when she got in. Did you know they're involved? Romantically."

"C'est un secret de Polichinelle."

An open secret. "So everyone knows?"

"But no one talks about it." He slowed to let a pale pink Moke full of beautiful girls roar past on the narrow road, their hair whipping in the wind. "I think Tyson imagines it is for his benefit."

I snickered. "Blinded by his own ego."

"Yes."

"Do you know anything about Samira's first marriage?" I asked.

He glanced at me. "Another thing we do not talk about."

"Encore un secret de Polichinelle?"

He smiled. "Yes."

"But you know what happened?"

"I do not think anyone knows what happened."

Right. "Do people think she did it?"

"Some people."

"Do you?" I pressed.

He shrugged. *"It is not for me to say."*

I bit back my frustration with his discretion, staring out my window as we came to a halt at a stop sign. "Do you want to see the site of the De-Sal center?" he asked.

"If we have time," I answered more tartly than I intended.

But he didn't seem to notice, calmly checking his watch before turning onto the one-way road, so steep my stomach leaped to my throat as we plunged downward. Branches scraped along the roof of the van, and a black-and-white cat sauntered along the top of a stone retaining wall so close I could have reached out and petted her if the window had been open.

Past a cluster of small green-roofed houses whose doors opened directly onto the street, the road curved to the right, but he made a sharp left turn onto a patch of dirt and cut the engine.

"We go through those rocks there." He indicated a path that cut through two boulders between the dry bushes and scraggly trees. I looked down at my wedge sandals, wishing I'd worn flats as he came around the front of the van to offer me a hand down, which I accepted, then consciously released to close the door behind me before he could do it. He watched, amused, but didn't comment.

"The path is not so bad," he promised, noting my shoes as we made our way along the sandy shale toward the rocks.

He went ahead, turning back as he navigated a rock garden to again take my hand. I reluctantly let him, hating how aware I was of his smooth calluses against my palm.

The passageway opened onto a promontory that was perhaps ten by twenty meters, overlooking an inlet where turquoise water crashed against the cliffs below. To our left, the path continued along the rocky ridge; to our right, a sloping hillside tumbled down to a small beach. The view was breathtaking.

The sleeve of his fitted white T-shirt rode up, revealing his tattoo as he pointed at the bay. "The De-Sal center goes there," he said.

"And the developers have plans to build here." He indicated the hill-side.

"I can see why they're upset," I said.

"The land is . . ." He searched for the word, then switched to French. *"Devalued."* I nodded to let him know I understood, and he continued, *"But he won't win. St. Barth's has no natural source of water. We've been using desalination for over fifty years, but Tyson's system is far better. It is good for the whole island."*

"What will they do, the developers?"

He shrugged. "Sometimes you win, sometimes you lose, no?" His phone dinged in his pocket, and he checked it, his face darkening as he read whatever message was there. He tapped out a reply and pocketed the phone. "We should go."

He offered his arm to steady me on the way back, and I took it, holding the inside of his bent elbow. But he was preoccupied by whatever message he'd received, and all business, his movements efficient, no lingering glances or light touches, as he ushered me into the van.

The sudden shift reminded me of the secrets Tyson had mentioned. Laurent was helping me not because he wanted to, but because Tyson was holding something over his head, as he was with me. I wondered if Laurent's secrets were as dark as mine.

He turned on the radio as we pulled onto the narrow road and the sound of Jimi Hendrix's guitar wailed from the speakers as he answered a call, telling whoever was on the other end in French that he was dropping a guest in Gustavia and would have only thirty minutes.

We came around a bend and Gustavia appeared at the bottom of the hill, green mountains sloping down to the red-roofed buildings that circled the port. Sailboats and catamarans were moored in the center, a variety of pleasure boats docked along the promenade, with larger yachts closer to the mouth of the harbor.

When we reached the town, we turned onto a one-way street, immaculately clean and paved with gray cobblestones, lined with well-maintained palms and benches where shoppers rested in the shade, licking cones of gelato. It felt like a perfect blend of European and

Caribbean culture, sophisticated yet laid back, the architecture colonial, the brands luxury. The usual suspects were there: Louis Vuitton, Chopard, Dior, Bulgari, Prada, Cartier, Hermès, their storefronts featuring selections from their resort collections, nestled among restaurants and upscale boutiques.

Laurent stopped at a corner and pointed to a shaded alleyway that ran between two buildings. "This is the nearest I can go in the van," he said. "At the end you will see the white building with two balconies. Text me when you're ready for pickup."

I nodded, opening the door. He didn't move to help me down. I wanted to read into it, but I didn't let myself. "Where is the council meeting being held?"

"At the pink civic center building a block east of Gary's. But they won't let you in without an appointment."

I nodded. If I wanted to find a way in, I would, but I didn't think it would be necessary today. "You're driving them home after?"

He nodded.

"I'd like to be in the car."

"Then be outside the civic center at one."

After trying on a number of suits in the sunlit changing room of Gary's, I selected a black-and-green zippered shorty with long sleeves, a black mask, and the cheapest dive watch they carried, which was still far more expensive than any I'd ever owned. It had been years since I'd updated my gear and I was grudgingly thrilled by my new duds, regardless of who was paying for them.

Shopping bag in hand, I stepped into the warm day, contemplating the nearly empty street from beneath the brim of my sun hat. It was twenty 'til one.

I located the civic center in my maps app and set off toward it in the shade of the palm trees, stopping in front of shop windows to gaze at mannequins wearing crocheted bikinis and designer sunglasses, jewel-encrusted sandals and four-thousand-euro Missoni cover-ups. I looked into a real estate office whose windows advertised newly built villas not unlike the one we were staying in for the low, low price of eighteen million. The cheapest one I could find was a one-bedroom apartment with no view for one point six million.

Where did the people who worked here live? Surely Laurent wasn't paid enough to afford a two-million-euro apartment? Or maybe he was. Maybe I was the only asshole around here who couldn't afford twenty euros for a minuscule lemonade in the shop next door.

I was about to continue up the sidewalk when I recognized a picture of the developers' land overlooking the site of the De-Sal center Laurent had just shown me, paired with renderings of the houses they planned to build there. There were ten of them, ranging in price from fifteen to twenty-five million. Roughly two hundred million gross for the developers. I wasn't sure what they'd paid for the land, but it couldn't have been cheap, and with the cost of building on an island, their margins likely weren't wide.

It made sense that they were angry about the placement of the De-Sal center. I would be too, if I were them, regardless of what it would do for the island. It's one thing to be civic-minded when you're not the one being asked to sacrifice your livelihood for the good of the community; it's quite another when you're the sacrificial lamb.

Across from the civic center, the Sprinter van was at the curb right where it should be, engine running. Laurent waited outside the open back door, typing on his phone. He looked up as I approached, reaching out to take my bag. "You found what you needed?"

"I did."

The front door of the civic center flew open and Tyson stormed out, his face a mask of fury. Allison and Cody were on his heels, looking none too pleased themselves, followed by the two guys I'd met at the house when I arrived yesterday and a handful of other worried-looking people I guessed were their assistants.

"Sit in front," Laurent murmured.

I accepted his hand into the front of the van as Tyson, Cody, and Allison piled into the back.

"Go," Tyson barked before Laurent had even closed his door.

Laurent fired up the engine and pulled away from the curb as the side door slid shut.

"What the fuck was that?" Tyson spat. "They should never have had that information. Someone on our team leaked it to them."

"We'll hire someone to dispute it," Cody said calmly. "It's only a delay."

"A delay? What planet are you living on?" Tyson demanded. "This could tank us. Now every center is going to want to do their own environmental report—"

"And when they do, they'll find everything is fine," Allison said. "Won't they?"

"I don't need this right now," Tyson growled.

"Is there something you're not telling us?" Cody asked.

"Nothing you need to know," Tyson snapped. "You don't have the balls to make the decisions that need to be made."

"This sounds like a conversation we should have in private," Cody said pointedly.

I didn't have to turn around to know he was shooting a glance at Laurent and me in the front seat.

"I trust them more than I trust either of you," Tyson retorted.

"Would you like me to raise the privacy partition?" Laurent asked.

"Yes, please," Allison said.

Laurent pressed the button, and the screen began to rise. Once it was in place, we exchanged a glance as the voices in the back intensified, their content muted by the partition. Whatever it was they were so upset about, Laurent and I both knew it was Allison who'd leaked it to those two men from the city council last night.

The question was what I should do with that information.

A couple of weeks after the Fourth of July, I was asleep in Tyson's bed when I awoke with a start to the sound of a buzzer and banging somewhere in the house. Tyson continued to sleep as I sat up, looking around in the pitch-dark room. The banging seemed to be coming from the sliding glass door out to the pool. I tapped my phone, bringing up the time: 2:24 A.M.

"Tyson," I whispered, jostling him.

"Mmmpf," he said, rolling over.

"There's someone at the door downstairs."

He turned quickly, suddenly awake, listening. In a flash, he was on his feet, reaching into the bedside table to pull out his handgun. He released the safety, swinging open the bedroom door and creeping onto the landing in his boxers as I pulled on a T-shirt and gym shorts and went to the window that looked out over the pool, lifting the blackout shades.

I gasped as my eyes caught sight of the flames erupting from Ian's trailer, a column of black smoke rising into the night sky.

I swiped my phone from the bedside table, dialing 911 as I dashed out the door and down the stairs, not bothering to find shoes. I could see Andie banging at the glass but flew past her into the kitchen on Tyson's heels, reciting the address into the phone. "We need the fire department, fast," I said.

Tyson dropped the gun to the island with a clatter and pulled a fire extinguisher from beneath the sink, tossing it to me. "I'm grabbing the other one," he said as he went into the laundry room off the kitchen.

I ran to the sliding glass door and flung it open. Andie was in sleep shorts and a ripped T-shirt, her hair wild, ash streaked across her face. "You have to help me," she cried. "Ian's not waking up and I can't drag him by myself."

"There's someone in the trailer," I said to the operator on the phone. "He's unresponsive. Please send help fast."

I waited for confirmation before hanging up, then looked at Andie. "What's he on?"

"I don't know," she said. "He was pretty fucked up when he passed out."

I gripped the fire extinguisher to my chest as we sprinted across the pool deck and out the back gate. "But he's breathing?"

She nodded, her eyes scared. "He was when I left."

The ground was still wet from the rain, leaving the path to the trailer slippery and pocked with puddles, and I slid in the mud, catching myself with the base of the fire extinguisher. "Where is he?" I asked, getting back to my feet.

"In the bedroom," she answered. "I went out the window. The fire's in the kitchen."

The flames reflected in the surface of the lake as we raced around it, and a chemical smell accosted my nostrils. "Is the bedroom door closed?" I asked.

"Yeah."

As we neared the trailer, I saw that only the glass door was shut. I hit the bottom of the fire extinguisher into the latch, coughing when it swung open and a plume of smoke billowed out.

I covered my face with the bottom of my shirt, remaining on the top step just outside the living room as I pulled the pin on the fire extinguisher and aimed blindly in the direction of the flames, firing in a sweeping motion. In a flash, Tyson was beside me, doing the same.

"What are you doing?" Andie cried. "That's not gonna work. We have to get him out."

She was right, our efforts didn't seem to be doing much good at all. But the windows were so far off the ground that we needed something to stand on to get up to them. "Do you have a ladder?" I asked.

"No."

Tyson continued to work on the fire as Andie and I glanced around the yard. We saw the plastic chair at the same time. She grabbed it and started running toward the back of the trailer.

"Come on," I yelled to Tyson. "We need your help pulling him out."

Tyson cast a glance at me as he continued spraying the fire. He said something, but I couldn't make it out with the roar of the flames and his elbow covering his nose and mouth.

"What?" I shouted.

"We should wait for the fire department," he repeated.

I shook my head. "He could be dead by the time they get here!"

"We're not risking our lives for him," Tyson said.

I drew back, shocked. "We have to try."

"He's put us in a very bad situation. We're better off without him."

It was true, we were under Ian's thumb, running the sales deflation program constantly to be able to pay him the cash he demanded. But it had never occurred to me not to save him.

"I'm not letting him die," I said. "And I will never speak to you again if you do."

When I reached the back of the trailer, I saw Andie standing on the chair, struggling to pull herself up on the window frame. I came up behind her and hoisted her into the open window.

"Use your shirt like a mask," I called out to her as I placed my hands on the windowsill and struggled to lift myself up.

I'd gotten my chin and shoulders through when Tyson showed up. "We're gonna regret this," he said, giving me a boost from behind.

Andie was already tugging on Ian, her shirt covering her nose, when

I dropped through the window onto the mattress. The room was thick with smoke as I pulled my own shirt up over my nose, my eyes stinging.

I took Ian's wrist in my hand, placing two fingers over his pulse. It was weak, but present. "He's alive," I said, slapping him across the face.

He didn't wake. I slapped him again, to no avail, as Tyson came through the window.

"How are we gonna get him out?" Andie asked.

"We can prop him by the window, then you and I can push him out," I said to Andie. "Tyson will be outside to catch him."

Tyson nodded grimly, already hooking his arms under Ian's armpits. He dragged him across the bed, set him up by the window, then went out backward. "Okay," he said. "Pass him to me."

I grabbed one foot and she grabbed the other and we pulled until his legs were dangling out the window. "Okay," I called to Tyson, coughing.

Andie and I lifted Ian and gave a push.

He was stuck on the frame and then in an instant, his weight shifted, and he was gone, ripped from our hands by gravity. Andie cried out as he fell on top of Tyson, knocking them both to the ground.

I turned to gesture for her to go out first, but she was rummaging through the closet. "Come on," I called. "We need to get out of here."

"I'm coming," she said. "Go. I just have to get something."

I didn't have it in me to argue. I was beginning to feel weak from smoke inhalation as I stuck my head out the window to see Tyson dragging Ian away from the trailer. The chair was on its side, but the drop wasn't more than six feet. I swung my legs over the windowsill and tumbled to the mud. I felt the jolt all the way through my body when I struck the ground, falling to my knees. "Come on," I called to Andie.

But the window remained empty. After a moment, I heard a loud bang from somewhere in the trailer, and the glass of the window cracked. "Andie!" I yelled, panic rising in me. "Get out of there!"

A backpack came crashing out the window, then Andie's head appeared. Her shirt had fallen and her face appeared drained of blood, her eyes blinking slowly. Something was wrong. As her hand gripped the windowsill, I saw it was covered in blood. I grabbed the chair and pulled it over to the window, reaching up to her.

"Come on," I said. "I'll catch you."

She stepped through the window with the slow, unsteady movements of someone heavily intoxicated, and I caught a glimpse of dark crimson smeared across her torso as she plunged into my arms. I lost my balance on the flimsy chair, and we toppled to the ground. My body absorbed most of the shock as she fell on top of me, and I was grateful for the thick layer of mud.

Once I'd caught my breath, I scooted out from under her and she groaned, seemingly unable to sit up. "Are you hurt?" I asked, sitting up to look her over. "Oh shit," I said when I saw the blood oozing from a long, jagged wound across her torso, just above her left hip. I pulled my shirt mask over my head and pressed it to the wound. She yelped in pain.

"The ambulance will be here soon," I promised, praying that was true. "What happened?"

"The door exploded," she said weakly. "A piece of it hit me."

I heard sirens in the distance, and tears of relief sprang to my eyes. "It's gonna be okay," I said, holding the blood-soaked shirt to her wound. "They're almost here. Just breathe."

Tyson got to his feet, leaving Ian lying in the grass, and waved his arms overhead as he ran toward the flashing red and white lights, his shadows jumping and twisting in the glare of the flames.

CHAPTER 12

"Tyson," I called as Laurent helped me down from the Sprinter van in front of Le Rêve, "I'd love to chat with you if you have a moment."

Tyson paused his stride halfway across the parking court, his mouth in a hard line. I knew that this was not a good time. But what I'd learned thus far had only left me with more questions.

I squinted in the direct sunlight. "It won't take long," I promised.

He kicked off his shoes and pushed through the front door, leaving me fumbling with the straps of my stupid wedges. By the time I'd stepped out of them, he was gone. I scurried down the outdoor staircase to the lower floor, where I found the door to his lair ajar.

"Tyson?" I called out as I stepped inside, allowing my eyes to adjust to the dark after the brightness of the day.

A crack of light shone along the edge of the partially open door to the patio, so I headed in that direction, my eyes once again adjusting to the change in light as I stepped into Tyson's garden. The space was lush with a variety of leafy plants and succulents, the walls covered in creeping vines, green grass sprouting between the square pavers. A fan spun in the wooden slat ceiling, above two white couches that faced each other in front of a gurgling fountain.

He sat on the couch facing the view, so I took the one opposite. "Phone," he said, holding out his hand.

I took out my phone and turned it off, then set it on the table between us.

"You seem awfully chummy with the butler," he scoffed.

As anxious as Tyson made me, at least I didn't have to keep up my veneer of congeniality around him. I hardened my gaze. "You told me to use him, so I am."

"So? What have you found out?"

"Why didn't you tell me Samira was implicated in her first husband's death?" I asked.

He crossed his arms. "I wondered how long it would take you to figure that out."

I swallowed, refusing to give him the satisfaction of my aggravation. "You had her reputation cleaned up online."

He shrugged. "And?"

"Did she do it?" I asked.

"Are you asking me if my wife's a murderer?"

"You're the one that thinks she might be blackmailing you," I pointed out.

"No," he said. "My wife's not a murderer." He uncapped his bottle of water and took a swig. "Unless, of course, she is."

My muscles twitched with the desire to smack him.

"Is that all you've discovered?" he asked, emphasizing the word "discovered" in an obvious attempt to belittle my job title.

"I was thinking about who might hold a grudge against you, outside your inner circle," I said evenly.

He crossed his arms, his jaw tightening. "And?"

"Do you remember Andie? Ian's girlfriend?"

"The Australian girl? Barely. She wasn't exactly memorable."

It was true we'd never spent a lot of time with Andie, and it had been more than a decade since we'd seen her. But still. "I know she went back to Australia, but we'd be remiss not to at least look into her."

He was already shaking his head. "It's not her."

"How do you know?"

"She's dead."

I raised my brows in shock. "When? How?"

"Not long after Ian disappeared. Her car went off a bridge."

"Shit," I said, unnerved. "Are you sure?"

A sharp nod told me that no matter how dimly he might remember her, he'd checked, and thoroughly. Tyson was nothing if not cautious.

"That's so . . . sad."

"Is it?" he asked, his eyes full of meaning.

I shook off his implication, abruptly changing the subject. "What happened at the meeting today?"

"The city council put a hold on the permit, pending further investigation."

"I gathered," I said evenly. "Why?"

"Monterey tightened environmental regulations recently, and the city decided to hire their own inspector, who provided a report that differed significantly from the one our inspector had supplied."

I raised my brows as he continued. "Someone on the council here got hold of that report, and they're now demanding that an independent inspector be contracted to perform an environmental assessment before the permit to break ground can be issued."

"Why were the results of the assessment in Monterey different from what was reported by your inspector?"

"I don't know. That's not my area of expertise."

"No," I said, narrowing my eyes. "But you told me long ago that your area of expertise is recognizing brilliance and harnessing it for your own purposes. Did you not hire a service you thought was brilliant?"

"I hired a service to perform the job at a level that suited my needs," he said.

A level that suited his needs. The depth of his duplicity hit me like a truck.

He was so worried about the Monterey report leaking and all the other centers wanting to perform their own independent assessments because they would all find discrepancies. Centers would need to be shut down all over the world, adjustments made at great expense to the company. That is, if he even had the technology to produce the kind of environmental reports he needed to keep De-Sal afloat.

I met his confrontational gaze, holding on to my composure by a thread. "Do Cody and Allison know this?"

"They do now."

"But they didn't before today?"

He shook his head, and it dawned on me what a colossal mistake Cody and Allison had made in leaking that report without knowing the full story. They'd believed it was a one-off. That it would slow down development in St. Barth's, pushing back the potential contract with France just long enough that Tyson would consider bringing on the investor that would allow Allison to pay off her debt to the bank. They had no idea that whatever company Tyson had hired was a sham, working under his thumb, and every De-Sal center in the world would be affected.

Instead of slowing down the construction of a single center, they'd potentially brought the entire company to its knees.

"What does this have to do with my blackmailer?" Tyson demanded.

"You think the blackmail comes from your inner circle, you have to consider motive," I pointed out. "Which means you have to consider all angles. So yes, the unilateral decision you made that could tank your entire company has to be considered."

"It'll be fine," he growled. "I'll figure it out. Like I always do."

There was a hint of fatigue in his voice, and for a fleeting moment, I caught a glimpse of the man inside the monster he'd become, before his mask slid back into place and he tilted his head, his dark eyes penetrating. "I always win. By whatever means necessary. Don't forget that."

Shit, you couldn't write this stuff. It was like he'd taken lessons in vice from a comic book villain. If it weren't so real, it would be laughable.

"We're on the same side," I reminded him.

He didn't reply, gesturing to the door as he rose. "I won't be at dinner tonight, but you should go. They'll talk more if I'm not there."

But I wasn't going to be dismissed so easily. The shock of his accusation yesterday had worn off, and I'd had time to strategize. "You claimed yesterday that you have evidence I created the SADEP," I said calmly. "Show me."

He didn't move.

"Show me, or I'm going home, and you can figure this shit out on your own," I said, crossing my arms.

His swiped his laptop from where it rested on the counter, clenching his jaw and dropping back into the chair he'd vacated. My heart rate sped up as his fingers flew over the keys. I'd been hoping he was bluffing, but apparently that was not the case.

Finally, he spun the computer toward me and hit Play on the video that filled the screen. I saw a blur of motion as a camera whipped from the computer monitor in Tyson's dad's office to me in my bikini, a strand of red, white, and blue plastic beads around my neck.

The video Ian had shot on the Fourth of July, nearly eleven years ago.

Onscreen, I stared at Ian in shock, asking him what he was doing. I watched horror spread over my face as he told me from behind the camera that he was admiring my work and demanded we cut him in. I saw me pull out my phone and text Cody and Tyson to come upstairs, watched as I pleaded with Ian, telling him the money was for my mom's cancer treatments, until Cody and Tyson burst into the room and the phone blurred again before the image cut.

I gaped at Tyson, processing what I'd just seen. "How'd you get this?"

He just scowled at me.

"Where's the rest of it?" I asked.

"I think this is plenty to prove your guilt." He snapped the laptop closed. "I need to get to the gym. Let me know what you find out tonight."

CHAPTER 13

I was still reviewing the video in my mind as I changed into my swimsuit in my room. I'd imagined its contents so many times over the years, but I'd had it all wrong. I'd thought it ended where it began. Had Ian accidentally pressed Stop instead of Record and vice versa? Or had he been bluffing about filming when I walked in all along?

Maybe there was more to the video, and Tyson was only showing me the part that implicated me. Because I was certain that clip was not what had gotten Cody arrested. If that was what Ian had shown the cops, I would have gone to jail with—or in place of—Cody.

Fortunately, arrest and police reports were in the public domain in Florida. I powered up my phone and typed out a message to Rosa:

You have time to go down to the Central Records Bureau today?

She gave my message a thumbs-up immediately, adding:

What do you need?

Cody's arrest record.

She wanted to talk, but I didn't trust Tyson not to have listening devices throughout his home, so I typed out a message urging her not to get sunburned and promised to fill her in later.

Ian might have been bluffing, but Tyson wasn't, though I still didn't understand why he was treating me like I was the enemy. Was he really paranoid enough to think I'd try to blackmail him, or was there something else going on? And if he didn't trust me, why had he dropped the compromising information about the faked environmental reports in my lap?

Of course, he hadn't said it outright, and I didn't have any evidence. But still, I couldn't quite see his angle. And I was damn good at spotting angles.

I found Jennifer by the pool, parked in the sun in a white one-piece that showed off her tan, her hair curled, makeup flawless. "Dinner should be fun," she said, putting down the Emily Henry novel she was reading. "Tyson's not coming."

I settled into the lounge chair next to her. "Do you guys not get along?"

She laughed. "Tyson doesn't 'get along' with anyone. He's generous sometimes, I'll give him that, but—" She shook her head. "He makes things very difficult for all of us. And I'm not even inner circle."

"How long have you and Cody been together?"

"About a year." She took a sip of her Perrier. "But it feels like longer."

"How did you meet?"

"At the coffee shop in our neighborhood."

I smiled. "I'm glad to see him happy. He's a good guy. So, cheers to you."

She tapped her Perrier to mine. "Ooh, I have the perfect dress for you tonight."

"That's so nice of you, but I think I'm a little bigger than you," I said, eyeing her pint-size frame over the top of my sunglasses.

"I never know what size I'm gonna be because of these," Jennifer said, indicating her ample chest, "so I always order things in two sizes. I threw a couple of doubles in my suitcase, and one of them would be stunning on you. I can do your makeup, too, if you want. I used to do tutorials on TikTok, before I met Cody."

Makeup tutorials on TikTok. I snapped my fingers, suddenly realizing why Jennifer had seemed so familiar when we were introduced. "Oh my gosh, that must be where I know you from," I said, smiling.

"Oh, yeah," she said. "I didn't want to say anything when you asked if we knew each other because it's awkward to be like, 'You probably know me from TikTok,' but it happens."

I nodded, understanding. "I'm not a TikToker myself, but I think my best friend Rosa follows you. She is obsessed with makeup tutorials and sends them to me all the time. Not that they do me any good. What's your handle? I'll have to tell her."

Her sigh was laced with regret. "I took them all down after Cody and I got together."

"Did he make you?" I asked, surprised.

She shook her head. "But I could tell the idea of me being out there so publicly made him uncomfortable. He's very private."

"Well, I'd love your assistance with my appearance tonight," I acquiesced with a smile, glad I was making progress with at least one of Tyson's guests. "It's very sweet of you to offer."

She shrugged. "It's nice to have someone to hang out with. Gisèle and Samira do their own thing, and Allison mostly keeps to herself."

"Do you like her?" I asked.

"Sure." She paused, considering her words. "It's not that she thinks she's better than everybody, it's just that she is, if that makes sense."

"What do you mean?"

"She had multiple Olympic medals at eighteen and a billion-dollar company by the time she was thirty. I think it makes it hard for her to relate to us normal people."

"But she's close with Tyson and Cody?"

"Close, yeah." Jennifer leaned in, lowering her voice. "I mean, she hates Tyson—more and more, that much is clear. She and Cody get along, though—honestly, I was a little jealous when we first got together, until I saw the kind of guys she dates."

I motioned for her to go on.

"Athletes," she said. "Pro basketball players, football. Big muscly guys. With swagger. Not my sweet Cody."

It was sounding more and more like Allison was likely Tyson's blackmailer—if blackmail was even the right term. There hadn't been any demands. Not even a warning. Just the article. But Allison had known Tyson long enough and well enough that she would have guessed the impact it would have on him.

I closed my eyes, letting the sun warm my skin. I just needed some kind of evidence, then I could go home. Allison was in her suite now, but perhaps if I waited here long enough, she'd leave, giving me the opportunity to search her room.

I was dead to the world on my lounger a few hours later when Samira and Gisèle came in, laughing. Jennifer was no longer on the pool deck, and the sun had dropped in the sky. Annoyed with myself for falling asleep, I checked my phone, hoping Rosa had sent me what I asked for, but I had no new messages.

"I told you he was great," I heard Gisèle rib.

Cabinets opened and closed. *"It's not that I didn't think he would be great,"* Samira answered. *"It's that I didn't want to be murdered by my husband. Where are the pods for the Nespresso machine?"*

"Just wait till you see the pictures," Gisèle said. *"It takes forever because he develops them all in his own darkroom, but so worth it."*

"The longer the better. I'd like to live until I'm twenty-six. I can't find the pods anywhere."

"Frame one for Tyson," Gisèle encouraged. *"Say you did it for him."*

Samira snorted. "Laurent," she called. "Hello?" I heard the door to the servants' area open and close. *"Where is he?"*

"He's not here," I answered, rising from my lounger. An espresso sounded divine, and this seemed like a good opportunity to connect with Samira and Gisèle, who had yet to say so much as a word to me.

"*Putain,*" Samira exclaimed, clutching her chest in shock as she collapsed against the island. Both girls were barefoot in bikinis and cover-ups as if they were coming from the beach, but their hair and skin looked suspiciously perfect. "*I didn't know anyone was there,*" she continued, recovering. She peered at me warily. "*You speak French?*"

I nodded.

They exchanged a surprised glance but didn't comment, nor did they switch to English.

"*Is Tyson here?*" Gisèle asked.

I nodded. "*Downstairs.*"

"*Merde,*" Samira muttered, lowering her voice. "*He didn't go to that meeting?*"

"*I don't know,*" I said, unsure of what she was referring to. "*They had the hearing this morning—*"

She shook her head. "*Never mind.*" She went to the mirrored backsplash and evaluated her reflection, wiping at the makeup around her eyes.

"*I have face wash in my bathroom if you need it,*" I offered.

She paused, again surprised. "*Thank you, but it's so dark down there, I don't think he'll notice before I shower.*"

I gestured to the bottles of vodka and Kahlua on the island. "*Are you making something?*"

"*We wanted espresso martinis, but we can't find the Nespresso pods,*" Gisèle said.

I opened the side of the machine and showed them the row of pods. "*They're stored in here.*"

"*I've never seen that,*" Gisèle said, peering at the machine.

"*I have the same version at home,*" I said. "*Do you want me to make you an espresso?*"

Samira held up two fingers. "*For the martinis. Unless you want one?*" she added.

It was an afterthought, and she likely didn't expect—or particularly want—me to accept, but it was a chance to get on her good side.

And I could use a pick-me-up before dinner. *"Sure,"* I said, pressing the button on the Nespresso machine. *"Are you guys coming out tonight?"*

"Where?" Samira asked.

"I can't remember the name of the restaurant. A seafood place in Gustavia, I think. Then La Petite Plage?"

In the reflection of the mirrored backsplash, I watched them exchange another glance, and I had the distinct feeling that they could read each other's minds. *"Who is going?"* Gisèle asked.

I filled a cocktail shaker with ice. *"Everyone, I think. Except for Tyson."*

"Ah," Samira said. *"We'll see if he lets me go."*

I poured our shots of espresso into the cocktail shaker and handed it to Gisèle, who added liberal amounts of vodka and Kahlua, then capped it and shook it over her shoulder.

"You look like a professional," I commented, grabbing three martini glasses from the shelf.

"She was a bartender in Paris," Samira said. *"Until she was discovered by a modeling scout and started booking so many jobs she didn't need to work in a bar anymore."*

Gisèle uncapped the shaker and poured the dark liquid into our glasses. Each of us took a stem, cautiously raising the precariously full drinks.

"Santé," I said.

We carefully clinked glasses, then slurped off the top before we could spill them, laughing when we realized how ridiculous we all looked. "Damn, that's good," I said, taking another sip of the chilled, rich martini.

"My favorite," Samira said.

"We always have them before a night out," Gisèle added conspiratorially. They smiled as we sipped, the frostiness they'd exhibited toward me since I arrived thawed.

"Did you two meet modeling?" I asked.

They shook their heads, and again I could feel the intense connection between them as their eyes met. *"We met in dance class when we were teenagers,"* Gisèle said. *"She was already a successful actress."*

"I was a little successful in Belgium," Samira said. *"Which is . . ."* She shrugged.

"You would have been successful everywhere if you'd stuck with it," Gisèle chided.

"Plans change," Samira said. As she tossed back a large gulp of her drink, I tried to imagine her leveling a shotgun at her first husband's head and pulling the trigger. But for some reason, it was Gisèle I saw behind the sight.

"I've got to get dressed," Samira said, setting her glass down on the counter with a clink.

Gisèle seemed pensive as she watched her friend stalk down the stairs to her quarters. I lingered, hoping she might talk to me, but she didn't, instead shouldering her beach bag and starting for the stairs up to her room, glass in hand. *"À plus tard,"* she said.

As I sipped my drink, I was already thinking about later, about how to break through Allison's aerodynamic exterior and get the information I needed so that I could go home. Everyone had an Achilles' heel. I just needed to find hers.

I cast a glance toward her suite. Maybe luck was on my side, I thought as I padded across the living room to her door. I knocked softly, calling out, "Allison?"

There was no answer. I knocked again. "Hello?"

After a moment, I laid my hand on the doorknob, holding my breath.

But the door was firmly locked.

Tyson paced along the boardwalk beside the marshy waterway, running his fingers through his hair. "Can you believe this motherfucker is still demanding money from us, even after we saved his life?"

I leaned against a palm tree, taking refuge in its small slice of shade. The day was sweltering, but I hadn't wanted to talk about Ian in my mom's house and couldn't leave her long enough to go to Tyson's, so we'd met at a park down the street.

My mom had done so well after the first treatment, but the second one hadn't been as smooth. One of the side effects she was now suffering from was vertigo, which meant she needed me by her side to make sure she didn't fall and hurt herself. I didn't feel comfortable leaving her for more than fifteen minutes, which meant I hadn't seen much of Tyson since we'd last returned from Naples.

"We would have been better off letting him go up in flames," he groused.

"Not funny," I said, though I was beginning to worry he was right. It had been three weeks since the fire, and instead of gratitude for risking our lives on Ian's account, we'd only received increasingly steeper demands from him for money.

"I'm not joking. And now he has the balls to demand we cover his and Andie's hospital bills. He's hired a lawyer to claim the fire was our fault for not maintaining the trailer properly, when he's the one that left a fucking burner on and passed out!"

"Are your parents coming back to deal with it?" I asked.

"What, and leave Lake Como?" He snorted. "They don't trust me, but they've hired their own attorney and have insisted Cody come babysit me, like any of this is my fault."

I refrained from pointing out that he'd failed to tell his parents Ian was dealing drugs out of the trailer on their property, not to mention making all kinds of modifications with his inventions.

He kicked a pebble into the water. "I can't wait to go back to school next month."

I looked up at the milky blue sky, wishing that that didn't smart as much as it did. "We're going to have to come up with some kind of deal with Ian," I said. "The way things are going, I don't know whether they'll let my mom do another treatment after this, and we can't just leave the program running indefinitely."

Despite my protests, Tyson was skimming off the proceeds as well now, with the reasoning that if Ian was profiting, so would he.

"Shoulda let him burn," he muttered again.

I checked my watch. "I have to get back. You wanna come over for dinner? Maybe stay the night?"

He grabbed my hips and pulled me in for a kiss. "I wish I could, but I told Cody I'd grab a bite with him after I drop off this money to Ian."

"Where's Ian staying now?" I asked.

"In a shitty apartment about ten minutes east of here."

"Do you know how Andie's doing?" I asked.

"I'm not exactly inquiring after his girlfriend's health when I'm dropping off the money he's blackmailing me for."

I nodded, gripping the handlebars of my bike and releasing the kickstand. "I'll see you tomorrow."

He nodded, mounting his bike, and we rode off in opposite directions.

That night, I lay in my bed tossing and turning, unable to sleep for my anxiety over what to do about Ian. Finally at around midnight, I texted Cody:

We've got to figure out what to do about Ian. This can't go on forever.

It was late, but I knew Cody was a night owl, and I figured if he'd already fallen asleep, his ringer would be off. The three little dots appeared immediately, and he replied:

100. But how are you texting me right now

I stared at the phone. What was he talking about? I held down the text and gave it the question mark.

He texted back the monkey covering its ears emoji, followed by:

I can hear you guys

I sat up, feeling like someone had just dumped a bucket of cold water over my head, my thumbs flying over the keyboard:

R U fucking with me?

My stomach clenched as I hit Send. Had Tyson lied to me when he said that he and Cody were going to grab a bite tonight? After all his tender words about how much he cared for me, his claims that he was collecting money from the SADEP to pay for my education, his promises about our future . . . had he called some other girl to come over and satisfy his needs?

The three little dots appeared, and then disappeared. Then appeared again, and disappeared again.

Shit.

Finally the three dots appeared again, followed by the text that sent an ice pick through my heart:

I'm sorry.

I flipped on the bedside lamp and threw back the covers, blindly pulling on whatever clothes were on my floor. I grabbed my mom's car keys from the top of my dresser, then reconsidered. Biking would cool me off. And if anything was going on, Tyson wouldn't hear me pull up.

I crept down the hallway and peeked in on my mom, confirming she was sleeping soundly, then slipped out the back door and mounted my bike. The night air was cool against my skin as I hurtled down the dark streets, in and out of the yellow pools of light cast by the streetlamps, my heart racing.

Maybe Cody was wrong. Maybe I'd rush over there just to find Tyson watching porn. We'd laugh and I'd feel like an idiot, bike home with my tail between my legs.

All was quiet as I pulled into the driveway and leaned my bike against the side of the house. I knew Cody was probably on the couch downstairs watching television, but if what I thought was going on was really happening, I didn't want to put him in the position of being the one to let me in. Instead, I slipped through the side gate and around the back of the house to the pool deck, grabbing the key to the laundry room door from beneath the potted plant where I'd insisted Tyson stash it after the last time I'd gotten locked out. I fitted it into the lock and silently pushed the door open.

I could hear a laugh track on the television in the living room as I tiptoed through the kitchen toward the stairs. Cody turned, startled, his eyes widening when he saw me. I put a finger to my lips as he shook his head.

"Don't go up there," he mouthed.

I darted for the stairs before he could stop me, flying up the marble staircase and across the landing like the wind. My nerves stood on end as I came to a stop in front of Tyson's door and stood still, listening. I didn't have to strain my ears to hear the thunk of his headboard against the wall, the squeaking of the mattress coils interspersed with grunting I recognized and soft moans I didn't.

With a deep breath, I placed my hand on the doorknob and shoved open the door. Candles burned on either side of the bed, illuminating the surprised face of one of the American flag bikini girls from the Fourth of July party, looking up at me from beneath Tyson. I gaped at them, engulfed by rage.

I'd known what I was getting into coming here, but seeing it was so much worse.

I could feel the wrath rising from my skin like steam as I spun on my heel and marched out of the room. When I reached the bottom of the stairs, I found Cody standing at the edge of the living room, his jaw slack.

"I'm sorry," he said, following me toward the door. "I feel like this is my fault."

I stopped, turning to lay a hand on his arm. "Don't. It's not."

"Stay out of this, Cody," Tyson warned, sprinting down the stairs in his boxers. "It's none of your fucking business."

I swung open the front door and scurried out, their raised voices growing muddled as I grabbed my bike and pedaled off into the night. Fuck Tyson Dale. I hoped I'd never see him again.

CHAPTER 14

The vibe of the restaurant perched on the hill overlooking the port was more house party than fine dining establishment, with low lighting and plush couches in the bar area arranged to encourage conversation among the attractive clientele. Electronic lounge music thrummed over the speakers, and waiters maneuvered deftly between candlelit tables of tanned, laughing patrons dressed fashionably and imbibing decadently.

"Stop it," Jennifer said, swatting at my hand as I tugged at the too-short hem of the powder-blue spaghetti-strap number she'd lent me. "You look amazing."

It was true the dress fit me like a glove, the cutouts on either side displaying the tan I'd picked up by the pool today, and paired with the diamond waterfall earrings she'd insisted I borrow, I had to admit I looked good. Good enough that I'd been sorely disappointed when someone who was not Laurent showed up to drive us to dinner.

I'd convinced myself it was better that he wouldn't be there, but clearly I hadn't done a sufficient job, because when I heard Allison raise her voice in greeting and glanced over my shoulder to see Laurent, I felt a rush of excitement. He looked appropriately devastating in a crisp white button-down with the top few buttons undone and the sleeves rolled up, and was talking to Allison and Cody, but his eyes were fixed on the hem of my dress. My gaze collided with his and my body immediately betrayed me, producing a thrill that blazed all the way down my spine.

Trying in vain to snuff out the flame, I turned my attention to my phone, but the message I was waiting for from Rosa still hadn't come in. I fired off a text:

Any word on that arrest record?

Her reply came immediately:

Did the pix I texted not go through?

I gave her text a thumbs-down and asked her to email them, but a moment later when I checked my email, I couldn't access the attachment. The files were too large for the spotty cellular service on the island. I needed Wi-Fi.

I sidled over to the bar, signaling the bartender. "Excuse me," I said. "Is there Wi-Fi here that I could hook up to?"

He shook his head. "Sorry."

"Put your phone away," Jennifer teased, pulling me back toward our group. "Just be here."

Not wanting to look like an asshole, I acquiesced, stowing the device in my purse. When I looked up, my gaze again caught Laurent's, and I flushed.

Would it be such a bad thing to have a fling with Laurent? A very small, very discreet fling. Yes, he worked for Tyson, but what did it matter, really? I'd never see him again after this week, and Tyson hated me already.

Maybe I didn't need to always color inside the lines quite so faithfully, I thought as we followed the hostess to our table by a window open to the balmy night air. Maybe the lines were a prison of my own making, that held any power only because I gave them power. There was a whole philosophy based around that, wasn't there?

"What are you thinking about?"

It was Laurent, his voice husky in my ear, his hand coming to rest lightly on my hip as I turned toward him, grazing his chest as I kissed him on the cheek. My breath grew shallow at his scent, a scent I now realized wasn't just his cologne but the unique blend of his skin, fresh out of the shower, and his aftershave.

Hormones and pheromones, as my mom used to say.

My cheeks grew hot. I definitely couldn't tell him what I'd been thinking about. "How do you know I'm thinking?" I asked instead.

"Your eyebrows go like this," he said, imitating my furrowed brow.

I laughed, fishing for something I could say without showing my hand. "I was just trying to remember which philosophy says life has only the meaning we give it," I said. A bit pretentious, but close enough to the truth.

He raised his brows, pulling out a chair for me.

"You are thinking of existentialism," he said as he sat next to me. *"The confrontation of meaninglessness, in which you are the artist of your own life. Life does not give us meaning, we give it meaning."*

The noise of the restaurant retreated to a quiet hum as he laughed. "Don't look so shocked," he said, his eyes dancing. "I am French. Also, I specialized in philosophy in university. *Which is of course how I ended up in hospitality.*"

I liked how he flipped back and forth from English to French when he talked to me. It made me feel like we had a secret language. I smiled. "No, it's— I don't think I've ever heard it defined so simply. I honestly don't know that I've ever really understood it before."

"Ah, yes. It is a very misunderstood philosophy," he said with a glimmer of a smile. "Many people confuse it with nihilism, the belief that nothing matters, and life has no meaning. But existentialism gives us responsibility, whereas nihilism removes it."

"Was it Sartre who said that every man is condemned to be free?" I asked.

"Yes. Because he is responsible for everything he does."

I nodded, pointing. "Existentialism."

He shrugged. *"But within existentialism, there are many different interpretations. I prefer this humanist view, it is the more positive way to look at it.* You can go very deep and things become not so clear."

"The murky depths."

He took a sip of his champagne. "Yes."

I thought I might like to explore the murky depths with Laurent, and the way he was looking at me, it seemed that he might like it as well. But we were at a table with five other people, so that would have to wait.

As the champagne worked its magic, everyone loosened up, egging Allison on as she regaled us with tales from the Olympic Villages in London and Rio, where she'd learned to play poker between events and won jerseys off athletes from five different countries.

I'd been looking for some weakness in Allison, but the more I got to know her, the stronger she seemed. She was smart, focused, driven to succeed. Perhaps a shade too driven. Maybe that was her weakness.

"Talk about a walk of shame," she concluded a story that had featured a late-night strip poker game. "I had to wear an Italy basketball jersey home. My shirt never did turn up."

"Allison, I have never seen this side of you," Samira said.

Her cheeks reddened. "This is why I don't drink champagne."

"Everyone should drink champagne," Gisèle declared, and we all clinked glasses.

I'd begun the evening responsibly, imbibing slowly and drinking a glass of water after each glass of wine, but by the time we finished dinner, I'd stopped counting how many times my glass had been topped up. I'd learn more about this group the closer I got to them, I justified. Besides, without Tyson there to sour the mood, I was actually having fun.

Until I opened my phone to see a text from Rosa:

136 | KATHERINE WOOD

> FYI just heard from Deanna they've officially opened a murder
> investigation into Ian's death. I told her you were out of the
> country but expect a call from them tomorrow. They'll want a
> statement when you get back.

Suddenly the room seemed too crowded. I needed air. Swiping my
wineglass from the table, I pushed back my chair, mumbling something about the restroom.

Of course there was going to be an investigation, I reminded myself
as I wove through the restaurant, swigging wine to dull the shock-
waves radiating through me. I knew that. And of course I was going to
be interviewed.

I pushed open a side door and stepped into the balmy night. Thankfully, the small patio overlooking the street behind the restaurant was
deserted. I leaned against the stone wall, taking big gulps of air.

I'd been through this once before. The difference was that now I
had a lot more to lose. And now Tyson was threatening to—how did
he put it?—"change his story," if I didn't prove I wasn't the one who'd
sent him that damn article.

An alibi is only worth anything if everyone stands by it, and he'd
made it very clear that if he felt threatened, he'd have no qualms about
throwing me under the bus.

It was up to me to make sure that didn't happen.

CHAPTER 15

After the text I'd received from Rosa, my mood was far from celebratory, but there was nothing I could do about my predicament tonight, and the last thing I wanted to do was go home early and risk facing Tyson. So, I downed my wine and painted on a smile as we tripped down the boardwalk toward La Petite Plage, hoping to be numbed by the alcohol and buoyed by the exuberance of the group.

A yacht was docked in front of the club, the group of people on board singing along with the French pop song that emanated from its speakers. Men with their shirts partially unbuttoned and women in dresses as short as mine sat at tables on the sidewalk, smoking and laughing, moving to the music that emanated through the windows. I wished I felt nearly as carefree as they seemed to.

Laurent spoke to one of the bouncers, who ushered us inside, the bass booming as a guy in a black vest over a white button-down led us into a room with a high slatted wooden ceiling lit by dangling wicker-caged lights. At one end of the room was a bar where the waitstaff danced in unison, colored lights sliding over their skin, and two full sides of the space were lined with giant windows through which the harbor was visible.

As soon as we arrived at our booth, our waiter brought over a magnum of Dom Pérignon with fizzing sparklers and a glowing green label, holding the bases of two flutes in his mouth as he poured champagne into them. I gratefully accepted one as the music grew louder and Samira and Gisèle clambered onto the table, hips swaying to the music, beckoning for me to join them. *What the hell,* I thought. I checked my phone one last time to see that the photos Rosa sent still hadn't populated, then dropped my purse to the banquette as I climbed up, my worries alleviated by the effervescence of champagne bubbles in my blood.

I felt him behind me before I saw him, his body moving with mine. I didn't need to ask where he'd come from. He was here. I glanced over my shoulder, our faces close in the rotating lights. He had that look again, his changeable eyes glinting in the dark.

The room around us disappeared as he brushed my hair away from my neck, and we were alone in the crowd, his breath hot on my skin. My body buzzed pleasantly as he placed his hand on my hip, his fingers gently pressing into my pelvis low enough to be suggestive, dancing so seamlessly with me that it was like magic.

I knew I should break the spell. Walk away. This wasn't what I was here for, wasn't what I needed . . .

But damned if it wasn't what I wanted.

It had been such a long time since I'd had that spark of connection with anyone that I'd almost forgotten what it felt like. Before this trip, I'd almost convinced myself that that part of my life was over. I was thrilled to find that not only was I wrong, but he clearly felt it too.

And then the gentle pressure of him behind me was gone. I turned to see him on the banquette, holding his hand out to me. I took it, gripping his strong biceps with my other hand as he helped me down.

His tongue flicked out to wet his lips. "I'm going for a smoke."

"Are you asking me to come?"

He held my eye. "Do you smoke?"

I shook my head without breaking eye contact, the champagne making me bold. "Does that mean you don't want me to come?"

His lips tugged into a wicked whisper of a smile. "I wouldn't say that."

His eyes snapped to the window behind me, and a shadow passed over his face.

"What?" I asked, turning in search of what he'd seen.

"Tyson's here."

I spotted him as he said it, striding up the walk to the door like a storm appearing suddenly on the horizon. My buzz faltered. "He wasn't supposed to be here."

"Come on." The rest of our party were lost in the music, paying no attention to us as he slipped his fingers through mine and tugged me into the crowd.

We threaded our way around the far side of the bar, through a door guarded by a bouncer that Laurent traded fist bumps with. The alley behind the restaurant was empty, save for the cleanest-looking dumpster I'd ever laid eyes on. As the door closed behind us, the music quieted to a pulsing bass line, and suddenly we were alone in the shadows cast by the streetlights.

We took a few steps down the alley away from the dumpster and he released my hand, setting his whisky on the ledge that ran around the building as he reached into his pocket to extract a pack of hand-rolled smokes. He lit a cigarette and leaned against the brick wall, evaluating me as he exhaled. The smoke hung in the night air.

"What?" I asked.

When he didn't answer, I reached for his cigarette, and he let me have it. "It has hash in it," he warned.

I took a drag as he watched, amused. The smoke was sharp in my throat, and I coughed, handing it back to him.

"Been a while?" he asked.

I nodded, the hash tingling as I leaned my shoulder against the wall, facing him. "How do you stand working for Tyson?" I asked.

"I don't take it personally." He took a drag of the spliff. "And not all the guests are so terrible. *There was a man who had been coming here since the sixties. An old hippie—he was in his eighties when I knew him, still smoking ganja every afternoon—but very wealthy, friends with the Rockefellers, who used to own a big estate here. I took him surfing and he treated me like a son, taught me everything he knew about business, and when he died, I found out he'd written me into his will."*

Maybe that was how he could afford to live in this exclusive island paradise. "He's the one that gave you the car?"

He nodded.

"He must have really cared about you."

He exhaled a line of smoke, leaning his back against the wall. "I did for him as well."

I reached for the spliff, our fingers brushing as he handed it to me. I didn't cough this time when I exhaled. "It must be hard to maintain personal relationships, working as much as you do."

"Yes."

"Do you have a girlfriend?" I asked, fixing my gaze on the burning cherry.

He laughed. "I would not be standing here with you if I had a girl-friend."

"I don't know," I teased, relieved. "You are French."

"And you're Swiss. Do you take a neutral position on everything in your life?"

"I like to think I'm fair. But really, I'm American," I countered. "And we both know I own a firearm, so I think I'm doing a pretty good job of living up to the stereotype."

He laughed and dropped the smoke, stubbing it out with his heel, then took a sip of his whisky, coming to stand directly in front of me. "Nothing about you is a stereotype, Audrey."

Damn if I wasn't a fool for the way he said my name. I leaned back against the rough bricks, my breath shallow as he set his glass on the ledge and placed a hand on the wall behind me, his body tantalizingly close. His gaze dropped to my lips. "I don't get involved with guests," he whispered.

"No," I returned, my heart hammering. "You shouldn't."

He raised his free hand and ran his smooth fingertips along the strip of skin exposed by the cutouts in my dress. "This dress . . ."

I shivered with desire, our faces inches apart as he looked at me from beneath his brow. There was no better word for what his eyes were doing than "smoldering."

I couldn't stand it anymore. I reached for him, burying my hand in his thick hair as I brought his mouth to mine. The release was like a detonation inside me, sparks and smoke and hissing steam as he kissed me slowly, sensuously, his body lightly skimming mine, his hand stroking the skin of my rib cage.

It was even better than I had imagined it would be. I pulled him closer, pressing the length of my body against him, relishing the warmth of his lips on mine, the feel of his muscles against my chest. His tongue caressed the roof of my mouth as his fingers brushed the hem of my dress, our breath coming fast.

However inconvenient and ill-fated our entanglement might be, God it felt good.

Suddenly, the door at the far end of the alley on the other side of the dumpster burst open.

"I hate him so much I wish he was dead!"

Laurent and I broke apart to see Samira and Gisèle stumble into the alley in their heels, clearly trashed. "That motherfucker!" Samira screamed through tears, throwing her champagne glass against the wall and balling her fists as it shattered into a million pieces.

They were so wrapped up in their anger, they didn't seem to have spied Laurent and me, but it was only a matter of time if we continued to stand there slack-jawed. He sank to the ground, pulling me with him, the dumpster between us keeping us out of their line of sight.

"I can't do this anymore," Samira wailed.

"So leave him," Gisèle said. *"Fuck the money."*

"But then the time I've put in already is worth nothing," Samira protested. *"All this pain, worth nothing."*

One of the girls kicked something that went scuttling across the pavement. *"He may get rid of you before you have the chance to leave,"* Gisèle pointed out.

"If he does that, he has to pay me. Not as much, but something."

"So force his hand," Gisèle suggested.

Samira sniffed. *"It's like he gets off on torturing me."*

Gisèle grumbled something I couldn't make out.

In Laurent's pocket, his phone buzzed. He extracted it, frowning when he saw the number. "I have to take this. I'll meet you inside. Okay?"

I nodded, watching as he skulked along the wall away from the sound of Samira's tears until he rounded the corner out of sight. I was still high from our kiss, yearning for the pressure of his body against mine, but the heat of our connection left me cold now that he was gone. The reality of my situation once again weighed on me, his abrupt departure on the heels of Tyson's arrival bringing back all my doubts about his intentions and making me second-guess our connection.

Tyson had mentioned that Laurent had secrets, had insinuated that these secrets gave him power over Laurent, then thrown us together. Was our immediate attraction serendipity, or something more sinister?

ELEVEN YEARS AGO, AUGUST

The day was still but for the shrilling of the cicadas and the slight breeze that ruffled the palms in our backyard. Mom had gotten so she was cold all the time, so we were outside in the heat, passing the afternoon on lounge chairs in the shade. I finished a chapter of the detective novel I was reading and bookmarked the page, looking over to see she'd fallen asleep.

The past few weeks had been rough, with Tyson's betrayal followed closely by the official news that the second round of treatments hadn't taken, and a third was not recommended. I knew how badly she didn't want to see me suffer on her behalf, so I was strong for her when I was home, forcing positivity and tranquility, then collapsing in tears on Rosa's shoulder the minute I walked into her apartment.

My phone buzzed beside me, and I checked the number. Tyson again. This was the third time he'd called within the hour, leaving only one message asking me to call him immediately.

But I wasn't fooled.

In the two weeks since I'd found him with the blonde, Tyson had called and texted almost constantly, alternating between messages begging for my forgiveness and complaining about Ian, who was still asking for ever larger amounts of money.

A knocking roused me. "Audrey!" came Tyson's voice.

I groaned. He was at my front door. I stood and charged in the back entrance, through the kitchen and into the living room, where I jerked open the door to find Tyson panting on the stoop, his eyes panicked. "What do you want?" I demanded.

"We need to talk," he said.

"No, we don't," I hurled, slamming the door in his face.

But he blocked the door with his foot. "Not about us," he said urgently. "It's about Cody. He's been arrested."

I stared at him in shock. "Arrested?"

"This morning at work. His lawyer just called to let me know there's a bail hearing set for tomorrow morning."

I swung the door wide, allowing him to step inside. "Arrested for what?" I asked as I shut it behind him, hoping my assumption was wrong.

He frowned at me like I was an idiot. "The sales deflation program."

My heart stopped. "How?"

"Ian must have turned him in." He ran his fingers through his hair, distraught. "It's my fault. He kept coming for more and more money. I couldn't keep up."

"Fuck. This is bad," I said, the wheels in my brain spinning so fast I felt dizzy. "What do we do?"

"We can't do anything now," he said. "If we touch anything, they'll know he's not the only one involved."

I gripped the back of a chair to steady myself. "Surely they've shut the program down already."

"I assume so, but I don't know. I tried to check but I was locked out of the website because his credentials didn't work anymore."

"Shit. The bank account," I said, sinking into the chair.

"It's a numbered Swiss account," he said. "They shouldn't be able to get into it."

"Because it's linked to a Swiss citizen—my dad," I said, growing more upset as I began to grasp the gravity of the situation. "They'll figure that one out pretty quickly, then they'll come for me."

He perched on the couch across from me. "You're giving them too much credit."

"Won't they want the money back?" I asked.

"I doubt it's often that anyone gets stolen money back," he said. "And no one company lost enough for them to pursue it. We didn't leave a digital trail, and I don't think Cody will flip on you. Maybe on me, but not on you."

"He wouldn't do that to you," I said. "You're blood."

"You didn't see the fight we got in the other night," he muttered, studying the discoloration on his knuckles. "My face is just now looking normal again."

"I heard you beat him up pretty bad, too."

Anger flared behind his eyes. "You've been talking to him?"

"To find out what was going on with Ian," I returned. He opened his mouth to speak, but I went on before he could get a word out. "Don't start with me. You're the one who fucked things up between us, not Cody."

"You're saying he didn't tell you to come over?" he asked pointedly. "Because why the hell else would you show up at two in the morning?"

"That is completely beside the point," I snapped. "You shouldn't have been fucking some girl behind my back."

"It was a mistake," he pleaded, changing his tone as he leaned forward and took my hand. "I fucked up, and I am sorry. But it was a one-time—"

"I'm done, Tyson." I pulled my hand away, rising to my feet. "I hope you'll use whatever you stole to pay for Cody's defense."

"My parents are paying for his defense," he said, standing, "and they'll put up the money for bail. He'll maybe spend a few months in a fancy white-collar prison, then he'll be out. He'll be fine."

"No, he won't," I snapped, incredulous. "This will follow him around for the rest of his life. Try getting the kind of job he's qualified for as a felon."

"He can work for me—"

I looked around. "Where?"

"I'm gonna take this money and start a company—"

"And here I'd thought it was for my education."

"You said you didn't want it!"

I glared at him, stewing in my indignation. "Fuck off, Tyson."

"You'll forgive me when you see what I can do," he said.

I drew back. "You realize my problem with you has nothing to do with what you can or can't do."

Through the window, I could see my mom stirring, looking around for me. "You have to go," I said. "Don't come here again."

CHAPTER 16

Laurent didn't return from his phone call, and after a few minutes of hiding behind the dumpster listening to Gisèle comfort Samira, I worked up my courage to furtively slip back inside. The club was more crowded now, every surface turned into a dance floor where euphoric patrons gyrated in the spinning lights. I threaded my way through the throng to our table and scooted behind the table to grab my purse.

I pulled up short. Tyson was sitting on the banquette hidden by the crush of dancers, calmly nursing a Coors Light. He looked up at me, his face unreadable, obscured by shadow. Unsure what to do, I remained still as I weighed my options, as if he were a wild animal that might attack if I made any sudden movements.

"Happy birthday," I said finally. It had been nearly midnight when we arrived, so I figured it had to be tomorrow now.

He didn't smile, but raised his beer to me in salutation, which was something.

"I've just gotta get my purse," I said, reaching behind him to grab it.

"I'm paying you to find out who's blackmailing me, not to fuck my butler," he said in a low voice as I leaned past him.

I recoiled, steadying myself on the edge of the table behind me. "Excuse me?"

"I said I'm paying you to—"

"I heard you," I snapped. The champagne and hash that had lifted my spirits minutes ago now stoked the fires of my fury, loosening my tongue. "But who I choose to fuck is none of your business. And a newspaper clipping is not blackmail."

"What's this?" he asked, pulling a folded envelope from his back pocket and shoving it into my hand.

I sat next to him with a sigh. He smelled like a nauseating combination of patchouli and garlic, and I leaned away from him to unfold the envelope. Inside was a single sheet of plain printer paper with a short paragraph printed in Times New Roman. I pulled my phone from my purse and activated my flashlight to read:

E500K in unmarked bills in exchange for what I know. Tomorrow. 5pm. Amis in Grand Cul-de-Sac. Come alone.

"Keep it," Tyson said. "I have it memorized."

I was nearly certain it was Allison who'd leaked the environmental report, but I couldn't see how blackmailing her business partner for half a million euros could help her cause, when she was in the hole eighty million. Unless maybe her next payment was five hundred thousand? Regardless, I was not prepared to have that conversation right now at two in the morning after drinking all night. I folded the note into my purse.

"Where did you find it?" I asked.

"It was left under the windshield of my car while I was at the gym today."

"And you're just now mentioning it?"

His jaw clenched. "I have other things on my plate, Audrey."

"There were no cameras in the area?"

He shook his head.

"Well, now you know it's not me," I said. "And once we review the footage from the house, we can eliminate anyone else that was there while you were at the gym."

"You were the only one at Le Rêve at the time the note was left. Asleep, by the pool." He crossed his arms. "Remind me again what I'm paying you for."

I rounded on him. "So don't fucking pay me, Tyson!" This abuse simply wasn't worth it. "Now that you know I'm not involved, let me go home."

"No," he said flatly. "I don't trust you."

"We're on the same side! Stop being so fucking paranoid!"

The moment the word came out of my mouth, I wanted to take it back, but it was too late.

"Paranoid?" he demanded.

I held my ground. "Are you not?"

His eyes bored holes in me. "Paranoia is unjustified. I run a multi-billion-dollar company that everyone either wants a piece of or wants to fail. I'm being blackmailed, and someone inside my company is leaking confidential documents. Would you call my concern unjustified?"

I felt suddenly queasy. I was in no position to go toe-to-toe with Tyson tonight. I hadn't even expected to see him. If I'd known he'd be here, I wouldn't have allowed myself to let loose the way I had. But I should have known. I should've been smarter.

I squeezed my eyes closed, trying to shut out the booming bass and rotating lights. The world tilted, and my eyes flew open as I felt a wave of nausea.

He shook his head. "You're trashed."

"I'm not," I protested, focusing on the corner of the table to keep the nausea at bay. I was definitely trashed, and his acrid scent wasn't helping. "But yes, I was having fun. Until you showed up."

"By all means, don't let me interrupt your all-expenses-paid vacation," he spat, voice dripping with sarcasm.

"You smell like shit," I said as I stood, shouldering my purse, and walked away from him before I could say anything else I would regret.

Tyson had always been sharp-tongued, had always had a temper. But he'd never been spiteful before, never malicious. Now it was as though he believed the whole world was conspiring against him, and he wanted to make everyone bleed. Especially me.

I threaded my way through the throng, scanning the room for Laurent. I didn't see him, but it was just as well.

Outside, the night was quiet after the booming bass, and I immediately felt less dizzy with the breeze off the water cooling my skin, though no less stupid for allowing myself to get swept away tonight.

I followed the sidewalk along the harbor to the line of taxis waiting in the street and climbed into the first available cab. "Le Rêve," I told the driver.

"One hundred euro," the man said.

"Seriously?" I asked, taken aback. "It's five minutes away."

"Is going rate," the man said. "All driver tell you same."

I was too tired to argue. "Okay," I said, resigned.

There was a tap on the partially open window, and I looked over to see Cody outside. "Can I join?"

I nodded, relieved I wouldn't have to foot the exorbitant bill for the taxi, and he opened the door and slid in next to me. "Where's Jennifer?" I asked.

"She left with Allison an hour ago."

I tilted my face toward the air rushing through my window as we turned up the hill that led out of town.

"Did my brother scare you off?" Cody asked.

I nodded. "What happened to him?"

"I think you know what happened to him," he said meaningfully.

"But you went through worse and you're not a dick."

He rested his head against the cracked pleather seatback. "I don't have the emptiness inside that he does."

"How do you stand him, day in and day out?"

"I didn't have a choice at first. Not a lot of companies hire felons for high-level jobs. Now . . . I guess I feel a responsibility to the company. And there's an element of timing involved if I want to exit."

I looked over at him. "I'm so sorry, Cody."

"Don't be."

"I know I've said it before, but I'll never forgive myself for what you went through because of me."

"No," he said. "Don't do that. You were careful, you would never have been caught. It was Ian's fault. He was the one that turned me in."

I lowered my voice. "You heard about his foot?"

He nodded, eyeing me. "I thought it was awfully coincidental Tyson invited you down right after it washed up."

"Did he tell you why he invited me down?" I asked.

"He wouldn't talk about it."

I took a breath. I knew I was playing with fire by telling him, but it was time I made sure Cody was on my side. "Someone sent him the newspaper article about it," I whispered. "He wanted me to find out who."

He furrowed his brow. "And he didn't think this should involve me, too?"

"He wasn't sure it wasn't you."

"Why the hell would I—"

"I know. He accused me of it as well, if it makes you feel any better. And I think you deserve to know what's going on. Whoever it is, they're now demanding half a million to show their hand."

I pulled the note from my purse and handed it to him. His face darkened as he scanned it. "Goddammit," he said.

I tucked the note back into my bag as the taxi pulled through the gates of Le Rêve and Cody handed the cabbie a wad of cash. "You'll be here tomorrow?" he asked as we climbed out of the car. "It would be good for the three of us to sit down, make sure we're all on the same page."

As much as it pained me to be in the same room with Tyson, I knew he was right. "I'll be here if you want me to be," I promised.

I bade Cody good night in the foyer, then padded across the smooth floor to my room, a tornado of apprehension churning inside me.

Tyson was going to lose his shit when he found out I'd told Cody about the blackmail.

I collapsed on my bed and took out my phone, again hitting Download on the images of the arrest report Rosa had sent. Finally the pictures started to populate, one by one.

I zoomed in on the pages of Cody's arrest report, looking for some indication of the evidence that had been turned in. I found it in the handwritten notes toward the bottom of the second page:

Digital copy of video dated 8/2 included in evidence shows fraudulent program devised and run by suspect.

I pulled up my calendar app and scrolled back eleven years. August the second was a Sunday, the day after I caught Tyson cheating on me Saturday night. The day after he beat the shit out of Cody for not covering for him.

Tyson had played it so well, placing the blame for Cody's arrest on Ian. We'd both believed it, and I knew Cody did still, or there was no way in hell he'd be working for Tyson. But it was a lie. Ian hadn't been the one to turn Cody in, Tyson had.

If Cody found out, he might very well betray his brother the same way Tyson had him. I didn't have hard evidence of the falsified environmental reports Tyson had ordered, but Cody did, and if he discovered his own brother had been the one to send him to jail all those years ago, there would be nothing stopping him from turning those documents over to the authorities, which would destroy De-Sal.

I felt a surge of triumph, realizing that this knowledge gave me the upper hand.

It was time to fight fire with fire, before Tyson made good on any of his threats toward me. And I needed to do it now, while I was still fortified by rancor and champagne, before I lost my nerve. I didn't want to engage with Tyson, didn't want to give him the chance to respond. No, I wanted to have the last word tonight. Let him sleep on it, contemplate what damage I could inflict.

I was practically giddy as the printer in my room churned out the pages. I didn't need to leave a note with the arrest report, nor did I need to make any threats; Tyson's imagination would do the work, just as it had with the news article about Ian's foot. All I had to do was provide the information, folded neatly and left on his pillow.

Sweet dreams, asshole.

CHAPTER 17

I was shocked when I awoke in the morning to find I'd slept a full seven hours. It was past ten o'clock, and I felt remarkably good despite the copious amount of alcohol I'd consumed the previous evening. Then I remembered my altercation with Tyson, and my hangxiety reared its ugly head with a roar. I suddenly felt ill.

I also vaguely remembered telling Cody why Tyson had invited me down here. And then . . . the envelope I'd left on Tyson's pillow. I groaned, burying my head under my own pillow. But I didn't regret my decision. I'd be free to leave now, just as soon as Cody and I had the chat I'd promised him with Tyson.

I shakily popped three Advil and guzzled the entire bottle of water next to my bed. I checked my phone, my stomach doing a flip as I recognized the number for the police station in my messages. The voicemail was short:

"Audrey, it's Deanna. I know you're out of the country, but we've opened an investigation into Ian Kelley's death, and need you to come on down to make a statement when you return. Give me a call and we'll arrange a time."

Her voice was professional but calm, and in the bright light of day,

I was glad to find my pulse didn't skyrocket the way it had last night when I got Rosa's message. I'd known this was coming. And yes, I'd been caught backfooted by Tyson's accusations when I got down here, but now that I had some leverage, Tyson, Cody, and I would talk like civilized adults today, like we should have to begin with. Everything was going to be fine.

At least that's what I'd keep telling myself.

I was desperate for coffee, but I also didn't want to face anyone before I'd pulled myself together, so I showered and put on enough makeup to conceal the dark circles beneath my eyes before exiting my room.

The first person I saw was Laurent. He was wearing his uniform of khaki trousers and a white button-down, cleaning up the remains of breakfast with the chef and another server. He flashed a professional smile as I entered the kitchen, and immediately I was in that alleyway again, my hands tangled in his hair, his body pressed to mine.

"Good morning, Audrey," he said breezily.

"Good morning," I replied, flushed.

"Would you like some coffee?"

"Definitely," I answered, trying and failing to match his casual attitude. "Merci."

As he prepared my coffee, I turned to survey the veranda. Cody was on his laptop on the couch facing the view while Allison swam laps in the pool, moving so gracefully through the water that it was hard not to stare. Jennifer was parked on a lounger in a sun hat with the same book she'd been reading yesterday, next to Gisèle and Samira, who both appeared to be asleep on their stomachs, their long limbs splayed at odd angles. Tyson was nowhere to be seen.

Laurent appeared at my side, coffee in hand. "Thank you," I said, taking it from him.

He nodded, his gaze slipping away from mine too quickly. He certainly was doing a good job of treating me like any other guest this morning. So good, I wondered if he thought last night was a mistake.

Which it was, of course. Though just the thought of his lips on mine sent an echo of pleasure shimmering through my torso.

I beelined for a chair on the far side of the couch, as far away from him as I could get and remain in the shade. "Has Tyson made an appearance?" I asked, hiding my apprehension beneath a placid veneer as I pulled my feet up under me.

"He's not home yet," Samira answered without moving.

Not home. That meant he hadn't seen the arrest report. There was still time to retrieve it if I wanted to. But I didn't. Though the decision to leave it there had been fueled by champagne and rage, I felt confident it was the right decision.

"Do you know where he is?" Cody asked.

"Don't know, don't care," Samira muttered, pulling a hat over her face.

"Tyson is already on the yacht," Laurent said, coming to stand behind the couch.

We all looked over at him in surprise.

"He decided to sleep there last night," Laurent continued, his face neutral. "He's requested for you all to arrive at noon."

Allison emerged from the pool, wrapping her powerful body in a towel. "What is this?" she asked.

"Tyson wants us to go to the boat," Cody said.

"He said to let the two of you know he has a gift for you," Laurent said to Allison and Cody.

"Fun," Cody grumbled.

"The car will be ready at eleven-thirty to take you down to the airfield, where the helicopter is waiting," Laurent said.

Gisèle and Samira bent their heads together, whispering, as I checked my watch. It was nearly eleven. I turned to catch Cody's eye and he nodded, confirming our plans for a tête-à-tête with his tyrant of a brother. His mood seemed even darker today than it was in the cab last night, and I wondered if it was my fault for telling him about the blackmailer. But he deserved to know.

Jennifer looked at Cody as she rose from her lounger, tucking her book under her arm. "If you're in, I'm in."

Samira stretched, muttering something to Gisèle too low for me to make out. "We will come," she said. "Franco will be leading the dive?"

"Unfortunately, he has a cold," Laurent said. "Today we have Rémy. He comes highly recommended."

"So, you don't know him," Jennifer translated.

"I have not met him personally, but Franco dives with him often and recommended him. Also, I am a rescue diver and will be there to make sure you are all safe."

"Fine, then," Allison said, striding for the stairs up to her room.

"We need dresses for tonight?" Samira asked.

"Yes," Laurent said. "Plan to spend the night on the boat."

The helicopter was an unnecessary extravagance. The seven of us could easily have driven to the cove off which the yacht was anchored and taken the dinghy out, but I wasn't complaining. I'd never been in a luxury helicopter before—actually, I'd never been in a helicopter before, period. This one was white with a roomy tan leather interior featuring wood paneling and seating for eight, though Laurent sat up front with the pilot, who seemed to be a friend of his.

As we rose into the air, I looked out the window to see the mottled sea beneath us, an electric shade of teal. The island appeared to be alive from this angle, a dragon-like sea creature slithering toward the horizon, the jagged peaks of the mountains the spines of its back, the sandy beaches its soft belly, the rocky cliffs its claws. I snapped a pic and sent it to Rosa, who immediately replied with a picture of Benji's baseball game. Her message:

Same same.

I laughed as I replied:

Billionaire life isn't all it's cracked up to be. Please kiss the boys for me (if they'll let you!) xx

Beachgoers frolicked on the shore below us as we soared along the coastline, and countless white boats dotted the water. Within five minutes, a large white yacht came into view, anchored perhaps a mile offshore, near a small, rocky island. A handful of other boats bobbed on the waves nearby, but none of them were near the size of the only one with a helipad on the back.

The captain's voice crackled in our headphones. "You can see our ship, *Sea Ray,* down below. We'll be landing shortly."

I'd never been on a yacht before, either, and while I knew close to nothing about boats, I would definitely put *Sea Ray* in the megayacht category. It was a gleaming colossus of the seas, proof of Tyson's stupendous success for all the world to see. I wondered what would happen to it if Tyson sank the company. Was there a CarMax for yachts?

Jennifer grabbed my hand as our helicopter hovered above the ship and our captain slowly lowered us onto its helipad, the motion of the blades whipping the water beneath us into whitecaps.

The pilot helped each of us down, the wind from the slowing blades buffeting our skin. I was last to exit, and I gazed at the view of the mountainous island as I trekked across the helipad, paying no attention to my feet until I felt something squish beneath my sandal. The stench hit me as I lifted my foot, and I wrinkled my nose in disgust.

Dog shit. Just my luck. But also: what the hell?

"Oh no," a willowy crew girl in a navy polo and khaki shorts cried as she rushed over. "I am so sorry."

"Well, that was unexpected," I said, wincing.

I could almost laugh, thinking about the kick Rosa was going to get out of my stepping in dog shit on a megayacht when I told her, but at the moment, the smell was too foul to do anything other than gag.

"We had a dog here this morning. Two, actually. What are they called with the short nose?" She placed her hand on her nose.

"Bulldogs?" I guessed, clamping my fingers over my own nose to stifle the smell.

She shook her head. "Black and brown . . ."

"Pugs?"

Her auburn ponytail fell over her shoulder as she lifted my foot, removing my soiled shoe. "Yes! Pugs. They are very cute, but oh no. I do not know how we miss this."

"Oh gross, it's on my foot," I said, pulling a face as I noticed the smear of dog shit on the side of my foot.

"I am so sorry," she sympathized, indicating the room at the far end of the tarmac. "Right there, you can wash in the sink." She held the compromised sandal as far away from us as she could. "I will take both and clean them, okay? My name is Justine."

"Thank you, Justine," I said, stepping out of my other shoe. "It's no problem."

She lingered behind me, cleaning up the mess as I walked barefoot through the open glass doors into a chic cocktail bar that faced a rooftop deck featuring a large spa. Another pretty, smiling young woman in a navy polo and khaki shorts greeted me. "Welcome aboard *Sea Ray*," she said, her English lightly accented, like Justine's. She proffered a tray of cold hand towels. "For your hands."

"Um, I also need one for my foot," I said, smiling ruefully as I wiped my hands and the back of my neck with the towel. "I stepped in dog poop."

"I'm so sorry about that," she said, soaping up a rag.

"Who had dogs on board?" I asked. Tyson had never been a dog guy. Or a cat guy, for that matter. Not much of an animal guy at all. Which, again, should have been a red flag back when we'd dated. So many red flags I'd missed.

But the crew girl just shrugged silently as she applied the rag to my foot, then used one of the cold hand towels to wipe it down. Odd. I made a mental note to ask Tyson later.

"This way, please," she said once my foot was clean. She indicated the stairwell on one side of the room. "The primary suite is one deck down on level three, the game deck on level two, and on the main deck, level one, you will meet Evan, who will show you to your room belowdecks."

I nodded, trying to memorize what she'd said as I followed the stairwell down a level to what appeared to be a lavish gray and cream lounge, the front of which was completely open to the sea. I paused, gazing at the view. This place was incredible. *Succession* and *Below Deck* had given me glimpses of the interiors of yachts, but actually being on one was surreal. I felt a bit like Dorothy waking up in Oz.

Before I could continue down the stairwell, the door of the primary bedroom flew open and Cody burst out, fury radiating off him. Damn, he'd only beaten me downstairs by perhaps ten minutes, and he and Tyson had already gotten into it. I inhaled sharply, stepping to the side to let him pass, but he didn't so much as give me a backward glance.

So much for talking like adults.

CHAPTER 18

I prayed Cody hadn't ratted me out as Tyson emerged from his room, looking at me like a cat who'd trapped a lizard under his paw. He was shirtless, his emaciated torso tattooed with an array of symbols and runes I'd never seen, and he was holding a polished black rock the size of my fist in his palm.

"Audrey," he said, swinging the door wide. "Come in."

I felt my breath grow fast as I followed him into the large primary suite, also decorated in luxurious shades of gray and cream, with sleek ash wood accents and a king-size bed covered by a gray duvet. Like his lair at the house, the temperature was freezing cold, and blackout curtains covered the windows, the room lit only by the dim lamps on the bedside tables and the glowing humidifier responsible for the strong scent of rosemary and sage that permeated the space.

It was on the tip of my tongue to tell Tyson what I'd discovered in the arrest report, but now that I had a choice as to when to deliver that blow, I realized it would be more beneficial to have a civil conversation with him and Cody about how to deal with the investigation before playing that card. If a civil conversation was still on the table after the way Cody had stormed out of here a minute ago.

"Did you get dogs?" I asked instead.

He dipped his chin, looking at me intensely from beneath his brows as he rubbed his thumb over his rock. "Cody seems to think my inviting you down here has something to do with Ian's foot washing up," he said, disregarding my question.

"Because I stepped in dog shit upstairs," I continued. "And no one seemed to want to tell me whose dog it was."

"Audrey." There was warning in his voice.

But I was done letting him bully me, whatever the size of his yacht. "What, you don't like it when people ignore your questions?"

"I didn't get fucking dogs, okay?"

"So, whose were they?"

"Why are you so hung up on this?" he snapped.

"It makes it really hard for me to help you when you won't even tell me who you're involved with."

He uttered something unintelligible under his breath, then swiped his green drink off the bedside table and took a long swig.

"Fascinating," I said, my tone dripping with sarcasm.

"It's none of your business who was here this morning," he said, wiping his mouth with the back of his hand. "They aren't blackmailing me. Of that I'm sure. And after the conversation I just had with Cody, I don't trust you not to go back to him with anything I tell you, so I'm keeping the details to myself." He squeezed his black rock with all his might, then exhaled. "Why does Cody think you're here because of Ian's foot?"

I ignored the weirdness with the rock, keeping my face neutral as I crossed my arms over my chest. "He's not wrong, is he?"

His nostrils flared, and I felt a taste of victory at his irritation. "Did you speak to him about it?" he demanded.

"Did he say I did?"

"He sidestepped that question the same way you just did. Said the three of us should sit down."

"It's a good idea for all of us to be on the same page," I said diplomatically. "Have you gotten the call from the police yet?"

He jerked his head in a nod.

"Same." I took a breath, softening my tone. As good as it felt to get under his skin, it was in my best interest to keep things civil between us, so I needed to reel it in. "I know you don't trust me or Cody, but it doesn't work for us to turn against each other."

He snorted. "Tell that to him."

I cocked my head. "What happened just now?"

"None of your business."

I sighed. "Well, you two are gonna have to figure it out. We should also come up with a plan for how to handle the blackmailer."

"I pulled the cash out last night."

"Look, I want to know who is blackmailing you and what they have on you just as much as you do. But then what?"

He passed the rock from hand to hand. "We pay them to shut up."

"In my experience with blackmail, that's not how it works. It's not a give-and-take. It's just a take and take and take. You should know that better than anyone." A look of recognition passed over his face as our eyes met. "So you need to figure out how it is that you benefit from this exchange before you engage with them."

He paced over to the window and pushed open the drapes, letting in a sliver of light as he stared out at the sea.

"This blackmailer may or may not have anything that could touch you," I went on, "but once you engage with them, they know you're guilty of something, even if they don't know what, so they have you on the hook."

He evaluated me. "And if I don't engage with them, and they go to the police with whatever they have?"

"They won't. This isn't altruistic. No one here is trying to 'do the right thing.' They want money, and for that they need leverage. If they go to the authorities, they'll have played their cards and will have nothing left to blackmail you with."

"You've dealt with this before."

I leveled my gaze at him. "So. Have. You."

He turned back to the window. "We'll find out who it is when we meet them at five."

"We?"

"You and me."

"Tyson . . ." I dug my nails into my palms, reminding myself to stay calm. "They said to come alone."

"I will. You'll already be there, waiting."

"I didn't bring protection," I protested. "I don't want to get into a situation where—"

"I have guns, if that's what you need."

I shook my head. Packing my own registered weapon in Florida was a lot different than pulling out some gun of Tyson's in the territory of another nation. "I don't think that's legal."

"Now who's paranoid?"

I held up my hands. "This is getting a bit above my pay grade."

"You want more money?"

"No."

A rapping at the door, and he dropped his rock to the bed. "Five o'clock."

I fixed him with my gaze. "After the dive, you and Cody and I are going to sit down and have a conversation like adults."

He didn't answer, striding for the door. But I wasn't worried. As much as I preferred to tell him about the arrest report after we'd had a chance to talk civilly, if he refused to play ball, I'd have to force his hand.

Either way, I was done taking his shit.

I left Tyson chatting with the white-uniformed captain, a deeply tanned man in his forties with a blond man-bun, and descended the stairs to another sumptuous lounge one level down. This one featured a golf simulator, shuffleboard, and arcade games, as well as tables for pool, foosball, and poker, with an open sitting area and bar decorated in the same shades of gray and cream as the master suite.

"Welcome aboard, Ms. Collet," an attractive male crew member greeted me with a smile. Hell, they were all attractive—which after a few days in St. Barth's should've no longer been remarkable, but somehow I was still thrown by it, like I'd wandered into one of those utopia scenes in a movie where you know something nefarious is going on beneath the surface. Life simply wasn't supposed to be quite so perfect. "This is the game room," he went on, oblivious to my wariness about the symmetry of his face. "There is a gym and sauna directly behind the bar," he said, pointing, "and you will find pickleball and basketball courts on the deck beyond."

Good God, Tyson was rich.

Proof that money couldn't make you happy, I supposed, no matter how good-looking the crew of your yacht might be.

The guy indicated the wide spiral staircase behind him. "The stairs are here, please, when you're ready, madame."

As I reached the next landing, I was greeted by another fit male crew member with thick, short brown hair. His name tag indeed read EVAN, as the girls upstairs had said it would. "*Bonjour, madame.* You are Audrey Collet, yes?"

I nodded, shading my eyes against the glare off the sparkling rectangular pool. The main living area was decorated in that same soothing wealthy man's greige and cream with a circular bar in the center of the room. To one side was a long dining table beneath a modern LED chandelier, to the other a grand piano and seating area with a studied simplicity that came off as distinctly sophisticated. Off the hallway past the piano, I could see Jennifer and Allison chatting between the open doors of what must be their suites.

"Madame?" I turned my attention to the young man. "Your room is one more deck down," he said. "Number seven. Please meet on the pool deck ready to dive at one. That's in fifteen minutes."

I forced a smile. "*Oui, merci.*"

I descended yet another stairwell and followed the beige-carpeted hallway past doors four, five, and six to door seven. Past my room were two more doors, with another at the end of the hall marked CREW. Through the open door of the room next to mine, I could see Samira helping Gisèle unpack.

My cabin was small but well appointed, everything built into the space: polished wood queen-size bed with white linens, a dresser against the opposite wall with a television above it, and on the other side of the door to the bathroom, a closet.

As I shut the door to my suite behind me, there was a soft tap on it. "Who is it?" I called.

"Laurent," came his voice.

I gave myself a quick once-over in the mirror above the sink before opening the door to find him changed out of his uniform into swim trunks and a black rash guard that advertised a surfboard retailer, holding my suitcase.

"I have your bag," he said. His tone was professional, but his blue eyes were fixed on mine.

I peered into the empty corridor, then swung my door open wide.

He glanced over his shoulder before he stepped inside, leaving the door ajar. I started to close it behind him, but he caught my wrist and shook his head, so I pulled him into the bathroom, where we could talk out of sight of anyone that might be passing by. *"I'm sorry I left without saying goodbye last night,"* he whispered, leaning against the sink. *"The call I received was our dive master canceling. I had to find another dive master, then Tyson decided he wanted to come to the ship early."*

Our bodies were close in the tight space, the inches between us crackling with electricity. I wanted to feel him against me again, but wasn't about to be the one to make the first move when he was clearly uncomfortable being in my room at all.

"It's okay," I said. "Did you get any sleep?"

"I never sleep much when I'm working."

"Your job is hard," I sympathized.

"It won't last forever." I shivered as he ran his fingers lightly down the inside of my arm. "Audrey . . . Last night is between us, yes?"

I nodded. I didn't risk losing my job like he did if anyone found out about us, but it certainly wouldn't be a good look. "My lips are sealed."

His eyes flicked down to my lips, lingering.

In the hallway, someone called his name. "I'll see you upstairs," he said, pulling away.

"Yes," I said. But he'd already gone.

CHAPTER 19

Once I'd changed into my swimsuit and shorty, I descended the stairs at the far end of the pool to find ten tanks and dive vests laid out on the sugar scoop at the stern. Jennifer and Cody were already there, checking their equipment with the aid of the dive master, a wiry man with a shaved head who looked to be about forty.

"*Bonjour,*" he greeted me, flashing a smile. "I am Rémy, I will be leading the dive today. I love your—" He gestured to my shorty. "The green—" He kissed his fingers with such gusto, I wondered for a moment whether he was Italian. But no, the accent was definitely French.

"Thanks," I said. "I'm Audrey."

"Welcome, Audrey." He checked his clipboard. "Your dive partner is Laurent."

I nodded, pleased, as he crossed to the vest on the end. "This is yours," he said, looking me up and down. "I think the"—he grabbed the weight belt and stared at it, perplexed—"I have lost the word."

"Weight belt?"

"*Oui, oui.* The weight belt I think will be good, but you see."

Allison appeared at the top of the stairs looking sleek as a seal in her wetsuit with Gisèle and Samira close on her heels in rash guards and bikini bottoms. *"Allô,"* he called out to them.

As he rushed over to get the others sorted, I took a seat on the bench to wait for Laurent so that we could do our buddy check, and Jennifer collapsed next to me. I'd washed my face and tied my hair back in a braid, but she was just as perfectly made up as usual. She was going to be a mess after the dive, but to each her own.

"You dive often?" she asked.

"Used to. What about you?"

"I got certified in Turks at Christmas," she said, zipping up her navy shorty. "But yeah, this will only be my third dive." She showed me her hand, which was shaking. "I'm kinda jittery."

Jennifer's inexperience worried me a little, but if the rest of us were seasoned enough, she'd likely be okay. "Just breathe," I said. "You'll be fine."

"Jennifer's better than she thinks she is," Cody said, coming over to join us as he checked his buoyancy control device.

Tyson jogged down the stairs, his eyes hidden behind mirrored aviators. "The swim-through is gonna be epic," he said with a grin, slapping his brother so hard on the shoulder that he nearly lost his balance. "Hoping we see some sharks."

"Sharks?" Jennifer asked, her eyes wide.

"Most likely nurse sharks, which are harmless," I said.

"Just don't provoke them," Tyson said, grabbing her knee so quickly she jumped. He laughed. I wanted to punch him, and Jennifer looked like she did too.

We weren't the only ones. Allison glanced up from her equipment at Tyson's back, a look of pure hatred crossing her face before she arranged her features into a more accommodating expression.

"We saw a beautiful hammerhead yesterday," Rémy said, joining us. Clearly, he hadn't heard Jennifer's minor freakout. "And a school of eagle rays. There's a little current that will take us through the Snares, easy."

"The Snares?" I echoed.

"This is the name of the tunnel through the reef," Rémy explained.

"Conditions look perfect," Cody said, casting a glance at the crystal-clear water.

"It's pretty cool all you guys dive," I said, taking the bottle of no-fog from Jennifer when she was done rubbing it into her goggles.

Tyson threw an arm around Samira's shoulders and she gave him a kiss. "Tyson told me he couldn't marry me if I didn't dive."

"What's up with that guy?" Jennifer asked, staring across the water.

I followed her line of sight to a nearby yacht—gray in tone and smaller than ours but still sizable—where a tall man in black board shorts and a rash guard was standing on the bow with his arms crossed, looking down at us with what appeared to be disdain. He was wearing sunglasses and I couldn't fully make out his features, but he definitely seemed displeased.

"That's Marcel," Allison answered, her voice low. "One of the developers who'd like to kill us."

Jennifer spun to face her, a look of alarm on her face. "What's he doing here?"

A crew member came up behind Marcel with a pair of fins in his hand, and Marcel turned to follow the man, out of our view. "Looks like he's diving," Cody commented.

Cody, Tyson, and Allison exchanged a dubious glance. "Seems awfully coincidental," Allison said.

I had to agree.

"Let's beat him to it," Tyson said.

I glanced behind me to see Laurent exiting a crew door under the stairs. Rémy pointed to his pile of gear, and he began checking it as I sidled over to him, my flippers and mask in hand. "We're partners," I said.

He smiled, rising as he adjusted his air supply knob. "You will like this dive." He breathed into the yellow emergency regulator, then shouldered his pack. "It's one of my favorites."

His eyes traveled the length of my body as I inserted my arms in the sleeves of my wetsuit and zipped it up. "What?" I asked.

He ran his tongue over his bottom lip. "Just memorizing your wetsuit so I don't lose you."

"Shit," I heard Tyson say. "My O-ring's broken."

Laurent and I both frowned as our eyes met. Without the O-ring, air would escape the tank or water would enter it, rendering the regulator inoperable and necessitating an emergency ascent.

"That wouldn't have been fun to discover in the water," Cody said dryly.

"This is why we check," Rémy said calmly. "Don't worry, I have another pack."

As he scurried over to fetch the other pack, Tyson pointed a finger at the rest of us. "One of you fuckers trying to knock me off?"

Allison slapped Tyson on the back, her lips curling into a smile that didn't reach her eyes. "If any of us were trying to knock you off, I think we'd do a better job than that."

It was meant to be funny, but it fell flat.

Rémy handed Tyson the extra pack, and they carefully checked it together as the rest of us found places to sit to slip on our fins and adjust our masks. Once Tyson was satisfied that his new gear was working perfectly, Rémy came to stand at the back of the boat and whistled for our attention for the pre-dive briefing.

"Today we will dive in St. Barthélemy Natural Reserve. As you can see, the water is very clear, so we will have lots of fun and see lots of fish. Rays, *tortues*—turtles," he corrected himself. "And maybe sharks too."

At this, Jennifer gripped Cody's arm.

"We will go down here and swim along the reef toward the big rock you see there, then we will go through the Snares to reach the wreck." Rémy's English seemed to have improved as he got into his groove. "The little boat—"

"Dinghy," Jennifer supplied.

"Merci—*dinghy*—will wait for us on the mooring ball closest to the wreck and we can surface there."

Nods all around.

"We will have a safety stop for three minutes"—he held up three fingers—"at five meters. If you need to surface early, the *dinghy* has extra gear and a kit *médical*. Is everybody ready?"

A smattering of claps and a chorus of "Yes" and "Let's do this," and Rémy grinned. "Okay, divers, in the water."

A splash, then another, and another, as Tyson, Samira, and Gisèle plunged into the water. I looked back at Laurent, pulled my mask down over my eyes, and stepped off the back of the boat.

CHAPTER 20

The sea was the perfect temperature, refreshing but warm enough on the surface that it shouldn't be terribly cold down below. I felt a shiver of excitement as I inserted my regulator in my mouth and sank into the calm blue water. One of the things I loved most about diving was the inability to think of anything other than the present moment, something I was especially looking forward to today.

Beneath the water with masks, packs, and wetsuits, it became difficult to tell everyone apart, but Laurent stayed by my side as we descended as a group. Like most of the guys, he was wearing a black rash guard and face mask, but his red shorts stood out, so he was easy to keep track of as we began to swim toward the reef.

The water was deep near the boat, but so transparent I could easily make out the sandy bottom. I felt powerful and free as I moved through the water, my fins propelling me, breathing in and out rhythmically. Almost immediately, Laurent nudged me and pointed beneath us, where I saw a four-foot-long nurse shark swimming slowly through the depths, paying no attention to us. I pointed it out to Allison as we continued on our way, hoping Jennifer hadn't seen it.

Up ahead, the reef rose from the ocean floor like a city in the desert, the coral in vibrant shades of purple, yellow, and brown, some of it shaped like leafless trees, some like bushes, some like brains. A school of striped angelfish mingled with fat black fish at the edges of an outcropping of what looked like giant undersea mushrooms. I spotted rainbow-colored parrot fish, and deeper in the reef, a grouper that had to weigh two hundred pounds. I'd never seen one so big. A turtle at least three feet in diameter sailed peacefully past, gazing at us curiously before taking off into the reef, and Samira pointed out a spiny Caribbean lobster backed into a clump of tubular coral. I could hardly believe our luck. The dive would have been successful with these sightings alone, and we'd only just begun.

Coral rose up around us and fish darted into crevices as we entered the swim-through, the reef tightening around us. The visibility was incredible, the sunlight filtering through the turquoise sea to illuminate the underwater world as we passed weightlessly through the reef. We moved slowly, taking time to appreciate the colors and textures, the little silver and orange fish that flitted between the veiny sea leaves, the fluttering fingers of sea anemone and ubiquitous iridescent parrot fish.

Allison pointed out a pair of gorgeous eagle rays far below us, their spots rippling as their giant fins undulated, kicking up sand along the bottom. The water grew cloudier, which was odd, given how far above them we appeared to be, but it was hard to determine depth in the water, and the rays could have been closer than I imagined.

The visibility continued to decrease, the coral above us shutting out much of the sunlight as the water grew more and more opaque. I didn't know what was going on, but Rémy continued without looking back, so I kept swimming.

I thought I heard the ping of a tank-banger coming from somewhere behind me, and I turned back to Laurent, who had also turned. There was a blond swimmer behind him—it was too milky and crowded in the water to tell whether it was Jennifer or Samira—regardless, she didn't seem concerned. Someone's pack hit my shoulder as they passed, but the water was so cloudy that I could hardly make out their fins in front of me, much less determine who it was.

I felt my heart rate quicken at the changing conditions and reminded myself to breathe evenly. Rapid breathing burned oxygen. I checked my gauge console. I had plenty of oxygen left. Everything was okay. It was just murky.

Very murky.

After a few long minutes, the coral opened up around me and I saw the slanted deck of a submerged watercraft so close ahead of me that I almost swam headlong into it. We'd reached the shipwreck, but the visibility was so poor that I couldn't ascertain which part of the boat I was looking at. Nor could I distinguish who was who as the other divers poured out of the Snares and dispersed around the wreck. I looked back for Laurent's red shorts, but everything appeared blue in the deep water.

Was the diver ahead of me Rémy? He was too big to be Rémy, I realized as I caught up, and when he turned back toward me, his features were unfamiliar. I sucked in a gulp of oxygen as a bolt of adrenaline shot through me, but before I could be sure of what I'd seen, he was gone.

For a moment I lost which way was up, and I grabbed on to a corroded railing until I could orient myself, pushing down my panic as I searched for Laurent among the fins and masks in the swirling sand. Who was that man? Or was I suffering from nitrogen narcosis, seeing things that weren't there?

No. I wouldn't let myself think like that. I was agitated, but I wasn't hallucinating. That man was real, and I was okay. Laurent had said this wreck was a popular diving spot, it was entirely possible another group was down here.

I spotted what looked like red shorts and released the railing to reach out and tug on Laurent's arm, but when the diver turned, it was Cody.

I felt a tap on my shoulder and spun to see Laurent, finally. I breathed a sigh of relief as he flashed the OK symbol. I gave him the so-so hand motion, gesturing to the water around us. He nodded, motioning for me to calm, his eyes never leaving mine as he breathed in sync with me until my pulse returned to something like normal.

I pointed up, and he nodded, indicating the other divers scattered around the wreck. I heard another tank-banger, this one louder, and Laurent and I both looked around for the source. We swam toward the sound, converging on Jennifer, who was holding tightly to the mast of the ship, her air bubbles coming much too fast. I hovered close by as Laurent did the same check with her that he'd done with me. Once he'd calmed her, he pointed to the two of us and indicated we should hold on to the pole and stay there. I gathered he was going to look for Rémy so he could take us to the surface before Jennifer passed out or made any dumb mistakes.

Cody swam over to us as Laurent glided away, immediately going to work to calm Jennifer. Gisèle appeared out of the murk, followed by Samira, who both grabbed on to the mast too, clearly nervous.

It was only two minutes before Laurent returned, but it felt like two hours. He pointed up, and my anxiety began to ease as we rose toward the surface. By the time we paused for our five-meter safety stop, I was feeling silly for getting so freaked out. I knew better. Anxiety caused mistakes. The best thing a diver could do in any situation was remain calm.

Once our three minutes were up, we rose toward the light, surfacing into the full glare of the afternoon sun like waking from a nightmare. The swell was mild, the skies blue, the faintest breeze blowing over the surface of the azure water, no sign above of the turmoil beneath. Our yacht bobbed on the horizon, a monster of the seas.

Two of the male navy-shirted crew members I recognized from before leaned over the side of the dinghy to grab our hands as we emerged awkwardly with our giant packs from the water, once again susceptible to gravity. I let Jennifer, Gisèle, and Samira go up first, pulling off my fins and handing them up before I grabbed the ladder. As my feet struck the bottom rung, I realized my legs were shaking.

One of the crew members radioed to the yacht to send another tender as I dumped my pack on the pile with the others and collapsed onto the inflated side of the dinghy, pulling off my mask. Jennifer was still visibly upset, her hands trembling as she untangled the strap of her mask from her matted hair, her makeup streaked down her face. "It's okay," I said, sitting next to her. "You're okay."

"That was really scary," Gisèle muttered.

"I thought I heard a tank-banger in the Snares," I said. "Was it one of you?"

Everyone shook their heads. "Did anybody see Tyson?" Samira asked, her eyes concerned.

"I saw him with Rémy," Jennifer said.

"Me too," Gisèle said. "Or I thought I did, it was really cloudy down there."

Samira nodded, relieved. "I lost him."

"What do you mean, you lost him?" Cody asked Samira as he came over the side of the boat.

"We were at the back and he kept swimming off by himself—"

"Like he always does," Cody grumbled, pushing up his mask as he sat next to her.

"It makes me crazy," Samira agreed. "This is why I don't like to partner with him, but—" She shrugged with a sigh. "I tried to make him keep up, but I was afraid to leave everyone. Every time I turned back, he was there, but then it got so cloudy, I couldn't see. I was scared and I had to keep going forward. Then in the shipwreck, I was looking for him, but I found you guys instead."

Laurent climbed the ladder with urgency, ripping off his mask as he boarded the boat. "What the fuck?" he demanded of Cody.

Everyone's heads snapped toward him, startled. The fact that Laurent was usually so even-keeled made his sudden outrage that much more shocking.

"You abandoned your dive partner to confront another diver not in our group," he continued, hurling his pack onto the pile.

"Chill, man," Cody said. "I didn't abandon her, I was right there."

"You never leave your dive partner, and you never confront another diver under the water. It's dangerous. If you have a problem, figure it out once you surface." Laurent shook his head, water dripping from his curls as he collapsed on the side of the dinghy next to me. "What were you thinking?"

"I wasn't," Cody said, holding up his hands. "I'm sorry, man. My bad."

Laurent swallowed, and I could feel his biceps tense against my arm before he nodded, accepting Cody's apology. "Okay. Just . . . don't ever do that again."

Cody put an arm around Jennifer, who was still shaking. "Sorry, babe," he said. "You did great."

Jennifer nodded weakly, putting on a brave face, but after today, I'd be shocked if she ever dove again.

Gisèle raised her brows at Cody. "Who did you confront?"

"That asshole Marcel was down there muddying the water to ruin our dive," Cody grumbled.

So that was who I'd seen down below.

"Is that why it was so cloudy?" Samira asked.

Everyone looked at Laurent, who shook his head. "I don't know. Cody is right. It could have been him. But also maybe a current."

He bit his lower lip as he gazed toward the dinghy hurtling over the water toward us from *Sea Ray*. When it was close, one of the crew members started our engine and backed off the mooring ball, the water slapping against the side of the boat as we moved aside to let the other dinghy have our place.

"*They have enough oxygen for twenty more minutes, but Rémy told me they'd be up in five,*" Laurent shouted in French to the other boat.

The captain saluted him, and we puttered away, our speed increasing until we were skipping over the tops of the waves toward the giant yacht lurking on the horizon.

CHAPTER 21

Our dinghy docked at the stern of the yacht, bobbing on the gentle swells as the crew secured the ropes and helped us one by one over the side and onto *Sea Ray*.

"No, no, leave your equipment, please," a petite crew girl chastised Gisèle as she attempted to hoist her own pack from the pile at the bottom of the boat. "You, too," she said, stopping Laurent, whose pack was slung over his shoulder.

He began to protest, and she chided him in a playful tone. *"You are not working here, Laurent. You are a guest."* She caught his eye and smiled, pulling her long caramel braid over her shoulder. *"Let us take care of you."*

The flirtation in her voice hinted at an intimacy that sparked a searing flash of jealousy in me, followed by embarrassment. I had no grounds to be jealous. Of course these would be the girls Laurent dated. They had things in common that we never would. He should date them.

I allowed the girl with the braid to help me out of the dinghy, the dregs of adrenaline rendering my legs noodle-like as I stepped onto the teakwood stern. "Leave your wetsuit here," she said, pointing to the pile of wetsuits. "We wash for you."

I scanned her name tag as I unzipped my shorty. "Thank you, Marielle."

The inside of my suit was rough, my skin coated in fine grains of sand as I peeled it off, making sure my bikini was in place. When I looked up, Laurent was under the shower shirtless, head tilted back, the tattoo that wrapped beneath his arm and up his back on display as he ran his hands through his hair while water cascaded over his chest.

I must have been staring, because Marielle gave me a knowing smile as she took my wetsuit and started the shower opposite Laurent's for me.

I quickly turned away to wash the sand from my body, undoing my braid to rinse the seawater from my hair. When I cut off the water, I found Marielle holding a towel out for me. I squeezed out my hair and took it, thanking her. She and another girl gathered the wetsuits while I wrapped the towel around me and followed Laurent up the stairs.

Cody and Jennifer had disappeared somewhere inside, but Gisèle and Samira were by the pool, topless as usual, rehashing their experience below as they slathered themselves in sunscreen.

"Can we get two double vodka sodas?" Samira called out to the crew guy setting up towels on the loungers around the pool. She turned, spying Laurent and me. "You guys want drinks?" she asked.

Laurent and I both shook our heads as he steered me gently past the pool with a hand at the base of my spine. I saw Samira's gaze flit to his hand, then to me, with a flash of interest before she returned her attention to Gisèle, lathering her back with SPF50.

"Are you okay?" Laurent asked as we reached the railing on the far side of the main living area.

I nodded. "I got freaked out for a minute down there, but I'm fine."

I raised a hand to shield my eyes from the glare of the sun and gazed across the water at the developers' gray-toned yacht, watching as their crew unloaded scuba gear from their dinghy.

"You are wondering whether they clouded the water as revenge for Tyson's behavior yesterday," Laurent said.

I nodded. "Cody sure seems to think so. But how?" I asked. "And is that even legal?"

"I don't know about legal, but possible. *A few weeks ago, a guest sank an underwater scooter, and it got lodged under coral that pressed the power button. Made such a mess we couldn't find it until it ran out of juice and the sea calmed.*"

"But aren't those things made to float?"

"So are boats," he said with a shrug. "Sometimes they sink. What I am wondering is who told them where we are diving today."

He shifted his gaze from the yacht to our second dinghy, still tied to the mooring ball where we'd left it when we motored back to the yacht. I could make out only two people on board. He checked his dive watch and frowned.

"What?" I asked.

"They should be up by now," he said. "They only have five to ten minutes of oxygen left."

A jolt of alarm went through me. "Shit. Who's still down there?"

He thought for a moment. "Tyson, Allison, and Rémy."

"What should we do?"

"Let me—" He glanced around, looking for a crew member. "Marielle," he called out as she crested the top of the stairs from the landing pad. She came toward us, shading her eyes against the sun. As she drew nearer, he pointed to the walkie on her belt. "Have you heard from the other dinghy?"

She shook her head.

"Can I?"

She palmed the walkie and pressed the button. "*Moon Two*, this is *Sea Ray*, can you hear me?"

"Go for *Moon Two*," crackled a male voice through the speaker. Marielle handed Laurent the walkie, and he spoke into it.

"*This is Laurent. Divers should be up already. Any sign?*"

"*Nothing.*"

"Do you have extra tanks on board?"

"Three, fully loaded," came the reply.

"Is either of you ready to go in the water?"

"This is Evan," came a second male voice. *"I can suit up."*

Laurent released the button and looked at Marielle. *"Take me over?"*

She nodded, and he spoke into the walkie. *"Headed to you,"* he said. *"Suit up, we're going down."*

Laurent met my eye only briefly, but I could see the worry in his face as he turned to cut across the deck toward the stern with purpose, Marielle trailing in his wake.

CHAPTER 22

I stood at the railing for a moment, watching *Moon Two* for any sign of movement before I returned to the pool.

"Can I borrow that sunscreen?" I asked Samira and Gisèle.

I heard the motors of the dinghy fire to life as Gisèle tossed me the bottle and I squeezed a generous amount of coconut-scented cream into my hand.

"Where's Laurent going?" Gisèle asked.

I cast a glance at Samira as I rubbed SPF50 into my face. I didn't want to worry her unnecessarily, but I also didn't want to lie. "To the other dinghy."

"Why?" Samira asked, picking up on my hesitation.

I squeezed more sunscreen into my hand, working it into my chest and arms. "To make sure the rest of the divers surface smoothly."

"They're not back yet?" Samira rose and crossed to the railing, squinting across the dazzling water at the bobbing tender.

Gisèle pulled on a loose crop top and we joined Samira, watching as *Moon One* skipped over the waves toward *Moon Two*. "They should be back by now," Samira muttered.

When the boats were side by side, Laurent climbed into *Moon Two*, and I could make out him and Evan shouldering their tanks while the others conferred. Then they splashed into the water on the far side of the dinghy.

"Shit." Samira pressed her fingers into the bridge of her nose.

"It's gonna be fine," I said, willing my voice to sound more relaxed than I felt.

Gisèle glanced at me, understanding the need to calm her friend. "Tyson probably swam off and they had to make him come back."

Samira was breathing more rapidly now, her knuckles white as she gripped the railing. "What if he got lost?"

"Laurent and Evan know the area and they have full tanks," I assured her.

Samira took a gulp of her drink. "I told you I lost him. I couldn't find him in the shipwreck."

"I saw him," Gisèle said. "And so did Jennifer."

She leaned into Samira, whispering something in her ear too low for me to make out. Samira shot her a frown with a sharp shake of her head.

Out on the dinghies, there was a commotion as the two guys on *Moon Two* rushed to the back of the boat. "What's happening?" Samira asked.

The boats were too far away, the light off the water too bright to see any detail, but it looked like they were pulling divers from the water.

"They're back," I said, patting her shoulder. "Everything's okay."

"What's going on?" I turned to see Jennifer, freshly showered and made up in a teal one-piece with a colorful sheer caftan, giant white sun hat, and sunglasses. Cody trailed behind her in fresh swim shorts and a polo, holding two white plastic *Sea Ray* cups.

"It's the other divers coming back," I said.

Cody checked his watch as they joined us at the railing. "They took their time."

I nodded. "Laurent went over to make sure everything was okay, but it looks like they're loading into the dinghy now."

Samira took another long draw of her drink, showing us her shaking hand as Gisèle rubbed her back, soothing her like a baby.

"You feeling better now?" I asked Jennifer.

She nodded. "I don't know that diving is my thing."

"That was just a fluke," Cody placated. "In over twenty-five years of diving, I've never had that happen."

"It wasn't fun," Gisèle concurred. "But did you guys see that turtle right before we entered the Snares?"

Watching Gisèle with Samira now, I could see the calming effect she had on her friend and had a new appreciation for her grounded energy. "It was so cute," I agreed.

"The nurse shark was my favorite," Samira said. "I love sharks."

"There was a shark?" Jennifer asked, alarmed.

"And it didn't hurt you!" Cody laughed, shaking his head.

Jennifer glanced over her shoulder toward the indoor dining area. "I'm starving. Do you think they—"

"They're setting something up for us on the deck up there," Gisèle said, pointing to the next level. "I think it's pizza."

My mouth watered, conjuring up warm, salted crust and melted cheese. I hadn't eaten since breakfast and suddenly realized that I, too, was starving.

"But they'll bring you anything you want," Samira added.

"I'm gonna go find someone," Jennifer said.

"Tell them I need another one of these," Samira requested, tapping her drink before she set the empty cup on a nearby table.

As Jennifer wandered away, I turned back to the water, watching *Moon One* pull away from *Moon Two* trailing a white wake as it headed back toward the yacht. But there appeared to be only two people aboard. Marielle was driving, and I couldn't make out who the other passenger was, nor could I tell what was happening or how many people remained on *Moon Two,* where everyone seemed to be clumped together at the stern.

The corner of Cody's mouth tugged downward as he took in the tender speeding toward us. Gisèle cast a concerned glance at Samira, who leaned over the railing as though getting a foot closer would help her determine what was going on.

After a moment, Cody pulled away from the railing, heading toward the stern. Samira quickly followed, stopping by the pool to don her sunglasses and slip a cover-up over her head before jogging down the stairs to the sugar scoop with Gisèle and me on her heels.

A male crew member awaited the dinghy's arrival, the radio clipped to his belt crackling with the voice of someone wanting to know what time food should be served. As the dinghy approached, I saw it was Allison on board.

Where was Tyson?

Allison appeared stricken, her face pale, as the crew tied up the boat. Unease shot through me.

Something was wrong.

CHAPTER 23

Allison's perennially calm countenance was cracked, her face like a broken mirror reflecting all our anxiety right back at us.

"Where's Tyson?" Samira asked as Allison climbed aboard the yacht.

"They went to get him," Allison said. Her usual confidence had been replaced by a jittery energy that seemed all wrong on her.

"What?" Cody asked.

"Where is he?" Samira overlapped, her voice rising with panic.

"He— We— We don't know," Allison said quietly.

"What do you mean?" Cody asked.

"We couldn't find him," Allison answered.

"Oh my God," Samira muttered, her hands covering her mouth.

Allison swallowed. "Rémy and I searched until we were running out of air—"

"He's down there without air?" Samira cried. "He's gonna die!"

"Shh . . ." Gisèle said, wrapping her arms around Samira, whose legs seemed to have turned to noodles.

"He's a very experienced diver," I offered, hoping I was projecting more confidence than I felt.

"*Oh my God,*" Samira said again, pressing the heels of her hands into her eyes. "*Oh God. Shit. Oh my God.*"

"They're gonna find him," Allison said unconvincingly.

"How much more oxygen does he have?" Cody asked.

"I don't know," Allison answered. "It varies from—"

"I know it varies," Cody snapped. "How much did you have left when you surfaced?"

"Five minutes."

"We need tanks," Cody said, turning to the crew members, who were flapping around helplessly. "Now. We have to go help them look for him."

"I'm sorry, we don't—" Marielle started.

"They don't have any more tanks," Allison finished. "And even if they did, they won't let us go back down unless we're certified rescue divers. I already asked."

"Goddammit." Cody clenched his fists, turning on the crew. "We have to do something! My brother's down there running out of air right now. What can we do?"

Two male crew members hurried down the stairs, their arms laden with safety rings and life jackets, their faces anxious. "*We're taking the dinghy out to scan the water, see if he came up somewhere else,*" one of them said to Marielle in rapid French. He jumped into the tender, starting the engines as the other guy quickly untied its rope.

"I'll come with you," Cody said, rushing over.

Marielle stopped him with a gentle hand to his chest. "I'm sorry, we can't allow you to go."

"He's my brother, I'm going," Cody said, pushing past her.

"It's a liability issue," said the guy with the rope. "Please . . . there is not a lot of time."

Before Cody could protest, the guy had jumped into the tender and they were off, skating across the water, one driving while the other held binoculars to his eyes, scanning the water.

"Our crew know the area well," Marielle said in a soothing voice. "And the rescue divers all have full tanks. It is a good situation."

"A good situation?" Cody echoed, his face dark.

"I'm sorry, what I mean, if anyone will find him, they will."

If her intention was to calm us, it didn't work. Allison broke away, running up the stairs as a wail escaped Samira's throat and she sank to the ground, pulling Gisèle with her.

"Goddammit," Cody repeated, balling and unballing his fists as he paced the teak deck. "God*dam*mit."

Samira was letting out a high-pitched keening, clearly in shock as she rocked back and forth on the floor, her face buried in Gisèle's chest.

"Somebody needs to call Search and Rescue," Cody said. "Has anybody called Search and Rescue?"

"Yes," Marielle said. I could see she was holding on to her composure by a thread. "We are in communication."

I was aware of the boat rolling beneath my feet, the sun warming my shoulders, the rivulets of water from my wet hair dripping down my back. Yet simultaneously I felt nothing, an odd numbness buzzing beneath my skin.

I could see the scene from above like a drone shot in a movie as I glided back up the stairs to the main deck, where the crew members conferred in low voices, their routines disrupted. I found my way back to the place on the side of the boat where I'd stood with Laurent, out of the fray and shaded from the Caribbean sun by the hulking upper floors of the yacht. Leaning on the railing with trembling arms, I fixed my eyes on *Moon Two,* gently rising and falling with the ocean swells, the large rock looming above the tender like a guardian. From this distance there was no sign anything was amiss.

Not yet.

Tyson would be out of oxygen by now. Sure, there was a possibility he had surfaced somewhere else, but it wasn't likely. I had the strangest sense of déjà vu, the sinking sensation of knowing how it would all turn out.

Out of the corner of my eye, I saw someone coming toward me and glanced over to see Jennifer, looking lost. "Hey," she said. "The crew said Tyson's missing?"

I nodded. "It doesn't look good."

"My God," she murmured, joining me at the railing. Close up, I could see she was pale with shock, the lines of her makeup contouring dark against her blood-drained face.

We stood shoulder to shoulder, watching as an angular Search and Rescue boat cut across the water and tied up on the mooring ball next to the one where *Moon Two* was moored. The back of the rescue boat opened like the tailgate of a pickup truck, and two divers splashed into the water.

"Cody's gonna be a mess," she murmured. "And Samira, God. Nobody wanted him dead."

My head snapped toward her. "No."

She quickly registered my discomfiture, fumbling to walk back what she'd said. "I just mean, even if he was an asshole and maybe sometimes people talked about wishing he would die, they didn't mean it."

"Right," I agreed.

But I was unsettled by her declaration, even more so by her attempt to walk it back. Tyson's death—if he was even dead, which was as yet unconfirmed—was an accident, surely.

Or was it?

I thought of the blackmail, the falsified environmental reports . . . and I had in fact heard more than one person in the last twenty-four hours express the wish that Tyson would die. I couldn't say I hadn't thought it myself.

Other than Cody, I hardly knew these people, I realized. They *seemed* nice. That didn't mean they were.

I considered the shark-gray yacht lurking in the water not a hundred meters from our boat. If the developers had muddied the water, was Laurent safe down there?

He was a rescue diver, I reminded myself. Diving with other rescue divers. He knew the area, and what he was getting into. He was fine.

"Sorry," Jennifer said, picking nervously at her nail polish. "I always say the wrong thing."

I turned my attention back to her, shaking my head. "It's not you. It's just—" I glanced over at the neighboring yacht.

Jennifer followed my gaze across the bright water. "They were down there at the shipwreck," she said, turning back to me, slack-jawed. "You don't think they could have killed Tyson?"

I grimaced. "I think we should probably wait for more information before we start pointing fingers."

"Sorry," she agreed. "You're right. I watch too much true crime."

The sound of yelling drew our attention to the pool area, where I saw Cody berating a crew guy, his fists clenched, face red. I'd never seen him so angry. "Do something!" he was yelling. "That's my brother down there!"

Jennifer scurried across the deck toward Cody, placing a calming hand on his back as she approached. He shrugged her off, wildly gesticulating at the poor crew member before storming into the main living room with Jennifer trailing behind, apologizing to the guy as she followed Cody toward their cabin.

I turned back to the sea, scanning the surface of the water for any movement, but all was calm.

A gull swept down from the sky and scooped a wriggling fish from the sea, its silvery scales glinting in the bright sun as it struggled against its fate. Across the water near the back of the Search and Rescue boat, a head emerged from the water. And then another.

T he skies opened just as I shouldered my purse to leave Rosa's apartment.

"Damn it," I said, peering out the window at the pouring rain.

"Do you have to go?" Rosa asked.

"I wish I didn't."

But I needed to take advantage of the time I had while Rosa's mom was with mine tonight.

It had been two weeks since Cody's arrest. He was out on bail, his ankle bracelet confining him to his and Tyson's parents' house, but I had yet to see him because their parents had returned to oversee preparation for his trial and had been watching over their sons like hawks. They'd spoken to their offspring so little during the summer that they didn't even know Tyson and I had been dating again—much less that we had broken up again—and we thought it was better if I stayed out of the picture completely.

Tonight, though, Mr. and Mrs. Dale had gone to a charity ball in Miami, so Tyson and Cody had invited me over to catch me up on everything and make sure we were all on the same page before Tyson returned to school in Boston next week. Of course I couldn't tell Rosa any of this.

"You better not be seeing Tyson again," she said.

I shook my head. "I just have errands to run."

"At night?"

Thunder cracked overhead. "It's only eight."

"Okay," she said, pulling me in for a tight hug.

I drove to Tyson's parents' at a snail's pace with the windshield wipers on high, but still it was hard to see through the sheets of water that poured from the sky. Which was probably why I didn't spot Ian's black pickup truck until I was parking next to it in front of the house. I groaned, staring at it while the rain pounded the roof of my car, considering whether to leave. I wanted to see Ian even less than I wanted to see Tyson, but I needed to talk to Cody, so it looked like I was going to be seeing all of them.

I cut the engine, again hugging my purse to my body as I dashed up the steps to the front door and pressed the doorbell. I could hear it ringing throughout the house as I waited under the narrow overhang that did little to protect me from the wind and rain. It wasn't long before Tyson jerked the door open a crack, poking his head out and looking around before opening it just wide enough to let me in.

"Something bad happened," he whispered urgently as I stepped inside.

My pulse quickened and I focused on his face as he shut the door behind me, noting that while he was dry, he looked worse than I did, the color drained from his skin, his eyes haunted.

"I can't fucking find it!" came Cody's voice from somewhere in the house.

"What happened?" I asked.

His gaze shifted to a point behind me, and I turned.

I gasped, one hand flying to my mouth as the other gripped Tyson's arm for support, my knees buckling beneath me.

Ian's body lay crumpled at the base of the sweeping marble staircase, his limbs at unnatural angles, a pool of blood seeping from beneath his head onto the gleaming beige floor.

"What the fuck, Tyson?" Cody demanded as he strode from the back of the house, his eyes flitting to me before fixing on his brother. "I told you not to let her in."

"We need her help," Tyson said. "You can't leave the house."

Cody shook his head, glowering at him. "She shouldn't be involved in this."

"Is he . . . ?" I asked, staring at Ian's unmoving form.

Cody nodded slightly, his mouth in a grim line.

My mouth watered as nausea curdled my stomach. I released Tyson's arm and ran on wobbling knees, the slick floor tilting beneath me as I careened into the kitchen and hurled into the sink. I gripped the counter to steady myself as my body convulsed again and again until I'd emptied my stomach, leaving me shaking and unnaturally cold. Mechanically, I washed out the sink and slid to the kitchen floor, wrapping my arms around my legs and dropping my head between my knees.

Ian was dead.

Cody was at my side in a flash, his hand on my shoulder. "You should go," he said, squatting on his heels beside me. "He should never have let you in. You didn't see this."

"What happened?" I managed, raising my gaze to his.

"He fell down the stairs."

"Which one of you pushed him?" I asked, my voice trembling.

His jaw tightened, and I caught a glimpse of the chasm of despair inside him.

"He wanted more money and there is no more money," Tyson said, striding over to hover above us. "He was high as a kite. We got in a fight, and he fell. That's all."

"Have you called the police?" I asked, looking at them in turn.

They glanced at each other. "Not yet," Cody said.

"They're gonna think the same thing you did," Tyson said. "The guy who turned Cody in dies at the bottom of our stairs two weeks after he's arrested? It doesn't look good."

"But he was high," I protested. "They'll test his blood and see how inebriated he was—"

"It doesn't matter. People get high all the time, and they don't fall down stairs and die. Cody will go to jail for murder," Tyson said. "Or we both will. We can't call the police."

"Then what do you plan to do?" I asked.

"We have to get rid of his body," Tyson said.

I looked at Cody. "Do you agree with this?"

"I don't like it," Cody grumbled, collapsing to the floor with his back against the kitchen island.

It was then that I noticed the bottle of bleach and box of rubber gloves resting on the counter above him. "This isn't a discussion," I said, realizing. "You guys have already decided."

"Tyson's right," Cody said. "It looks like we killed him. And since he turned me in . . . they'll have a motive, even without knowing about the extortion."

"Did you kill him?" I asked. I knew Tyson would lie, so I focused on Cody, fixing him with my unrelenting gaze.

"He slipped and fell," Cody repeated hollowly.

"We should have let him burn in the fire," Tyson growled. "But what's done is done. Now we have to get rid of the body before Mom and Dad come home and find him ruining their marble floor."

"I don't want any part of this," I said, wiping the tears I didn't realize had fallen from my eyes.

"I need your help," Tyson said, dropping to his knees beside me. "Cody's on house arrest, he can't leave. I have to load Ian into his truck and dump him in a canal somewhere in the Everglades, then park the truck at a lot in a different part of the park. I need you to dispose of his phone somewhere in Miami and come back to get me."

I stared at him. It was a good plan, but I wanted nothing to do with it. "Are you crazy? No."

"Audrey, you're already entangled in this, and not just because you've been here and seen his body," he said, his eyes pleading. "Ian knew you and I were involved in what he got Cody arrested for. I'm sure the only reason he didn't narc on us too was so he could continue to extort us. There's no telling what he has on us. If we call the cops now, there will be an investigation into his death regardless of what we say. They'll search his apartment and find whatever evidence he has against us, and all three of us will go to jail, even if Cody and I manage to somehow not get convicted of his murder."

I evaluated him. "What makes you think Andie won't turn us in anyway?"

"She'll never know we had anything to do with his death. She'll think he OD'd somewhere, or got himself killed in a shady drug deal. He's involved in some bad shit. There are lots of ways he could die that don't involve us."

That, at least, was true.

"You can walk away now," Tyson went on, holding up his hands. "But we have a lot better chance of not getting caught if you'll help me get rid of the phone and the truck."

I took a shaky breath as darkness settled over my heart. I knew it would haunt me for years to come, but I saw the accuracy of Tyson's logic, and I didn't want to go to jail. "We'll need a tarp. And something to weigh the body down with when you throw it into the canal."

PART II

CHAPTER 24

"Madame?"

I wiped the spittle from my mouth with the edge of the towel wrapped around my waist and turned to see a navy-shirted crew member hovering at the edge of the pool deck, her hands clasped before her.

"Are you okay?" she entreated.

I nodded, my eyes fixed on the Search and Rescue boat, where the divers were loading Tyson's body into the stern. It was the same every time I went into shock. Shaking morphed into nausea and then back again. You'd think my body would have learned to handle it by now, but no.

Behind me, Allison stared across the water, her arms wound around herself, too absorbed in the scene unfolding at sea to have noticed me vomiting over the railing.

"May I bring you some water?" the girl inquired.

"You don't have to—I can come," I said, starting toward her with wobbling legs. There was nothing left to see now, anyway. The other divers had fished Tyson's body from the sea, hauling him into the boat and removing the oxygen tank from his back so they could lay him on the deck. My tongue felt like cotton as I tried to formulate words. "Is he . . . Tyson, is he—dead?"

I knew the answer to the question, but I had to ask.

The poor girl's eyes welled with tears. "I am sorry, madame. There was nothing they could do."

I nodded, following her out of the shade of the side deck onto the main deck, where the pool sparkled in the dazzling sun. Over the sound of the chill trance music that still pumped from the speakers at low volume, I could hear Samira keening below on the sugar scoop. Samira, who it struck me had now lost two husbands at the tender age of twenty-five.

"Someone should probably cut the music," I muttered.

"Yes, I will take care of that," she said, grabbing a bottle of water from an ice bucket and handing it to me.

The dissonant wail of sirens announced the arrival of the police boat. I watched as it pulled up alongside the Search and Rescue boat, blocking our view of Tyson's corpse. *Moon One* and *Moon Two* bobbed nearby, a morbid flotilla on a bright Caribbean day.

I sat on a lounger and took a deep breath, focusing on the horizon. The shock combined with the physical exhaustion from the dive and the dregs of my hangover had made me woozy and weak. I could probably stand to eat as well. With all the trauma, I'd forgotten how hungry I was.

The edges of my vision darkened as I stood, and I gripped the back of the lounger, closing my eyes until my head rush subsided.

"This can't get out." I opened my eyes to see Cody striding toward me, Jennifer on his heels. "The media can't find out Tyson's dead until we've decided how we're going to handle it."

Dazed, I blinked up at him. "Of course."

"We'll need to make an announcement," Cody said to Allison as she joined us. "I'm having the attorney draft an addendum to the NDAs the crew signed when they were hired. We'll need to make sure all the divers and the emergency personnel sign them as well. The three De-Sal centers in development could all pull the plug if it gets out."

"I'll come up with a statement," Allison said.

"We can stop the bleed by having a plan in place before we announce," Cody said. His face crumpled and he choked back a sob before taking a deep breath and resetting his face. "We need to come up with that plan," he finished.

"I'll call my publicist," Allison said. "She's a friend, and she'll know what to do. Take a minute to breathe. You're in shock. We all are."

Cody reached out to a passing crew member, clearly not hearing Allison. "Excuse me, can you show me how to print?"

"The printer is in the office on the primary level," the guy said. "This way."

"I need you to round up the crew," I heard Cody say as he followed the guy toward the stairwell, Allison trailing behind with a hand on his back, still trying to calm him. "We need to make an announcement."

I was so queasy, and the sun was so bright. It would take them a minute to print the NDAs, and no one was paying any attention to me. I headed down the stairs to my room.

In my cabin, I ate a banana from the snack table to steady my stomach, then brushed my teeth, showered, and changed into a cream shift dress, letting my hair air-dry into messy waves. I deliberated whether I would appear insensitive, wearing white, but it was what I had. This was an unexpected circumstance.

A man was dead, and I was wondering what to wear. It seemed wrong.

But what was right in this situation?

It was shocking. I was in shock. Allison was right, we were all in shock. I kept thinking of that word, "shock." Was it an onomatopoeia? It felt like one.

I thought of my boys, wishing intensely that I could wrap my arms around them right now. I picked up my phone to see a text from Rosa wanting to know where Benji's shin guards were. I answered, then tapped out a message asking her to tell the boys how much I missed them.

As I sat on the bed waiting for the message to go through, I imagined the hugs I would give Alex and Benji when I got home. Though it wouldn't be tomorrow, I was relatively sure now.

Tyson would have no more tomorrows.

The realization hit me like a truck, the finality of it. He would never have a chance to grow old, to see his children grow up, to become a better man. Because as much of an asshole as he was, there had still been some scrap of hope inside me that he might change someday. That as surely as the darkness had claimed him, the light might recover him in the end.

Even though I hardly recognized the man he'd become, I'd loved him when he was a boy. And though he'd hurt me, I still wanted to believe he had goodness in him, somewhere deep in the recesses of his soul. The seed of it still remained in the generosity he sometimes displayed. But now that seed would never sprout.

A red exclamation mark appeared next to my text and I hit Send again, but the Wi-Fi signal indicator was dark. I'd try again later, I thought, taking one more deep, centering breath before I grabbed my hat and sunglasses and closed my cabin door behind me.

CHAPTER 25

Upstairs, I found Cody in the midst of his announcement, the crew gathered around him on the pool deck. Allison and Jennifer were there too, but I didn't see Gisèle and Samira anywhere. I hovered at the edge of the crowd as Cody spoke, fascinated by his transformation this afternoon. For as long as I'd known him, he'd always seemed so unassuming; the milder-mannered, meeker brother. But it had been years since I'd spent any time with him, and I'd never seen him in a business environment. Perhaps this stronger, sharper Cody was who he'd always been at work. He did run a multi-billion-dollar company, after all.

And now . . . would Tyson's shares go to Cody? Or to Samira?

"We appreciate your discretion during this trying time," Cody concluded as the chief steward handed out NDAs and pens. "Any questions?"

A hand went up and Cody pointed. "Are you all still having dinner on the boat tonight?" the chef asked.

Cody looked over at Allison. "We have to eat," Allison said.

"We'll be staying overnight," Cody added. "For containment purposes."

"When will the Wi-Fi be turned back on?" a guy in the back asked. So that was why my text to Rosa hadn't gone through.

"After the public announcement has been made tomorrow morning," Cody said.

As the crew signed their documents and handed them over to the chief steward, I made my way to the railing on the far side of the ship. Even with the protection of my hat and dark glasses, the glare from the sun on the sea was so bright that it was hard to make out any details across the water. Our dinghies were no longer moored in front of the big rock, but the Search and Rescue boat and the police boat were still there.

I wondered where they'd found Tyson and what had happened to him, what his final moments had been like. I thought of Laurent, of how harrowing it must have been to discover Tyson unresponsive. It had been an hour now since they reeled him in. What were they still doing over there?

A heavy hand on my shoulder startled me and I turned to see Cody. "Audrey, can you come with me?"

I nodded, uneasy as I trailed him up the two sets of stairs to the primary level and across the living area. Before we could step into the office, the door to Tyson's suite opened and Gisèle emerged, closing it behind her with unsteady hands.

"How's Samira doing?" I asked.

"Not well."

Cody loitered in the doorway of the office, waiting for me. "The crew's on the main deck, if she needs anything," he offered.

She nodded, starting down the stairs as Cody beckoned me into the office, shutting us inside.

A large built-in lucite desk faced the view, with two barrel-backed white velvet chairs opposite it and a wall of mostly empty white shelves behind it. Cody sat heavily into the white leather desk chair and dropped his forehead to his hands. I took the chair opposite him, waiting for him to compose himself.

"Sorry," he said after a moment, looking up.

"You're handling everything really well, all things considered," I said gently.

"Thanks." He sighed, massaging the bridge of his nose. "I'm glad it looks that way. I'm—" He closed his eyes and took a breath, stopping the tears before they fell. "It's not something I ever thought I'd have to deal with."

"Have you heard anything about what happened?" I asked.

"Not yet."

"You guys fought before the dive." It wasn't a question. We both knew I'd seen him exit Tyson's room enraged. But I hoped it would elicit some kind of explanation.

He leaned back in the chair. "I didn't mention that you and I had spoken last night, but I did tell him I realized the timing of your visit couldn't be coincidental. He got angry and accused me of blackmailing him, which I told him was preposterous. That's when you saw me storm out. You talked to him after that?"

I nodded. "He told me he'd taken out the money the blackmailer demanded and wanted to meet them this evening. I tried to talk him out of going, but he seemed set on it."

"Do you think this blackmailer has anything?" he asked.

I paused. "There were keys in the lining of Ian's shoe. My contact on the police force told me, but it hasn't been mentioned publicly. One was to his safety deposit box."

"Have the police opened it?"

I shook my head. "Figuring out which box would be impossible without any more information."

"Did you tell Tyson about the keys?"

"No. I'd planned to, but he was so antagonistic when I got down here, and so paranoid . . . I decided not to mention it. The blackmailer hasn't said anything about them either, but maybe that was what they planned to reveal at the meeting this evening. I mean, Ian told us he kept the keys in his shoe—he could have told anyone else too."

He nodded, following along. "You think Ian told people he was blackmailing us?"

"It certainly seems that way."

"So, Tyson would've been afraid there was some evidence inside the lockbox that Ian had been blackmailing us, which would have given us a motive to kill him."

"Exactly," I agreed. "But even if this blackmailer did know about the keys, they couldn't know for sure what was inside the lockbox. Hell, none of us know that."

I could see the gears in Cody's mind turning as we looked at each other, both of us at a loss. "Can you think of anything else they might have?" I asked.

He rubbed his bloodshot eyes. "No."

I couldn't either, unless there were things Tyson hadn't shared with me . . . which was entirely possible. Probable, even. But also impossible to know. I sighed. "Then I don't see what good could come of meeting them."

He clicked the end of his pen. "So how do we find out who it is?"

"Does it matter anymore?" I asked. "It was Tyson they were blackmailing, and he's gone. You've got bigger things to deal with now."

He let out a groan, dropping his forehead to his folded arms on the desktop.

"Did you have operating instructions in place in case Tyson wasn't able to perform his duties as CEO?" I asked.

He nodded. "I'm interim CEO."

"And do you know how his shares will be conferred?"

"No. That'll be in the will."

"The police will be asking, so you'll want to get ahead of it," I said.

"I'll make a call." He looked like a lost little boy. "Anything else I should do?"

"Get yourself a lawyer if you don't have one already. A criminal defense attorney. Sooner rather than later."

He blinked at me, unsettled. "You think that's necessary?"

"Yes."

"Okay." A tear escaped his eye, and he quickly wiped it away. "Thanks, Audrey."

"Have you called your parents?" I asked.

He shook his head. "I should do that."

"I'll leave you to it." I knew Tyson's relationship with his parents had been strained, but my heart went out to them, and to Cody, having to tell them they'd lost a son. I paused with my hand on the doorknob. "I'm sorry, Cody. You've always been there for me. If there's anything you need, please know I'm here."

He didn't turn. "Thanks."

CHAPTER 26

I descended the main staircase to see the police boat docked at the back of the yacht. My heartbeat quickened as a gangly older man with an impressive mustache stomped into the salon, followed by an officer so good-looking that if he turned up at a party in the figure-hugging shorts uniform he was wearing, I'd be more inclined to think he was a stripper than a real police officer.

Marielle was on their heels. *"Can I offer you anything? A glass of water?"* she inquired, rushing to head them off.

The older one plodded over to the coffee table and plucked a canapé from a tray. *"What are these?"* he asked, his bushy eyebrows knitting as he inspected it.

"It's a brie tart with fig jam," she answered. *"I have ham and cheese mini-quiches as well if you'd like?"*

He popped the tart into his mouth and nodded appreciatively as the younger officer smiled at her, revealing a dimple, the highlights in his brunette locks glinting in the sun. *"Water, please, for both of us,"* he said. *"Thank you."*

Marielle returned his smile, flustered.

"And yes to the quiches," the older one said once he'd swallowed.

As Marielle scurried away, their eyes landed on me. "I am Officer Lambert," the older one said, switching to English, "and he is Officer Gauthier."

"I'm Audrey Collet," I said. I peered past them, looking for Laurent. "Are the rescue divers with you?"

"They are showering on the lower deck," Officer Gauthier said.

"What is your relation to Monsieur Dale?" Officer Lambert asked, assessing me with a penetrating gaze.

"We were old friends. He invited me here to celebrate his birthday."

Officer Gauthier glanced around. "Where are the others?"

"I don't know. Can I ask . . . do you know what happened to him?"

"We will need to interview all of you," Lambert replied, sidestepping my question. He turned to Marielle, who had returned with a cold bottle of water for each of them. Switching back to French, he asked her, "*What room can we use?*"

"*Give me just a moment, I will find a room for you.*" And she was off again, bustling up the stairs.

"I can talk to you now if you like," I volunteered, wanting to appear helpful while gleaning whatever information I could.

Officer Lambert looked down his prominent nose at me, then threw his hands up and sat in a nearby chair, gesturing for me to take the couch opposite. I did as directed and Officer Gauthier sat in another chair, extracting a tape recorder and a notepad from the backpack I hadn't noticed was slung over his broad shoulder.

I considered the tape recorder, wondering whether I needed a lawyer. But I'd just volunteered to talk to them; backing out now would make me seem suspicious.

"This is Audrey Collet," Gauthier said into the tape recorder.

"Audrey, can you tell us about the dive?" Lambert asked.

While I talked, Gauthier took notes and Lambert kept his eyes trained on me, mustache swishing as he gnawed at one cheek and then the other. When I reached the part where we'd gotten caught in the murk, he stopped me, asking me to carefully recount who I'd seen, following up with questions about timing. I answered everything as best I could, with the caveat that it had been quite cloudy, and I'd been more focused on my own safety than who I saw when.

My words faltered as I saw Laurent, Evan, and Rémy emerge from the stairs beyond the pool wrapped in towels, their shoulders slumped, faces somber. Laurent caught my eye for just a moment, his gaze uneasy, before he followed them down the central stairwell toward our cabins.

"Did you talk to the owners of the gray yacht?" I asked the officers.

I could tell from the look that passed between them that I wasn't the first to ask. The hair stood up on the back of my neck. "Why?" Gauthier asked.

"We saw one of them down there. They own the land around the proposed De-Sal site, and apparently they were really upset with Tyson."

"How long had you known Tyson?" Lambert asked, abruptly switching directions.

"Since high school," I answered.

"And the last time you saw him before this trip was when?" he pushed.

I paused, knowing my answer would only elicit more questions. "Ten, eleven years ago."

"Why so long?"

While my exterior remained calm, my pulse skyrocketed. "Our lives went in different directions."

"So why did he invite you, who are not close to him and had not seen him in so long, to this intimate birthday celebration?" Lambert asked.

The wheels of my brain spun as I tried to decide how much to tell them. Should I reveal that he'd hired me to find out who was blackmailing him? But that would lead to other questions, questions neither Cody nor I could easily answer. Still, they would see the $50,000 he'd paid my firm up front if they looked at his bank statements, which, if this turned into a murder investigation, they definitely would. So I needed to tell them something.

"I'm a discovery agent," I said.

That got their attention.

"What is this?" Gauthier asked, pausing with a brie tart halfway to his mouth.

"I normally work with attorneys doing discovery before trial." I lowered my voice. "But Tyson was afraid someone in his inner circle was plotting against him, and he hired my firm to find out who."

"Plotting, how?" Lambert asked, stroking his mustache.

"He was a bit . . . paranoid," I said. "There were a few things, documents, that should have been confidential but were leaked. He wanted me to find out who was leaking these documents."

"And did you?" Lambert asked.

I shook my head. The only proof I had of Cody and Allison's duplicity was the pictures of her talking to those two men at Le Ti who were wearing costumes that concealed their identity, and I was not inclined to make accusations without evidence that would stand up in a court of law. "I've been here less than forty-eight hours. And the others don't know I am here in that capacity, so please don't mention it to them."

Lambert nodded as Gauthier madly scribbled on his notepad.

"Did Mr. Dale say or do anything while you were here that would lead you to believe he might be capable of harming himself?" Gauthier stepped in.

"No," I said, relieved that they didn't seem inclined to ask any more questions about my work.

"And can you think of anyone who might have wished Tyson harm?" he asked.

Literally every guest on this boat. But all I knew was hearsay, and I wasn't about to start pointing fingers without talking to an attorney first. I shrugged. "Sorry I'm not more help."

Behind the officers, I saw Marielle descend the central staircase, followed by Allison and Cody, who looked more composed than when I'd left him. Officers Gauthier and Lambert stood, hands extended, as Cody and Allison crossed to them.

"Cody Dale," Cody said.

"Allison Zhu," Allison followed up.

Gauthier's eyes lit up as he registered who Allison was. "You are the champion swimmer," he said, impressed. "I watched you beat our girl in every race."

Allison nodded. "Alaina was a great competitor. She beat me sometimes too."

"But not in the Olympics," Gauthier said, pointing at her. "My little sister is a swimmer. She had your poster on her wall in—"

Lambert cleared his throat, cutting his partner off. "We need to take statements from everyone who was diving today."

"Marielle told us you need a room," Cody said. "There's an office upstairs. I can show you."

"Do you need anything more from me?" I asked as they started toward the stairs.

"Not now," Lambert answered. "But you will be here if we have more questions."

I descended the stairs to my room, kicking myself for volunteering to speak to the police as I went over the half-truths I'd just told them about why I was here. Was there any way for them to learn about the blackmailer if I didn't tell them? I had both the article and the letter the person had sent Tyson hidden inside the pocket of my jeans in my suitcase. But where was the money he'd taken out?

Their questions about who might have had reason to harm him indicated to me that they thought his death hadn't been an accident, but they'd also asked whether I thought he might have been inclined to harm himself. So maybe they weren't sure yet what had happened to him and were just covering their bases, not ruling anything out.

Still, I couldn't help but think of Samira's other dead husband and her drunken vitriol last night, of Allison's almost eerie calm, and of Cody's preoccupation with having everyone sign new NDAs. All these things were suspicious. Yet each made sense: Allison and Cody still had a multi-billion-dollar company to run, and whether Samira was more upset that her husband was dead or her meal ticket was gone—because God only knew what his will said—she seemed the right degree of upset, under the circumstances. Hell, everyone did.

Sure, Gisèle and Jennifer were more shell-shocked than anything else, but their relationships with Tyson were the least close. And what of Rémy and Laurent?

Who was Rémy? And what secrets was Tyson holding over Laurent?

I paused between the door to my room on one side of the hall and Laurent's on the other. I raised my hand to knock on his door but stopped, knuckles inches from the wood, when I heard voices within. Male voices, whispering in tones so low I almost hadn't heard them.

I glanced up and down the hallway and leaned closer to the door. I could tell they were speaking French, yet their voices were so soft that I couldn't make out what they were saying. One of the men had to be Laurent, but who was the other? Rémy, most likely, I figured.

Rémy was a new dive instructor, and Tyson had appeared not to know him. Could he have been hired by someone to kill Tyson?

Laurent was who had hired him, I realized with a jolt of unease.

I hovered there, straining to listen, aware I could be caught at any moment if someone came into the hallway. But it was no use. Their voices were too low to make out.

I retreated to my own room, where I shut the door and lay on my bed, the wheels of my mind spinning as I listened for Rémy's departure. I was getting ahead of myself. I didn't even know yet what exactly had happened to Tyson.

A knock at my door jerked me out of slumber. I sat up, groggy and disoriented. Clearly the late night and stress had taken their toll, though I wouldn't have imagined sleep possible in my agitated state. I blinked and checked my watch, surprised to find that more than an hour had passed. "Who is it?" I called out.

"Laurent," came Laurent's voice, in a whisper.

I opened the door and he quickly slipped inside and shut it behind him, seemingly no longer worried about what people might think about the two of us being alone together. He was dry now, in a black T-shirt and gym shorts, and clearly on edge, his eyes sunken, jaw tense. Before I could ask him if he was okay, his voice was in my ear, low and urgent.

"Tyson was murdered."

CHAPTER 27

"Murdered?" I echoed. My knees felt weak, and I realized I was gripping Laurent's arm with claw-like fingers. "How?"

"*Someone turned off his oxygen,*" he whispered. "*That's why it was so hard to locate him. No bubbles. His tank was still half full.*"

My head spun. "How did you find out?"

"I was the one who found him," Laurent said. "He was in a cave off the Snares."

Laurent steadied me as I lowered myself onto the end of the bed, then sat beside me, his body angled toward mine. "Don't let anyone know I told you this," he continued, his eyes deadly serious. "They told us not to tell anyone."

"You don't think he could have gotten disoriented in the murk? He could have had nitrogen narcosis or something and turned off his oxygen himself—"

He shook his head, and I thought of how hard it was to reach your own oxygen valve when you were wearing your tank.

"Maybe he hit it . . ." I suggested, but my voice trailed off as Laurent again shook his head. The oxygen valve was a big knob that had to be spun. We both knew you couldn't accidentally turn it off.

But turning off someone else's oxygen wouldn't be easy either. If you did it from in front of them, they could fight you off, grab your emergency oxygen and breathe off that.

"You can mount the tank from behind," Laurent said. "Dive masters learn to do that to contain people who freak out."

"So you think someone lured him into the cave using the cloudy water as cover, then mounted his tank and turned off his oxygen?"

"Yes." His eyes were haunted.

I thought of the clang I'd heard somewhere in the murk. "Was his tank-banger still attached?"

He shook his head. "We found it on some coral nearby."

A chill went up my spine as the grim realization settled over me. "One of us. . . ."

"It might not have been one of us," he said quickly.

"You're thinking of the developers."

He nodded. "The police will check to see if there were other divers in the area as well."

I bit my lip, thinking. "I mean, muddying the water to fuck up our dive is one thing, but murder? What good would it do them? The site will go forward anyway."

"It does seem unlikely."

"Do you know them?"

"Not so much. They are not locals." He paused, studying his hands as if considering saying something. But he must have thought better of it, because he shook his head.

"Whatever you're thinking, you can tell me," I prompted.

A muscle in his jaw feathered. "It's not important."

"Anything could be important."

But again, he shook his head, tight-lipped.

I knew I'd have a better chance of getting whatever it was out of him later if I didn't push now. "Did you tell Tyson about seeing Allison with the guys from the city council at Le Ti?" I asked instead.

"No—you told me not to."

I evaluated him. "And you were more loyal to me, who you'd known less than twenty-four hours, than to Tyson?"

"What can I say?" The corner of his mouth twitched up as his gaze found mine. "I like you better."

"It's a low bar." I swallowed, looking away. "I can't imagine what you've been through today."

"When we stopped for the safety check, we all had to hold him down so that he wouldn't float away," he said quietly. "His eyes were open, and it felt like he was looking at me." He shuddered, trying to dislodge the image.

"I'm so sorry, Laurent," I said, just as a knock came at the door. "Who is it?" I called out.

"Gisèle. Can I come in?" she asked, pushing the door open.

"By all means," I returned wryly, gesturing for her to enter.

She shut the door behind her and took us in, her dark eyes troubled. "I need to talk to you," she said, crossing her arms over her Guns N' Roses T-shirt. "Both of you."

I gestured for her to go on.

"You were in the alley last night when Samira and I came out of the club after she fought with Tyson."

Laurent and I exchanged a glance.

"We don't care," she said, waving a hand at us, "about that. But the police are asking questions. We are hoping you will not tell them about her fight with Tyson."

"I already spoke to them," I said. "I didn't say anything."

"I didn't either," Laurent said.

"Oh, good." Her body sagged with relief as she leaned against the doorframe of the bathroom. "You know how these things can be. We don't want them to get the wrong idea."

"Of course," I said. Though I couldn't promise I'd continue to cover for Samira. As much as I sympathized with her for what Tyson had put her through, she did have reason to kill him. "How's Samira doing?"

"Not great." Gisèle pulled at a thread on her cutoff jean shorts. *"Their relationship was complicated, you know. But she did love him. She feels terrible that they were fighting last night. But it wasn't her fault. He wasn't . . . easy."*

"I know," I said, wondering if the same could have been said for her first husband. "Did you talk to the police yet?"

She nodded. "They asked us all to come to the salon."

"I should change," Laurent said, rising and going to the door. "I'll see you upstairs."

Gisèle followed him out, but I stayed put for a moment, thinking.

Laurent clearly knew something he wasn't letting on. I wished he trusted me enough to tell me whatever it was, because if he couldn't trust me, that meant I couldn't trust him, either.

Whatever I'd told myself about there being no danger in developing actual feelings for him, I had to admit I liked him more than I'd intended. But no matter my feelings or how genuine he seemed, he'd had opportunity to kill Tyson, and depending on whether whatever secret Tyson held over him was worth murder, possibly motive as well.

My heart sank.

I so badly wanted to trust him. And I could use his help, if I was going to try to find out who'd done this. Which I realized wasn't my place, of course. But it was in my best interest, and my brain was already working to put the pieces of the puzzle together, whether or not I wanted it to.

The same way my heart was finding ways to defend Laurent, whether or not I wanted it to.

Which was exactly why now, more than ever, I needed to maintain control, to repair the walls I'd so sloppily left unguarded. But if I was going to try to solve this—which, okay, obviously I was—I did need someone's help, and Laurent was likely the most willing candidate.

I couldn't trust him, though, couldn't confide in him or get lost in those absurdly blue eyes.

No matter my ill-advised affection for him, he was a suspect now.

We were all suspects.

CHAPTER 28

I emerged from the stairwell to find the sun low in the sky, glinting off the water and bathing the main deck in its golden rays. The soft notes of a melancholy song hung in the air, courtesy of Gisèle, who sat at the baby grand piano, fingers caressing the keys.

Jennifer listened with her eyes closed from a nearby chair while Rémy and Laurent talked in low tones at the bar. Samira sat alone on a couch that looked out toward the shining sea.

I'd just settled onto a divan near the piano when Officers Lambert and Gauthier came down the stairs, followed by Cody and Allison. They hesitated at the base of the stairwell for a moment, listening to Gisèle play until she noticed them and stopped midphrase, leaving the notes ringing.

"Is everyone here?" Lambert asked.

We gathered in the sitting area near the bar, Gisèle coaxing Samira into joining us with an arm around her waist as though she was an invalid. In her long black dress, Samira was a picture-perfect young widow, her shoulders slumped, her face tear-streaked.

But as she collapsed into a chaise longue, pushing her sunglasses up on her head to reveal red-rimmed eyes, I couldn't help but wonder whether she could possibly be as sad as she appeared to be. Yes, love was complicated, but her vitriol toward her husband last night had seemed much more deep-seated than a lovers' spat—not to mention whatever was going on between her and Gisèle.

The officers hovered at the edge of our seating area. "This is everyone from the dive, no?" Lambert asked.

"There were additional Search and Rescue divers with us when we recovered him," Rémy volunteered.

"We do not need them," Lambert said. He paused, his piercing eyes lingering on each of us in turn before he finally cleared his throat. "We have reason to believe that Mr. Dale's death was not an accident."

A strangled noise escaped Samira's throat as everyone stared at him, their faces etched with shock. Cody and Allison exchanged a glance. "What do you mean?" Cody asked.

"His death appears to be a homicide."

"He was . . . murdered?" Jennifer asked, her eyes wide.

"Mon Dieu," Samira murmured, dropping her head into her hands. Gisèle scooted closer to her, wrapping an arm around her trembling shoulders.

Looking around, I noticed that the captain was the only representative of the crew, leaning against the bar with his leathery arms crossed over his chest. The rest of the crew seemed to have evaporated—sent away by the police so as not to hear the grisly details of Tyson's demise, I assumed.

"Why didn't you tell us this to begin with?" Cody demanded.

"We wanted to be sure before we shared this development with you," Lambert said.

Gauthier nodded, putting his stamp of approval on this message. But I knew it wasn't true. Laurent said they'd known immediately when they found Tyson that he'd been murdered, and if Laurent knew it, surely the police did as well. No, they were withholding that information in the hope that someone would slip up and give them a lead worth pursuing.

I felt sick, thinking how I might have unwittingly done just that by keeping the blackmail scheme from them. But no one knew about it, except for Cody, who had as much interest in keeping it under wraps as I did.

I thought of the arrest report I'd left on Tyson's pillow last night. He'd never see it now, but the police would find it when they searched the house. Would they know the significance of it? And would they show it to Cody? Tyson's duplicity had been spelled out in the small print all along, if Cody had ever cared to look. But clearly he hadn't.

I'd never really wanted to tell Cody about his brother's deceit; I'd only planned to use the arrest report as collateral so that Tyson would let me go home unscathed. It would be a cruel twist of fate for Cody to discover the depth of his brother's deception now that Tyson was dead.

As Lambert went on to describe how Tyson's oxygen had been turned off, I feigned surprise, scanning the faces of the others in the room for any signs of guilt. Cody was clearly distraught, while Allison was more stunned; Samira was a wreck; Jennifer and Gisèle were appropriately disturbed and supportive of their significant others; Laurent and Rémy were fittingly resigned.

"But who killed him?" Jennifer asked once Lambert had finished explaining all the things Laurent had already told me.

"That is what we will find out," Lambert said.

"Did you talk to the developers who—" Cody started.

"They were diving with GoPro cameras mounted to their chests that recorded their entire dive," Lambert cut him off. "We've reviewed the footage, and they are no longer suspects."

"Wait, you don't think one of *us* did it?" Jennifer interjected, her tone incredulous.

"Everyone who was in the water at the time of Mr. Dale's death today is a suspect," Lambert confirmed wearily.

Laurent met my eyes as a ripple of dismayed murmurs went around the room.

Cody looked at the captain, the only one in the room not implicated. "Not a word of any of this to the crew," he said.

The captain nodded.

"We recognize that this is a delicate matter and have agreed not to report the fact of Mr. Dale's death until tomorrow morning, which will give you time to make your own announcement. As this is an active murder investigation, we will not disclose any facts about the case, including the manner of death, and we encourage you to keep the details private so that the investigation can proceed without interference from the public. Any questions?"

Everyone just stared at them, dumbfounded.

"You will stay here overnight. Please do not plan to leave St. Barth's. Our office will be in touch," Lambert finished, turning to march across the pool deck toward the stern, Gauthier on his heels.

No one spoke until the engine of the police boat fired to life, when finally Allison voiced what we were all thinking. "They think one of us did it," she said.

Samira lay back on the divan, flinging an arm across her eyes.

"She should eat something," Gisèle said. "She hasn't had anything but alcohol since this morning."

Outside, the sun sank toward the sea, sending amber rays bouncing around the boat, the beautiful, calm evening at odds with the tense mood aboard the yacht.

"Where's the crew?" Jennifer asked, looking toward the captain.

"We've asked them to leave us alone unless summoned so that we can talk freely," Cody said.

"Dinner will be served on the deck of the game room at seven, which is in thirty minutes," the captain said. "You can ring me or the kitchen if you need anything before that."

Nods all around as he took leave of us and disappeared through the crew door.

I caught Laurent's eye and nodded toward the balcony.

He rose and I followed, joining him by the railing where we'd stood earlier this afternoon before we knew the turn the day would take.

"You have friends on the crew?" I asked, gazing out over the luminescent water toward the boats bobbing on the horizon.

He nodded. "Some."

"I need to get into the security room so I can tap into the cameras.".

"Why?"

Because while I realized I should probably let the police do their job, I'd seen them fail enough in my line of work that I couldn't trust them to do that. What if they got it wrong, and Samira went to jail when Allison had done it? Or Cody went to jail when Samira had done it? Or what if they started digging into our past and decided *I* was to blame? I couldn't let that happen.

"Because we're on that suspect list," I said. "And I have the best chance of anyone of finding out who did this."

He nodded. "Give me ten minutes. I'll see what I can do."

CHAPTER 29

Ten minutes later, I was in front of a bank of computer screens in the windowless security room belowdecks, staring at a grid of camera feeds throughout the boat.

Marielle glanced into the hallway as she shut the door behind us and came to stand behind me, next to Laurent. "There's another page," she said, pointing to the arrows at the bottom of the page.

I thanked her, but I was after more than a glimpse of the camera feeds. I needed to link them to my computer so that I could access them remotely whenever I wanted, and that required getting into the operating system, which I was pretty sure Marielle was not going to be comfortable with. Which meant I needed to get rid of her.

"This may take a minute," I said, clicking into the settings of the page.

She checked her watch, nervous. "How long? I have to serve dinner in fifteen minutes."

"It won't take longer than that," I promised. "Why don't you go ahead?"

"I don't know," she said, uneasy. "I'm not supposed to—"

"You're doing us a big favor," I said, buttering her up. "We don't want to get you in trouble. If you're not here, it won't be your ass on the line if anyone catches us."

"Right." She looked over my shoulder at the bank of cameras. "Unless they check the tape and see me letting you in here."

"Watch this," I said, clicking into the video. I snipped out the footage of us entering the security room and patched it with a clip of the static feed of the empty hallway so that the time stamp didn't jump. "See? We were never here."

"Oh, you're good," she said, impressed.

"It's really not that hard," I demurred, throwing her a smile.

She shook her head. "I can hardly do a Zoom call."

I laughed, hoping my friendliness was having the intended effect. "Well, I bet you know your way around a yacht a lot better than I do."

She nodded, looking from Laurent to me. "We won't mess anything up, we promise," Laurent swore.

"Okay," she said. "If anyone comes, the door was unlocked."

"I'll snip your exit too," I offered.

She nodded. "I'll see you at dinner in fifteen."

She slipped out the door and I went to work, my fingers flying over the keys while Laurent watched, standing behind me with his arms crossed. I threw a glance at him.

"What?" he asked.

"You're making me self-conscious," I said.

He laughed. *"Don't be. I'm amazed by what you can do."*

I tried to forget he was there as I peeled back the front-facing part of the server and located the code within that would allow me to access the cameras from outside the system, leaving no trace. I would have to hack into the Wi-Fi from my computer as well so that I could connect to the internet, but in comparison to what I was doing now, that would be a cakewalk.

"Shit," Laurent said when I'd been at it for about ten minutes, pointing at the feed from the camera in the hallway directly outside our door. "Someone is coming down the hall. I don't know that guy."

I glanced around the small room. There was nowhere to hide unless you crawled under the desk, which was in full view of the door, so not really a hiding place at all. "I'm almost done here," I said, sending myself what I needed.

"He's right outside," Laurent whispered urgently.

In a flash, I'd restored the page, but it was too late. On the screen, I could see the guy just outside the door. Laurent grabbed my hand, pulling me out of the chair and spinning me until my back was against the wall.

Our eyes locked and my heart quickened as he slipped an arm around my back, drawing me closer.

This was exactly what I'd promised myself I wouldn't do—but it was a ruse, I justified as our lips met, our tongues tangling as we made out with abandon, my hands in his hair, his pushing up my skirt. My body lit up like a phosphorescent sea as he pressed me into the wall. It was a tactic, sure, but I was enjoying every second of it, and I knew he was too as I wrapped one of my legs around his, my inhibitions negated by the need to put on a show for the guy I could hear pushing the door open behind me.

We didn't stop when he stepped inside, pulling up short. "Oh," he muttered, thrown.

Laurent and I separated, playing at being embarrassed. "Oh," I said, still panting.

"This room is private," he said.

"Sorry," Laurent said. "We were just looking for a place to—"

"I see," the guy said, looking away as I straightened my clothes. "Please." He gestured to the door.

"Please don't say anything to anyone," I said, batting my eyes. "He could get in trouble."

He nodded. "Please, go out."

"You got it," I said, threading my fingers through Laurent's as we slunk out the door, acting sheepish.

In the hallway outside the room, he again pulled me toward him, playfully biting my earlobe. "You know he's watching that camera," he whispered, his breath hot on my neck. "I'm just making sure he believes our story."

I knew it wasn't necessary, that I couldn't trust him and shouldn't let it happen again. But what was one more kiss? I tilted my face to his and my body flooded with pleasure as our lips met, my reservations melting in the heat between us.

"We're gonna be late for dinner," I murmured into his mouth, breathless.

He took my lip between his teeth, teasing, before pulling away just far enough to lock eyes with me. "We could skip it," he suggested.

I flushed as my body responded with a resounding yes. But we both knew skipping wasn't really an option—not to mention the decision I'd made just an hour ago not to trust him. "Ha," I said, pulling away. "We need to be there."

A hint of a smile flickered across his face as he ran a hand over my hair, smoothing it.

"What?" I asked.

"Nothing," he said. "Let's go."

CHAPTER 30

We were anchored with the bow facing the island, which meant the view from the stern was of the open sea, punctuated by the jagged rock we'd stared at while we waited for news of Tyson— a stunning vista, if it were not for the morbid memory it now evoked. The table was situated at the end of the game deck, open to the tranquil evening, where the sun had melted beyond the horizon, leaving the sky awash in shades of pink and purple. A light breeze blew off the calm water, flickering the candles and fluttering the petals of the white hibiscus in low vases.

Rémy was alone at the table facing the view, playing some sort of game on his phone. He quit the game and gave me a brief smile as I approached, and my eyes caught on the glowing image on his lock screen: two pugs, one with a pink bow tie, the other with a blue one. A strange sense of déjà vu came over me as I stared at the image.

"Cute dogs," I commented, sliding into the banquette across from him. "I love pugs. I had one growing up."

"Oh," he said, staring at the picture. "Oui. Merci. Mister and Sister. Faces only a mother loves." He laughed. "But of course, I am the mother."

"They have English names?" I asked.

"My partner, he is English," Rémy said.

"Ah. Well, they're adorable," I said, racking my brain for why the hell I would know Rémy's dogs when I hadn't even known he had dogs until thirty seconds ago.

Suddenly it struck me. The dog shit. The pile I'd so unexpectedly stepped in on the helipad what felt like years ago but was actually mere hours ago. The woman who'd helped me had said there were two pugs here earlier.

It seemed like a stretch, but was so coincidental that I had to wonder whether the pugs that were here this morning could possibly be Rémy's. But what on earth would they be doing on the boat? Could his partner be the person whose name Tyson had refused to divulge? That too seemed awfully coincidental.

I glanced at Rémy, but before I could ask him a follow-up question, Samira collapsed next to me on the banquette. She was no longer crying, but clutching the stem of her martini with a steel grip, as though it was all that was keeping her afloat. I noticed that her hand shook as she brought the glass to her lips and drained it. She looked so fragile.

In her current state it seemed implausible she could have killed her husband, but she certainly had a motive, and she was an actress.

Laurent slid in on the other side of me, while Gisèle claimed the chair next to Samira at the head of the table, never more than arm's distance from her friend. Gisèle, who'd been there when Samira's first husband died, too. Another coincidence?

"Should I go get Cody and Allison?" Jennifer asked, glancing toward the stairs that led up to the office as she hovered behind the seat next to Rémy.

No one answered, and she eventually sat.

White wine was already poured in our goblets and our plates brimmed with Lyonnaise salad, topped with bacon strips and a poached egg. I ripped off a piece of warm French bread, salivating as I coated it with salted butter.

"I'm starving," Jennifer said, picking up a strip of bacon with her fingers. "I can't wait for them."

Samira simply stared at her food as the rest of us tore into our dinner like a pack of wild animals. It felt inappropriate to enjoy such delicious food at a time like this, but we had to eat, and it was impossible not to appreciate the taste of the chef's efforts. I wondered whether Tyson would have rolled back his rules to dine with us tonight or sulked from his spot at the head of the table, disapproving of our vulgar appetites while he slurped his murky green concoction. What a tragedy that he'd had all this, and not been able to enjoy it.

I'd just finished my salad when Cody and Allison finally emerged from the office, looking spent.

"Everything okay?" Jennifer asked as Cody took his place at the head of the table.

Cody frowned at her as though she was speaking a language he didn't understand. "Okay?" he echoed.

I liked Cody—had always liked Cody—and he certainly seemed broken up about his brother's death, but I couldn't help thinking of their fight this morning. Had Cody finally had enough of Tyson's shit and snapped?

And what of Allison, whose perennial mask of impassivity made her so difficult to read? She reached for her wineglass as she settled next to Rémy, her sleeveless gray silk camisole showing off her toned arms. She was certainly strong enough to have killed Tyson, and quicker than any of us in the water. And she had cause, with Tyson standing between her and the money she needed. It wasn't hard to imagine her taking him out.

Cody had just opened his mouth to speak when a handful of crew members emerged from the stairwell bearing a second course of cheese soufflés steaming in individual ramekins. He held his tongue as they set them before us. "We'll let you know when we're ready for the next course," Cody said once they'd refilled our wineglasses. "Please, leave us until then."

"There is a phone there." One of the girls pointed to the wall. "Ring the kitchen when you are ready."

Cody nodded, and they all filed down the stairs and out of sight.

But he seemed to have thought better of whatever he had been about to say. Instead, he raised his wineglass in a toast. "To my brother, on his birthday." His voice cracked. "Tyson always marched to the beat of his own drum. Yes, we all know he could be difficult, but he was also a genius—as he so often reminded us—and he did more good for the world than . . . than . . ." He broke off, choked up.

"To Tyson," Allison finished for him, stoic. "A giant among men."

Everyone raised their glass and drank, except Samira, who clasped her goblet to her chest, her tears splashing into her wine. Gisèle reached out to pat her on the back. "Have some bread," she encouraged. "It's still warm."

Jennifer considered Samira from across the table, her head slightly tilted. After a moment, Samira looked up at her, not bothering to wipe the tears that cut tracks down her puffy face. "What?" she demanded.

Jennifer shook her head. "Nothing."

"You are looking at me like that all evening," Samira said. "If you have a problem with me, say it."

"I don't have a problem," Jennifer said, raising her hands.

"We're all upset tonight," Cody said, rubbing his temples. "Let's not—"

"No. I want to hear what she has to say," Samira said, her eyes focused on Jennifer.

"It's just . . ." Jennifer sighed. "He treated you like shit."

"He treated everyone like shit," Samira returned, "because of the great insecurity inside of him."

"It's true," Cody murmured.

"Okay, sure," Jennifer said. "But last night—I know you were all drunk, but I wasn't. I remember clearly every vile thing he said to you. And you told him you hated him, you wished he was dead—"

"Do you have to remind me?" Samira choked back a sob. "We were fighting, I was angry. It doesn't mean I didn't love him. I didn't mean—" Samira stopped, inhaling sharply. "Mon Dieu, you can't think I killed him?"

Her shock seemed incongruous, considering that everyone who's ever watched a true-crime show knows nine times out of ten it's the spouse.

Jennifer shook her head, though. "I'm not saying that. But if I were you, I might have."

"It's true you stand to gain the most," Allison said, studying Samira.

Samira's head whipped toward her, her jaw slack for a moment before she let out a bitter bark of laughter. "We were married only fourteen months. I do not get a cent until we are married three years."

"That's the prenup, not the will," Allison said.

Samira sighed. "He assured me it was for both. Everything goes to his children."

I took a sip of water to wash down the bite of soufflé that had lodged in my throat as Jennifer shook her head, mystified. "And you still loved him?"

"Oui—yes, yes!" Samira cried. "Did I always like him? No. Would I have been married to him forever? Probably not. But I did not murder him."

Samira was certainly convincing, and my heart went out to her, but that didn't mean it wasn't entirely possible that she was acting the part of the grieving wife.

"Okay, if we're going to play this game"—Allison fixed her eyes on Gisèle, a hint of amusement playing around her lips—"was it you?"

"Me?" Gisèle furrowed her brow, bewildered. "No. Why would I—"

"For Samira," Allison said, as if it were the most obvious thing in the world. "So she could be free of him."

Gisèle's mouth opened slightly as she stared at Allison, dumbfounded. "I did not kill him," she said finally. "But you are right I am not so sad about his death." She glanced at Samira apologetically, softening her voice as she switched to French. *"He dimmed your light and I am glad for your sake that he is gone."* She returned her focus to Allison. "What about you? You were under the water longer than anyone."

"And it's no secret that both Cody and I disagreed with him on a lot of things," Allison admitted. "I'd be a liar if I said I didn't fantasize about killing him sometimes."

Cody gave Allison a discomfited glance. "Don't bring me into this."

"But I didn't do it," Allison said. "Not that I'd tell you if I did," she added dryly. "I'm just saying, we all had a motive. Even you might have killed him on Cody's behalf, Jennifer."

"Okay, okay," Cody said.

But Allison was on a roll, turning to Laurent. "And I don't know what it was that he was holding over your head, but he trusted you, and he never trusted anyone he couldn't ruin." She pointed her fork at me and Rémy. "Even you two. I don't know either of you, but you show up and then he's dead. That's pretty suspicious."

Beneath the table, I felt Laurent's fingers brush my thigh, lingering on my skin, and I wished I could trust him. But would he trust me, if I told him the whole truth?

"I never met Tyson before today," Rémy said.

"How do we know you are not lying?" Gisèle asked, her tone more sardonic than accusatory. "You could be anyone. You could be a person you hire to kill."

Jennifer guffawed. "A hit man?"

I'd had the same thought, of course. But while it was possible, it was also improbable. This wasn't a spy novel. What I found more intriguing was the question of Rémy's dogs. Did he have a connection to Tyson that neither of them had wanted anyone to know? And whatever that connection was, could it have driven Rémy to kill him?

Rémy shrugged. "I could be this hit man, maybe. But, no. I did not kill Tyson."

"And neither did I," Cody said, his patience growing thin. "This is ridiculous."

"It will be more easy to run the company without him, no?" Gisèle prodded, her gaze bouncing between Cody and Allison.

"No." Cody's chair scraped the deck as he pushed it back and stood. "You know nothing about it."

Samira raised her chin, a note of warning in her voice. "You will be surprised how much he told me."

"At this point, I wouldn't be surprised by anything my brother did,"

Cody said darkly as he strode toward the phone on the wall. "But that doesn't mean I had anything to do with his death."

"Which brings me back to my earlier point," Allison said coolly. "Tyson was a complicated man, and we all had complicated relationships with him. It doesn't do us any good to turn on each other."

"But one of us did kill him," Jennifer pointed out.

"And that person isn't going to confess just because you accuse them," Allison leveled.

She was right about that. Accusations would only make the killer more careful about covering their tracks.

"We'd like dinner now," Cody said into the receiver. "And please send up staff to take care of us. We no longer wish to be left alone."

He hung up and spun to face the table. "Enough of this. We'll have a civil dinner."

As he sat heavily into his chair, running his fingers through his hair exactly the way his brother used to, I had to blink to make sure I wasn't seeing a ghost.

CHAPTER 31

Shortly after the chateaubriand arrived, I excused myself from the table. The steak was delicious, but I realized this might be the only time before we left the boat tomorrow that everyone was in one place, allowing me to slip away and explore their rooms.

No matter their protests, someone at this table was a killer, and I didn't want to think about what might happen to me if that person caught me snooping.

No one asked where I was going, but as Samira moved aside to let me out of the banquette, I muttered something about needing to take my medicine. I had no medicine, but I didn't want anyone to wonder why I felt the need to go all the way downstairs, when there was a powder room on the other side of the game room, just a few steps away.

Unfortunately, the entry to the primary suite was up the stairs, which were in full view of the table, so instead I hurried down the staircase, hoping for the chance to pop into Cody's and Allison's rooms on the main deck. But that was not to be, either, as the staff was busy in the lounge cleaning up our mess from earlier in the evening.

"Can I help you?" one of the girls asked as I passed.

"Just forgot something in my room," I said.

I scurried down to the cabin level, relieved to find it quiet and empty, and slipped into my room, where I disconnected my phone from the charger and pocketed it. I had just stepped back into the hallway when a crew girl carrying cleaning supplies came down the stairs. She smiled at me as she went into Rémy's room.

That left me a choice between Gisèle's and Laurent's rooms.

It was only becoming harder for me to be impartial about Laurent, so if he was involved in Tyson's death, the sooner I found out about it, the better. With a furtive glance over my shoulder, I quietly opened the door to his cabin and slipped inside.

It was laid out exactly like mine, a queen-size bed centered in the room, the gym clothes he'd been wearing earlier left in a pile on the comforter, next to his open canvas duffel bag. Feeling like a traitor, I ruffled through his stuff, relieved when I found nothing out of the ordinary. I extracted a French paperback and flipped through it, but Laurent was apparently not a person who annotated as he read.

His bookmark, however, caught my attention.

It was a printed receipt from a company called EazyShip, for the amount of €3,950 for the transport of one 1995 Land Rover Defender from St. Barth's to Port of Calais, France, departing on April 10.

That was roughly three weeks from now. Laurent hadn't mentioned shipping his car back to France, but perhaps he was selling it, or giving it to a family member? Regardless, I snapped a photo of the paper and replaced the book in the bag, then stepped into the hallway, taking comfort in the fact that I hadn't found any incriminating evidence in his room.

I could hear the vacuum going in Rémy's cabin, so I stole across the hallway to Gisèle's.

Her room was a mirror of mine and Laurent's, her silver hard-shell suitcase stowed in the corner, two dresses hanging in the closet. The bathroom was spotless, her matching monogrammed toiletries and makeup bags resting on the counter. I hoisted Gisèle's suitcase onto the bed and unlatched it to find her clothes neatly folded inside.

I'd just started to go through a stack of T-shirts when I heard the door to Rémy's room open and close. I looked desperately around for a place to hide, but the closet was tiny, the bed built into the floor. Praying that the maid would go into Laurent's room, I darted into the bathroom, closing myself inside just as I heard the door open and someone enter. I held my breath, listening to the maid whistle as she began to clean Gisèle's room. There was nowhere to hide in the tiny bathroom, not so much as a shower curtain. I had to get rid of her before she came in and found me.

I swallowed my nerves.

"*Excusez-moi,*" I said in French, manipulating my voice as much as I could to sound like Gisèle's. "*I'm in the bathroom. Can you come back later please?*"

"*Oh!*" I could hear the surprise in the girl's voice. "*I'm so sorry, I didn't know you were here. I'll come back.*"

I breathed a sigh of relief as the door closed. I could hear her entering my cabin next door as I stepped into Gisèle's bedroom and bent over her suitcase, quickly returning the items I'd removed to their places.

But as I restacked her T-shirts, I noticed that the bottom of the suitcase was uneven.

I removed the shirts once more and swept my hand over the nylon fabric. There was something under it, though there didn't appear to be another packable compartment beneath. I moved her bag of swimsuits to see that the lining had been ripped at one end, the slash in the fabric hidden by clothes.

I reached my hand into the slit, and my fingers immediately struck what felt like a stack of paper bills. My jaw dropped as I removed what, according to the band around it, was €10,000.

Jackpot.

I stuck my hand back into the suitcase and extracted another, then another, and another stack of hundreds. I'd taken out twenty-five stacks—amounting to two hundred fifty thousand euros—when I heard the door to my room open and close.

There was still more money in the compartment, and I could see the fabric on the other side had a rip in it as well, but I was running out of time. I snapped a picture of the money I'd extracted, then put it all back, carefully arranging the clothes as they had been before returning the suitcase to its rightful place.

The gears in my brain turned as I stepped out of Gisèle's room, my phone gripped tightly in my hand. The cash had to be the €500K Tyson had pulled out of the bank to give his blackmailer at the missed meeting this evening. I could think of no other reason Gisèle would have that much cash. She must have taken it to hide it from the police before they searched the boat earlier.

Which raised two questions: First, was Samira aware she'd taken it? And second, did she—or they—know what it was intended for?

I realized the answer might be on the camera feed, but I still needed to hack into the Wi-Fi and download the software to connect to the cameras, which I knew would take me more time than I could afford to spend right now.

The maid was currently in Laurent's cabin, but she'd already done Rémy's, which meant I was probably safe there. With a glance over my shoulder, I slunk across the hallway into Rémy's room, quietly closing the door behind me.

On the floor of his closet I found a black-and-gray Gucci overnight bag, which seemed extravagant for a dive instructor, but this was St. Barth's. God only knew what his going rate was. Inside were neatly folded clothes—all high-end labels—and a matching Gucci Dopp kit. But the drawers were empty, and his phone was with him at the table.

Satisfied that his room contained no answers to the pug question, I checked my watch. Shockingly, I'd been gone only seven minutes. If I took the exterior stairs up to the primary level, I might just have time to do a quick sweep of Samira's room before I returned to the table.

I flew up the stairs to find the crew vacuuming the main deck. No one paid any attention as I exited the side door.

The sky was dark, save for the moon reflecting on the black water. I could see the gleam of St. Martin in the distance, and the twinkling lights of other boats at sea, but we were alone in our bay. No floodlights blazed, the side deck lit only by the path lights as I stole toward the bow, where I'd noticed an exterior staircase earlier.

Outside, I quietly ascended the stairs, past the pickleball and basketball courts on the game level to the private deck off the primary level, where I paused, listening. I could hear voices filtering up from the game room as I exited the stairwell. The lights were dim on the deck but blazed inside the office, making it easy to determine that no one was inside.

I slipped through the hatch, my heartbeat thudding in my ears as I dashed toward Samira's room like a thief in the night, casting furtive glances over my shoulder. There was no denying I was up to something now, if I happened upon anyone. I stood still for a moment at the door straining to hear whether there was anyone inside, and when I was satisfied it was empty, placed my hand on the doorknob and turned.

CHAPTER 32

Luck was on my side. Samira and Tyson's room was indeed empty. Though the humidifier was no longer running, the faint scent of rosemary and sage lingered in the dimly lit room as if Tyson had just walked out, sending a chill up my spine. The gray silk blackout drapes over the windows were closed, the clothes Samira was wearing earlier folded neatly on a chair.

I quickly opened and closed the drawers of the bedside tables, but they were all bare, and her closet contained nothing more than a solitary dress and a few things folded on the shelves. I unzipped her Louis Vuitton overnight bag and riffled through it, finding only a black satin negligée and a change of clothes.

A noise on the other side of the closed door drew my attention and I froze, my nerves standing on end as I quickly scanned the room for a place to hide. The nearly empty closet was too risky, the bathroom too far. I gasped as the doorknob turned, and seeing no other option, darted behind the nearest set of curtains.

I held my breath as the door swung silently inward.

Praying I was out of sight, I pressed myself against the window behind me, aware that anyone who walked past outside would see me clear as day. I could feel my heart thumping in my chest so loudly, I was afraid it would be audible to whoever was standing in the entrance to the room.

Through the gap where the panels of curtains met, I watched as Allison entered, looking as guilty as I must have.

She surveyed the room, her shoulders tense, then strode toward the bed and jerked open the drawers in the bedside tables just as I had, only less carefully. She spun, moving in and out of my field of vision as she scanned the room, clearly looking for something—something specific, it seemed; something she knew should be here. Her gaze went to Samira's empty suitcase, then to the door to her closet, then to another suitcase on the opposite side of the room, which had to be Tyson's.

It struck me as odd that the police hadn't taken Tyson's bag as evidence, until Allison turned it upside down and I saw that it, too, was empty. I lost her for a moment when she entered Tyson's closet, but she quickly reemerged empty-handed. I held my breath as she strode toward Samira's closet and yanked open the door, not two feet from where I was hidden.

The curtains billowed with the rush of air; my nose suddenly tickled. No. I couldn't sneeze. My eyes watered as I moved my hand noiselessly to my nose and rubbed it violently, willing the tickle to subside. Allison hastened from the closet to the bathroom, and I stifled the smallest sneeze.

Should I risk exiting while she was in the bathroom? But she'd left the bathroom door ajar, and I could hear her rummaging around in there. I was likely better off right where I was. As long as I didn't sneeze. I squeezed my eyes shut, wrinkling my nose.

My eyelids flew open as Allison burst out of the bathroom, desperately clenching and unclenching her fists as she studied the room. I could practically see the waves of anxiety radiating off her. She clearly hadn't found whatever it was that she was looking for.

She lunged at the bed, feeling beneath the pillows to no avail before lifting the mattress and reaching her hand beneath. I saw the relief hit her before she withdrew her hand, gripping a manila envelope. She opened the top and peered inside, then, satisfied with whatever its contents were, lifted her shirt and tucked it into her pants. With the envelope hidden, she righted the pillows and exited the room as quickly as she'd entered.

I deliberated for only a moment before I pushed aside the curtains and darted across the room, slipping out the door behind her.

The few seconds I'd waited to follow Allison had given her enough time to vacate the primary level, but I knew she'd likely use the outdoor staircase to avoid detection by the staff, so that was the direction I went as well.

When I reached the game deck, it appeared dinner was over, the guests dispersed. Only Rémy sat at the bar, his face lit by his phone. I crept down another set of stairs and along the dimly lit outer walkway on the main level, trying to appear casual but also sticking close to the wall so that it would be harder for anyone inside to spot me. I was grateful for the cover of darkness as I edged closer to the long line of windows and peered inside, all the while scouring my brain for some explanation should Allison catch me following her. It did not escape me that if she was the killer, she might well kill again to protect her secret, if she thought I was on to her.

The living area was softly lit and deserted but for Allison, who stood in the center of the seating area closest to me looking toward the door to her bedroom, which I could see was partly open with a vacuum cleaner parked outside. Thwarted by the cleaning crew, she scanned the room, clearly assessing her options. I watched as she strode to the built-in bookshelves that framed the giant flat-screen television, pulled down a thick coffee-table-size book with a cover that showed a picture of a green door, and shoved the envelope inside.

As she replaced the book on the shelf, I retraced my steps to the exterior stairwell, darting up the stairs two at a time, exhilarated. All I needed to do was wait for that lounge to be empty, then I could retrieve the envelope and find out what it was that Allison had stolen from Samira's room.

Gratified by the results of my cursory search, I exited the stairwell on the game deck and went to the railing, pretending to simply be enjoying the view while I gave Allison a few minutes to clear out of the area before I returned to collect whatever she'd left inside the book.

I could feel my heart still thudding in my chest as I gazed across the dark water toward the twinkling lights of the island, plotting my next move.

The sound of swift footsteps behind me interrupted my reverie, and I turned.

CHAPTER 33

I awoke to crushing pain and voices conferring rapidly in French.

Where was I?

My eyes fluttered open to the sight of a light shining so brightly in my eyes that I quickly squeezed them shut again, my head throbbing.

"She's coming around," a man shouted in French.

"Give her space," a woman added.

I coughed, suddenly feeling as if I was drowning as salty water shot out of my mouth and nose, and I rolled onto my side.

"Audrey?" The voice was male, familiar.

I wheezed, my body racked with shivers as water dripped onto the deck, mixing with something darker. Red. Was I bleeding?

"I need you to open your eyes," the first man said, in English this time.

I obeyed, blinking up at a young man in a navy polo with a name tag that read EVAN. The name rang a bell, but I couldn't quite make the connection. "The light will be bright for a moment only."

I cringed as he shone the flashlight into my pupils. I could hardly see him for the red dots burned into my vision as he gave a similarly dressed woman the thumbs-up, seemingly satisfied with whatever he'd found in my eyes.

"Can you tell me, where are you?" Evan asked.

I looked around. I was on a boat. Tyson's yacht. My head pounded as it all came flooding back. Tyson was dead and I was on his boat. But why was I wet? And why was I lying on the sugar scoop, bleeding onto the teakwood planks?

"*Sea Ray,*" I answered, my voice hoarse. I coughed again. "What happened?"

"I saw you go over, and I jumped in after you," Cody answered.

I pushed up to my elbows to see Cody sitting on the deck a few feet away, panting and just as drenched as I was, an orange lifebuoy ring and expanse of tangled rope between us.

"I was on the deck below you when you fell, thank God," he explained, accepting a towel from a crew member.

As the red spots left by the flashlight waned, I could make out all of Tyson's guests, as well as the captain and what must've been the majority of the crew standing around us, their faces etched with concern. I realized the woman on her knees next to Evan was Marielle as she leaned forward and gently applied a towel to the back of my head. Pain seared through my skull as the towel made contact.

"Ah!" I cried out. "That really hurts."

"You hit your head," she said. "But do not worry, we do not think you have a . . ." She looked up at Laurent. "*Commotion cérébrale?*"

"Concussion," Laurent said, his face dark.

I could see he was angry, his eyes flashing as his glance went to the others, then back to me.

"Wait," I said, trying to recall. I remembered dinner had been tense. Then I'd left, found cash in Gisèle's suitcase . . . and Allison. The envelope. I remembered her storing it in a book and returning it to the shelf. Then . . . nothing. "How did I fall in the water?"

No one spoke as they exchanged uneasy glances.

"You were pushed," Laurent finally answered, his voice tense.

My body went cold as I realized the implication of his words.

"We don't know that," Allison said diplomatically.

I focused on Allison's calm countenance. Had she caught me following her and doubled back to push me off the boat? Her dark eyes met mine, ever impenetrable, and I was confident she would have no trouble eliminating me if she thought I was in her way.

"We should call the police," Laurent insisted.

It seemed this was not the beginning of this argument.

The captain looked from Cody to Samira, unsure who was in control now that Tyson was dead. "What do you want me to do?"

Samira's face crumpled. "I'm too tired to deal with the police again tonight."

"None of us want to talk to the police," Cody agreed. "And we don't know that she was pushed."

"If I wasn't pushed, why is my head bleeding?" I asked.

"You might have hit it on the way down," Evan chimed in.

"It does appear someone hit her in the head," Marielle dissented. "And pushed her over."

"Did anyone check for a weapon on the deck?" Jennifer asked.

"There was nothing," a crew guy somewhere behind her answered.

I pulled my knees into my chest, suddenly very afraid. One of the people on this boat had tried to kill me. And if not for Cody being in the right place at the right time, they might very well have succeeded.

"*Please, take her to the infirmary,*" the captain instructed Marielle.

"Can you stand?" Marielle asked me gently.

Evan slipped an arm around my back as I struggled to rise, and Laurent was quickly at my other side, helping me to my feet. My head felt like it had gone through a blender and nausea crested inside me as the edges of my vision darkened. I closed my eyes, trying to steady myself.

"*I can carry her,*" Laurent said. "*Is that okay?*" he asked me.

I wanted it to be okay, and while it was far more likely that it had been Allison who had tried to kill me than Laurent, I couldn't be sure. What if he dropped me now to finish what he'd started?

I shook my head, wincing. "I can walk."

The crowd parted to allow us through, their faces contorting in sympathy as I passed. Marielle and Justine, who I recognized as the girl who'd cleaned the dog shit off my foot earlier, trailed behind as Evan and Laurent walked me past the pool and main deck living area and through a door marked CREW at the end of the hall between Allison's and Cody's rooms.

On one side of the crew area was the industrial kitchen, on the other was what appeared to be a captain's office and a small infirmary, with one bed and shelves full of medicines and medical gadgets. Laurent and Evan sat me on the bed, and Marielle waved them out of the room. *"Okay,"* she said. *"I can take it from here."*

But Laurent lingered, casting a worried glance my way. "I can stay," he said.

"It's okay," I replied, nodding to Justine and Marielle. "I trust them."

"Please don't leave her alone," he said to the women, and they nodded.

"Actually, Laurent," I said—he turned, brows raised—"could you bring me the dress hanging in my closet?"

He nodded. "Of course."

Once he'd left, Marielle shut the door behind him and gave me a pain reliever, which I washed down with water, then asked me to turn onto my stomach so that she could evaluate the cut in the back of my head. "It is not so deep," she said. "But I must clean it and put the bandage."

Justine handed me a palm-size rubber ball to squeeze, tapping my shoulder to distract me as Marielle poured cleaning solution into the wound. I let out a yelp as my scalp burned with the heat of a thousand fires. "Sorry," she said, patting it dry. She showed me the bottle of derma-glue. "Now I put this to hold it together, and we are finished."

I gripped the ball as she applied the glue to the cut while Justine held my hair out of the way. "Has anyone checked the cameras?" I asked through clenched teeth as the adhesive dried.

Marielle and Justine exchanged a glance. "I don't know," Marielle said.

There was a knock at the door and Laurent's voice came from behind it. "I have the dress."

"Come in," I called.

He pushed open the door and hung the long blue dress from a cabinet, setting the towel he'd brought next to me on the bed. "How do you feel?" he asked.

He looked genuinely concerned, and I again wished I could trust him.

"I'm okay," I said. "My head hurts, but I'll live. Have they checked the camera feed?"

He nodded, and I could again see the anger simmering beneath his calm veneer. "The cameras were off," he said.

I gaped at him. It would be quite a coincidence if the cameras just happened to have shorted out right when someone tried to push me off the boat.

"You mean whoever pushed me disconnected them," I said, the hairs on my arms standing on end.

"That is what I told them, but the—" He stopped, glancing at Justine's and Marielle's backs as they put away the medical supplies. "Anyway, they were not working."

It would make sense for Allison to have turned off the cameras before sneaking into Samira's room, and once she realized I was following her, she would have known she could then push me overboard without its being recorded. You'd need some computer savvy to wipe the cameras, but it wasn't rocket science. I knew she was proficient enough with computers to have done it.

But hell, so was Cody—though he had jumped into the sea to save me—and Laurent would probably have been able to figure it out after watching me earlier today. With her TikTok experience, I didn't doubt Jennifer knew a thing or two about computers, and while Samira and Gisèle might not work in tech, they were young enough that I was pretty confident they knew their way around an operating system. My bet was on Allison, but until I was sure, I couldn't rule out any of them.

"Did you guys see anything?" I asked the three of them.

Justine shook her head. "We were in the kitchen, cleaning from dinner."

"I was on the cabin level, looking for you," Laurent said.

I nodded. "Give me a second to get changed."

Once Marielle had closed the door behind them, I peeled off my wet clothes and rinsed the seawater from my skin with fresh water from the sink, drying myself with the towel before pulling on the soft sleeveless dress. Using a rubber band I found in a drawer, I pulled my tangled hair back into a loose ponytail that covered my wound, then wiped off the mascara that had smudged beneath my eyes with the corner of the towel. I'd looked better, but my bedraggled appearance was the least of my concerns right now.

I opened the door to find Laurent waiting outside alone. "Where did Marielle and Justine go?" I asked.

"The captain called them," he said.

"What were you going to say about the cameras a minute ago?"

"The guy who came in when we—"

I nodded, remembering exactly what we'd been doing when the crew member had unexpectedly entered the control room.

"He said we were responsible for the problem with the cameras."

I frowned. "You and me?"

He nodded.

"But that's not true," I protested. "I did nothing to the camera feed, I just created an access point so that I could tap into it."

"I know," he said.

"So there's nothing on the cameras at all after we left there?" I asked.

"The entire feed is wiped." He laid a hand on my shoulder, his gaze troubled. "They are saying your fall was an accident."

CHAPTER 34

Laurent and I emerged from the stairwell on the game deck to find Rémy and Cody, now in dry clothes, engaged in a game of darts on the far side of the salon area where everyone else lounged, drinking champagne, seemingly all too glad to write my near death off as an unfortunate accident.

I paused, taking advantage of their self-absorption to observe them for a moment before they noticed us. Ever perceptive, Laurent stilled beside me.

The hair on the back of my neck stood up as I zeroed in on Allison, reconfirming my suspicions about her. She was leaning against the bar, a glass of champagne casually dangling from her hand, placid as the moonlit sea. If anyone on this boat could kill someone and get away with it, it would be perennially cool Allison. Anyone who'd seen her swim knew a cutthroat competitor lurked just beneath that calm exterior. And with Tyson gone, she'd be free to bring in an investor to pay off her debt.

Frustration curdled my blood. I was exhausted and scared; I wished more than anything that I knew without a doubt Allison was guilty. It would mean I'd have only one person to evade to avoid being killed myself, not a whole room full of them. But I knew better than to let my theory about one suspect hinder my ability to see the others.

"I guess the real question," Samira said from where she lay on the couch with her head in Gisèle's lap, "is which of you profits most from my husband's death."

No one answered.

Samira was displaying the biggest show of grief, which was fitting, but I kept coming back to the question of whether it was real? She might have glimpsed me leaving her room, recognized I might be on to her, and decided to make sure I couldn't out her. She'd certainly been resistant to having the police return tonight.

Though it would be almost too obvious for Samira to be Tyson's killer: the long-suffering spouse who'd already had one husband die under mysterious circumstances. Not to mention her insistence that she'd receive nothing in the will.

Regardless, it was possible she'd been pushed past her limit.

Or could it have been Gisèle—or better yet, the two of them together? And what of the money in Gisèle's suitcase? Had they somehow realized I'd found it and wanted to make sure I couldn't tell anyone? Yes, despite the cliché of it, they were both strong suspects.

My wound smarted as I watched as Rémy let a dart fly, striking the very bottom of the target. I recalled seeing him here in the game room, so close to where I'd gone over the railing, just a few minutes before my fall. Yet he claimed not to have seen anything. What reason might he have had to push me?

Cody's aim was surer, his dart flying directly into the board, a near bullseye. He grabbed his champagne glass and downed half of it in one gulp, brooding. But was his anguish over his brother's death or over the prospect of being caught? He'd saved me, which would be odd behavior for someone who had pushed me . . . unless of course he'd planned it that way. Which seemed like a big risk to take for an uncertain outcome.

All of this was bizarre, everyone sitting around swilling champagne like they were celebrating something when Tyson had been murdered and I'd nearly met the same fate less than an hour ago. It made me think of that Agatha Christie novel in which all the suspects had murdered the victim together.

All of them had reason to want Tyson dead. Could they all have been in on it?

Which would mean they'd all been in on the attempt to silence me as well.

Fear curled around my bones like an icy vine, making it hard to breathe.

Act normal, I reminded myself. While this was definitely the closest I'd ever come to being killed, it wasn't the first time my life had been threatened on the job. There were reasons I now carried a gun. And I knew from experience that whoever had attempted to murder me needed to think I wasn't a threat in order to be dissuaded from finishing off the job.

I watched as Jennifer leaned forward from her place on the couch and cut herself a slice of the chocolate cake that sat untouched in the center of the coffee table, "Happy Birthday, Tyson" scrolled on it in curling gold letters.

A birthday, I realized. That's what they were celebrating. The food and liquor had been purchased in anticipation of Tyson's birthday dinner tonight. Which was why they were drinking his Dom and eating his cake while he lay in a refrigerated cabinet somewhere, his blood congealing in his veins.

Had it been their plan all along?

The thought made me shudder.

"Oh," Jennifer said, catching sight of Laurent and me as she reached for a fork. "You're back. How are you feeling?"

Everyone's expressions were solicitous as they watched us approach, but I didn't buy their sympathy. They clearly weren't my friends. One of them had tried to kill me, and regardless of whether the rest had been in on it, they hadn't thought it necessary to call the police.

Jennifer patted the seat beside her on the sofa opposite Gisèle and Samira. "We were all so worried about you."

"Thanks," I said, perching next to her. *You catch more flies with honey.* I forced a pained smile. "They got me patched up."

Laurent made no attempt to disguise his wariness as he sat next to me, a German shepherd ready to attack. I couldn't say it wasn't attractive.

Rémy's dart went wide of the target and he cursed, swaying as he lined up his next shot. He wasn't the only one who seemed to have become a bit sloppier while I was being patched up. In fact, everyone but Jennifer appeared well oiled. Which could work to my advantage.

My head still pounded, though thanks to the glue and the pills, the pain wasn't quite as sharp as it had been. I couldn't give in to the cocktail of terror and exhaustion that swirled inside me. I was alone here, my fate hanging in the balance. One of these people wanted me dead, and no one but me—and possibly Laurent, if he was for real—seemed to give a shit.

"What happened when I went over the railing?" I asked, consciously not using the word "pushed." A light touch was always more effective.

"I'd just come out of our room and was heading up here when I saw you fall," Cody said, pulling his darts out of the target.

"Did you hear anything?" I asked. "A scuffle or a scream—"

Cody shook his head. "Nothing. I just saw a body, falling from the deck above. I didn't even register it was you until I jumped in after you. Someone on the crew heard me shout 'Man overboard' and threw me the donut."

"Were you with him?" I asked Jennifer.

She shook her head. "I was in our suite."

Alone. No alibi. Though it was hard to imagine rabbit-like Jennifer overpowering me. Or getting the better of Tyson, for that matter, especially with her subpar diving skills.

"What about you guys?" I asked Samira and Gisèle. "Did you see or hear anything?"

They both shook their heads. "We were smoking on the sun deck," Gisèle answered. "We heard the shouting after and came to see what happened."

Of course. They'd been alone together, as they had when Samira's last husband died. The thought gave me little comfort.

"What about you?" I asked Allison, wondering what fib she'd come up with to cover her tracks.

"I was in the powder room on the main deck," she said. "The steak did not agree with me."

It was a good lie. Simple, impossible to refute, a touch of embarrassment to prevent follow-up questions. And she showed no signs of dishonesty. But of course Allison would be a good liar.

"Did you see anything?" I asked Rémy.

"No, I was on the basketball court trying to get my phone to work," Rémy admitted. At Cody's disgruntled glance, he shrugged sheepishly. "Sorry. I was not able to call my partner and I know he is very worried about me."

"Do you remember what you were doing before you fell?" Cody asked.

I shook my head, feigning memory loss, though I remembered exactly what I'd been doing.

"Maybe you saw something in the water and leaned too far over the railing," Allison suggested.

"Or maybe one of you pushed her," Laurent said.

"But why would any of us push her?" Samira asked.

I wasn't about to admit to sneaking into their rooms. "Maybe the murderer wanted to use me as a scapegoat," I suggested. "It's a lot easier to pin a murder on someone who's not around to protest."

No one responded, the room so quiet that I could hear a motor somewhere out on the water.

Laurent rose and went to the bar, pouring himself a glass of Scotch. He leaned against the bar as he swilled it, looking more like someone who traveled on yachts than worked on them. His face was unreadable, his demeanor cool.

Not dissimilar to Allison, I realized.

Laurent was clearly a chameleon who was far sharper and more perceptive than the people he worked for realized. And there was the matter of whatever secret Tyson held over him. Could it have something to do with the car he was shipping back to France? Was he planning to make a break for it?

It would be just like me to fall for a guy who turned out to be a murderer.

But he did seem awfully protective of me since someone had tried to kill me. Which could just as easily be a cover as a sign that he genuinely cared. Regardless, I shouldn't risk being alone with him again until I had more information.

I shouldn't risk being alone with any of them.

The sudden sound of raised voices drew my attention to the back of the boat. Cody went out onto the open deck, followed by Rémy, as the rest of us sat up straighter, peering after them.

"What is it?" Allison asked, striding over to join them.

"There's a dinghy docked at the stern," Cody said, dropping his darts to a side table and jogging for the stairs.

"*Please turn around,*" I heard a crew member shout.

Alarmed, I rose and went outside to see a handful of crew members chasing a tall man dressed in black across the pool deck down below. He looked vaguely familiar, but I couldn't place him.

"*Sir, please,*" another crew member cried. "*You have to go back to your boat.*"

"Hey," Cody called out, marching toward him. He seemed to recognize the guy. "What are you doing here?"

As Laurent came to stand by me, the captain and another male crew member attempted to stop the man, but he was stronger and pushed right through them.

I could feel Laurent tense the minute he laid eyes on the man. "*Shit,*" he murmured, turning to bolt after Cody.

What the hell?

My pulse raced as I leaned over the railing, watching Laurent rush toward the man. "I got this," Laurent said to Cody.

But Cody didn't back down, following closely on Laurent's heels.

"*It was you,*" the man said, pushing Laurent squarely in the chest.

My hand flew to my mouth.

"Get the fuck off our boat," Cody said, drawing back his fist.

Laurent placed a hand over Cody's fist before he could do any damage. "I'll handle it."

The crew hovered around them, ready to step in, but Laurent waved them back. *"What are you doing here?"* Laurent asked the man.

"You knew," the man shouted at Laurent. *"You fucked me over."*

Next to me, Gisèle grabbed Samira's elbow. *"Is that the guy from the gray yacht?"* she whispered.

"Marcel," Samira confirmed.

I knew as she said it that she was right.

But what business did he have with Laurent?

Laurent waved him toward the sugar scoop at the stern, his level of confidence impressive. *"Let's talk down there,"* he said.

"Without them," the man said, pointing at the crew and Cody.

"It's okay," Laurent said to Cody. I could tell Cody didn't want to let him go, but Laurent was insistent. "It is my problem. I can handle it."

Disappointment weighed on me as I watched Laurent lead Marcel past the glowing pool. Even though I'd known he had secrets, that I shouldn't get attached to him and couldn't count him out as a suspect, seeing it play out before my eyes made me realize just how much hope I'd held out.

Once again, I'd been wrong.

CHAPTER 35

Laurent sank into the chair at the head of the dining table on the main deck, where we'd all gathered while waiting for him to finish talking to Marcel. It had been only ten minutes, but it had felt like a lifetime, my nerves standing on end while I waited for him to return, knowing that potentially one of the people seated at the table with me wished me dead.

"What the hell was that about?" Cody demanded.

In the soft light of the chandelier, I could see that the confrontation had drained Laurent. He grabbed the bottle of Scotch from the center of the table and topped up his glass. "I own the LLC that sold him the land," he admitted.

For once, Allison actually appeared surprised. "Wait, you're Ciel Bleu?"

Out on the water, the lights of the dinghy shrank into the distance, its motor growing quieter as Laurent nodded. "I inherited it from Bruno Leroy. The company was a shell for the land, which I sold most of to Marcel. I kept just enough to build my own home and lease a plot to De-Sal."

I felt a lightening of the pressure that had settled into my bones when Laurent chased the man onto the deck. *So this was his secret.* And while I was disappointed that he hadn't trusted me with it, it didn't seem a plausible reason to kill Tyson. And if he hadn't killed Tyson, he likely hadn't pushed me overboard either.

"Tyson knew about this?" Cody asked.

Laurent nodded, rubbing the bridge of his nose. "As you know, the lease on the center is a percent of revenue, so we both had interest in its approval."

"But you made tens of millions in that deal," Cody said. "Why are you still working as his butler?"

Laurent sighed. "Tyson and I had a common interest in the deal going through, and he agreed not to tell anyone I was Ciel Bleu while I worked for him."

"But he lied," Cody said.

Laurent nodded. "Marcel will not be back. There is nothing he can do, the deal is done."

"After this, there may not be a center in St. Barth's anyway," Allison muttered.

Laurent rose, extracting a pack of cigarettes from his pocket as he looked at me, his gaze an invitation. *"I need a smoke."*

Was his admission enough to definitively clear him of Tyson's murder? Maybe not, but I had to go with my gut instinct, which was screaming at me that I was a lot safer with him than I was with this pack of jackals. Ignoring the glances of the others at the table, I pushed my chair back and followed him.

When we reached the game deck, I paused, looking toward the place where I'd been standing when I was pushed. "I just want to see . . ."

He nodded, and I exited the stairwell and went through the hatch onto the walkway. Nothing seemed out of place; there was no debris, no sign of a struggle. The railing was hip-height on me, not so high that it would be impossible to fall overboard if you were incredibly drunk or uncoordinated. But I was neither, despite the number of times I'd been righted by Laurent's strong arms in the past few days.

I leaned out, scanning the hull for the kind of bloodstain that might have been left by my head striking the white siding. But the side of the yacht was pristine.

Laurent followed my gaze and understood. "You didn't hit your head on the boat," he said heavily.

"I didn't think I had," I said. "I just . . . held out some hope, I guess."

He gazed down at the inky water. "Whatever they hit you with is down there."

I nodded. "Unfortunately, the ocean has a way of destroying evidence."

We were quiet the rest of the way up the stairs, both of us lost in thought as we ascended. When we reached the sun deck, my head wound was pulsating from the exertion of climbing. I stopped, reaching for his Scotch, and tossed back half the glass, the burning in my throat briefly drawing my attention from the searing pain in my skull.

The lights were low, the night balmy as we threaded our way past the glowing spa toward the smoking area at the very precipice of the bow, where a small sign that read ZONE FUMEUR was affixed to the railing behind two built-in banquettes arranged in a V shape beneath the stars. We sat side by side facing the twinkling lights of the island, where a mix of modern mansions and older bungalows was built into the hillside above the dark beach. I could feel the whisky beginning to work, dulling the throbbing in my head as Laurent lit a hand-rolled cigarette.

"Bruno was the client you used to surf with, that gave you the car?" I asked.

He nodded. "He did not have family. He tried for years to bring De-Sal to the island, and he trusted me to do it once he was gone."

"Which you did."

He exhaled a line of smoke. "Sorry I did not tell you before."

"I understand," I said. "We've only known each other a few days."

Though so much had happened since we met that it felt like much longer than that.

"No one knows, except my family at home. I am moving back to Paris next month, after the De-Sal center breaks ground."

So that explained the shipment of his car. I was so relieved I could have cried. Or maybe that was the mixture of adrenaline, fear, and whisky coursing through my veins.

He cut his eyes to me, and despite the glue holding my scalp together, I felt the urge to forget our circumstances and pick up where we'd left off in the security room earlier. But my rational mind intervened, reminding me this wasn't the time for that. "I'd been following Allison when I got knocked over the railing," I said quietly.

He raised his brows, giving me his full attention as I caught him up with everything that had happened before I'd ended up in the sea.

"And you think this money was Tyson's?" he asked when I'd finished, zooming in on the picture of the stacks of euros I'd found in Gisèle's suitcase.

"It has to be the half a million he intended to pay his blackmailer," I confirmed.

Laurent raised his brows. "His blackmailer?"

Right. I hadn't yet disclosed that bit of information either. I paused, looking up at the shimmering pinpricks of lights flung across the dark sky. He'd told me his secret, but mine wasn't nearly so glamorous—or so forgivable.

"Just before I came down here, a foot washed up on the banks of a canal in the Everglades," I began.

He listened intently as I outlined everything that had happened the summer I turned twenty-one, admitting to my hacking crimes but omitting any details about Ian's disappearance, save the fact that his foot had turned up last week, opening up the can of worms that brought me down here. In the dark, it was hard to read his expression, but when I'd brought the story full circle, he threaded his fingers through mine, his face solemn. "I'm sorry about your mom."

"You don't think I'm a horrible person?"

He shook his head, alleviating my fears. "If my mom was ever in that position, I would do whatever I could to save her. It would not be with computers, but . . . I understand."

"There is a lot more to the story, which I will tell you another time," I said. "Suffice it to say, Tyson wouldn't have wanted it getting out that the guy who went missing had been extorting him."

"Who else knows this?" Laurent asked.

"Cody," I answered.

He ran his fingers through his hair, thinking. "So the question is, how did this blackmail money end up in Gisèle's suitcase?"

"Right," I said, grateful he'd connected the dots without digging further into my sordid past. I paused. "Do you think Samira's grief is an act?"

"I don't think so," he said. "They did fight a lot. But also they made up a lot."

"Did they?" I took another sip of his whisky.

"I think maybe she is a little . . . *masochiste*? That word I do not know in English."

"Masochistic," I supplied.

He pointed at me. "Yes, that. The maids tell me the things they find."

Interesting. Perhaps Tyson and Samira were better suited than I'd realized. "Samira said she won't get anything in the will. A few hundred thousand would better than nothing, now that he's gone."

"So she finds the money and has Gisèle hide it in her suitcase—"

"Because she knew the police would be searching Tyson's room," I finished, watching the headlights of a car wind down the mountain on the island. "Which means Samira's telling the truth about believing she's cut out of the will. Which essentially eliminates her and Gisèle as suspects."

"Yes," he agreed.

"It's a start," I said. Leaving four other suspects, other than Laurent and me. Three, if I could cross out Cody for having saved me.

"There you are," a female voice behind us called.

Laurent and I whipped around to see Marielle moving toward us across the deck. "They are looking for you," she went on, slipping past us to collect the ashtray as we rose. "Cody wants to talk to everyone in the salon. He says it's important."

CHAPTER 36

Laurent and I found everyone reassembled in the game deck salon. The room buzzed with tension, all eyes on Cody as he paced in front of the bar, sullen.

As Laurent and I took our places on the couch, Cody cleared his throat, and everyone stilled. "I've just spoken to Tyson's attorney, who will serve as executor of his will." His gaze landed on Samira. "Samira gets all the properties—"

Samira gasped as she sat up, her hand flying to cover her open mouth. "What? But he—"

Cody held up his palm to silence her. "And the rest of his estate will be split evenly between Samira—"

"Oh my God." Tears pooled in Samira's eyes as she gaped at him.

"—and his five children."

A wave of nausea crested in my stomach as everyone exchanged confused glances. "But he only had three," Allison said.

"Satellite, Nibiru, and Dalí Dale, and Benjamin and Alexander Collet."

I tried to breathe, but I couldn't remember how.

"Benjamin and Alexander Collet?" Jennifer echoed, frowning as she tried to place the names.

At the same time, Gisèle turned to Samira. "Did you know about them?"

Samira shook her head. "I didn't know about any of this."

"Wait a minute," Jennifer said, her eyes fixed on me as realization dawned. I stared at my hands, bracing myself for what I knew was coming next. "What did you say your children's names were?"

All heads swiveled toward me, their attention rapt.

I couldn't speak.

"Yes," Cody said after a moment. "Collet is Audrey's last name. Benjamin and Alexander are the children she shares with Tyson."

"Oh my God," Jennifer said.

"What the fuck?" Samira murmured.

I was frozen, unable to meet their eyes. Of all the times for Tyson to be generous . . . I took a deep breath and looked up at Cody, whose mouth was set in a grim line.

"Tyson and I were together a long time ago," I explained to the others, my eyes flitting from one shocked face to another. I couldn't bring myself to look at Laurent. "I found out I was pregnant after we broke up, and he advised me to terminate the pregnancy. So I let him think I did, and we never spoke again until this week."

Cody eyed me. "But they were born nine months after you broke up."

"And I've raised them alone without ever asking him for anything," I protested, my voice catching in my throat. "He didn't want to be their father, and I honored that. His name isn't even on the birth certificate. They're mine and mine alone."

"Not biologically," Cody said. "There was a DNA test with the rest of the paperwork."

I could feel everyone staring, their expressions somewhere between incredulity and relish. "But . . . why?" My brow furrowed, my heart beating faster. "And how? I never submitted permission. The boys never took one—"

"I don't know," Cody said. "But the results were conclusive."

I dropped my head to my hands, overcome with shock and indignation. "That motherfucker." I took a shaky breath and looked up at Cody. "After he said he wanted nothing to do with my children, he went and stole their DNA to prove they were his."

"I guess he changed his mind," Cody said.

"*Merde,*" Gisèle said, brows raised.

"I don't want his money," I said, looking at Cody. "I never have. I don't want anything to do with this."

Cody's smile was sour. "Not up to you. He didn't give the money to you, he gave it to your children. It will be held in a trust for them until they're eighteen, at which point they can make the decision what to do with it."

I pinched the bridge of my nose. "Fuck."

"I don't know why you're so upset," Jennifer commented. "Your kids just got set up for life."

Her flippant words stung. "My kids, who don't know he's their biological father?" I asked bitterly.

No one spoke, all of them silently judging me.

"Wow," Jennifer said finally, weighing me up. "I have to say, I didn't expect it of you. You seem so . . . *nice.*"

The way she said it wasn't a compliment. But what came next was worse.

"I don't know anymore, though." She drummed her long nails on the table. "You show up out of nowhere, and two days later, Tyson's dead, one-third of his fortune going to your kids."

"Someone just tried to fucking *kill* me," I protested.

"Maybe you tried to make it look like you were pushed to throw off suspicion," Jennifer suggested. "Maybe you jumped."

"Don't be ridiculous," Laurent argued. "Did you see the cut in her head?"

Grateful for Laurent's defense of me, I tried to catch his eye, but couldn't.

"Could be an accident," Samira suggested.

"Whatever you've just inherited would be worth a few stitches," Jennifer concluded.

I could feel my face growing red as the frustration built inside me. "I told you, I don't want his money," I insisted, doing my best to keep my voice calm. "I know what it looks like, but I've never wanted this." I caught Cody's eye. "You of all people know that."

"But you're a mom," Jennifer said. "You'd sacrifice whatever weird morals you claim to have against Tyson's money to benefit your kids."

That, at least, was true. Our eyes met and I swallowed, my throat tight. "Regardless, I didn't have any idea they were in his will. And I didn't kill him."

But their gazes were all tinged with suspicion now—the same suspicion I felt toward each of them. I could claim innocence all I wanted, but the genie was out of the bottle, and there was no putting it back in.

CHAPTER 37

Jennifer set her empty champagne flute on the coffee table with a clink and rose, yawning. "I'm gonna call it." She looked at Cody. "Shall we?"

Allison stood, stretching. "Same."

Laurent extracted his pack of cigarettes from his pocket as he stood, and I glanced at him, but again he didn't quite meet my gaze. My heart sank. Did he suspect me too now?

"I could use one of those," Samira said to Laurent in French as she got up, extending a hand to pull Gisèle up off the couch.

Whether or not they wanted anything to do with me, Laurent and the girls were the only people I was relatively certain hadn't tried to kill me, and my desire not to die superseded my ego. So, swallowing what was left of my pride, I rose to follow them.

But Samira held out a hand to stop me. "We need to talk to him," she said.

Laurent glanced from Samira to me, finally meeting my eye. But I couldn't read him. It stung more than I wanted it to.

Cody, Jennifer, and Allison had retreated down the stairs to their cabins on the main deck. But that didn't mean I was safe. Just the thought of walking to my room alone sent a shard of terror through me.

Whack. The sound of a dart hitting the board drew my attention to Rémy, whose focus was trained on the target. Behind him, Marielle and Justine wiped down the bar. I took a calming breath. Marielle and Justine had been kind to me, and neither of them had any reason to try to off me. I'd be safe as long as they were around. Right?

"Audrey—"

I turned back to find Laurent still loitering at the bottom of the stairs, his eyes fixed on me.

"I'm fine," I said woodenly. "Good night."

His jaw feathered and I thought for a moment he might say something else, before he gave me a stiff nod and jogged up the stairs behind Gisèle and Samira.

I'd never felt more alone as I strode toward Rémy. But there wasn't time to stew in the sea of emotions frothing inside me. All that mattered now was discovering who had killed Tyson before it was pinned on me.

"May I join you?" I asked as I approached, checking again that Marielle and Justine remained in the bar.

My voice distracted Rémy as he let the dart fly, and it went wide of the target. "Okay," he said. "But I must warn you, I am terrible."

"I'm not so great either," I admitted, though it wasn't true. I was a damn good shot. But being terrible would serve me much better in this situation.

I grabbed a half-empty bottle of Dom off the bar, topping off Rémy's and my glasses as I scoured my weary brain for an organic way to ask him about his dogs. "So, who are Mister and Sister staying with tonight?"

"My partner," he said.

"Oh, I get it," I teased. "The dogs made the lock screen but the partner didn't." My jocularity was forced, and we both knew it, but he let it slide. A kindness.

"What can I say, their little faces . . ." He shrugged.

I took a handful of darts from the table behind the couch and stepped up to the line, aiming for the wall just above the target. I hit it, and cursed.

"Cody says you must let it go *comme ça*," Rémy said, sending a dart flying so low it nearly hit the floor.

He didn't seem wary of me, which I took as a good sign. "My mind isn't all here," I admitted.

"I understand," he said.

Justine was cleaning up the cake now while Marielle fluffed pillows. There didn't appear to be much more for them to do in the room, which meant that I would soon be alone with Rémy unless I said good night now. But I didn't yet have the answers I needed.

I took aim to the right this time, and my dart lodged in one of the outer rings. "I didn't kill Tyson," I said. "Just to be clear."

"Okay." He met my eye with a shrug, apparently taking my declaration at face value. "And I did not kill him also."

"But no one thinks you did," I said bitterly. "They think I have a motive, but I didn't even know the boys were in his will."

"Can you prove this?" he asked. "To the police? It is not important what these people think." He flourished his hand vaguely in the direction of the stairs.

"I don't know how I would." I leaned against the couch. "But if I can figure out who did it . . ."

"Do you have an idea?"

I sighed. "Not really." Here was a chance to make sure he wasn't on the defensive with me. "It wasn't me, and I'm pretty sure it wasn't you or Laurent. But the rest of them . . ."

"I think earlier they all seem so nice," he confided, lowering his voice with a glance toward Marielle and Justine. "*Alors*, at dinner they are so—*vicieux?*"

"Vicious, yes," I agreed. This was good, we were chatting like confidantes.

"Can we get you anything else?" Marielle asked, her hands clasped behind her back.

"I would love a Perrier," I said. I wasn't terribly thirsty, but I wanted her to have reason to come back, and I'd noticed earlier that we'd drunk all the Perrier in the bar fridge.

"Same," Rémy said.

"Of course," she said with a nod.

"I didn't fall overboard," I whispered once she and Justine had disappeared down the stairs toward the kitchen. "Someone pushed me."

"I believe you," he said. "I tell them call the police, but nobody listen to me."

"Thank you," I said, hoping this meant he might confide in me. "Can I ask you something?"

He nodded.

"When we got off the helicopter, I stepped in dog poop, and one of the crew girls told me there had been two pugs on board this morning. Were your dogs here?"

I could see the gears turning in his brain as he looked out toward the dark sea, and I realized that stepping in that pile hadn't in fact been bad luck on my part, but good luck, because the answer was written all over his face. I held my tongue as he considered how to reply, stifling my instinct to jump in with some kind of apology to make the moment less awkward. His dogs had been here, we both knew it. But whether he would tell me the truth about why depended on whether he felt he could trust me.

Finally, he turned his eyes on me. "Okay," he said. "I tell you this, but please, it is *entre nous*, okay?"

I nodded, hoping my eagerness wasn't as obvious as it felt.

"My partner was here earlier today. He has to meet with Tyson and he bring the dogs. He bring them everywhere."

"Why was he meeting with Tyson?"

He sighed, looking at me from beneath his brow. "He is . . . Rick Halpern."

Now it was my turn to gape. Like seeing someone completely out of context and not recognizing them, it took my brain a moment to catch up. "The same Rick Halpern whose potential investment in De-Sal Cody and Allison were fighting with Tyson over?"

He nodded, and as badly as I wanted to jump in immediately with all the questions that this information brought up, I knew he'd tell me more if I kept quiet, so I simply inclined my head, waiting for him to go on. But before he could continue, Marielle appeared with the mineral waters we had requested.

"Please, if you need anything else, you can use the phone, there," she said, indicating the phone on the wall next to the bar.

We thanked her, and she retreated to the crew quarters, leaving Rémy and me alone. Fortunately, with his admission about Rick, I was no longer worried he might off me while we were unsupervised.

"The environment is Rick's passion, and he wants for years to work with De-Sal, but they say no," Rémy said, settling onto a barstool. "Allison and Cody want to work with him, but Tyson is always the problem." He shook his head. "Then this morning, Tyson calls Rick to meet him here on this boat and says okay, he can come in the company. I don't know everything—we speak very little after because I am coming here—but Rick was so happy."

I climbed onto the barstool next to his, leaning an elbow on the bar. "Do the others know?"

He shook his head. "They don't know I'm Rick's partner. He's very private. This way we can live a normal life."

"I can understand that," I sympathized. "But, your partner was trying to close a deal with Tyson while you were leading his birthday dive. That seems . . . awfully coincidental."

He sighed. "Rick ask me to lead the dive and maybe discover more information about why Tyson will not let him put the money in the company. I know how important this is to him, so I agree."

"The other dive instructor isn't really sick, is he?" I asked.

He shook his head. "We get him VIP concert tickets on St. Martin. When Tyson call this morning and ask Rick to meet, it was too late for me to not come here today."

"What a mess," I said sympathetically.

"I did not know Tyson will die," he lamented, his anxiety apparent in the shadows beneath his eyes. "How can I know that? Now I can lose my license, and Rick can lose the deal he tried for years to close."

"But surely the deal will go through," I said as he took a fortifying gulp of champagne. I had my doubts as well, but I wanted to make him feel better. "It's what Cody and Allison wanted, and they're in charge now."

"Maybe." He shrugged. "Or maybe when they learn I am Rick's partner, they will not want to work with him anymore. If there is no papers to prove Rick make the deal with Tyson, then I can be a suspect too."

"Shit," I said, understanding. "No wonder your darts aren't hitting the target tonight."

"Yes," he replied with a sad little smile.

My suspect list was rapidly dwindling.

CHAPTER 38

After Rémy walked me back to my room, I locked myself inside and sat on the bed, pulling my computer into my lap. As bone-weary as I was, I had to keep pushing.

Cody had turned off the Wi-Fi, but the satellite link was still live, and I'd created another access point when I was in the security room earlier. Using the credentials I'd pilfered, I logged in to the site where the camera feed was hosted, then adjusted the view to show nine cameras at once, covering most of the indoor areas of the boat.

As Laurent had told me, the feed went back only two hours, coming online about fifteen minutes after I'd been thrown off the boat.

I scanned the video feed from that point, watching as Laurent and Evan walked me to the infirmary. I followed Laurent's path when he went to get my dress, observed everyone drinking champagne in the lounge while they waited for me, traced each person's movements as they visited the restroom or had a private conversation away from the others. But without sound, it was impossible to determine the content of those conversations.

I groaned aloud, rubbing my eyes. I'd hoped I'd find something useful on the camera feed, but it appeared that was not to be. I was too terrified about becoming the fall girl to stop digging now, but I was hitting a wall. I reached for the screen, about to close my laptop, when I saw movement at Cody and Jennifer's door. I'd left the feed running, and the time stamp in the corner showed that what I was watching now had happened about ten minutes ago. I squinted at the screen, observing as Jennifer exited her suite, glanced around furtively, and carefully shut the door behind her.

What was she up to?

I followed her path down the spiral staircase to the cabin level I was on now, my heart thumping faster as I observed her move stealthily along the hallway. A jolt of adrenaline went through me as she placed her hand on the door handle to my room and disappeared into my cabin. I glanced around. I was alone. Nothing was out of place.

Onscreen my cabin door opened again and Jennifer stepped into the hallway, moving quickly up the stairs and back into her suite.

She'd been in my room less than a minute. Had she taken something? Or left something? Or had she just been snooping, as I had earlier?

I set the computer aside and quickly opened the bedside table drawers, only to find them empty. Same with the drawers of the bureau; the closet contained nothing more than the dress I'd hung there earlier, the bathroom my toiletries. My suitcase was just as I'd left it, and when I rifled through it, I found the blackmail note still in the pocket of my jeans and nothing out of place.

What did she want?

Jennifer was the last person I'd expected to have anything to do with Tyson's death. Not that this meant she did. But clearly she wasn't as innocent as I'd assumed.

I enlarged the video, capturing it with my phone for good measure as I rewatched Jennifer's entrance and exit of my room, studying every aspect of the image. I couldn't make out her expression, but her hands were empty, and there appeared to be nothing in her pockets either. No indication as to what she was up to.

As I scanned through the feed again looking for some clue, it dawned on me that I'd never seen Allison come back for the envelope she'd stored on the bookshelf shortly before I was pushed. I zeroed in on the camera that showed that angle of the main deck, but unless Allison had retrieved the envelope before the feed went back online, she hadn't returned for it. Which meant it might still be there.

Did I dare leave my room alone, after someone had already tried to kill me once tonight?

But I wouldn't be blind now, I realized. I could view the security cameras on my phone.

Within five minutes I had the camera feed up and running on my phone. It wasn't as user-friendly as the app that worked with the cameras at Le Rêve, nor was as it as clear as it was on the computer, but I felt a lot safer knowing I'd be able to see if someone was following me.

Currently, it appeared the only people out of their rooms were Laurent, Gisèle, and Samira, whom I could make out chatting in the smoking zone on the sun deck.

My heart racing, I locked my computer and left it on the bed, then palmed my phone, my eyes glued to the live camera feed as I slipped out of my room and darted up the stairs at the end of the hallway to the quiet main deck.

Wasting no time, I went straight to the bookcase, where I located the book with the green door on the front, a retrospective on the style of French country estates. I had the feeling I was being watched, the hair on the back of my neck rising, my scalp prickling. But the camera feed was empty, and the yacht was silent, its shadows still as I carried the book past the bar and into the powder room behind the piano area. I shut myself inside, sat on the closed toilet lid, and opened the pages to the envelope in the center.

Bending back the brad prongs, I lifted the flap and inserted my hand into the envelope, pulling out some kind of medical lab report. Allison's name was at the top, with a date in 2018, the year she'd retired from swimming. She'd been expected to compete in the 2020 Olympics, but she'd surprised everyone by announcing halfway through her 2018 season that she was hanging up her swim cap.

I gathered the report was some sort of blood test, though it contained rows of numbers and letters I didn't understand. Regardless, I photographed the pages quickly with my phone, then reinserted them in the envelope, which I put back in the book. The main deck was fortunately still empty, and I hurried across the room, leaving the book on the shelf exactly where I'd found it.

I wanted to share what I'd learned with Laurent and get his take on it, but I wasn't sure he wanted anything to do with me anymore. I felt a stab of contrition, asking myself again whether I should have told him about the boys' paternity. But I'd never told anyone other than Rosa and my mom—not even my children themselves—nor had I realized it was pertinent information until I learned that Tyson had included Benji and Alex in his will, which I'd never even considered a possibility.

I hadn't yet contemplated what Tyson's shocking generosity would mean for my little family. I'd think about that later. For now, I would take my chances with Laurent and the girls.

CHAPTER 39

With the aid of the camera feed, I made my way carefully to the sun deck, where I found Samira, Gisèle, and Laurent in the *zone fumeur,* silhouetted against the lights of the island, the ends of their cigarettes glowing in the dark. Samira exhaled a long line of smoke, eyeing me in a not entirely friendly fashion as I approached, but she didn't speak; neither did Gisèle, taking her cue from Samira, as usual. But Laurent held my gaze this time, offering me a cigarette. I was so grateful he didn't totally hate me that I accepted it, inhaling shallowly while he lit it.

"Anyone know why Jennifer might have been snooping in my room just now?" I asked, taking a seat on the bench next to Laurent.

Gisèle cut her eyes toward me as she blew a line of smoke over her shoulder. "Did you catch her?"

"I saw her," I said. This wasn't the time to explain what I did for a living and why Tyson had hired me. "But she didn't see me. I don't know what she was after."

"Probably some proof you killed Tyson," Samira said.

"Which I didn't." The words came out more defensively than I'd intended.

"Why would Jennifer be so interested?" Laurent mused.

I could read the rest of the question in his eyes, and I supposed it was possible she could be the blackmailer, but I couldn't see why.

Gisèle and Samira looked back and forth between us, registering that there was more to the story than we were giving them. "What are you not telling us?" Gisèle asked.

I leveled my gaze at her. "I found five hundred thousand euros in your suitcase."

Smoke caught in her throat, her poker face wavering. So Laurent hadn't told them about my discovery. Would I be reading too much into it to hope that it meant his loyalty still lay with me?

"It was Tyson's money," I went on. "When he died, the two of you decided to hide it in Gisèle's suitcase, knowing that if you didn't, the police would search the primary suite and take it as evidence."

When neither of them protested, I focused on Samira. "If you'd known you were getting anything in the will, you wouldn't have needed that money and wouldn't have taken the risk of stealing it. So, you didn't know, which means you didn't kill him. You've already put up with him for fourteen months. You only needed to do twenty-two more to get a hundred million dollars."

Samira and Gisèle exchanged an anxious glance, thrown. "I told you I didn't kill him," Samira said, vindicated.

"You're smart," I said more gently. "Too smart to give up a hundred million dollars. Besides, it wasn't all bad between you, was it? Sure, he was a dick, but you didn't mind that in bed."

"You are not wrong." She shrugged, relaxing slightly. "I hated him, but I also loved him."

"And you," I said, switching my gaze to Gisèle, "love her. You really care about her happiness. As much as you probably wanted Tyson to bite the dust, you wouldn't have gotten in the way of Samira's happiness, which included Tyson and his money."

Gisèle and Samira looked at each other and back to me, unsure how to respond.

"Everyone knows you're more than friends," I said. "Except maybe Tyson."

It was endearing how shocked the two of them appeared. "How long have you known?" Samira asked Laurent.

"A long time," Laurent said. Then, off Gisèle and Samira's bewildered look, *"I have discretion but I'm not deaf or blind. You say—and do—things right in front of me all the time."*

Samira's face crumpled. *"I'm sorry, Laurent."*

"I don't care," he said. *"I'm used to it. It's part of the job. And no, I won't say anything to the police. Though I'm not sure the others won't."*

"You're probably best getting ahead of it and telling the police the three of you had a special relationship." I let that land before I moved on. "Regardless, the police have as much reason to believe you killed him as they do me, especially considering what happened to your last husband. So you have as much reason to find out who really killed him as I do. Maybe we can help each other?"

"What do we get out of it?" Samira asked.

"I'm assuming you don't want me to tell the police about the money you hid?"

She sighed. "What kind of help do you need?"

"I took a look around your room earlier as well," I said. She drew back, displeased, as I continued, "Right before I was pushed off the boat. And I wasn't the only one. Allison came in while I was there and swiped something that was hidden beneath the mattress."

She frowned. "What?"

I pulled out my phone and displayed the shots I'd just taken of the medical records. "It's a blood test," I said. "I can't read it, but I'm guessing whatever it says wouldn't be good for Allison if it got out, and Tyson was using it against her. Any idea why?"

Samira shook her head.

"Did you know he was suspicious that someone in his inner circle was responsible for leaking the environmental report to the city council?" I asked.

She nodded, and I stifled a yawn that pulled at the glue holding my scalp together, wincing at the pain. The day was catching up with me, but I needed to push through. "Did he say anything to you about bringing in an investor?" I pressed.

"Yeah, the man Allison wanted. Rick Halpern?"

I nodded, recognizing the name of Rémy's partner.

"Allison wanted to sell some shares to him," she went on, "but Tyson was giving him new shares—I do not know the word."

"He was diluting shares. Which would have pissed Allison off," I said.

"He wanted to punish her," Samira said. "I don't know why."

The image of Ian's body splayed at the foot of Tyson's parents' staircase flashed before me. "Tyson did like to punish people," I muttered.

But someone had finally turned the tables on him.

CHAPTER 40

Once we'd said our good nights, Samira and Gisèle retired to the primary suite while Laurent and I descended the stairs to our sleeping quarters.

"Do you think Jennifer is the blackmailer?" Laurent asked, his voice low.

"It's possible," I said. "Cody could have shared information with her which she used to blackmail Tyson. But I'm missing a motive."

"Maybe she wanted to leave Cody but doesn't have any money of her own," he suggested.

I paused, considering that. "But why would she kill him before she got the money? And why would she push me off the boat when I didn't have anything on her?" My brain was fried, and we'd reached the cabin level. "I think I need to sleep on it. It's been a long day."

"Yes," he agreed.

Anticipation rose in me as we paused in the corridor between our rooms. My head was tender, and I was beyond spent, but the idea of leaving him made me cold. Was it crazy to think about spending the night together after all that had happened today? I dared a glance at him to find him considering me, his gaze lingering.

"I'm sorry I didn't tell you about Tyson being my boys' father," I said.

"It's okay," he said, and the gentleness in his voice told me he meant it. "I am sure you are a great mom."

I smiled. "I try to be."

"It was interesting, getting to know you better today," he said.

I cocked my head. "Interesting?"

He reached out and tucked an errant strand of hair behind my ear, his fingers trailing along my jaw. "I like the way you think."

I laughed.

He leaned a shoulder into the wall, his eyes fixed on me. *"How you reacted under pressure was . . . impressive."*

"Thank you. But we still don't know who did it, and tomorrow . . ." I could feel the anxiety building in my chest again. "What if the police don't believe I was pushed either? What if they think I did it?"

"Audrey . . ." The sound of my name on his tongue was like a spell. He placed his hands on my shoulders, his gaze calm and grounded in the semidarkness. "It's not you. It will be okay."

He wrapped his arms around me, and I laid my head on his chest, allowing myself to feel safe in his embrace. I noticed the warmth of his skin through his shirt, the fresh scent of his aftershave, the density of his muscles. As I relaxed, my body awoke, my fatigue falling off me like a coat dropped to the floor, and I became very aware of every detail of his body pressed to mine.

My problems would still be there in the morning, but he was here tonight.

"You're tired," he said. I could feel his voice reverberating, his heartbeat quickening. "I should let you sleep."

But neither of us moved.

I pulled back just enough to look up at him. His blue eyes were dark, locked on mine. "I don't want to sleep just yet," I murmured.

My breath grew shallow as he bent his face toward me, hovering just a moment before he brought his lips to mine, kissing me tenderly. My anxiety melted under the pressure of his tongue, the events of the day receding from view as my skin lit up in response to his touch.

"I don't want to hurt you," he whispered.

"Just be gentle," I said.

"I don't know if that is possible."

I tangled my fingers in his thick hair, shivering with desire as his lips slipped down my throat and his hands swept up my legs. I fumbled behind me for the doorknob, feeling it unlatch as I twisted and pulled him into the cabin with me.

Inside, I locked the door behind us, and he cupped my head protectively in his hands, the heat between us growing with every flick of his tongue. It was more than want. The trauma of the day had unlocked something primal in me, a need to feel alive, and I could sense it in him too as he kissed me with raw abandon, like a man headed to war.

Yes, gentle was going to be difficult. I wrapped a leg around his waist, my skirt bunching as our hips connected and he let out a low groan.

His desire stoked the fire inside me and I tugged at his clothes, desperate to feel his skin against mine. His shirt came over his head and I ran my hands over his chest, tracing his tattoo with my fingers as he pushed the straps of my loose dress off my shoulders and let it fall to the ground.

The skin contact made me desperate for more, and I drew him to me, pressing my body into his as we stumbled toward the bed and he pulled me down on top of him. There was nothing other than us in this moment, nothing but his mouth against my skin, nothing left to separate us as the rest of our clothes came off and our bodies fell into sync.

ELEVEN YEARS AGO, DECEMBER

It didn't feel like Christmas without my mom. I hadn't put up a tree, hadn't wrapped any presents or made the caramel and chocolate Christmas Crack.

She'd had been gone for two months now, and my grandfather had transferred the house into my name, but I was still sleeping in my childhood bedroom. Thankfully, her life insurance had paid out a decent amount, because between the pregnancy and grief, I'd been barely able to get out of bed for months.

The symmetry of losing my mother and becoming a mother within the same breath was not lost on me or my mom. She'd bought cribs as well as tiny clothes and an assortment of baby-related gadgets for me before she passed away, and we'd decided to name the boys Alexander, after her, and Benjamin, after her father. She wouldn't be here physically, but she would be with me every step of the way.

Unlike Tyson, who wanted nothing to do with any of it. I hadn't expected him to be my partner in parenthood, but I also hadn't anticipated just how brutal his response would be. When I told him I was pregnant the night before he went back to school, he first asked if I was sure it was his. I'd "made him use condoms" every time we had sex, so I must have been "raw-dogging" with someone else. Once I'd convinced him that that was not the case, he proceeded to lecture me for not taking the birth control pills he knew made me emotionally unstable, while pulling wads of cash out of the safe so that I could "take care of it somewhere nice."

I tried to turn down the cash, tried to tell him that while I appreciated having a right to choose, I'd already made my choice. But he said I'd come around. I was twenty-one. Motherhood would ruin my life. Was I "crazy or just stupid?"

But I didn't want what he wanted out of life. I valued love and family above all else, and my only real family was about to pass out of this world. I saw the pregnancy as a gift. A child—or, as it turned out, children—would give me something to live for.

In the end, I accepted the cash and promised to use it, relieved that it meant he wouldn't be a part of our lives. I knew of course that he would realize I'd lied when I gave birth, but I also knew he'd never challenge me. The one thing we agreed on was that it was better for him not to be my children's father.

I'd promised my mom that I'd move into her room and make the house my own by the new year, so three days before Christmas, Rosa turned up on my doorstep with a box of trash bags. We both cried as we sorted through my mom's stuff, bagging the things I didn't want to keep, then loaded our trunks and drove down to the Goodwill to donate them. While employees in the donation center cataloged everything, we wandered the aisles, looking for maternity wear for my ever-expanding belly.

I was sorting through a rack of dresses when I saw her. My stomach dropped as our eyes met. "Andie," I said, my voice barely a whisper.

Her dark hair was pulled back into a ponytail, her bangs falling into her eyes, and though she was dressed in baggy sweats, I could tell she'd put on some weight, in a good way. Her eyes and cheeks were no longer hollow, and her skin had lost its sallowness. Perhaps Ian's disappearance had done her good.

Her eyes darted past me as if scanning the area for danger. Tyson, I realized. She was looking for Tyson.

"Tyson and I broke up," I said, coming around the rack so that she could see my belly. I saw her register my state and do the math, but she didn't comment.

She took a step toward me, lowering her voice. "I've been trying to get in touch with you."

"Oh?"

She narrowed her eyes. "I know Tyson had something to do with Ian's disappearance."

My pulse quickened. "What?"

"Don't play stupid with me. I know Ian was at his house the night he didn't come home."

"But they found his phone in Miami and his truck in the Everglades," I said, feigning confusion. "So even if he did go by there, he clearly left."

She shook her head, crossing her arms. "I went over there the next day looking for him, and Tyson answered the door. Threatened me, told me he would make me sorry if I ever stepped foot on his property again."

"That was wrong, and I'm not defending him—he's a dick, which is why I'm not with him anymore. But you know as well as I do that Ian had been extorting him," I said gently.

"Which is why Tyson killed him," she levied.

"That's a leap," I said, my heart in my throat.

"The police wouldn't listen to me either," she said bitterly. "Said he was an addict and drug dealer, and it was only a matter of time until he didn't come home. But he'd stopped dealing drugs once he started *extorting* Tyson."

Blood rushed in my ears as the nausea I'd thought I was past resurfaced and my knees grew wobbly. I steadied myself on the clothes rack. "At least you have that money," I said weakly.

"I don't, though," she said, advancing on me. "Ian kept one key to his safety deposit box on his key ring and one in his shoe, and now they're both gone. We weren't married, so they won't let me into the box without a key, even though my name is on the list. I have nothing."

"I'm so sorry," I managed, the edges of my peripheral vision darkening.

"Audrey?" Rosa's voice was tinged with worry as she rushed down the aisle of clothes racks toward me, but she sounded very far away. "What's going on here? Are you okay?"

"He thinks he's won, but he hasn't," Andie whispered. "One day he'll pay."

PART III

CHAPTER 41

A heavy rapping at the door ripped me from slumber. Laurent's arm was flung across my waist, the sheets tangled around our bodies as we jerked awake, discombobulated. Light bled from the edges of the blackout shade over the window.

What time was it?

The rapping came again, louder this time, as I fumbled on the bedside table for my phone: 7:36 A.M.

"Police," came a male voice. "Open up."

I sat bolt upright. "One second," I called out, blood rushing in my ears. "I'm not dressed."

I rolled out of bed and opened the shade, flooding the cabin with light. Laurent's hair was mussed, his cheek dented with the wrinkle of the pillow as he rubbed sleep from his eyes and stepped into his pants. My heart squeezed as I looked at him. I wished our circumstances were different, but I didn't regret one minute of last night.

I went to my closet, pulling on a T-shirt and ripped jeans shorts with shaking hands. I heard the rapping again, this time on Rémy's door.

"I guess they wanted to surprise us," I said.

"Yes," Laurent said, pulling me in for a quick kiss. He was trying to be reassuring, but I could tell he was as spooked as I was.

I heard a clunk in Gisèle's room, and rapid male voices. Again, a rapping on my door, this time more polite. "Everyone to the main deck, please," said a female voice. Crew.

"Okay, one second," I called out.

While Laurent dressed, I splashed water on my face and quickly brushed my teeth in the bathroom, then downed ibuprofen for my head, which was fortunately not hurting as badly as I'd feared it might.

"Let's go." That was one of the cops. "Leave all your things in your room."

Thinking fast, I fished Tyson's blackmail note out of my bag and stuffed it in my back pocket along with my phone, debit card, and ID. I wasn't yet sure yet what to do about the blackmail note, but I figured it would be better for me to it hand over than for them to discover it.

Laurent and I exchanged a glance. Apparently, the police weren't going to conveniently step away so that he could slip out of my room and into his without anyone the wiser.

I realized, as he opened the door, that this was worse for me than it was for him. He was the one person who could vouch for my where-abouts during the dive, and now the police would think he was biased because we were involved. They might even think I'd seduced him to cover my tracks.

This was very, very bad.

I followed him into the hallway, where Officer Lambert leaned against the wall with his arms crossed, looking down his nose at us. If our appearing together was a surprise, he didn't let on. He pointed to the stairs. "Main deck."

Through the open door to Gisèle's room, I could see the police bag-ging the money she'd hidden in her suitcase. So much for my promise to keep it a secret. In my mind, I scanned my room for anything they might find suspicious in my own belongings, but since I'd removed the blackmail note, I didn't think I had anything. That was something, anyway.

When we reached the main deck, we found everyone else already assembled at the dining table, hastily dressed and on edge, seated before an untouched spread of pastries, eggs, and fruit. Jennifer looked like she'd slept in her makeup, and even always-put-together Allison looked disheveled, her perennially smooth hair kinked in the back, bags under her eyes.

An officer was stationed in the hallway between the doors to Allison's and Cody and Jennifer's rooms while additional officers searched their cabins. All the officers were ripped, confident. There might not be a lot of crime on St. Barth's, but these guys seemed unnervingly ready to handle whatever was thrown their way.

One of the crew girls offered me a coffee and I took it gratefully. My brain was foggy from the lack of sleep, not to mention all the alcohol I'd consumed yesterday, and I needed to be sharp today. I added a dash of milk as I slid into a seat next to Samira.

"Are they going to let us back in our rooms?" Jennifer asked of no one in particular. I watched as she spun her hair into a bun atop her head. Why would she have been blackmailing Tyson? And if she had been, could she also have killed him? She was pint-size, and such an inexperienced diver—unless she wasn't. An advanced diver would know how to mount a tank to control another diver, no matter their size difference. "I need a shower," she complained. "I didn't even get to brush my teeth."

"None of us did," Allison said.

"What the hell are they looking for, anyway?" she asked.

"They're doing what they should have done yesterday," Cody groused from his spot at the head of the table, one side of his polo collar upturned. He checked his watch and glanced at Allison. "The announcement goes out in ten minutes."

Jennifer reached beneath the table and stopped his jumping knee. "Calm down."

But she seemed just as fidgety as he did. What was I missing about her?

"They're bringing us in for questioning," Allison said.

I caught Samira's eye and looked pointedly at the side deck, then rose, taking my coffee with me. No one asked where I was going as I exited the dining room and skirted the shimmering pool to stand at the railing, just out of sight of the table. My eyes burned with the brightness of the day as I squinted across the turquoise sea toward the hilly green island, and I wished I'd thought to bring my sunglasses upstairs with me.

After a moment, Samira joined me, leaning over the railing on her elbows. As beautiful as she was, she looked like shit, and I could tell by the dark circles beneath her puffy eyes that she hadn't slept.

"They found the money," I said, my voice low. "I saw them bagging it."

"*Merde.*"

"It may be better for you in the long run, it backs up your story that you didn't know you were getting anything in the will."

"Thanks for telling me." She took a sip of her coffee, glancing back toward the table. "How is your head?"

"Sore," I answered. "But better than last night."

"Good." Her gaze lingered on me. "So, you and Laurent . . ."

I stared at her, unsure what to say.

"*Come on. Of all the women I've brought down here before, none have gotten so much as a kiss from him.*"

"*Really?*" I asked, surprised.

"*And not for lack of trying.*"

"*I didn't . . . I wasn't sure. If this was something he did.*" I stared down at the clear water.

"No," she said. "*Not that I know of, anyway.*"

I held back a smile. I'd convinced myself to be totally fine with it if it turned out he was some kind of butler lothario, but I couldn't deny that learning he wasn't felt good. A spot of sunshine on a horizon darkened by thunderheads.

The sound of boots on the deck, and we turned to see Lambert stomping around the pool. "Ladies, please join us." He gestured to the police boat moored a short distance from the yacht.

Behind him, the others were rising from the table, taking last sips of coffee, grabbing pastries for the road.

"We need to pack up," Cody said.

But he shook his head. "We will bring your things."

"We're not even wearing shoes," I protested.

"The crew will provide you with the shoes you were wearing when you arrived."

"My computer—" I started.

"We will return it to you." He gestured to the stern. "Please. We go to the station for interviews, then you are free to go home."

"Like, home to America?" I asked, though I knew the answer.

"We ask that you remain on the island for now," he said, waving us toward the back of the boat. "Please."

Samira and I joined the others as they filed around the pool and down the steps to the sugar scoop, looking just as disgruntled as we did. At least I had my phone. Some of the others weren't so lucky.

At the bottom of the stairs were two baskets of shoes, but I could find only one of the sandals I'd worn yesterday. The one that had been soiled was nowhere to be seen. "Where is my other shoe?" I asked one of the girls sorting a pile of discarded dive gear.

She held up a yellow flipper without a pair. "Is it this one?"

"No, my street shoes," I said, showing her my sandal. "You guys took my other one to be cleaned."

"I'll find it," she said, setting the flipper down to trot up the stairs, speaking into her walkie.

Another crew girl held up a dive compass attached to a carabiner. "Whose is this?"

Jennifer raised her hand and reached for it. As she clipped it to her belt loop, I frowned. What was a novice diver like Jennifer doing with a dive compass? How to use it underwater wasn't something you learned until advanced open water dive training. Perhaps she wasn't as inexperienced as she claimed.

"The announcement just went out," Allison said, looking at her phone from behind big black sunglasses.

As the police began to load us into the dinghies to transfer to their boat, the girl who had gone to find my shoe returned empty-handed, apologizing profusely. My shoe was nowhere to be found. "Can I please go get my other pair of shoes?" I asked Officer Lambert, but he shook his head.

"We must go now."

"Here." I looked up to see Marielle jogging down the stairs, a pair of Havaianas in her hand. "Have mine."

"Thank you," I said gratefully, taking the shoes from her. They were a size too big, but better than nothing.

She helped me into the dinghy, and I sat next to Allison. We pulled away from the yacht, the wind whipping our hair as we motored over the top of the waves toward the police boat. If Allison had been the one to push me off the boat, I felt certain she wouldn't try anything here, under the watchful gaze of the police, so I could afford to be direct. I seized the moment, leaning into her, my voice barely rising above the sound of the motor. "Is there any reason I shouldn't tell the police about the blood test Tyson was blackmailing you with?"

She stilled.

"I have pictures of it, so there's no use denying it," I said, locking the cage. Now to show her a way out. "But I don't want to throw you under the bus if there's a plausible explanation."

She glanced at Rémy and Laurent, who sat on the opposite side of the boat, out of earshot with the sound of the motor. The others were on the first dinghy. "Fine," she acquiesced. "It was a stupid mistake. I was using EPO to increase my red blood cell mass after a hiatus, and it worked so well . . . I got sloppy. That blood test ended my career."

"But no one ever knew about it," I said. "You retired before it came out."

"That was the deal I struck."

"How did Tyson get hold of it?"

She shook her head. "Who knows. But he'd decided Cody was to blame for leaking the environmental report, and he was using the blood test to pressure me to vote him out. If I didn't, he'd slip that blood test to the press."

"Is that why you killed him?" I asked.

Her head whipped toward mine. "I didn't kill him. I was getting what I wanted. Tyson was bringing in another investor and had agreed to let me sell some of my shares to him once I voted Cody out."

"So you were willing to screw Cody over, even though it was you who leaked the environmental report?" I pressed.

"I didn't—"

"I saw you, Allison. I was at Le Ti that night."

Her jaw tensed. "I didn't have a choice," she muttered. "I didn't like it, but I had to save my own ass." She leaned closer, her voice urgent. "I may be a liar, but I'm not a murderer."

She could be lying about that too, of course, but in my line of work, I'd learned to trust my instincts, and I didn't believe she was. Allison might be duplicitous, but she was too rational to let her hate for Tyson get the better of her if she was already getting what she wanted from him. "Did Cody know Tyson was trying to vote him out?"

She shook her head. "No."

We docked next to the angular police boat and the officers helped us board, directing us to the interior, which was gray and bursting with gadgets and screens. The sides were lined with benches, and I took a seat next to Laurent, who gave me a reassuring glance as we lurched forward.

The engine was loud enough that conversation was next to impossible as we cruised around the edges of the island, my dread growing heavier the closer we got to Gustavia. A pair of Jet Skis streaked by, and I could see surfers waiting for waves offshore and beachgoers frolicking on the golden sand, oblivious to the morbid scene on this police boat.

A phone dinged, and then another. We were back to service. I felt my own device vibrate and pulled it from my pocket to see my home screen lit up with messages that had come in since the news of Tyson's demise had been posted fifteen minutes ago. Rosa alone had texted me seven times, increasingly worried when I didn't respond.

I pulled up my news feed to see that word of Tyson's death had spawned a cornucopia of articles about him, spanning the gamut from his professional achievements to his tumultuous personal life, but thankfully, no one had yet gotten hold of the information that he had not three but five children. I knew I needed to break the news to Benji and Alex before they learned it from someone else, but I wasn't about to make that phone call in front of everyone.

As I composed a text to Rosa telling her not to let the boys watch the news, my phone began to ring, and her name flashed on the screen. I considered. The engine was loud, but Cody and Allison were both talking on their phones. I should at least let her know I was okay. "Rosa," I answered.

"Oh my God Audrey, what the hell?" she cried.

"I can't really talk right now, I'm on a boat and it's loud."

"I can hear that. I read it was a dive accident? What happened?"

"We're still trying to figure that out," I said. "But yeah. I'm not gonna be able to come back immediately. Are you okay keeping the boys a few more days?"

"Of course. Don't even worry about it."

"You're an angel, thank you," I said. "Tell the boys I love them and I'll be home soon. I'm just a little sunburned."

"Got it," she said, receiving our code word. "Stay safe."

"Oh, and Rosa," I said, catching her before she hung up. "Please don't let them watch the news."

Once we'd hung up, I pocketed my phone, looking out the window to see the green trees give way to red rooftops, the buildings getting closer together as we neared Gustavia. I rubbed my sweating palms on my jeans, scanning the faces of the others on the boat, who all looked just as anxious as I felt.

I knew Laurent would vouch for me, and I felt relatively certain Rémy would as well. Samira and Gisèle might, though I doubted they'd stick their necks out for me if it might compromise their own defense in any way.

The captain cut the engine and the water slapped the side of the boat as we cruised into the harbor. Jennifer rose from the bench to peer out the window behind me at the row of docked yachts, but the boat rocked, sending her stumbling backward. As she reached up and caught a grab handle, her shirt lifted, and a jolt of recognition went through me.

On the left side of her torso was a long, jagged scar.

CHAPTER 42

The waiting room of the police building was windowless, out-fitted with large-format tile floors and thinly padded uphol-stered chairs. Shivering in the blasting air conditioning, I desperately searched for anything about Andie's demise on my phone while the police prepared the interview rooms. But I couldn't even remember her last name, much less the when or where of the car crash that had supposedly taken her life.

Though it wasn't exactly a crash, was it? The car had gone off a bridge, Tyson had said.

Which meant that just because she was assumed dead didn't mean she was. Perhaps her body hadn't been recovered. Perhaps there was no body. Perhaps she'd used the accident—if it even was an accident—to disappear and start a new life. How, I wasn't sure. But it was pos-sible, and she'd surely made some shady contacts through Ian's drug dealing business.

My memory of Andie's face was hazy after all these years, but there was a possibility I had an image of her stored in the depths of my iCloud.

Grateful for the free Wi-Fi in the station, I pulled up my account and scrolled back to the summer I was twenty-one. There I was with Rosa, our faces fuller, eyes brighter. There was my mom, her favorite turquoise scarf tied around her head. And so many pictures of Tyson, tan and fit, his arms around me. As I flipped through the Fourth of July pictures, I spotted Ian in the background, smoking a joint.

And there she was. Andie, approaching him, looking just past camera.

Electricity crackled inside me as I zoomed in, studying the structure of her face. She was pale, dark-haired, and waiflike, with bangs that fell into her eyes, whereas Jennifer was tan and blond and curvy, and her nose and cheeks had certainly been altered, but the resemblance was unmistakable, confirming my hunch.

Holy shit. Jennifer was Andie.

Officer Gauthier appeared with a small plastic bin. "We will need your phones until you have been interviewed."

I locked my phone and obediently deposited it in the bin, my head spinning as Gauthier informed us that they'd be doing individual interviews in two rooms. We were not to speak to one another while we waited, nor were we allowed to return to the waiting room once we'd been questioned.

A small television mounted next to the security camera in the corner played a series of French soccer games as the group slowly dwindled over three long hours, until only Laurent, Rémy, Gisèle, and I were still waiting beneath the buzzing fluorescent lights.

"What is your plan when you leave here?" Laurent asked me, his voice low, mouth barely moving in deference to the security camera.

"I don't know," I whispered. I was desperate to tell him my suspicion about Jennifer, but we hadn't had a moment alone since this morning.

"You can stay with me if you like."

I couldn't deny the rush of affection I felt for him as I accepted his offer. "That would be great, thank you." I dropped an elbow to my knee and my head to my hand, so that the security camera wouldn't record my mouth moving. "Are you guys going back to the house?" I asked Gisèle.

She copied my posture. "Samira and I are returning to the boat," she said. "Allison's going to the hotel where the rest of the staff is staying."

"Cody and Jennifer?" I asked. My two remaining suspects, one of whom had killed Tyson—if it hadn't been the two of them together.

"They'll be at the house, I think."

A police officer appeared in the door to the hallway. "Gisèle Breydel and Laurent Auguste?"

Rémy sighed. "We'll be here."

Laurent squeezed my hand. "Text me when you're finished and I'll come get you."

Another thirty minutes went by before the handsome Officer Gauthier appeared once more in the doorway. "Mr. Durand, you are with me," he said to Rémy as we followed him through the door into a short hallway off which were two doors. "Ms. Collet, you are in there"—he indicated the room across the hall, where Officer Lambert waited with a female officer.

As I entered, the female officer rose, closing the door behind me. Even with her face bare of makeup and her dark hair pulled back in a ponytail, she looked like an actress playing a cop on television. But her attitude was all business.

"Legs wide," she said gruffly.

I complied as she patted me down, then took a seat in the chair across from her and Officer Lambert. "This is Officer Trudeau, and I am Officer Lambert," he said.

"I remember." I smiled, forcing friendliness though I was sweating with apprehension. "We met yesterday."

He nodded, evaluating me with sharp eyes. "Your children are Benjamin and Alexander Collet, yes?"

I nodded, shivering. Why did they have to keep it so cold in here?

"Please, say it aloud for the tape," he instructed.

I cleared my throat. "Yes."

"And the father of Benjamin and Alexander Collet is Tyson Dale?" Lambert asked.

"Yes," I said. Adding quickly, "But he was never involved with the children."

While Lambert asked the questions, Trudeau jotted things down in her notebook, observing me as if she knew something I didn't. It was unnerving.

"Did you ask him for money?" Lambert pressed.

"No."

He evaluated me with hawklike eyes. "He owns a billion-dollar company, and you reported an income of ninety-two thousand dollars last year." So they'd done their research, and fast. "Why did you not ask him for money?"

"Because the choice to have the boys was mine alone," I said, turning my palms up to show I had nothing to hide. "I don't want his money. I never did. But someone else here does. Someone was blackmailing him."

The two officers exchanged a glance as I took the blackmail note from my pocket and slid it across the table. Lambert picked it up and studied it, his brow furrowing.

"You found the money he intended to pay them off with in Gisèle's room. But it wasn't her." I waited until they returned their focus to me to go on. "I have reason to believe it was Jennifer."

Lambert swished his mustache. "Explain, please."

I took a breath, wiping my palms on my jeans. "I'm nearly certain she was the girlfriend of a guy named Ian Kelley, who lived in a trailer on Tyson's parents' property the summer we . . . conceived my children. She looked different then, and went by a different name, spoke with a different accent even, but she believed Tyson was responsible for Ian's death."

Both officers kept their composure, but I could tell this was news to them. "His death?" Lambert asked.

"He disappeared. He was a drug addict and dealer, so it wasn't terribly surprising, unfortunately. His remains were recently recovered in the Everglades."

Lambert frowned. "And you believe Jennifer was his girlfriend?"

I nodded. "I didn't see it at first, because her appearance is so altered. Not to mention that we weren't close, and it's been over ten years since I last saw her. But she has a scar on her stomach. I was there with her when it happened. And once you see the resemblance, you can't unsee it."

"Does Cody know this?"

Did he? I wasn't sure. He'd spent even less time than I had with her back then, and she was an entirely different person now. It wasn't just the physical alterations; she'd transformed her whole personality. Gone was the surly, drugged-out Australian trailer park girl, replaced by a bubbly, sober American Barbie.

It wasn't until I saw the scar—which I now realized she intentionally kept covered—that I put two and two together. Cody had seen it, obviously. But he hadn't been there the night of the fire, hadn't kept pressure on her wound until the paramedics arrived. He was aware she'd been injured that night, but he might well not have known exactly what wounds she sustained, certainly hadn't seen the damage.

Sure, it was possible that she and Cody had reconnected after all these years and kept her true identity from Tyson. But it was more probable that she'd targeted Cody to get close to Tyson to exact her revenge. In which case, half a million was definitely not her end goal. She would have increased her demand when she and Tyson met, and she told him about the keys in the lining of Ian's shoe. Because even though the keys found with the foot hadn't been in the news, she knew about them. She'd been the one to tell me, all those years ago. She probably didn't even know whether the keys were still with the shoe, but she knew Tyson well enough to know he'd respond to the threat, however vague it was.

Or had she decided to scrap the whole blackmail scheme in favor of inflicting the ultimate vengeance?

Either way, it was a shockingly risky plan for a single mom. I couldn't imagine putting my children's fate on the line for—well, any-thing.

Wait a minute. . . . Her son was my boys' age, thin with dark hair, from what I remembered of the picture she showed me. *Could he be Ian's son?*

Holy hell.

I hadn't noticed that Andie—Jennifer—was pregnant when I ran into her at Goodwill, the last time I ever saw her—but she'd been in baggy sweats, and I'd ended up in an ambulance, so I might have missed it. Her kid *must* be Ian's son, which would explain why Jennifer was still set on revenge all these years later.

"She wants revenge," I said, my confidence growing. "It has to be her. Andie was her name back then." I closed my eyes, attempting to pull her full name from the depths of my memory, but too much time had gone by. "If you look up the police records around Ian's disappearance—"

But I seemed to have lost the officers' attention. Trudeau scribbled in her notebook as Lambert pushed a clear plastic evidence bag across the table to me.

"Are you guys listening?" I asked desperately. "I'm telling you, I'm almost certain Jennifer killed Tyson."

Lambert raised his formidable brow. "Ms. Collet, I must remind you that you are a suspect in this case, not a detective." I blanched, alarm bells ringing in my head as I realized they didn't believe me. He tapped the document inside the evidence bag. "What is this?"

I turned my attention to the bag, my heart going to my throat as I saw what it was. "It's a DNA test showing that Tyson is Benjamin and Alexander's father."

"Yes," Lambert agreed. "And do you know where we found this?"

"I'm guessing Tyson's lawyer gave it to you?"

"There was a copy with the will he sent over, but no. This"—he tapped it—"is the copy we found in your suitcase this morning."

Shit. How had I missed that? I gaped at him, my head spinning. "I don't know where that paper came from. I've never seen it before. It's not mine, I swear."

"Ms. Collet, it was found hidden in your suitcase."

I wanted to protest, but when I tried to speak, nothing came out.

"You were using it to get money out of your children's biological father. And when he wouldn't give it to you, you murdered him."

"No!" I choked out. "Someone is trying to set me up! And whoever it is pushed me off the boat last night, nearly killing me."

"You say this, but you were the one who turned off the cameras before you went overboard," he said.

"No," I protested, "I didn't. I swear." My brain spun back to watching Jennifer enter my room on the security camera. "It has to be Jennifer. She came in my room last night when I wasn't there. There's footage of her entering my room on the security cameras. She must have planted that in my suitcase."

I just needed to prove it before they came up with enough "evidence" to arrest me. The thought made me go weak with fear.

"Yes, Jennifer told us you asked to speak to her last night, but when she went to your room, you weren't there."

"That's not true!"

Panic rose in my chest. The idea of being a suspect had been abstract before. There was always a voice in the back of my head reassuring me that everything would be fine in the end because I was innocent; there would never be any evidence I'd murdered Tyson because I hadn't. But if someone—Jennifer, or Andie—was actively plotting against me, that changed everything.

This was a high-profile murder case on an island with a murder rate of zero, where high net worth tourists came to feel safe. These guys were under enormous pressure to tie this up, and I was a convenient scapegoat. A suspect to throw in jail to placate the masses who would be demanding answers. Even if they never had enough evidence to convict me, I could spend months—years—in jail while they figured that out. I couldn't let that happen.

I rose, trembling. "Am I free to go?"

"We have a few more questions."

"I didn't blackmail or kill Tyson. Someone is setting me up, and I need to prove my innocence before you lock me up for a crime I didn't commit, or they succeed in killing me. So if I'm not under arrest, I need to leave. Now."

Lambert held up his hands. "As you wish."

I felt the world crashing down around me as I turned on my heel and swung the door open.

CHAPTER 43

The warmth of the sun was a relief after the frigid temperature of the police station, but I cringed in its glare, squinting at the screen of my phone as I stopped at the top of the stairs to read Laurent's text:

You finished yet?

I took a breath. I wasn't totally alone. Someone, at least, believed my side of the story. I shot him a message telling him I was done, and he immediately replied that he was on his way.

I descended the handful of steps to the sidewalk and took a seat on a bench in the shade of a palm tree, formulating a plan while I waited.

I couldn't go to Cody. He'd already saved my hide once by going to jail for the crime I'd committed, and though I'd done nothing wrong this time, I had a feeling he'd be more interested in saving himself—and perhaps his girlfriend—than doing me any more favors. And if Jennifer had planted that DNA test in my luggage and pushed me off the boat last night, who knew what else she would do to make sure I remained the prime suspect? Confronting her could be dangerous and should be a last resort. What I needed was to find incriminating evidence against her. Something concrete, that the police would have to take more seriously than my word. What that might be, I wasn't sure. But Le Rêve would be a good place to start.

The Land Rover pulled up to the curb, and I got in. Laurent's eyes were covered by sunglasses, but I could see the concern etched in his face. "How'd it go?" he asked as we roared away from the police station.

"Not great," I said with a sigh. "Someone planted the DNA test in my luggage, and they seem to think I killed Tyson."

He glanced over at me. "Jennifer?"

"That's my guess."

As he drove up the hill, I told him what I'd realized about her on the boat.

Unlike the police, he didn't doubt my judgment or question whether I was sure of her identity, accepting my conclusions at face value. "Did Tyson have anything to do with her boyfriend's death?" he asked when I'd finished.

I bit my lip. I didn't want to lie to him, but I also couldn't be sure he wouldn't turn on me if he knew the whole truth. Regardless, if I was asking him to help me now, I owed him some kind of explanation. I had to take that chance. "This has to stay between us," I said finally.

"Of course," he said, turning off the main road onto a winding, narrow street.

"I don't know whether it was an accident or intentional—I wasn't there—but Tyson and Cody were involved. There had been a fight. Ian was asking for money. It's probably best if you don't know any more than that."

He nodded, stoic, and I felt a modicum of relief that at least he hadn't pulled the car over and kicked me out.

"Is this your house?" I asked as he parked in front of a well-kept bungalow with a wide porch overlooking the sea. Two surfboards leaned against the railing in front of a pair of rocking chairs.

He nodded, turning off the engine. "Want to come in?"

"I do," I said. "But I need to go to Le Rêve to try to find something to prove my innocence."

He furrowed his brow. "If Jennifer killed Tyson, she is dangerous."

"It's a risk I have to take."

He nodded, accepting my competence without question. A rare man indeed. "How can I help?"

"Can you get me into the house without anyone knowing?" I asked.

"The gates have motion-activated cameras that ring the house." He drummed his fingers on the steering wheel, thinking. "The wall goes past the gate, down the hill, but the front of the property has no fence, and that side of the house is never locked. It's steep and overgrown, though."

"The hill on the side that faces the sea?" I asked.

He nodded. "The view side. I can come—"

I shook my head. "You'll be more useful to me watching the cameras somewhere nearby."

"I don't have access—"

"I do. I can log you in," I said.

He unlocked his phone and handed it to me.

"Will you drive me there now?" I asked, navigating to the site where the camera feed was hosted. "The police aren't gonna be happy that I left without answering all their questions. I get the feeling I'm on borrowed time until they issue a warrant for my arrest."

He started the engine and pulled away from the curb.

"Thanks for not trying to stop me," I said as I logged in with the credentials Tyson had given me.

"*I trust you know what you're doing,*" he said, glancing at me. "And also, you do not seem like a person who can be told no."

I laughed. "No."

He made a sharp turn onto a street that plunged at a death-defying angle toward the beach, and my stomach dropped in anticipation of what I was about to attempt. I appreciated that he trusted I knew what I was doing—but truthfully, I didn't. I never went into dangerous situations without a blueprint, and here I was, walking straight into the lion's den with no plan beyond seeing what I could find. I knew I should have a better strategy, but I didn't have time to come up with one.

I scanned through the feed of the cameras at Le Rêve, watching Jennifer and Cody arrive and enter the house.

I needed to get into Jennifer and Cody's suite, which meant waiting for them to emerge. "This may take a while," I said, handing Laurent his phone.

"Okay," he said as he brought the Land Rover to a halt in front of a row of green-roofed bungalows that hugged the street. He pointed to the hillside beyond. "The house is on top of the hill, five down. It has big concrete pillars. You can go in through Tyson's patio."

I nodded. "Got it."

"I'll park just past the gate and watch the cameras. How will I know if you need help?"

"The feed has sound, so you'll be able to hear me," I said. "And I can text you. But if I'm in a situation where I can't, and I throw up a peace sign, call the police."

"I'll text you if I see anything. *That's the best place to cut through,*" he said, pointing between two houses. "Please"—he caught my hand, forcing me to look at him—"be careful."

Impulsively, I leaned in and kissed him. He cupped the back of my head and I savored the sensation of his lips lingering against mine. "I'll see you soon," I promised, pulling away before desire could override my intention.

Casting a glance around to make sure no one was watching, I jumped down from the car and slipped behind a truck parked on the concrete pad between two of the houses. As Laurent drove away, I peered over the waist-high cinderblock wall beyond, wishing I had better footwear than the borrowed too-big flip-flops. The drop from the top of the wall to the ground was perhaps seven feet, but at least the landing would be in soft dirt that had slid down the hill to rest against the wall.

I pulled off the Havaianas and tossed them over, then jumped up on top of the wall and held on to the edge, lowering my feet until I dangled a foot off the ground. My fingers scraped over the rough surface as I released my grip and landed harder than I'd expected, immediately falling backward in the uneven soil.

I surveyed the hill, plotting my path through the tangled underbrush as I slipped the flip-flops back onto my feet and brushed myself off.

Sticking close to the thick row of bushes atop the retaining walls of the houses that backed up to the mountain, I scrambled over rocks in my flimsy footwear, picking through spiny branches that grasped at my hair and clothes. It was slow going, my ankles buckling as loose stones slid beneath my weight, my exposed forearms stinging with the scratches of coarse-leaved shrubs.

From below, it was nearly impossible to tell the difference between the mansions that towered above me, anchored by massive concrete pillars that plunged into the earth, and I had to stop to count the houses more than once.

As I scrabbled upward, grabbing roots and trunks to hoist myself, I lost a sandal. I kicked the other one off and kept going, fighting my way through the underbrush to the rocky dirt beneath the house, my bare feet slipping in the loose topsoil as I climbed.

But when I finally reached the top of the hill, exhausted and covered in dust, my head wound smarting, I saw that the railing of the outdoor hallway was a good eight feet above me, out of my reach. My only option was to continue up the hill toward the patio off Tyson's room and hope his door was unlocked.

Outside the shadow of the house, the dry brush was so thick that it was easy to haul myself up, but the trade-off was the abrasion of the prickly branches. I groaned as a long bougainvillea thorn lodged itself in my heel, and when I released my hold on the bush I was grasping, one of its limbs snapped back, swatting me in the face.

My skin smarted and my eye stung, watering so profusely that I could hardly see to pull the thorn out of my foot. As I removed the barb from my throbbing heel and surveyed the hill ahead of me, a rooster crowed close by, and I startled, almost tumbling back down the slope.

When at long last I reached the waist-high wall that surrounded Tyson's patio, I scrambled over, into an entirely different world. Soft green grass grew through the spaces between the large square paving stones and tropical plants bloomed in the well-tended beds that surrounded the pristine white couches. I had to stop myself from shedding my clothes and diving into the gurgling fountain, instead plunging only my feet and hands into the water.

Once I'd splashed my face and scrubbed the dirt from my feet, I could see how deep the puncture from the thorn was, a steady drip of blood oozing from the wound. I dried my hands on my shirt and pressed my heel into my shorts, slowing the blood flow. It needed attention, but I had nothing to wrap it with, and I needed to keep moving.

As I approached the door to Tyson's room with my weight on the ball of my foot, I could feel the blood trickling down my instep. The reflection in the glass showed a wild woman, leaves in my hair, my skin and clothes streaked with dirt and blood. I raked the debris from my hair with my fingers and, saying a silent prayer, turned the door handle.

To my relief, it was unlocked.

I stepped over the threshold into the dark room and paused, allowing my eyes to adjust to the gloom. Even with the blackout curtains closed against the afternoon sun, I could see the room had been ransacked—by the police, I supposed. Drawers stood open, the mattress was half off the bed, clothes and personal items were strewn about.

As my eyes adjusted to the gloom, I noticed a built-in glass cabinet, dimly illuminated by the light through the partially open bathroom door. I crept over to it, confirming what I'd thought I'd seen: guns, neatly displayed behind the glass, as other people might display their china. There were two handguns and space for two more, plus two shotguns and a rifle.

No wonder Jennifer didn't kill Tyson here. He was armed to the teeth.

St. Barth's was a territory of France, which had incredibly tough gun laws, and it was illegal for nonresidents to possess firearms, but I supposed that that didn't matter to Tyson. He had ways and means.

I tried the handle of the cabinet, but it was locked, and when I tapped the glass, I could tell it was shatterproof. Dammit. I would have felt a lot better with a weapon at my side.

I pulled my phone out to find a new text message from Laurent:

Cody going downstairs

I glanced back at the door, considering bolting, but what if he came in here and locked it? I'd be stuck outside with no way in. No, I needed to hide.

As I scanned the room for a place to take cover, I heard the click of a door latch in the next room. Light poured in from outside, spilling into the bedroom through the open double doors that led to the rest of the suite. I dived into the triangle of space between the mattress, the bed, and the floor, peering out to see Cody enter.

I lost sight of Cody as he moved away from me toward the theater, and typed out a text to Laurent:

Where's Jennifer?

His response came immediately:

In her room

With Cody in the theater and Jennifer upstairs in her room, this might be the best chance I had to sneak upstairs, where I could hide out in the suite that had been mine to wait for an opportunity to enter Jennifer and Cody's room. I knew they didn't have access to the interior cameras of Tyson's home; they didn't even know they were there.

Tyson had hidden them so that he might catch his guests doing whatever it was he was sure they were doing.

A lot of good that had done him. But it was fortunate for me.

I could feel my injured heel throbbing with each beat of my heart as I carefully backed out of my hiding place, scanning the floor until I found an errant sock. Hoping it was clean, I slipped it over my foot to stem the blood flow, then edged around the bed toward the door that led to the exterior hallway. I held my breath as I slowly turned the handle and pulled.

I opened the door only a crack and slid through, blinking in the sudden daylight as I stole down the outdoor hallway. I turned at the stairwell and dashed up the stairs two at a time, pain shooting through my injured foot every time it touched down. I felt my phone buzz in my pocket, but I didn't have time to stop and check it. Cody could reemerge from the theater at any minute.

Once I reached the main level, I bolted across the open space like the wind, headed for my bedroom door. But before I could reach it, I heard footsteps coming down the stairs from the upper level and saw Jennifer's legs. I would never make it to my room. I needed a place to hide immediately.

I darted behind the kitchen island, where I crouched low, trying to quiet my breath as my heart hammered in my chest. I heard the patter of her feet reach the bottom of the stairs, then . . . nothing. Where was she?

I pulled out my phone to see the text from Laurent that had come through while I was on the stairs, warning me that Jennifer was leaving her room. Another text came through.

Blood on the floor

She's on to you

Fear shot through me as I looked down to see blood had seeped through the sock onto the pale gray floor. I'd left a trail leading right to my hiding place.

CHAPTER 44

"Audrey."

I looked up from where I cowered behind the island to see Jennifer hovering over me, her blue eyes piercing. She was freshly showered and dressed in workout clothes, like she was about to go on a run, except for the gun dangling from her right hand. One of the guns missing from Tyson's cabinet, I assumed.

"What are you doing here?" There was an edge in her voice, her doe-eyed charm vanished. Yes, this was more like the Andie I'd known.

"Jennifer." I slipped my phone into my back pocket as I rose with shaking knees and held up my hands. *Play dumb. She doesn't know you know anything.* "Why do you have a gun?"

She looked at the gun, adjusting her grip as she raised it and pointed the barrel at me. "For protection."

I felt like I'd swallowed glass. "Against me?"

"You're wanted for murder."

"But you had it on you before you saw my footprints," I said.

"I saw you coming up the hill from my bathroom window. I waited until you came upstairs so we could talk in private. Why are you here?"

"I didn't kill Tyson," I said, dropping my hands.

She flinched. She was definitely jumpy, and she didn't look like she was used to handling a gun. A dangerous combination. "It sure looks like you did," she said.

She might be the one brandishing a weapon, but she didn't know about the cameras recording our conversation in crystal-clear audio and video, thanks to Tyson's paranoia. I just needed to get a confession out of her without making her want to pull the trigger. "Please, put the gun down. I didn't kill Tyson, and I don't want to hurt you."

She shook her head, keeping the firearm trained on me.

I desperately scoured my brain for anything I could use to compel her to confide in me rather than shoot me. *Treat her like an ally?* It was worth a try. I swallowed. "We have a lot in common," I said. "Both of us single moms. Neither of us can go to jail, we have our children to think about. If you'll just tell me what happened, I can help you."

She laughed. "You, help me?"

I softened my face and steeled my resolve. "I did once before, remember? The night of the fire. I kept pressure on your wound until the paramedics could get there. I saved your life, but you still have the scar."

She choked up on the gun, blinking rapidly. "I don't know what you're talking about."

"I always liked you, Andie." I tilted my head at what I hoped was a sympathetic angle, aware I was taking a risk. But Laurent was watching the camera feed. Would he have called the police already? I hadn't given the signal, but he might have thought it necessary when he saw the gun. If he had, I didn't have much time to get a confession out of her. "And I like you even better as Jennifer. Sobriety looks good on you. So does"—I gestured to her body—"all of it. Good for you, turning your life around."

"You're not making sense," she said, but there was acknowledgment in her eyes.

"I can help you stay out of jail, if you'll just tell me what happened."

"You're the prime suspect in Tyson's murder," she said, her voice unsteady. "Not me."

"Because they haven't verified your true identity yet," I said, feigning confidence. "But they work fast. We don't have much time to come up with a plausible story. If you'll just put the gun down, we can talk."

She didn't put the gun down, but I could tell she didn't know what to make of me, which was at least better than her wanting to shoot me. She'd already tried to kill me once; this time she might succeed. "I didn't realize you were pregnant when I ran into you at Goodwill," I went on. "But it's so clear now, that your son is Ian's."

She adjusted her grip on the gun.

"I understand why you wanted revenge on Tyson," I continued. "You felt he was responsible for Ian's death—"

"He was," she snapped, cutting me off. "You know it as well as I do."

She realized once she'd said it that she'd betrayed herself, but the cat was out of the bag and there was no putting it back in. She was jittery, her finger on the trigger as she backed away from me.

I considered giving Laurent the signal to call the police, but whose side would they be on when they showed up? Probably not mine. Not yet, even if Laurent had patched them in to the feed from the cameras overhead. I needed to get more out of her. "I can help you," I offered, putting my whole heart into it, though I had nothing to back it up. "We can help each other."

"How?" She was going for derision, but the quiver in her voice betrayed her.

"The police didn't listen to you back then when you tried to tell them Tyson was involved in Ian's disappearance, because Tyson was the son of a prominent businessman, and Ian was just another missing drug addict. That must have hurt."

"You have no idea," she said bitterly.

"But you were smart. You played the long game, taking on a new identity and worming your way into Tyson's inner circle so that you could tighten the noose around his neck."

The fact that she didn't respond told me I was on the right track.

"What was your plan?" I pressed. All of this had been set in motion long before Ian's foot washed up. "Your end goal?"

"I wanted to ruin his life, the way he'd ruined mine," she admitted finally. The gun began to sag as she paid more attention to her bitterness than to the deadly weapon in her hand, and I briefly wondered whether I could charge her and grab it. But what good would that do? I hadn't yet gotten a murder confession out of her, and Cody was downstairs and would surely come to her defense if he heard a scuffle. "I was the one who alerted the Monterey De-Sal center that their environmental impact report should be double-checked."

I swallowed my surprise, focusing on the barrel of the gun to keep my poker face straight. A thrashing fish had to be reeled in carefully. "How did you know—"

"I'm not as dumb as I look," she cut me off. "But when Ian's shoe washed up, I saw my opportunity to take care of my son in the way that Tyson prevented Ian from ever being able to take care of him."

"You blackmailed him for five hundred thousand," I said. "Was that all you wanted?"

She shook her head. "I just wanted the cash as a guarantee he'd play ball. Once I told him what was in the lockbox and threatened to tell the police, he would have agreed to transfer the millions I planned to demand."

"But how did you know the key to the safety deposit box was still in the lining of the shoe?" I asked. "That wasn't reported publicly."

"I knew that even if it was no longer there, Tyson was paranoid enough to respond to blackmail," she said, confirming my suspicions.

"So you sent him that newspaper clipping," I said.

She nodded. "And it did the trick, just like I knew it would. I didn't realize he'd invite you down here, but it ended up working in my favor."

I wanted to ask why she'd tried to kill me on the boat, but it seemed like a bad idea to remind her of her failed attempt while she was holding a gun that could finish the job, so instead I asked the question that had been bothering me since Tyson had shown me the blackmail note. "What was in the lockbox, that you were so sure he'd pay you?"

"Proof that Tyson had stolen the De-Sal technology from Ian."

I stared at her, my mind suddenly blank. "What?" I choked out.

She cocked her head, surprised. "You didn't know?"

Shock washed over me as I shook my head. But it explained so much . . .

"He was working on it in the plastic pools behind the trailer," she said. "You saw it, I'm sure you did."

A blurry image formed in my mind. A dead snake on a humid summer night. "The hydroponics?" I managed. "I thought that was for growing weed."

"I mean, he did intend to grow weed with the water it produced, but the experiment was using the brine left over from the desalination process to power the system."

I blinked, processing. "Which is what's made De-Sal so successful."

Had Tyson simply taken advantage of Ian's death to use his technology? Or had Tyson murdered Ian with the intention of stealing it? Regardless, the fact remained that if Jennifer was right, Tyson's entire empire was built on a lie. And the worst thing Tyson could've imagined was anyone finding out he was a fraud.

"If you couldn't get into the safety deposit box, how did you know what was inside?" I asked.

"After I saved Ian's notebooks from the fire, I made him promise to lock them up there to keep them safe."

But her logic wasn't totally sound. "If the notebooks were in the lockbox, then how did Tyson get them?"

"Ian kept an extra key on his keychain. Tyson stole it when he killed him."

The lockbox must have been where Tyson found the video that Ian had shot of us on the Fourth of July, too. But . . . "Then there would be nothing left inside, no reason for him to fear exposure from the keys," I pointed out.

"I don't know," she snapped, growing annoyed. "I never got that far. But I do know Tyson killed Ian and stole his technology, and he was scared enough about what might be in the safety deposit box that he took out the money to pay me."

The triumph of being right about Tyson's blackmailer not having anything on him rang hollow in the light of all that had followed.

"I don't understand," I said, trying to fit together the pieces of the puzzle. "If you had your ace in the hole, why did you decide to kill him?"

She snorted. "I didn't kill him. You did."

I paused, confused about why she was turning things around on me now, when she'd confessed everything else. "No, I didn't." At her disbelieving look, I raised my hands. "Don't you think if I wanted his money, I would have come after him with a paternity suit years ago?"

"Maybe you changed your mind."

I shook my head. "My life with my kids is great. We may not be rich, but we want for nothing. Staying out of our lives was the one kindness Tyson afforded me. I was as surprised as anyone that they were in his will."

"Then why did you kill him?" she demanded.

"I didn't!"

"Then who did?"

I stared at her. Did she really think I'd killed him? No, she had to be bluffing, trying to convince me she hadn't done it herself. "Look, I know you did it," I said, eying the gun still clutched in her hands. "But I want to help you find a way out."

"I did not! He was going to give me what I wanted. I'm losing millions now that he's dead."

"Then why did you plant that DNA test in my luggage?"

"Because if they found out he was being blackmailed, I wanted them to think it was you, not me," she said with an exasperated groan. "And I can hardly dive, you think I could have killed him underwater? He was twice my size."

"But you have a dive compass," I pointed out. "They don't even teach you how to use a dive compass until advanced open water training."

She rolled her eyes. "That was a gift from Cody. I had no idea how to use it, I just wore it to make him happy."

I thought back to the dive, remembering how genuinely terrified Jennifer had seemed. We stared at each other, both of us wary but quickly realizing we'd each been wrong about the other.

She lowered the gun, placing it on the island between us, a peace offering. "It's not even loaded."

I stared at the deadly weapon resting casually on the counter like a discarded cup. By power of elimination, the killer had to be Cody.

But why now, after all these years? The timing with the foot was too coincidental to be chance.

"Does Cody know who you really are?" I asked.

She shook her head. "And he can't find out."

"I saw him leave Tyson's room yesterday before the dive, looking like he wanted to kill him," I said. "I didn't think anything of it at the time because people often looked like they wanted to kill Tyson—but I think Cody actually did."

"No," Jennifer protested, fearful. "No, that can't be right." But her face told me she felt otherwise.

A flicker of movement near the stairwell drew my eye, and a shudder went through me as a hulking figure stepped out of the shadows, his eyes black as night.

CHAPTER 45

Jennifer and I both jumped back at the sight of Cody at the top of the stairs. I threw up two fingers in a gesture I hoped looked like some kind of greeting or warning to him, but would read as the signal to call for help to Laurent.

"How long have you been listening?" Jennifer asked, trembling.

"Long enough." He paced toward her, his eyes dark. "You used me to get to my brother."

She shook her head vehemently. "It started out that way, but I love you, I really do."

He watched warily as she slunk toward him like a chastised dog, her eyes pleading. When she'd nearly reached him, his hand shot out without warning. She didn't have a chance to react before he'd slapped her so hard across the face that she flew backward.

"Cody!" I cried as she hit the floor. He stood there, stunned, staring at his hand as though it had betrayed him while Jennifer curled into a ball and I cowered behind the island, afraid to rush to her for fear of what he might do to me.

Had he changed his mind after he shoved me overboard? Or had he staged the whole thing, knowing it would look as if the killer had pushed me, making him appear less suspicious by saving me?

He choked back tears, taking a gun from the back of his waistband, his eyes fixed on Jennifer. "I loved you." He said it like a defense, like of course he had to slap her after what she'd done to him.

I could see blood dripping from her nose onto the floor as she pushed herself up on her elbows and lifted her face toward him. "Don't do this, Cody."

"He took everything from me. Everything! Including you," Cody bellowed, kicking the leg of a nearby table so hard that it toppled over.

"I'm here," Jennifer whimpered, wiping her bloody nose on the back of her hand. "I'm not going anywhere."

"You were only with me because of him," he snapped, jabbing the gun in her direction. "Tyson was always telling me you must want something from me." He threw his head back. "God, it kills me that he was right."

His spittle landed on Jennifer where she cowered on the floor, looking up at him fearfully. "I'm so sorry," she repeated. "I love you."

"All of it was fake," he cried. "I had a ring. A fucking ring!"

Fear shot through me. He was volatile, infuriated, and—I was sure now—a killer. I had to do something before he hurt her again. "Tyson was an asshole," I said, forcing my voice through my dry throat.

He looked at me as though just registering my presence, his eyes dark with rage.

"You were the smart one," I said gently. "The kind one. He was nothing but a thief and a bully."

"I went to prison for you," he growled.

"For which I will be forever grateful."

"Fucking prison! Do you have any idea what that was like?"

The anguish in his face was both heartbreaking and terrifying. "I'm so sorry, Cody."

"Audrey—" I could tell Jennifer was trying to warn me with her eyes that he wasn't in his right mind, but that was what I was banking on. Yes, there was a harrowing chance he might shoot us in this state, but there was at least an equal chance that he might confess, and if I could induce him to do the latter, all of this would be over.

"All these years I'd thought it was Ian who turned me in," he lamented, wiping his tear-streaked face with the bottom of his shirt as he paced the floor. "And he paid with his life. For nothing!"

I swallowed my horror and glanced at Jennifer, who gaped at him with a look of shock and outrage as that sank in. Would she still claim to love Cody now that he'd admitted to killing the father of her child? She was smart enough to hold her tongue, for the moment at least.

From the beginning, my gut had told me Tyson and Cody had lied about Ian's death being an accident, but I'd always assumed it was Tyson who pushed him, not Cody. Though in context, it made sense that Cody would have been angry enough with Ian for turning him in to inflict harm on him. "But Tyson finally confessed to turning you in?" I asked.

"He didn't even have the decency to tell me in person," he groaned, more to himself than anyone else.

Dread settled heavy in my bones. "So, how did you find out?" I asked, though I had a bad feeling that I knew.

"My arrest report."

My heart stopped. It was my fault Tyson was dead.

"Samira gave it to me the morning after La Petite Plage."

I could hardly control my voice. "Samira . . ."

"Because he was too much of a fucking coward to tell me himself," Cody spat.

That much was true, at least.

"I saw her hand you that envelope," Jennifer interjected. "I don't think she even knew what it was. She just said it was yours."

"Did you ask her about it?" I asked, trying to follow.

He shook his head. "I didn't need to. There it was, in black and white . . ." His voice trailed off.

"There what was?" Jennifer pressed.

"The date of the video submitted as evidence against me wasn't July fourth, so it wasn't Ian's video."

So he'd come to the same conclusion I had.

"It was dated August second," Cody went on, focusing on me, "the day after you caught Tyson cheating on you, which he blamed me for. Tyson turned me in, not Ian." He bunched his free hand into a fist as he paced back and forth, agitated. "If we'd ever gone to trial, it would have come out in court, but I copped a plea, so I was never the wiser."

"But why tell you now, after all this time?" Jennifer asked.

"Because of you," he said, spinning on her with accusing eyes. "Your blackmail scheme made him crazy with paranoia. The idea of everything coming back up." His eyes cut to mine. "He wanted to hurt me, wanted me to know he'd been the engineer of all my pain all these years, and he'd hurt me again if he needed to."

Behind him, a flash of movement caught my eye, and I was shocked to see Laurent peer around the corner of the wall that separated my room from the covered patio. He must have come in through the servants' entrance off the balcony, gone through my room and out the sliding glass door that faced the view.

"So you killed him," I said, careful not to glance in Laurent's direction.

Cody continued to pace and sweat, so distressed I could practically see the anxiety radiating off him. "When I confronted him on the boat, he laughed. He actually laughed! Thought he was so smart. Said no one crosses him."

"So you lured him into that coral cave, mounted his tank, and disconnected his oxygen," I said.

"He ruined my fucking life," he shouted, running his shaking hand through his thinning hair. "Sent me to jail. His own brother! And he had no remorse. Ian may not have deserved to die, but Tyson did. I had no choice."

Behind Cody, Laurent crept across the open space to crouch behind the half-wall around the staircase, a body length from Cody. I could hardly breathe.

"You always have a choice," I said in as soothing a voice as I could muster. "And you still do. You can do the right thing, turn yourself in—"

"Sure," he said darkly. "Go back to jail. Or I can let them think you did it, that you came here and threatened my family, and I did what I had to do to protect us."

Fuck. Where were the police?

"Cody," I said as calmly as I could muster, "I'm your friend—"

But the Cody I'd known had disappeared, replaced by a man with hell in his eyes. "I should have let you drown last night, but I was too weak."

"You did the right thing," I said. "And you still can."

He shook his head, his mouth in a hard line. "I paid for your sins, now it's your turn to pay for mine."

He saw my gaze flick to the gun on the counter. "I heard her say it's not loaded," he said caustically. "But this one is."

I pointed toward the ceiling, where the camera was hidden somewhere above us. "It's over, Cody. There are cameras throughout the house recording all of this, and the police are watching."

"Oh yeah? Then where are they?" he demanded.

A blur of motion, and Laurent was on Cody, tackling him from behind, his arms around Cody's waist as they tumbled to the deck with a crash. Jennifer screamed and jumped out of the way as Cody's gun skittered across the floor to rest beneath a lounge chair on the far side of the two men. From my position near the island, there was no way I could get to it before they could.

Cody had a good fifty to seventy-five pounds on Laurent, but he wasn't nearly as fit as Laurent was, making them evenly matched as they tussled, grappling for the gun. Laurent was faster, though, and first to reach the firearm, seizing it as Cody pinned him to the deck with his body weight.

I heard sirens in the distance. Finally.

"Go." I pointed Jennifer to the door, and she scurried toward it.

In the split second I'd looked away, Cody had somehow ended up with the gun, which he slammed into Laurent's skull, sending him falling backward, dazed.

The sirens grew louder as Cody got to his feet, the weapon dangling from his hand.

"Put it down," I said, wrapping my fingers around the handle of the gun Jennifer had left on the counter. "It's over."

He hesitated as Laurent rose unsteadily behind him, clearly stunned and shaking his head. Time slowed as I considered my options, watching Cody's every movement. Finally, he pointed the barrel down and extended it to Laurent. I felt a wave of relief.

But at the last minute, Cody changed direction, swiftly raising the gun to point the barrel at his own temple before Laurent could grab it.

"No!" Laurent cried.

At the same time, I yelled, "Move!"

Time slowed.

Laurent dived out of the way, hitting the ground just as the deafening shot rang out. All sound beyond the reverberation of the blast was sucked from the room.

Red spattered the white wall, so bright in the afternoon sunlight. An image I knew instantly would be burned into my mind forever.

Cody's firearm clattered silently to the tile as he dropped to his knees beside it, blood oozing onto the floor.

The high-pitched ringing in my ears blended with the muffled sound of the front door opening. Laurent rose from where he'd fallen, his eyes glued to Cody.

I was still holding the gun as Jennifer entered my line of sight, sprinting for Cody, who writhed on the floor, clutching his arm, blood hemorrhaging from the bullet hole I'd put there. "You shot him!" she cried.

"He tried to kill himself and Audrey stopped him," Laurent explained, his voice hoarse.

I lowered the gun, my hand trembling. "A towel," I managed. "We need to stop the bleeding."

The sirens were close now, their wails melding with Cody's guttural howls. I placed the gun on the counter and tossed Jennifer a kitchen towel as Laurent scrambled to grab Cody's weapon from where it rested on the floor.

"I thought it wasn't loaded," Jennifer said shakily as she pressed the kitchen towel to Cody's wound.

Laurent set Cody's firearm next to the one I'd used to stop him from killing himself, then wrapped his arms around me. "There was one in the chamber. I could see the extractor was protruding," I said, leaning into him.

I'd known I was taking a chance, aiming for Cody's forearm. But in the split second I had to make the decision about whether to fire, I figured the worst that could happen was that I'd kill him, which wasn't any worse than what he was going to do to himself if I didn't take the shot.

I heard tires in the driveway, and one by one, the sirens abruptly cut. Footsteps, followed by someone pounding on the door, shouting, "Police!"

CHAPTER 46

The days following Cody's arrest for Tyson's murder were an emotional roller coaster. The recording from the kitchen security camera was enough for the police to charge him not only with Tyson's murder but with Ian's as well, and once he was detained, he quickly confessed, not wanting to go through the spectacle of a lengthy trial after already having admitted on video to what he'd done.

He also copped to having pushed me off the boat, having rationalized it would be a lot easier to pin Tyson's murder on me if I wasn't around to refute the story. But he changed his mind at the last minute and dived in after me, sorry for what he'd done.

To my relief, he didn't mention my part in the cover-up of Ian's death. Whether out of remorse for having tried to kill me or gratitude for my saving his life, I wasn't sure.

He was relocated to a holding facility in St. Martin, and Jennifer moved to a house there to be closer to him, though from what Samira told me, Cody refused to speak to her. I was surprised Jennifer still wanted anything to do with him after she learned what he'd done to the father of her child, but perhaps she really did love him. And Cody hadn't known that Tyson stole Ian's work.

My name was cleared immediately, though I was asked to stay on the island awhile longer to provide testimony. I didn't tell Samira that I'd been the one to leave the arrest report on Tyson's pillow. It had been the reason Cody killed him in the end, and she was already beating herself up for giving it to him, so I let her believe Tyson had been the one to leave it there, that he had inadvertently been the engineer of his own demise.

But I knew it was my fault Tyson was murdered.

I'd been so angry with him after I returned from La Petite Plage that I'd wanted to warn him I knew the truth of his duplicity. That I could hurt him more than he could hurt me. And I was right; in the end, I did, didn't I?

I didn't know that he wouldn't come home that night, that Samira would find the arrest report and, seeing Cody's name on it, hand it off to him. I didn't know Cody had killed Ian because he believed Ian had turned him in, or that Cody would kill Tyson as well when he learned the truth.

Poor long-suffering Cody. It was my fault he learned the truth, and though I can safely say I wouldn't have told him if I'd known how it would all turn out, I did also believe he deserved to know. I didn't want Tyson to die, didn't want Cody to go to prison. But I comforted myself with the knowledge that the truth is buoyant; like an Air Jordan buried for years in the Everglades, eventually it rises to the surface.

After a few days of my guilt eating away at me, I confessed my part in Tyson's demise to Laurent. But he had a different point of view, reminding me that it was Tyson's own paranoia that had made him susceptible to Jennifer's blackmail plot, setting off the chain of events that ended his life.

Tyson had chosen to turn his brother in all those years ago, had chosen to cover up Ian's death and steal his technology. And while those choices may have made Tyson a billionaire, over the years the lies had destroyed him from the inside out, transforming him from the driven young man I'd known to the cynical specter he'd become.

It's hard to comprehend the sprawl of the decisions we make, our choices colliding with those of others to create an impossibly tangled web that can come undone with the pull of a single thread.

But Tyson made his own decisions; he was both the creator and the destroyer of his own life.

Samira was too overwhelmed to plan a funeral straightaway, electing instead to do a celebration of life in a few months, when she'd had time to process Tyson's death. She and Gisèle planned to return to Paris once the loose ends had been tied up, but in the meantime, they'd moved back into Le Rêve, which was where I found them when I walked over to say goodbye the day before I was to be allowed to return home.

A heaviness clung to Samira as she lounged on a divan on the covered veranda, smoking cigarette after cigarette. "I know I should stop," she said, blowing a line of smoke out at the blue sky.

"Your husband just died," I said. "Give yourself time."

"I hope you'll come to the celebration of life," she said. "It will be in northern California I think, though I don't know where yet. You should bring your boys."

I took a sip of the green juice Laurent's replacement had prepared. "That's so kind of you. It would be good for the boys to meet you, and their other half-siblings."

My heart tugged at just the thought of my boys. I'd been away from them for a week now, the longest we'd ever been apart, and I missed them so much it hurt.

"How's Laurent?" Gisèle asked.

"Yes," Samira chimed in. "Tell us something happy."

I tucked my bare feet beneath me on the plush white outdoor couch, gazing out toward the calm sea. "Good, all things considered."

"Go on," Gisèle encouraged. "You've been staying with him, haven't you?"

I nodded.

Laurent's cozy two-bedroom bungalow was nothing fancy, but it was airy and bright and full of mementos from his travels and photos of his life. In the evenings, we sat in the chairs on the shaded front porch, talking until the sea below was swallowed by the night, when we went to bed early but didn't sleep until late. I told him the ugly truth, all of it, and he listened patiently, without judgment. He was able to intuit when I needed space and when I needed the graze of his lips on my neck, when I wanted to vent and when I wanted advice figuring out the mess my life had suddenly become, when I wanted to make love, and when I needed him to make me forget my name.

Laurent had been scheduled to work for Tyson through the end of the month, after which he'd planned to return to France, but he'd handed off his responsibilities to another butler early, the one who was now refilling my green juice as I considered how to reply to Gisèle. "I've had a hard couple of days," I said. "But he's made them easier."

My answer wasn't what Gisèle had been looking for, but she was perceptive enough not to press. I felt strangely protective of my budding relationship with Laurent. Had circumstances been different, had it been the vacation fling I'd imagined it would be, I would have been happy to tell her all about how incredible he was in bed. The man pressed buttons I didn't even know I had. But what we had was turning out to be more than physical, and as thrilled as I was by that, it was ours—just ours.

"What are you going to do when you get home?" Gisèle asked.

"What do you mean?"

"You have all this money now." It was true, Tyson's will set aside a generous amount for the boys' schooling as well as half a million per year for me as trustee, until the boys were twenty-one. To him, it must have seemed like pennies, but after living off far less than that for so many years, it seemed like a windfall to me. "Are you going to keep working?"

I nodded. "With the media circus around everything that happened, we have more cases pouring in than we know what to do with. But I'm going to hire a few people to do the legwork and take a step back for a minute to spend some time with my kids. They'll be out of school for the summer soon, and I've never had much of a chance to travel, so I was thinking we might take off for a while."

"Maybe visit Laurent in France?" Gisèle needled.

I smiled. "We'll see. Have you talked to Allison?"

Samira nodded. "She came by yesterday to check on me. It sounds like Rick Halpern, the investor Tyson brought on before he died, is a better partner than Tyson ever was."

"Rémy's partner," I said.

She nodded as my phone buzzed and I saw Laurent's name on the screen. "I've gotta run," I said. "Laurent's outside. He's taking me surfing since it's my last day."

Samira threw her arms around my neck. "I'll see you in California?"

I nodded, giving her a kiss on the cheek. "Until then."

EPILOGUE

The sky is awash in shades of pink and gold, the evening so clear I can make out the bridge across the bay miles away where the Sonoma Mountains slope into the sea. A breeze whips over the mountaintop, dissipating the heavy herbal smoke that unfurls from the stick of sage the Unitarian minister waves overhead.

I pull my trench coat tighter against the sunset chill as he chants in an unfamiliar language, his white robes rippling in the wind. Laurent circles his arms around me from behind, and I lean my head against his solid chest.

The group Samira and Gisèle have gathered to bid farewell to Tyson isn't large, consisting of his parents and a few other business associates and friends, his ex-wife, the woman he had a child with out of wedlock, Allison, Laurent, and me. Benji and Alex are with the rest of the children in the sprawling farmhouse at the bottom of the hill, having pizza and getting to know one another.

My boys took the death of the father they'd never known harder than I'd expected, but they were buoyed by the news of three half-siblings, and their mothers and I plan to get the kids together again to give them the opportunity to have a relationship with one another.

Notably missing from this gathering are Cody, who is at the beginning of his prison sentence, and Jennifer. They are no longer together, and Samira didn't feel it was appropriate to invite Jennifer after all the damage she caused.

But Jennifer wasn't completely abandoned. Ian's notebooks were recovered from Tyson's safe, and it turned out that the solution for the pollution problem Tyson had been falsifying environmental reports to cover up was in the notebooks all along. Allison came up with a plan to pay Jennifer—or rather, her son, Ian's beneficiary—a hefty sum for the use of the technology that included shares in the company. This lessened the guilt I felt about the money my children and I inherited from Tyson, though I've yet to spend any of the half million dollars that landed in my account once his affairs were settled last month.

The boys still don't know they're multimillionaires. I've told them they'll be able to go to college anywhere they want, but I plan to keep the weight of the privilege they'll now have access to off their shoulders until they're strong enough to bear it with grace.

Otherwise, their lives are not terribly different, except for the additional time I have with them since I've added three more agents and two assistants to my company, and the man who is often in our house. If things continue as they are, Laurent and I will likely buy a home of a more comfortable size for the four of us sometime in the future, closer to the beach where we surf. But there's no rush.

"I ask you to bow your heads for a moment of silent reflection as we remember Tyson Dale," the minister says, handing the urn to Samira.

I think of Tyson, the boy with big dreams who I'd been so smitten with in high school, the young man desperate to prove himself who'd broken my heart, and the billionaire who'd changed the world for the better but carried such darkness in his soul.

It's poetic justice, really, the corrosive nature of the knowledge that he didn't do the one thing that brought him notoriety and success. His deception became a cancerous tumor, crowding out all the light in him, withering his self-confidence and fueling the fire of his insecurity, which raged until his heart was charred.

Samira's black maxidress billows around her as she walks to the edge of the bluff, where she reaches into the urn and casts a handful of ashes into the fading evening sky.

Some have called Tyson's death at Cody's hand fate, some karma; but if that's true, it was a fate they authored by their actions, a karma of their own design. Both brothers made the choices that defined them, as did I, as do all of us.

The ashes scatter on the breeze, whisked over the canyon by the wind. "You are dust, and to dust you shall return," the minister says.

The days between? Well, I suppose we are condemned to be free.

ACKNOWLEDGMENTS

This book began with a trip to St. Barth's. I'd heard of the island, of course—the natural beauty, the exclusivity, the joie de vivre—but visiting with a group of twenty friends was an experience rich enough to inspire me to want to return every day in my head while writing this book. A huge thank you to Tripp and Jessica for planning such an incredible trip, and to the riotous band of adventurers who made it one for the books . . . or, rather, book. (I never could resist a pun.)

Thank you to my husband, Alex, and my BFF, Ashleigh, for their early reads—it's so hard to see your own work, and having your eyes on this story was like turning on a light!

I am so grateful for the whole team at Levine, Greenberg, Rostan Literary Agency, and especially for my incredible lit agent, Sarah Bedingfield—my champion, my co-conspirator, and the one person I trust to wander around in my head, whether untangling plot lines or helping me decide which stories have legs and which . . . don't. Thank you for always holding my hand and having my back! A huge thank you to my amazing film agent, Hilary Zaitz Michael, and the team at WME. I'm so fortunate to have you in my corner. You are the absolute best!

To Anne Speyer, thank you for your early read and suggestions that helped take this book to the next level. To the team at Bantam: Ted Allen, Carlos Beltrán, Sarah Breivogel, Jenny Chen, Caroline Cunningham, Corina Diez, Saige Francis, Jean Slaughter, and Samuel Wetzler—thank you for all your hard work bringing this book to the world!

And last, but certainly not least—thanks to you, dear reader, for reading.

ABOUT THE AUTHOR

KATHERINE WOOD is a native of Mississippi and a graduate of the University of Southern California. She is the author of the novel *Ladykiller,* and also writes under the pen name Katherine St. John. She lives in Atlanta with her husband, two children, a naughty pug, and a ferocious kitty.

thekatwritesbooks.com
@thekatwritesbooks